Magic's Not Real. But **Surging** Is.

Thirteen-year-old Finley McComb has just been invited to Brighton Preparatory School for Surgers. There's only one problem: he's not a surger. He can't summon superhuman gifts from electrical appliances. He can't will fantastic strength from lamps and clocks. The surger's glove—a tool designed with a rechargeable power source—does nothing for Finley.

So why the acceptance?

Intrigued, Finley leaves Southern California suburbia and heads to the prep school anyway, where classes prove tough, and the professors tougher. Finley's determined though, because despite the school's difficulties, he's found a sense of purpose, and the faculty believe there's untapped greatness inside of him.

Then, one evening, a mysterious ghost ship appears on the campus coast, creating panic. Classes are put on hold, the surging community is stricken with fear, and, strangely, Finley is told that the vessel's arrival is tied to his destiny.

Finley is faced with many tough choices in his first semester, but none will prove tougher than whether or not he should board the ghost ship...

...where, supposedly, his **true purpose** will be discovered.

{THE SURGERS}

Also by the author:

Capernaum

The Running Duology:
Running From Lions
Toward Uncertain Futures*

Finley McComb and The Surgers:
The Surgers!
The Kings Of The Night!*

Probably, Most Likely*

*forthcoming

To Mackenzie,
DON'T STOP WRITING!
So proud of you — can't
wait to read your book!

a novel by
Julian R. Vaca

SURGERS

This is a work of fiction. Names, characters, places and incidents either are the product of the author's imagination or are used fictitiously. Any resemblance to actual persons, living or dead, events, or locales is entirely coincidental.

Copyright © 2014 by Julian R. Vaca

All rights reserved. Published in the United States independently.

Visit me on the Web! www.julianrvaca.com

Summary: *Thirteen-year-old Finley McComb is summoned to The Brighton Preparatory School for Surgers, only to find out that he's not a surger—a person who can call on superhuman gifts by drawing from electricity. But feeling out of a place is soon the least of Finley's worries. A mysterious ghost ship has appeared, and the vessel supposedly holds Finley's destiny.*

Cover design by Katie Mae Vaca | www.katiemaevaca.com
Illustrations by Michael Cribbs | www.michaelcribbs.blogspot.com

{table of contents}

prologue	3
{book i}	7
Chapter 1 | Mr. Repairman	13
Chapter 2 | The Invitation	33
Chapter 3 | Professor Diffenbaugh	48
Chapter 4 | The Dissensions	69
Chapter 5 | The Caverly Twins	90
Chapter 6 | Chargeball	109
Chapter 7 | The Root	125
Chapter 8 | The Calling	150
Chapter 9 | Control	164
interlogue	179
{book ii}	183
Chapter 10 | On Lunging	185
Chapter 11 | Finley's Glove	205
Chapter 12 | The Games Of Illumination	221
Chapter 13 | The Electric Ghost	240
Chapter 14 | Professor Ambrose's Challenge	263

{table of contents} cont.'d

Chapter 15 | Stems	284
Chapter 16 | The Garden Of Glass And Ice	301
Chapter 17 | The Gatherer	326
Chapter 18 | Home For The Holidays	349
Chapter 19 | Orion Heights	361
Chapter 20 | What The Tide Brought In	383
Chapter 21 | The Black Ship	406
Chapter 22 | The Great A'alona, Thunderlight!	422
{book iii}	435
Chapter 23 | Trials Around The Bend	439
epilogue	457
acknowledgements	464
soundtrack	465
about the author	466

{to Katie}

"There will one day spring from the brain of science a machine or **force** so fearful in its potentialities, so **absolutely terrifying**, that even man, the fighter, who will dare torture and death in order to inflict torture and death, will be **appalled**…"

–Thomas A. Edison

'The surger wills for good; to those whose intent is ill, may their headrests be of stone, and their dreams cargo on the black vessel.'

'Virtue bears the diadem of lights…evil mans the fleet of black flags.'

'The surger is built of fortitude and patience, but the hasty and impetuous bring the curse of the black ship upon their lives.'

–Of The Old Proverbs

The Surgers

{Concerning The Text}

In this account you will read about surgers in great length, so it is important to understand what the five obtainable phases of surging actually are:

1.

<u>Lunging:</u> gives the surger the ability to leap great distances.

2.

<u>Fueling:</u> gives the surger the ability to increase speed.

3.

<u>Mending:</u> gives the surger the ability to heal faster + grant healing.

4.

<u>Enhancing:</u> gives the surger the ability to increase physical strength.

5.

<u>Understanding:</u> gives the surger telekinesis.

It is worth mentioning that a surger will always benefit more from utilizing electricity in its strongest form. So, when surging, choosing an appliance that is plugged in rather than battery-powered is always the better choice. Batteries are limited. Alternating currents offer continuous, replenishing electric power.

These different sources also play a role in how effective a surge will be. For example, Mending a broken bone is near impossible without alternating current as your form of power, while Lunging from one rooftop to another only requires a AAA battery.

PROLOGUE

There once was an old man who tinkered.

He sat at his desk for hours and hours, disassembling various electronic devices until his wrists were so sore his hands felt detached from his body, like marionette limbs held together by frayed strings. But the old man pressed on through the discomfort and pain, his desktop growing ever more cluttered with batteries and wires and the tiny metal things that make clocks tick and record players sing.

He was not looking for the knowledge of how these machines worked. No, that was not the old man's goal. You see, he labored and searched in the hopes of one day discovering the Root. He wanted so badly to find the Root, and, in doing so, reap the strange and wonderful powers it bestowed.

Finding the Root meant becoming a surger.

The old man had heard the stories—no, the *legends*—of men and women who could summon enhanced strength and energy from the Root of electronic power sources. Computers. Television sets. Washers, dryers, blenders, lights. They all held the key to absorbing superhuman gifts.

How this was done he did not have the foggiest, but what he was certain of was that surgers were capable of great, wondrous things. Miracles, some said, and a miracle is exactly what the old man's terminally ill wife needed.

One night, when the waxen moon had been in the cloudy sky for hours, the old man had a discovery, though not the one he had necessarily hoped for. He had set an analog clock before him, turned off every other electronic device in his study, and focused his narrowed eyes. He worked by candlelight—such as the limited resources on surging suggested to do—and fixed all his attention and thoughts on the analog clock. He begged it to do something, anything, until he felt beads of sweat form above his temples.

That was when the shadows cast by his candle began to swirl on the wall in dramatic, cylindrical patterns.

The old man leapt up from his chair, and a second later the shadows seemed to retract across the flat surfaces of the desk and wall and *into* the flickering flame with a faint *pop!* The next instant, the candle was snuffed out, and the old man stood in a strip of moonlight—panting.

Slowly, he began to catch his breath and collect his thoughts. What *was* that? Surgers were supposed to pull from currents of electricity. They manipulated power fields nested in the Root. This, however…this ominous movement of light and shadow…well, this was wholly different.

He slept in his study that evening. The next morning, before he could research the incident further, the old man who tinkered went unexpectedly missing.

{book i}

THE moment came with the ship, and the moment was rife with uncertainty.

Finley waded through the shallow ocean water as it splashed around his knees. He held his oil lamp aloft, though he didn't need the flame for light—the moon and stars were providing plenty of that. The water around his legs was terrible and cold, like frozen metal chafing against his skin. The sand beneath his sneakers was both spongy and hard.

What have I gotten myself into! Finley thought, the elements causing his teeth to chatter. He let out an involuntary grunt.

"Go on, Fin!" his best friend called from the beach. "We're running out of time!"

Finley tilted his head back. The old, decrepit Spanish ship was towering, and the fact that it was staying afloat was nothing short of a miracle. The holes and cracks in the ship's bilge should have stymied any chance the vessel had of functioning properly.

And yet there it was…looming above Finley with its torn sails and chapped rails. It was a ghost ship. Had to have been. What other explanation was there? Considering everything Finley had experienced in one semester's worth of time, he had no qualms accepting that the giant, ancient craft was otherworldly.

He took a step forward. His arm was starting to get tired, so he lowered the lamp, and that's when the neon lights blasted through the ship's fissures.

Finley dropped the oil lamp, and it sizzled as the flame was extinguished in the salty ocean water.

"Hurry, Fin! They're coming!"

The moment of uncertainty had passed, and now it was time to move. Finley sucked in a breath and took the coil of rope off of his shoulder…

"Here we go," he said aloud.

SIX MONTHS EARLIER

Chapter 1 | Mr. Repairman

Thirteen-year-old Finley McComb drummed his fingers on his leg as he sat in his uncomfortable desk and half listened to his balding English teacher drone on about the themes in *To Kill A Mockingbird*. He flipped his blonde, shaggy hair out of his eyes and focused his attention on the clock above Mr. Turner's head.

Okay, Finley thought, *this time it'll work. It has to.*

He stopped tapping his fingers and formed a fist under his desktop. He stared, fixated on the red second hand, and tightened his grip until his knuckles were bone-white.

C'mon...

Nothing happened. The clock did not speed up, like he had hoped, but then, he wasn't a surger, was he? Surgers didn't have to go to public school and endure the rote of boring, flawed education.

After a minute of Finley grunting silently under his breath and clamping his hand shut so tight that his arm started to shake, he gave up. Rolling his eyes dejectedly, he looked away from the clock and saw, with utter horror, that Melanie Plum had been watching him from two rows over.

Finley felt the blood in his body rush to his head, like he had been turned upside down. Melanie cracked a grin, however, and then turned to her notepad, where she scribbled something down on a sheet of paper. Next, she discretely tore off the sliver she had written on and waited. Mr. Turner eventually got up from his desk and turned to the board, and Melanie took this opportunity to pass the note over her shoulder.

Instinctually, the redheaded girl who sat behind her took the note, glanced down to see to whom the message was addressed, and passed it to her left. Finley watched, his mouth dry, as the note drifted from kid to kid in slow motion until it was eventually handed to him.

To: Fin, the lettering read in Melanie's sort-of-cursive handwriting. Finley swallowed and then folded the note back, opening it. *Do you need to see the nurse?* was all it said. Finley looked up from the chunk of college-ruled paper and caught Melanie watching him again. Her grin had changed into a full-fledged smile, and she tucked a strand of her velvety brown hair behind her ear.

Whoa, Finley thought and almost said aloud.

Thankfully, he caught himself, and instead pulled out a mechanical pencil from his backpack. *Must've forgotten my medication*, he wrote back underneath her sentence. He folded the note, tapped the shoulder of the kid in front of him, and gave him what was sure to be the cleverest thing Melanie would ever read.

Finley watched his message take the same route, in reverse order, and end up back in Melanie's hands. Trying not to look too obvious, Finley forced himself to stare at the blotch of sunlight that reflected off Mr. Turner's bald spot. Two painfully long minutes later, the note found its way back in his hand.

Before he could open it, the bell sounded from the hall and the classroom broke into its usual end-of-the-day frenzy. Ensuring no one would read Melanie's response over his shoulder, Finley stuffed the note into his jean pocket.

"Be sure to have your book reports on my desk first thing Monday morning!" Mr. Turner said hopelessly. His words were barely audible beneath the zipping of zippers and shuffling of sneakers.

Finley grabbed his backpack and skateboard, looked past the blur of his passing peers, and saw that Melanie had already left. Relief and disappointment sank in, but more of the former—he would not have known what to say if she had waited for him by the door anyway.

Finley trailed out of English class last, and he did not even notice that the clock above Mr. Turner's head had stopped working and was frozen in place at 2:48 p.m.

Finley cruised his Rad Tide board down the sidewalk, the school to his back and rows of palm trees above his head. Two weeks into his eighth grade year, and Melanie Plum had already noticed him. It was his wildest and craziest and most unrealistic dream come to fruition. The sky was the limit now.

He pushed off the concrete with his right foot—propelling him forward to maintain decent speed—and ran a dozen different scenarios through his head. One involved Melanie cutting to the chase and asking if he would be interested in that dance the school threw every fall. Normally, dances were lame, but dances with Melanie Plum were another thing entirely.

Another scenario involved Melanie getting cornered in an alley by some hooligans. Finley of course skated to the rescue, kicked up his board, and used it as a weapon, knocking out all three thugs. Melanie, overwhelmed with gratitude, leapt into Finley's arms and gave him a wet kiss on the lips.

Finley bent his knees, both feet in between the skateboard trucks, and shifted his weight slightly. He kickflipped off the sidewalk and onto the shoulder of the street. Eventually it would run into Pacific Coast Highway, and he could use this route to navigate to the burger joint on the pier, where he and his friends met up. Land Rovers and Beamers zoomed past him, flattening his tank top against his back.

Finley's friends would not believe him. They would not believe that Melanie had shown him the slightest bit of attention. But that did not matter, because he had proof. Proof in the form of her note. Together, he and his friends would read her response and—

Finley planted his right foot down on the tail of his board, tilted up, and grinded to a stop. Up ahead, in a strip mall parking lot, Dillon Trask and his cronies were "corralling" a sixth grader Finley had seen from school. They led the kid around back and out of sight. Finley knew what this was about: poor kid was about to get hazed.

Dillon was a freshman now, and, because he was undergoing his own personal, embarrassing initiation into high school, he was finding ways of vindication through torturing middle schoolers. It was kind of pathetic, when you thought about it, but Dillon did not see it that way.

Whelp, Finley thought, *it's not Melanie, but maybe she'll walk by and witness me saving the day.*

Realistically though, all Finley planned on doing was talking Dillon out of it. Coaxing him down from the ledge. He and Finley were not tight, but they were cool enough.

They used to get dragged to the same social events their moms coordinated in the suburban bubbles. Masquerade-themed charity dinners. Debutante balls. Pretty much anything that gave the adults a justification for setting up an open bar.

Finley picked up his board and jogged after Dillon and the group. He rounded the last store and saw Dillon leading the kid by his shoulder past a row of Dumpsters. They were headed toward a small, palm tree-lined field behind the staff parking lot, which dead-ended at an electrical fence.

"Yo!" Finley shouted, chasing after them. "Wait up!"

Dillon and his two lackeys stopped in their tracks and turned around. As Finley got closer, he noticed the sixth grader's busted lip.

Dillon narrowed his eyes, looking annoyed. "Fin? Need something?"

"Sup," he answered, dropping his board on the pavement when he reached them and putting his right foot on the tail. He nodded to the sixth grader. "Who's shortstop?"

"What do you care?"

"Looks familiar." Then, to the sixth grader, "I've seen you in the halls."

He did not respond. He stared at Finley's board.

Dillon: "Was there something you needed?"

"I was just trying to remember where I've seen him

from. Couldn't place it."

"Well, you go to school together. There, it's placed. See you around, Fin—"

"That's it—you have Ms. Sperry for homeroom! I had her in sixth grade, too." Finley whipped his bangs back idly, then laughed dramatically and added, "How crazy obsessed is she with bonsai trees, right?"

"Why don't you two do this Monday?" Dillon asked, only, he was not really asking. He then nodded toward the electrical fence, and his two henchmen took the sixth grader by his arms and towed him off.

"You should probably get home," Dillon told Finley in a low, threatening voice. Then, he about-faced and marched away. Finley watched him go, suddenly feeling hard-pressed, as if he had exhausted a large amount of energy.

I can't just go home, Finley realized, pushing off the ground and skating forward until the pavement cracked and split, and ended at grass and dirt. He leapt off his board and let his backpack fall from his shoulders, and then he sprinted down the field past Dillon.

"I'll do it," Finley said, turning and jogging backward. Dillon's cheeks flushed. "Whatever you were gonna have shortstop do, *I'll* do."

"Get out of here," Dillon said, setting his large jaw. "Don't make me ask you again." But together, they reached the humming electrical fence, where Dillon's lackeys were waiting with the all-but-whimpering sixth grader.

"What gives?" one of the lackeys said, a ninth grader with buzzed hair and a striped tank top similar to Finley's. He, the lackey, seemed anxious, almost *nervous*...

Their sixth grade victim stood, eyes downcast, subtly shaking.

Finley did not know where this urge to become the rescuer was truly coming from. He would like to think that it was because he once stood toe-to-toe against an oppressive and intimidating bully. That he knew what it felt like to have your eye bruised and your lip split.

Only, Finley McComb had not had an experience like that before. He had always been accepted into the right circles. He had always had the friends that afforded him the luxury to walk between classes without being pushed or slammed into a locker. This was not a privilege he had set out to attain, it just was.

"Let me do it," Finley continued, brushing past the kid wearing the striped tank top. "This? Were you gonna have him hold the fence until he wet himself?" Finley held out his hand and hovered it in front of the taut wires.

You kids just think you're invincible, Finley's mom was always scolding him when he would get into trouble. You act without weighing the consequences! His mom's sentiment had never been truer than right now.

That was when it dawned on Finley. Melanie Plum's

note. From English class. *That* was why he felt so indestructible, so determined.

Dillon cleared his throat. "Fin, wait—"

The next sequences of events happened in such fast succession, Finley would later have to strain to remember the order. He turned, meeting Dillon's gaze, but noticed that, in the staff parking lot by the strip mall, a few dozen yards off from where they stood, Melanie had appeared with a tenth grader who played water polo. They leaned against the brick wall, locking lips, and then the electrical fence smoked and flared behind Finley.

The sixth grader yelped, seizing this distraction to free himself. He bolted away. Dillon cussed, holding up his arms to shield his eyes from the cracking and spitting sparks. Finley had toppled to his knees, crawling away and bumping into one of Dillon's friends.

Then, an adult's voice spoke, "You kids all right?" and the electrical fence seemed to subdue, only crackling every few seconds now until even the wan hum from before had vanished.

Finley looked up from the ground, catching the backs of Dillon and his lackeys as they sprinted around the strip mall and disappeared. Melanie and the tenth grader were already gone, and for a second, Finley thought he had only imagined what he had seen, but then, with clenched fists, he decided that no, he *had* seen what he had feared he'd seen.

A hand came into focus beside Finley's head. He glanced over and saw a young, bearded man in an electrician's shirt, a cursive name stitched beside his heart that read, *Mr. Repairman*. He had blue eyes and a Dodgers ball cap, and he smelled of dust and fast-food hamburgers.

Finley accepted the man's help and got to his feet, attempting to wipe the grass stains from his jeans.

"Little laundry detergent will get those out," Mr. Repairman noted in a dully voice, taking off his hat and running his hand through tangled hair. "I get all kinds of stains from work. You okay?"

"Fine." Finley walked around the man and grabbed his backpack and skateboard.

"Wait. We should call your folks. You need to get to a hospital."

"I'm not hurt," Finley replied, turning to face the man and hazarding, "Was that you? Did you, you know, do that with the fence?"

"I was gonna ask you the same thing," the man said, a glint in his eyes.

"Nah, it was probably just a malfunction."

"Probably."

"Just a coincidence."

"Yeah. Good thing no one was hurt."

Finley spun around, dropped his board onto the cement, and flew off, leaving Mr. Repairman shouting that he should at least let him take Finley home. He knew not to accept rides from strangers, especially mysterious repairmen who seemed to materialize out of thin air.

After Finley deposited his skateboard on the marbled foyer floor, he strode through the great room, tossed his backpack onto the couch, and entered the kitchen, where his mom was washing and snipping a sprig of flowers beneath the faucet.

She was a kindly woman with a kindly face, but you never tracked dirt onto her carpet or complained about her cooking. She smiled at the appearance of her youngest child, but those sharp eyes of hers instantly honed in on Finley's dirty jeans.

"Make sure you change before dinner," she ordered Finley, arching an eyebrow disapprovingly. She placed the flowers in a vase and displayed them on the kitchen island, where Finley's dad sat reading the paper.

Don't people read the newspaper in the *morning*? Finley and his older sister, Erin, were always asking, to which their father only insisted that he was not like everyone else, and Erin and Finley would benefit greatly from this mindset. This got Mr. McComb in trouble when his children would argue that homework and chores and curfews should not apply to them, because, after all, they should not be treated like "everyone else."

It had to indefinitely be changed, Mr. McComb's

outlook, to *after* they turned eighteen. You should not be like everyone else *after* you turn eighteen, he would say with the most triumphant look, though all he had managed to do was confuse his children beyond saving.

"Finley," Mr. McComb said, lowering his newspaper and peering over the top of his circle glasses. "Try out for any sports today?"

"No, Dad," Finley said flatly, grabbing a Coke from the fridge and snapping it open. He guzzled down the fizzy drink and wiped his mouth when he was finished.

"Shame," Mr. McComb said, returning to his paper. "Your sister just made the varsity—"

"I know, Dad," Finley said, rolling his eyes and heading into the dining room, where dinner was already set.

Erin sat in her usual spot at the table, talking on her cell phone to one of her senior friends about why Landon was such a jerk and should just break up with Meredith already. Finley set his Coke can down and walked up the stairs to his bedroom.

He backed into the half open door, swinging it forward, and kicked off his Vans after turning on the light. He pulled down his pants and balled them up, throwing them across the room. Then, he dug through his dresser and eventually found a clean pair of gym shorts.

He took his time changing. He had not thought much on his way home, and actually opted to skip his hangout at the pier. Instead, he had skated straight to his neighborhood, purposefully getting lost and having to back track, which, in turn, ate up almost two afternoon hours.

Now, in his haven, in his bedroom, the one place untainted and unmarred by the outside world, Finley could finally think. Melanie had only been leading him on. She had no intention of ever doing more with Finley than innocent flirting.

It's just as well, Finley thought, closing his dresser drawer with extra oomph. *She went all this time without talking to me, so really, nothing's changed.*

Only, it had changed, because she had talked to him, albeit in a childish note in English class. Finley realized he wished that exchange never happened.

"Finley! Dinner!"

He left the light on in his bedroom and padded down the wooden stairs. In the dining room, his dad sat at the head of the table, pouring a hefty portion of rice onto his plate. His sister still chatted on the phone. His mom was using a pair of tongs to meticulously mix the salad.

And everything seemed...off.

Finley stayed near the stairwell, cocking his head. Everything was as it should have been, in its right place, down to the clinking of silverware and the smell of the sea breeze as it drifted inside through the open French doors. Why, then, did the atmosphere feel misaligned, off-kilter?

On the wall that separated the kitchen from the dining room, where the flat screen television hung, the image flickered like a candle set before an air vent. Bending, waving, almost wreathing. This was not uncommon, though, because ever since Finley's dad had upgraded to the supreme sports package with their cable provider, their reception would go in and out at the most inconvenient times, like when the host of Mrs. McComb's favorite reality show was seconds away from dubbing this season's champion cat masseuse.

Mr. Repairman stepped in from the kitchen, his Dodgers ball cap on backwards now, and Finley understood the change in the dining room. Everything was going a little slower, almost imperceptibly. The way Finley's dad cut into his salmon. The way Erin twirled her hair while she gossiped on her phone. The way Mrs. McComb lathered her salad with dressing.

"Any luck?" Mr. McComb asked from his place at the table, raising a forkful of fish to his mouth.

His voice came out at a normal speed, not matching his moving lips. It was like a poorly dubbed foreign film, only not as bad. If Finley had been tired and groggy, he might not have caught the discrepancy at all.

"Bad connection," Mr. Repairman said, *tsk tsk*ing and shaking his head.

His motion and gestures were fine, however, causing Finley to take a backward step up the stairs. His palms suddenly felt sweaty. His heart beat in his temples.

What's going on? Finley thought, eyes glued on Mr.

Repairman. *Did he follow me home?*

"Ah, there you are Finley!" Mrs. McComb said, waving for her son to come down. "Eat your dinner before it's cold. We're finally getting our reception fixed. Can you believe that! I know you don't like fish, but it's good for you."

Finley stayed where he was, his feet on two different level steps. "Not hungry. Actually, I'm not feeling well. Think I'm just gonna knock out my homework and pass out. Fridays are always tough."

"Because you said you'd do your homework," Mr. McComb said between bites, "I'm even *less* inclined to believe you. Plus, you need to eat!"

"You know," Mr. Repairman said, locking eyes with Finley. He did not seem threatening, Finley decided, but that was exactly why he seemed threatening. "If your kid's not hungry, he could always give me a hand? Might be fun for him to mess with the power tools."

"I'm not seven," Finley said, glaring through his yellow bangs at Mr. Repairman.

"Finley, don't be rude," Mrs. McComb snapped in her characteristic tone, but in an equally uncharacteristic, gradual way. It was not necessarily slow motion, it just was not what it should have been. "Help the nice repairman and then eat your dinner."

"Do what your mother says," Finley's dad added for good measure.

He, Finley, could not believe his ears. He watched Mr. Repairman wave for him to follow, and it took that simple gesture for Finley to conclude that the odd stranger with the Dodgers ball cap was somehow responsible for what happened at the electrical fence.

Finley took the route through the living room to the front door, which was open and gave view to Mr. Repairman's silhouetted form in the sunset—walking down the exterior steps and heading to his parked van in the driveway.

"Wait," Finley called out, staying on the front patio. Mr. Repairman froze, then eventually turned around. "Why did you follow me?"

Mr. Repairman smiled a toothy smile, and, instead of feeling weirded out or off put, Finley found himself strangely at peace. Whoever this man was, if he wanted to hurt Finley or his family, he probably could have done that by now.

So what *did* he want?

"I didn't follow you," he replied, standing still on the patch of lawn and picking his beard. "But, well, yeah, I kind of did, only not how you're thinking."

"That makes complete sense," Finley said sarcastically, folding his arms. "I should call the cops."

"Yeah, you could," Mr. Repairman said with a sigh. "But, the school would find another way of recruiting you, Finley, even if the boys in blue kept me away."

"School? What school?"

"Here," Mr. Repairman said, pulling something from his jean pocket and tossing it forward. Finley caught it in both hands. It was a silver, nondescript, electric lighter.

"What's this?"

"That," Mr. Repairman said, turning the bill of his hat forward and walking toward Finley, "is your test. If you pass, I'll explain the rest."

Finley was a breath away from throwing the lighter back at Mr. Repairman and slamming the front door shut in his face. But something inside Finley tugged at him. Yet, it was not something, but rather some *things*. Stories he heard. Rumors.

…Legends.

As far back as Finley could recall, kids in his school—grades equal, beneath, and above him—would randomly disappear right before the start of each semester. It was only one or two at a time, but it was enough to notice and set off chains of quick-spreading gossip. Boarding school? That was the logical explanation, because their parents remained in Huntington Beach, so they had not moved away.

But when summer rolled around, and Finley's peers returned from wherever they had been shipped off to, there was a noticeable change in them. A spark in their eyes. They stood taller, straighter. They seemed *happier*. When asked where they had been, they replied simply,

Away. We've been away.

A couple of years ago, in the middle of summer break, Finley had walked into the school gym on the weekend to borrow the sack of community kickballs, and he thought he had seen an eighth grade girl jumping the distance of the basketball court—disappearing behind the bleachers. When Finley rushed over, no one was there, so he quit Red Bull cold turkey the next day.

So is that what this is about? Finley thought, running his index finger across the cool lighter lid. *Surging?* This test, whatever it was, made no sense then, because surgers summoned and willed powers from electricity, not fire.

"Well?" Mr. Repairman asked expectantly, though he did not sound agitated.

"What do I do?" Finley looked up, hoping for instruction. Mr. Repairman gave none, leaving Finley to do the only sensible thing.

He flicked back the lid, delicately touched the thumbwheel, and pulled down against the flint. There was a tiny grinding noise, like two pieces of sandpaper being rubbed together, but that was all that happened.

Finley tried again. Nothing. What was he doing wrong? He'd seen it done a hundred times over in movies and on TV shows. He must have attempted to trigger the flame at least twenty times because his thumb was beginning to feel raw.

"I was afraid of this," Mr. Repairman said, holding out

an open palm for Finley to return his lighter. It was the first time Finley had heard disappointment in the man's diction.

Finley suddenly found that he was embarrassed, like that dream where you show up in class wearing nothing but underpants and mismatched socks. He swallowed, gave one last, desperate flick of his thumb, and started with surprise.

A miniscule flame appeared above the windscreen.

"Well," Mr. Repairman said, chuckling. He looked slightly cross-eyed as he gaped at the tiny, flapping fire. "On behalf of Brighton Preparatory School for Surgers, I'd like to extend to you an invitation for enrollment."

Finley blinked, closing the lid and snuffing out the flame. "That's it? You expect me to believe that?" He tossed the lighter back to Mr. Repairman who, because he wasn't expecting this, juggled it before finally securing it in his hand.

"Turning on a lighter is going to get me into some exclusive school?"

"Finley—"

"No, you know what? I should've called the cops. This isn't right—*you're* not right. Goodbye."

"There wasn't any lighter fluid, Finley."

This gave Finley pause, his hand grasping the shiny brass handle on the front door.

"*What?*"

"Yeah," Mr. Repairman said, pulling back the lid and attempting to reignite the lighter. The thumbwheel spun and spun, producing nothing but that soft grating noise. He then unscrewed the top of the lighter and held it upside down above the grass, proving that it was in fact empty. "Congratulations. You passed the test."

Chapter 2 | The Invitation

The sun set and disappeared behind the Californian hills, leaving the McComb front lawn twilit, and Finley laughed because it was the only response he knew to give.

"You're a recruiter?" Finley asked Mr. Repairman.

"Yes."

"For a surging prep school?"

"Uh hu."

"And because I was able to work that lighter, you want me to go back with you. To that school?"

"That's the gist of it."

Finley wanted to laugh some more, but kept the reaction inward. He wasn't trying to be rude or disrespectful, or even irritable. It was just, well, he didn't believe a single word this man spoke. That business with the lighter? It had to have been some kind of trick. No way Finley summoned fire out of nowhere. That was impossible. Plus, what the heck did any of this have to do with surging?

"And let's say I believe all this," Finley said, shifting his weight as he stood on the front patio. "What makes you think my parents are just going to pull me out of school and let me go, two weeks into the semester?"

"I think you will find them quite willing," Mr. Repairman replied, pocketing the lighter, "given that this honor is comparable to the highest of accolades."

"Is it?" Finley shook his head, grabbing the door handle behind his back. "I wouldn't know. The whole surging thing is kind of a taboo, isn't it?"

"Finley—"

"Look, as much as I want to believe you, I can't. I've never been able to do anything that remotely resembles surging. You've got the wrong kid."

Finley turned on his heel and pulled opened the door all the way, when the light above of the entrance flickered, and the next instant the handle slipped from Finley's fingers as the door seemed to close of its own accord with a *bang!*

Finley spun around, staring wordlessly at Mr. Repairman.

"This may come as a shock to you," he said, pulling a sealed envelope out of his breast pocket, "but I don't think you're a surger, and neither does Brighton Prep. No, you just proved with that lighter, Finley, you are something more."

Finley took the square envelope, which wasn't bigger than a Polaroid picture. How was this happening to him? Finley wasn't special. He didn't excel at anything. He didn't aspire to do much more than survive the school week so he and his friends could escape to the beach. There were expectations, sure, set in motion by his father, who wanted him to pursue sports, and his mother, who wanted him to maintain flawless grades and consider AP courses, because, after all, *Erin* had followed this path, and look how many colleges are practically begging her to grace their campuses with her presence!

Finley found those expectations lofty, at best, and never met them.

Now he was being told by a surger—an actual *surger!*—that he had a place among the elite, clandestine community of miracle workers most people said only subsisted in campfire tales and bedtime stories.

I should sit down, Finley thought, plopping onto the ground just before his wobbly knees gave way.

"I know this is a lot to process," Mr. Repairman said, blinking his blue eyes and scratching his swirly beard. "Usually we recruit months before each semester, but, well, you're not exactly usual, are you?"

"I think that was a compliment?"

Mr. Repairman chortled like the fake Santa Clauses at the mall. "It was."

"What happened back there? At the electrical fence?"

"That wasn't me. My guess? You started inadvertently drawing from the currents and voltage. Did you have a pins and needles sensation? Running through your hands and arms?"

"No."

"Curious that is," Mr. Repairman said, tapping his hairy chin thoughtfully. "Of course, you may not experience the same type of effects and reactions that a surger does after he or she has drawn from the Root."

"What exactly am I then?" Finley forced himself to stand, and, because he was on the bottommost step of the patio, he was level with Mr. Repairman's eye line.

"Ah, see, that's for you to find out. Along with Brighton Prep's finest, of course."

Finley ruffled his blond hair and then looked down at the envelope in his hands, which, in tall, skinny type, was addressed to him, reading happily, *Finley McComb!*—exclamation mark and all.

"Are you ready to have an adventure, Finley McComb?" Mr. Repairman put his hand on Finley's shoulder, reeling in his attention.

"I…," he trailed off, quite literally at a loss for words, before clearing his throat and stating, when nothing else came to mind, "I just want to be thirteen."

Mr. Repairman's eyes twinkled. "I would eliminate that word from your vocabulary as soon as you get the chance. From this moment on, you'll never *just* be anything ever again."

Finley wanted to swallow, but there was a knot in his throat that wouldn't let him. *I'm going to let the school down. I know it. They have the wrong—*

"Instructions are in the envelope." Mr. Repairman turned toward his van. "You leave first thing tomorrow morning!"

He waved over his shoulder without looking back, got into his van, took off his ball cap and propped it on the dashboard beside a Bobblehead, reversed out, and was driving off before Finley could form a response.

"Okay," he said aloud, walking back into the foyer and closing the door. Standing beneath the hanging stain glass light, he ripped open the envelope and read the hurried, informal message:

Mr. Finley McComb!

Excited? We are. In fact, you might even say we're thrilled. Sorry about the hurried, informal message. We're two weeks into the fall term, actually, but we just had to make an exception for you *because, well, you're exceptional, and if you don't know that by now, you will soon enough! The bus pass included in this letter will bring you straight here, to campus, and we'll get your courses, materials, and rooming situation squared away immediately!*

Dean Margaret Longenecker
Brighton Preparatory School for Surgers
Est. 1967

Finley fished inside the envelope again, positive the only contents had been this letter, but was surprised to find one ticket for a 6:00 a.m., nonstop trip to Brighton Preparatory School for Surgers.

Holding both the letter of acceptance and the bus pass, Finley found himself still incapable of believing all that had come to pass in the short, short span of one single afternoon.

I won't believe it until I step foot in the school, Finley decided, ruminating to himself as he walked through the house and into the dining room, where his parents still worked on dinner, his sister still talked on the phone, and the flat screen TV still projected the terrible, shoddy reception. Only when Finley sat down across from his sister, the image seemed to right itself, and now an orange woman with big lips was telling the room why Gilda's jewelry couldn't be beat.

"I hope it's fixed for good," Finley's mom said, pointing at the TV with her fork.

Her voice and lips were still a little off, but it wasn't as obvious now, and Finley figured it had to do with Mr. Repairman's presence. Standing in the midst of a surger must have that effect, and Finley wondered if, to Mr. Repairman, Finley's voice and mouth were off rhythm, too.

Mr. McComb took a sip of his wine and said, his smile so big his circle glasses slid down his nose, "Couldn't be more pleased to have someone in the family heading to Brighton Prep. Make sure and finish your dinner, Son."

"There's lemon in the fish," Finley's mom tacked on. "Lots of lemon. You *love* lemon."

Finley had always claimed, at the top of his voice, that his parents were the strangest, and he'd meant it, promising his friends that *their* parents didn't stand a chance in terms of comparisons.

Finley cut into his lukewarm fish, sighing inwardly, and he decided that now, officially, his parents truly were the strangest of them all, but it was okay, because he was leaving soon, and he'd probably miss that strangeness. Probably.

How they had already known he was going to Brighton Prep before he'd said anything was a mystery, but Finley was in too much shock to question it...

That night, Finley skipped desert (Oreos drizzled in ice cream with a glass of almond milk to combat the sugar) and went straight to his bedroom, where he threw as many pairs of jeans and T-shirts that would fit into his red gym bag. Then, he dug through his desk drawers and searched for every pencil and folder and ruler and school supply he owned.

I have to tell someone, Finley thought, zipping up his backpack and setting it on top of his duffle bag by the door. *Maybe then it will all start to sink in.*

The problem was that Finley didn't know whom he could call, because of his closest friends, he didn't know who was closest, really, and that forced him to fall on his bed dramatically with a wry frown and his arms outspread.

Finley knew a lot of people in school. He was always busying himself on the weekends and making sure that his time was spent away from home. Yet, at the end of the day, whom could he refer to as his best friend? What number could he dial when, say, he had news about getting enlisted in a surging prep school and he would be leaving Huntington Beach indefinitely?

Thinking about all the people Finley knew made him feel more alone than he'd ever imagined.

He rolled over on his bed, spun the plastic crank below

his window, and opened the glass. Wind that was coated in sea salt blew inside. Finley looked out over the tops of houses and palm trees, thinking and then realizing that no one at school would notice his absence. The vast Ethel Dwyer Middle populace wouldn't lose sleep over his sudden disappearance.

Scolding himself for this rueful disposition, Finley turned over, set his alarm clock for 5:30 a.m., and shut off the light.

Stop moping, Finley said in his heart. *I've just been accepted into a surging prep school.*

He didn't feel as if he'd earned this right, but the right had been granted to him all the same. It was time to embrace this reality and look ahead. Somehow, he'd made fire appear using an empty lighter, and, regardless of the fact that he didn't know how to duplicate this phenomenon, it had happened. It wasn't an illusion. He'd felt the warmth of the flame against his thumb—smelled the scent of fire. Something magnificent had occurred on the front patio, Finley just didn't know what that magnificent thing was, or where it had come from.

Lying in the dark above his covers, he tried guessing at what tomorrow would bring, but his thoughts overlapped one another, stirring up doubt and confusion and scary scenarios, like him showing up on campus and being told by the faculty a mistake had indeed been made, and they were sorry for the misunderstanding, and he shouldn't tell a soul about this place, or about surgers as a whole, because theirs was a secret and wonderful society, and Finley McComb didn't belong there.

When he returned home from this awkward experience, he was met by the laughter and heckling of his parents and sister, but eventually that laughter and heckling became something real, only, it was Finley's alarm clock, which he smacked rather zealously when his senses came to him.

He slugged through the mess on his bedroom floor, stubbed his toe on his nightstand, and fumbled with the light. He threw on his backpack, put on some jeans and sneakers, picked up his duffle bag with a tired hand, and took one last look at his room as if he would never see it again. He left with the light on.

Finley passed by his parents' bedroom in the hall, hearing his mother's soft breathing and his father's sporadic spurts of snores and inhales. When he was younger, and the dark had laid claim to him, creating monsters and shadows, hearing his parents sleep had always seemed to set things right.

I should wake them up…they'll be mad if I leave without saying goodbye.

Finley hesitated, staring at their door wistfully, but then ultimately moved further down the hall, pausing outside Erin's bedroom. The only thing he could hear was the hum of the cycling ceiling fan. Erin had to have her room cold, because what was the point of wrapping up in your comforter if you weren't cold? she'd say.

Finley laughed inwardly, tiptoed down the stairs, and left through the kitchen door. Outside, the grass was wet and the sky wasn't quite pink yet. He strode through the side yard, passed his mother's gardenias, and turned up the sidewalk. He swallowed, blinked his eyes to wake himself up more, and pointedly avoided looking over his shoulder at his house. The sight alone might convince him to stay.

Are you ready to have an adventure? Mr. Repairman had asked yesterday after passing Finley his sealed invitation. Finley still didn't know how to answer that. Was anybody ever ready for adventures? Exactly how does one ready themselves for an adventure?

Finley walked past a stop sign, crossed the street, and the neighborhood lampposts began to turn off. He eventually rounded the last yard and emerged onto Sunflower Blvd.'s sidewalk, where a newspaper kiosk, trashcan, and bus stop awaited. There were only a handful of cars on the street this early, one of which was a large blue bus that lumbered to a loud stop before Finley even sat down.

That's when he started to panic. Finley never had to use public transportation before—his parents took him wherever he needed to go because, after all, that's what parents were for. But he knew enough about traveling to discern the difference between city buses and Greyhounds. There was no way this ride would be enough to get him to

Brighton Prep! Unless, of course, Brighton Prep was closer than he figured it was.

"Let's go, kid," a voice barked.

Finley flinched; he hadn't noticed the bus doors opening or the uniformed driver staring down at him. Finley let his feet carry him up the steps, and he set his duffle bag down and pulled out his ticket, handing it to the thickset driver warily. The man lifted up his sunglasses and stared at the ticket, and Finley was sure he was going to laugh in his face and order him off his bus. All he did, however, was grunt something that sounded like, Okay, and then pull the lever that closed the doors.

Finley picked up his duffle bag and traipsed to the back of the empty bus, collapsing onto the last row of seats right as the bus started forward.

They passed through six streetlights before Finley pulled his music player and headphones out of his backpack and blasted Blink 182 into his ears. Finley was surprised to find that the driver didn't make any other stops. They drove by a few benches, where angry men and women shouted after the bus, but not once did the large driver even react.

They turned onto Pacific Coast Highway, zooming by the piers and beaches. The ocean was in beautiful form this morning, and Finley saw dozens of surfers out and about. Some used finesse as they glided over and through breaking waves, whereas others paddled on their stomachs out by the wave crowding.

An hour passed. The bus still didn't stop.

Finley leaned back in his stiff seat and set his feet on top of his duffle bag. He lazily turned up his music, hoping the volume would keep him awake so he could see where they were headed exactly, but his heavy eyes won.

Almost three hours later the bus was jerking to a stop, and Finley woke from his nap. The music player had long since stopped playing, so he pulled out his headphones and looked outside. To his left there was still beach, but it was empty. A shoreline with nothing but the waves and sand. To his right there were endless hills.

"Why are we stopped?" Finley called out. The bus driver said nothing. He stuffed his music player in his back pocket and grabbed his bags. He walked toward the front, almost tripping over his feet once, and then repeated, "Why are we stopped?"

"We're here."

"Here *where*?"

The bus driver took off his sunglasses. "Look, kid, I don't have time for this. I gotta get back into the city. I brought you to the address, all right?"

Address? What address? All the bus ticket had said in the way of destination was Brighton Preparatory School for Surgers.

Finley said, "Yeah, but—" A phone rang, cutting him off.

The bus driver reached into his pocket and pulled out a cell phone, answering it. He laughed a hollow, resounding laugh, and told the person on the other line something about poor scheduling and why he would never work on Thursdays and Sundays.

Finley shrugged to himself, turning and walking down the steps. Once outside, the accordion doors snapped shut behind him with a loud, mocking *phff!* When the bus drove away, Finley checked for oncoming traffic (even though he didn't have to, because there weren't any other cars in sight) before crossing the street to the beach.

He was the only one around for miles. Finley didn't think deserted beaches like this even existed anymore, at least not in Southern California. The late morning sun beat down on him in its hot September way, and he walked across the sand to the water. He set his bags on the ground and put his hands on his hips, surveying the Pacific Ocean with a heavy sense of dread welling inside him.

If it weren't for Mr. Repairman's display of surging—closing the McComb's front door without using hands—Finley would conclude that this was all some kind of twisted, cruel joke. But Mr. Repairman *had* used surging. Finley *had* passed his test. So what was wrong?

Finley sat at the ocean's edge, pulling his knees up and resting his hands on the sand. *Well*, he thought resolutely, *if this is as close to the school as I'll ever get, might as well enjoy the view before finding a way home.*

That's when a boisterous voice shouted: "Dude, *that's* how you came dressed for your first day at Brighton?"

Finley swiveled his head and saw a tall, pretty woman wearing a casual business suit and standing on the beach. She had stark red hair, and behind her, on the street, was a parked woodie with a surfboard rack, and behind the wood-paneled wagon, where before there had only been hills, was an enormous, city-like campus.

Finley McComb had arrived.

Chapter 3 | <u>Professor Diffenbaugh</u>

"You *are* Finley McComb, right?"

Finley McComb stood up on trembling legs and feet. He stared past the pretty redhead and old-school-looking car at the tall, stucco buildings that made up what he figured was Brighton Preparatory School for Surgers. Flags jutted out of the tile roofs and whipped in the breeze. A massive, yellow hot air balloon was ascending into the cloudless sky. He heard the low, faint hum of far off chatter and excitement.

Finley forgot how to talk.

"Great." The woman turned, calling out to the driver who sat in the idle woodie and shouting, "It happened again, Wally. Wrong kid. That's twice in two years—!"

"Wait!" Finley yelped after he found his voice. He

scooped down and snagged his backpack off the sand, putting it on. Then he carried his duffle bag at his side as he jogged toward the redheaded woman. "I'm Finley. Finley McComb."

"Good!" she said, pausing until Finley caught up and then leading him to the street. "The paperwork I have to fill out when the wrong kid shows up is tedious. It's much easier for the both of us if you're Finley McComb."

Finley laughed, but then stopped when he wasn't sure if that had been a joke or not. The driver—the man she called Wally—got out of the wagon and relieved Finley of his bags. Wally had messy, bushy hair and wore a loud Hawaiian shirt and khaki Bermuda shorts. He had a young, enthusiastic face that seemed lively and full of sincere determination.

"So it's him?" Wally asked the woman rhetorically as he put Finley's things in the trunk. The driver moved quickly, bumping into the trunk door twice and snort-laughing in response. Then, he opened the side door for Finley and the woman. She insisted that he go in first, so he did, sliding to the other side and immediately looking out of the window at the campus.

"I'm Dean Longenecker, by the way," the redheaded woman said, taking her seat beside Finley and shutting the door. Wally got into the driver's seat and put the wagon in drive. Roy Orbison played from the cassette deck.

"Hi," said Finley, turning to shake her hand. How the

dean wasn't repulsed by his sweaty, clammy hand was beyond him. He couldn't help it though. This was all actually, really, *legitimately* happening.

"We have to make a few stops this morning before getting you settled into the dormitories," the dean said, crossing her legs. Finley saw that she was wearing sneakers with her suit. "Need to get you the Brighton uniform first. But don't worry, it's got a rad design and isn't the ugliest thing you'll ever wear. You like crab tacos?"

"Er..."

"Good!" She tucked some red hair behind her left ear. "After lunch, we'll get your course schedule set up, arrange for tutoring sessions, set you up in your dorm, assign you a student preceptor for the spring, and, well, I think that covers it. Right, Wally?"

The bushy-haired driver snort-laughed again and nodded in the rearview mirror, turning the woodie up the paved entrance to the prep school. With a start, Finley noticed that Wally's hands weren't on the steering wheel; he was sipping what smelled like coffee and perusing the arts and leisure section of the newspaper. And yet, somehow, the steering wheel veered a little and guided them on course.

Surging! Finley thought, his heart beating quickly. *Is he drawing from the car battery and steering it with his mind? Going to have to get used to stuff like that...*

Wally turned around and faced Finley so fast that his

motion was a blur, and Finley thought for sure the coffee in his mug was going to spill. "You're going to love this place!" Wally shouted, his coffee still swishing around in the mug, the steering wheel still keeping them on track without needing the driver's full attention.

"Yeah," Finley said uncomfortably, "can't wait." Wally faced forward and turned his newspaper over.

Open steel gates admitted them entrance, and the single lane road was lined with lampposts and sideways banners. EXCELLENCE one of the banners read. PERSEVERANCE another banner read. PURSUIT OF PERFECTION.

Finley gulped. "S-So you're both surgers then?" he asked, looking away from the intimidating promises that the banners boasted.

"Yup," Wally said. He glanced up at the road every now and again.

"That's right," Dean Longenecker said distractedly, flipping through a folder of important-looking documents that Finley hadn't seen her pull out. "Everyone at Brighton Prep is"—the dean cut herself off—"except for you, of course, because you're *exceptional*."

"Right," Finley said, finding that he was getting annoyed with words like "exceptional." *Guess I'm going to have to get used to that, too.* Just then, three streaks of hot pink whisked past Finley's window with an echoing shrill, causing him to squeal and jump back.

Wally fist-pumped, but didn't look up from his reading. "Love when they see Fueling for the first time," he said to himself.

"What was that!" Finley demanded, almost panting.

"Ah," Dean Longenecker said, setting her folder on her lap. "Probably freshmen. Working on their Fueling."

"'Fueling?'" Finley repeated, cranking his window down and sticking his head outside. The slightest hint of the intense, neon colors tarried in the air, eventually fading like floating fireworks.

"Fueling," the dean said again as Finley sat back down. She put a hand on his shoulder and added, voice low, "Listen, Finley. Things being what they are, with you already two weeks behind in the semester, you'll most likely get overwhelmed."

"Nah," Finley joked, "can't see that happening."

"Plus, we're asking a lot of you to just accept this new culture and 'go with the flow.' So, right now, before we get out of this car, I want you to make me a promise." Her tone was still low and now serious. Even though Finley had just met the dean, he could tell this was uncharacteristic.

"Um, sure?" Finley chuckled nervously.

"If things start to get too intense for you," she continued, eyes filled with concern, "if your classes and studies seem to suffocate you, promise me you'll come find me. Promise me you'll let me know. There's absolutely no shame in walking away."

In the front seat, Wally cleared his throat and then sipped some more coffee. After a few seconds, the woodie lurched and then stopped.

"Promise me," the dean whispered, and Finley could see, through her window, a man descending wide steps from the top of what appeared to be the campus's biggest building.

Finley couldn't explain why, but he suddenly felt tense. "I-I prom—" The dean's door opened, revealing a man in his twenties with handsome features and straight short hair. He had a tucked-in shirt and a polka-dotted bowtie.

"He made it!" the young man said in a high-energy exclamation.

He stood aside, and before Dean Longenecker left the wagon, Finley caught her exchanging glances with Wally. She passed the driver her folder, and he couldn't be sure, but Finley thought he saw her sliding a note inside the collection of papers before Wally accepted it from the dean.

"Professor Diffenbaugh," the dean said, putting on her happy face and getting out of the wagon. "You're just in time! Look who we found at the beach."

Before Finley opened his door, he tried reading Wally's face, but the driver was putting the dean's folder in the glove compartment and getting out of his seat—all while showing the most deadpanned, apathetic expression one could fathom.

Finley got out of the wagon after Wally opened his door and walked around to meet the professor.

"Yes, yes, Finley, it's a pleasure!" the young professor shook Finley's hand with both of his. The professor had a rolled-up newspaper under his arm, but it fell to the ground with his arms outstretched. He was beaming, like he had just been introduced to the president of some country.

"Hi," Finley said, whipping his bangs back. He offered to help the professor gather up the fallen newspaper, but Diffenbaugh was already scooping it up.

"By Ohm's Law...," he said, looking up with a wide, genuine smile. "That was quite remarkable what you did with the lighter, Finley. The faculty's been buzzing about it all morning. We can't wait to welcome you to our school—blown fuse, maybe you can even teach *us* a few things!"

Finley didn't have time to feel uncomfortable, because the professor and the dean were already leading him away from the wagon and up the marble steps to a wide landing surrounded by beech wood pillars. Two floor-to-ceiling glass doors led inside, and they each had a fancy crest painted in the middle in white.

"Shouldn't I grab my things?" Finley asked Dean Longenecker.

"Wally will leave your bags at your dorm," she said,

checking her wristwatch. "I need to leave for a bit, contact your parents and let them know you had a safe and uneventful arrival. Safe and uneventful is good, trust me. Professor Diffenbaugh here is going to take you to get your uniform, and he'll show you around campus.

"I'll meet you for lunch in just a bit, and we'll discuss your classes and schedule. Good? See you soon!" Then, the dean vanished from the spot she was standing in and blew past Finley and the professor in a flash—leaving behind more of those neon streaks of light Finley had seen in the car earlier.

Because his eyes still weren't used to seeing and perceiving that speed, Finley saw stars and started to feel a little dizzy this time. Professor Diffenbaugh held his arm, and that's when Finley realized he'd been swaying.

"Easy, easy," the professor said, guiding him to the glass doors. "You'll have to pardon the dean; surgers here often forget that using their abilities in front of eighth graders before they've had their arrester can be—"

" 'Arrester?' " Finley asked, stopping by the looming doors.

"Right, sorry," Professor Diffenbaugh laughed apologetically. "Arrester here at Brighton Prep refers to your first week or so in the surging community. It's a slow, easy transition into the wonderful lifestyle and goings-on of a surger."

Finley raised his eyebrows.

"Think about it like this," the professor continued. "If you didn't know how to swim, would you want to be cast into the ocean? The salt water would fill your lungs before you knew what to do with yourself! Here, at Brighton Prep, new and strange and amazing things await, but, if you just get pushed into the tumultuous excitement without your lifejacket on, you just might drown."

Finley nodded, trying not to look unsettled.

"Bad analogy?" Professor Diffenbaugh asked, misreading Finley's expression. "You'll soon find that I'm full of those. Let's get your uniform!" And then he pulled open the eight-foot glass doors so Finley could step inside.

They entered the sphere ceilinged atrium together, and now Finley was sure he'd pass out: The large space was the size of a football field, lined with the tallest bookshelves Finley had ever seen. Students who looked much older than him were walking up and down the aisles, carrying on casual conversations, but encyclopedias and tomes and books were *floating* out of their places on the shelves and landing in expecting hands.

Finley saw four or five electrical towers at the edge of the room, towering over the shelves like ancient Greek columns, and, in the air, disappearing as swiftly as they had appeared, were more clips of fading neon colors. They went off, like tiny splashes, near every book that was being summoned, and the vivid tints of yellows remained as afterimages for only a second or two.

Finley froze by the door, paling. "You call *this* an easy transition?"

Professor Diffenbaugh nodded, hands in his pocket. "Sure. See, Understanding is much easier on the eyes than Fueling. Wouldn't you agree?"

"What's that? 'Understanding?'"

"It's my favorite stage of surging," the professor replied, looking around the room like he was witnessing the wonder for the first time. "When you will power from the Root, and channel it into Understanding, you can leverage telekinetic capabilities. Like in Star Wars, whenever they'd call upon the Force and—" Professor Diffenbaugh cut himself short, noticing Finley's blank stare. "What? That was a much better analogy."

Finley shrugged and followed the professor through the heart of the atrium. "This," Professor Diffenbaugh explained, "as I'm sure you've surmised, is the library. Seniors come in here on the weekends to practice Understanding."

"When do I get to learn Understanding?" Finley asked in the professor's shadow, watching a heavy-looking book glide down through the air in a weightless way and eventually plop into a girl's hands. She caught it in stride, not once breaking from her conversation with her peer.

"In the last year of your training, I'm afraid," the professor answered, turning a corner and heading for the exit. Finley, who had stopped walking to turn in a full circle below the network of flying books, sprinted to catch up.

"It's the toughest phase of surging," Professor Diffenbaugh was saying, "and, as such, it's reserved for your senior year."

"What will I be learning this year?"

The professor reached the exit and clasped the handle, but hesitated so he could reply, "Assuming your curriculum will be in line with the rest of the eighth graders, you will be studying the art of Lunging. This way, Finley."

They walked out the double doors and onto a sunlit greenway. Palm trees sectioned off a park area, where kids were lounging around on the grass or tossing a Frisbee back and forth. Flocks of seagulls quested in the sky for the ocean. A couple of teenagers skateboarded past Finley and the professor, kickflipping in the air on the paved trail, only, their jump was much further than Finley ever dreamed possible, covering over twenty-five yards before landing masterfully.

Surging-enhanced skateboarding, Finley thought, shaking his head with his mouth agape. He saw evaporating snippets of neon green trailing behind the wheels like sparks. *This is too good to be true!*

Professor Diffenbaugh led them over the grass, where long tables were set up and students were peddling their respective clubs. "Check out the inventors' guild—this term, we'll be collaborating on ways to make the glove less bulky!" ("What's the 'glove?'" Finley asked, nudging the professor. "All in due time," he replied, taking a flyer from the inventors' guild.) "Yo! Try out for the Brighton band, we take electric instruments to their fullest potentials!" "*You* look like you want to try out for the Games of Illumination!" "Join the chess club. Please. I'm the only member."

Above the tops of the palm trees and surrounding buildings, Finley saw even more buildings, and he quickly began to wonder just how big the Brighton grounds were. Together, he and the professor turned up an exterior hall made of more beech wood pillars and overarching flower displays.

"I-I have to ask, Finley," the professor said, striding at Finley's side and sounding rather giddy, like the time Finley had met his surfing idol, Felipe Toledo. "Exactly how did you get here? To Brighton Prep?"

"Um, a bus brought me."

"A bus!" Professor Diffenbaugh clapped his hands once. "That's hilarious. Here, right through here."

They weaved around a godlike statue of a man—dressed in late 18th century clothing and holding an Edison bulb—before they walked into a rectangular building that sat sandwiched between two much larger buildings.

Inside, the air conditioning was set to freezing, and an old, bespectacled woman sucking a lollipop sat behind a high counter. She wore an electrician's shirt, one identical to Mr. Repairman's, only her name read *Rose Y. Hyde*.

"Help you?" she said in a hoarse voice, looking up from her electrical typewriter, which punched letters onto a page without the woman having to strike the keys, and, consequently, neon yellow sparkles popped lightly above the keyboard.

She pulled out her red sucker with a squishy sliding noise. Finley cringed.

"Hi Rose! You're looking especially irritable today." Professor Diffenbaugh leaned on the counter, and Finley stood a few paces behind him. "Did someone rub you the wrong way before I had the chance?"

The woman named Rose Y. Hyde was unimpressed and simply grunted, holding her lollipop aloft like a sugary weapon of warding.

"Right," the professor said, fiddling with his bowtie idly. "We're here to collect Finley's uniform. You should have his sizes on record now."

Rose rolled her eyes behind her glasses and disappeared into a back room, and the typewriter paused.

"Since I got hired a few years back," Professor Diffenbaugh told Finley with determined eyes, "I've made it my personal goal to get that woman to smile. She's like my Mt. Everest, you see."

Finley deadpanned.

"Yeah," Professor Diffenbaugh said, sighing. "That

sounded much better in my head. Anyway, Rose is the master clothier, so if you try out for the Games of Illumination, you'll have to gather your jersey and gear from her."

Finley opened his mouth, but the professor added, "Sorry, you don't know what the Games of Illumination are yet. But you will. Our school breeds champions, Finley, and you'll see what I mean soon enough."

"Professor," said Finley, joining him at the counter. "What do you teach?"

"Only the most stimulating course we have to offer! Surging: A Complete History Of Its Invention, Progression, and Perfection."

"History," said Finley, pushing his bangs out of his eyes. It was his least favorite subject. "That's my favorite subject."

Professor Diffenbaugh beamed. "Mine too! Ah, here we are."

Rose returned with a flat bag that had a hanger at the top, and, because of the plastic covering, Finley couldn't see the uniform. The professor took the flat bag by the hanger and handed it to Finley.

"Don't worry about putting it on just yet," he told Finley, "students here aren't required to adhere to a dress code on weekends."

They both thanked Rose (she sniffed in response and returned to her typewriter, sucking on her lollipop repulsively), and headed back into the sunlight, where Professor Diffenbaugh guided them across the greenway and off to the mess hall—all the while talking up his class and expounding on the importance of knowing one's cultural and societal roots.

Finley couldn't say that he was looking forward to his studies, but he *was* looking forward to having Professor Diffenbaugh as a teacher. *He's like a breath of fresh air*, Finley concluded, but then he immediately cursed himself for the clichéd simile.

The professor, it seemed, was already rubbing off.

The mess hall was a vast, covered patio area with picnic benches and food carts. Finley carried his covered uniform over his shoulder by the hanger and tried desperately to keep in toe with the professor's long strides. Finley expected every pair of eyes to be fixed on him as he zigzagged around tables and through the busy mess hall, but he was relieved to find that everyone was fully enthralled with each other's gossip.

They found the dean at a table by the taco cart, and Finley draped his uniform bag over the seat while he sat down. The professor took his order and left Finley sitting with Dean Longenecker. Now that he had the dean alone for a few breaths, he hoped to list off all the questions that had been nagging at him ever since Mr. Repairman claimed he'd passed the ultimate test. For instance, if Finley wasn't a surger, what exactly *was* he, and how did Brighton Prep intend to teach and equip him?

Before the question fully formed on his tongue, the dean was sliding a piece of paper across the picnic table. Finley reached over and picked it up, scanning the typewriter font:

```
-Literature for the Surger w/ Prof.
Templeton 8:00-9:30
-Surging and Its Basic Historical
Origins w/ Prof. Diffenbaugh 9:45-
11:15
-Free Period Tutoring w/ Prof.
Ambrose 11:30-12:15
-Lunch 12:30-1:30
-The Science of Surging w/ Prof.
Guggenheim 1:45-3:15
-Control: Elements of Offensive &
Defensive Surging w/ Prof. Ambrose
3:30-5:00
-(extracurricular elective) 5:15-6:30
-Dinner 6:30
```

Finley swallowed, folding his schedule and stuffing it into his pocket. If he wasn't nervous before, and everything that he'd felt had simply been first-day jitters, *now* he really was nervous.

Dean Longenecker said, between bites, that she hoped Finley would take his extracurricular elective seriously, because, she explained, that was where most surgers found their "niche," and, ultimately, decided what to pursue as a potential career in the surging world.

Career? Finley just wanted to be thirteen...

Professor Diffenbaugh returned with two trays of tacos, a basket of greasy chips, and three different types of salsa. While they ate and crunched away, the dean told Finley his room (which he'd be sharing with three other boys) was ready, and his dorm mates were stoked to meet him.

Any other adult who said "stoked" or "rad" might come off as sounding desperate, but the dean was natural and selective about her usage. *It's probably her way of making kids feel less uptight*, Finley thought, dipping his taco into the salsa labeled El Diablo's Armpit.

Finley sighed when he remembered the unnerving list of classes in his pocket, and decided the dean's cool, level lingo wasn't working, if her intention truly was to make him feel even keel.

"Tonight," Dean Longenecker said, dabbing her lips with a napkin, "is our annual fall bonfire at the beach. We have one every year, a couple weeks into the semester, to get the student body excited about the G.I.s." ("Games of Illumination," Professor Diffenbaugh mouthed when Finley gave a quizzical look.)

"Yeah, uh," Finley took a drink from his water bottle, "that sounds tight."

The dean's face dropped slightly. "Remember our

promise, Finley." Then, after adjusting her posture, she said, "Ready to see your dorm?"

As they left the mess hall and crossed the grounds, it happened four more times. Bright strokes of pink rocketed past them, leaving behind spark-like particles that fell slowly, as if they shared the same properties as bubbles.

Finley tried not to be sick, but it was tough. The quick movement was just so foreign to him.

On the west side of the Brighton campus there sat a collection of four Mission style buildings with about six stories apiece. Students moved to and from the dormitories, some riding bikes and skateboards, others just walking. They all said *Hi!* to the dean and professor politely, but didn't acknowledge Finley. Going unnoticed was all right with him, because he knew that, with tough classes and uncertainty on the horizon, the last thing he needed to deal with were ripples of stares and whispers.

They walked into the first building on the left, and Dean Longenecker stepped aside so Finley could take in the view of the lounging area. High back armchairs and couches were arranged in groupings, lining the wide room, which had beautiful ceramic tile flooring. Multiple sets of French doors and tall windows let in ample sunlight, warming the lounging area in a magical kind of manner.

"What do you think?" Professor Diffenbaugh asked, putting a hand on Finley's shoulder.

"It's...," Finley said, staring at the middle of the

lounging area, where a circular fire pit was built into the center. Salmon colored hearthrugs surrounded the brick base. In one corner, there was a stack of surfboards, and in another, a pile of folded community towels. The tall ceiling was crisscrossed with beams, and strings of lights hung like drooping Amazonian vines.

"It's amazing," Finley finished, turning to face the professor and the dean.

"Now, the girls' dormitory is on the other side of the path," the dean said, putting her red hair up while she spoke, "but we've taken certain 'precautions' to prevent any sneaking or peeping, so don't get any ideas."

Finley flushed. "I—"

"You wouldn't, I know," she reassured him, her hair now in a ponytail. "But I've got to say it anyway. What kind of dean would I be if I wasn't at least a little mean or intimidating?"

Finley wanted to say that she wasn't mean or intimidating at all, really, especially not compared to his Aunt Lucille, who put cough drops in piñatas and gave Yanni CDs for Christmas gifts, which was the definition of mean, if you asked him.

"Your things are upstairs, fourth floor," Dean Longenecker said, ushering for the professor to follow her out. "Why don't you get settled in? Bonfire's not till 7:30. If your dorm mates aren't up there, they should be back from lunch soon."

Professor Diffenbaugh patted Finley on the back, waved, and left the lounging area in stride with the dean.

Okay, Finley thought, still clutching his bagged uniform over his shoulder, *fourth floor*. He walked across the room to a flight of stairs between two bookshelves. When he reached the fourth landing, he saw that, like the previous two floors, his shared quarters had an open-concept layout with two bunk beds, four desks, a few tables, and two doors that, Finley assumed, led to a bathroom and a walk-in closet.

The two top beds were clearly taken because one was unmade and had gobs of dirty clothes, and the other bed, also unmade, had an assortment of electronic devices strewn about, such as a fan, speakers, a hairdryer, and other things Finley couldn't identify at a quick glance.

He chose the bed closest to him and set his uniform down on the covers, eagerly pulling open the bag's zipper. Inside there were three, sky-blue shirts, three ties, and three pressed pairs of khaki pants.

Finley pulled out one of the shirts, running his thumb over the patch that was stitched on top of the breast pocket. The Brighton crest was comprised of a bulb, a jagged high voltage symbol, a fuse, and a fork of lightning, all bracketed inside two white wreaths.

For some reason, holding his official uniform while standing in the empty dorm room, Finley felt as if he were transported out of his skin...like he was having an out-of-body experience. He was a ghost, hovering in the air, watching a scared, nervous, in-over-his-head eighth grader agree to something he didn't deserve. Finley wanted to remain as that ghost, he realized, so he could float out of the dorm room window and get carried off with the sea breeze, leaving that *barely* pubescent shell of a child to fend for himself.

"No," said Finley aloud, and the ghost was gone. "I'm here for a reason." He straightened up, tossed his school shirt down, and turned around with a refreshed, invigorated sense of purpose.

That's when a cloaked figure fell from the ceiling and, using what felt like ramped-up voltage, electrocuted Finley McComb into unconsciousness.

Chapter 4 | <u>The Dissensions</u>

When Finley came to, his mouth was as dry as sun baked wood, and he sat propped up in a chair in the middle of a field at the head of a trestle table that was laden with steamy, delicious smelling Italian food.

The sun was about a quarter of an hour away from setting, and the result was that the field and the table and the food were sepia toned. Finley licked his lips, let out a soft groan, and sat up slowly. His head spun. He could smell the scent of dried blood, but when he checked around his body for cuts or wounds, he found none.

There were no palm trees around. He could not hear the ocean. The grass was knee-high. An old, round man with a walrus mustache sat at the other end of the table. Finley had not noticed him before because the stacks and tiers of food were piled in great heights.

"Hello, Finley," he intoned, his voice soft but asserting. "I'm James Olyphant. How's your head?"

Finley did not answer. Instead, he tried stretching his memory as far back as he could will it. How had he gotten here, to this field? There was Brighton. Yes, that had happened. Then, there was Professor Diffenbaugh. A tour. His uniform. His dorm room—

I was ambushed and shocked unconscious.

"Finley, I'm afraid that won't do." The old man who called himself James Olyphant crossed his legs under the trestle table. "Our time here is limited. They'll be coming for you. Please, lend me your attention. It's in your best interest."

He spoke without any trace of an accent, and his enunciation was proper and intentional, suggesting he was either extravagantly educated, or merely pretending to be.

"That why you attacked me?" Finley said, finding his voice. He rubbed his head, wincing when he felt a lump. "For my 'best interest?'"

"It was the only way I could get you here. And, for the record, that wasn't *me* who attacked you."

After he said this, a second person appeared behind Olyphant's chair—a figure wearing a long gray cloak and a purple masquerade mask with an enormous hooknose. Because of this person's posture, the way they held their gloved hands on top of Olyphant's chair, Finley could tell it was a she, and he knew, somehow, *she* was the one who had blindsided him and knocked him out cold.

Finley felt goose bumps forming on his flesh.

"How did you get me here?" he demanded, putting his hands on the table and pushing to stand, only, he quickly found that some invisible restraint was keeping him from doing much more than that. "What's going on!"

Olyphant cut into some lasagna and served himself a hefty portion as he spoke: "Finley, I know you're probably excited about your future education and endeavors at Brighton Preparatory School for Surgers. But I brought you here this afternoon to tell you it is all a show. A dance. A farce. The faculty have no idea what you really are…what you're really capable of. They just think there's potential in you. That's it. They're hoping that you, their *prize*, will go through their motions, apply your abilities to surging, and that one day they'll just *poof!*"—Olyphant set his glass plate down for emphasis—"Figure. You. Out."

Finley leaned back in his chair, and then said, "And? Are you going to tell me you know what I am?"

"I know what you are, but that's not why I brought you here." Olyphant took a bite, and Finley waited as the old man chewed. "I brought you here to ask you to leave. Walk away."

Finley laughed through his nose. "Walk away? From *Brighton*?"

"Walk away from Brighton," Olyphant repeated, taking

another bite out of the stretchy, steamy cheese, "and come with me."

"Why would I even dream of doing that?"

All Finley knew about this odd pair—the aged man with crinkled skin and his masked companion—was that they had used illegal means to get him here, wherever here was. That was enough for Finley to make up his mind about these two.

"Because," Olyphant replied between bites, "you're being lied to, and you're on the wrong side. *I* have the answers you seek."

Finley chuckled in his head. *On the wrong side of what?* But when Olyphant gave no further explanation, Finley felt an eerie sense of vulnerability spring up from nowhere. He was scared, then, for the first time in the field, and he wanted very much to leave and get back to campus.

"No, I'm going to Brighton," Finley said simply, thinking of Professor Diffenbaugh. "They may not know what I am, but they believed in me enough to recruit me. I want to figure stuff out with them. With the school."

Olyphant did not respond immediately. He simply used his fancy fork to take chunk after chunk out of the lasagna, and, Finley discovered that the longer he watched, the hungrier the old man looked. Olyphant's masked accomplice started to squeeze the back of his chair, and Finley could not tell if it was impatience, or because of Finley's decision.

He was betting the latter.

Then, "Finley, you must realize this is a terrible choice." Olyphant's emotionless, monotone voice had not changed, and Finley wondered if he had ever met someone so cold, so tired sounding. The old man was such a contrast to Dean Longenecker and Professor Diffenbaugh.

"I'm thirteen," Finley said with a shrug, "and pretty good at making terrible choices."

The trestle table shot into the air. A violent, cyclonic wind shook the field and its high grass. Olyphant stood, and, for some reason, he did not have to shout over the loud wind. Finley, who trembled in his chair, could hear every spoken word:

"You don't know what you're doing. You're just a child." And, louder: "Tell that school of yours the Dissensions were never buried. We're back, and you, Finley McComb, had your chance."

Then, Olyphant and his companion evaporated into billions of bright lights, and Finley felt sweaty, and then those bright lights were stars, behind his eyelids, and someone was holding him up, while he blinked and panted, by his shoulders in the Brighton dorm room. He could smell the ocean again, hear the seagulls, and he was relieved.

"Dude, dude," a voice was saying in breaths, "hang in t-there, dean's on h-her way."

Finley looked over as a chubby boy with thick, unruly

hair helped him across the dorm room and into one of the desk chairs. He had olive skin, and that thick, crazy hair of his appeared singed and fried, like he had been electrocuted recently.

After the boy helped him sit, Finley rolled his head in a long circular motion, feeling sore all over.

"What happened?" he croaked.

"Dude," the boy said, wheezing, as if he had just competed in a triathlon, "c-came up here to, to change before the b-bonfire, and I saw you all, like, just passed out, yeah? You're heavy."

The boy continued to pant, leaning on dual Lofstrand crutches, and Finley wondered how he had been able to pull him up off the ground in the first place—especially considering that his walking aid was braced around each of his forearms.

There was a moment of partial silence filled only with Finley's dorm mate's panting, a passing seagull, and barely-audible banter from outside. Finley heard and *felt* his ears ringing, and, when he reached up to touch them, he felt droplets of blood against his fingertips.

"There's tissue in the bathroom," the boy said, turning on his crutches and heading off, but before he made it all the way, Dean Longenecker, Professor Diffenbaugh, and a host of other staff members burst into the dorm room in a berserk frenzy.

"Finley! Are you all right?"

"Blown fuse, he's bleeding!"

"Get him a damp towel, fast!"

"How many fingers am I holding up?" Then, when Finley hesitated to moan, "The boy's *blind*!"

"N-No, I'm not," Finley said above the yells of concern.

He stood up slowly, fighting through the wooziness, and the faculty gasped. Professor Diffenbaugh came to his side and held him by the arm, telling the swarming staff that Finley just needed space, which was true, but he mainly wanted them to clear out of the room so he could sort out what had happened with Diffenbaugh.

"You need to lie down."

"What he needs is water."

"True, he needs to be hydrated."

Finley gritted his teeth. *"What I need are answers."*

Then the room fell silent. Finley tried reading the expressions in the room, but his vision was still a little blurry, so he just stared at his Vans until someone decided to cut into the awkward silence.

Professor Diffenbaugh: "Let's get you to the nurse."

The nurse had her own wing, adjacent to the administration building. There were two doors in her office: one that led in, and one that led into a long hall, which had dozens of other doors lining both walls. Each patient's room had a window, a bed, and a terracotta fireplace, or, at least Finley assumed each room had these things, because the room they were in did, and he felt it was a little—

"—excessive. I'm fine, really."

He tried sitting up in the bed, but the nurse gently eased him back down. She was a pretty, fair-haired lady wearing what Finley guessed waitresses in 60s diners might have worn—down to the paper hat. Her plastic nametag read, *Jasmine*.

"You're not," Nurse Jasmine said, "but you will be after a rest. Hear, drink this." She handed him a jar of yellow and orange liquid, which, upon close examination, was fizzing a little.

Finley looked past the nurse to Diffenbaugh, who stood by the door between the dean and another man. He was a tad older, maybe late forties? Looked to be somewhere around Finley's father's age. He had wavy hair, a chiseled jaw, and a lazy eye. He wore a pressed, expensive-looking suit, and his solemn expression conveyed a self-aggrandizing air.

Professor Diffenbaugh nodded to the jar in Finley's hand, so he drank it in four gulps. It was not repulsive, but it was not pleasant.

"There," the nurse said, taking the empty jar and rising from her stool. She turned to the dean and said, "Only thirty minutes, okay? You get thirty minutes with the boy, but then he needs to rest. I don't think going to the bonfire is such a good idea."

"Wait," Finley found himself saying, "I mean, wait, no, I can't *not* go. I mean, I've had a long day, you know? I kind of need this."

Nurse Jasmine sighed, but said nothing else after excusing herself. Diffenbaugh and Dean Longenecker strode toward Finley's bed, but the man in the suit remained by the door, arms folded across his broad chest.

"Finley," the dean said, taking one of his hands, "I'm sorry about what happened back there. For what it's worth, we've *never* had a breach of security like this. Ever."

"Until now," Finley said, chuckling. He added sarcastically, "Guess I really am special, hm?"

He whipped his bangs out of his eyes and exhaled. This was proving to be the longest twenty-four hours of his life, and he could have never expected his first day at Brighton to play out like this.

"I'm sure this is the last thing you want to do," Diffenbaugh said, putting his hands in his pockets, "but, for us to properly sort this out, we need you to walk us through what happened—down to the last detail."

"And then you'll answer my questions?"

Professor Diffenbaugh smiled. "The ones we can."

Finley was not entirely sure what that meant. As in, the ones you know the answers to, or the ones you are allowed to answer? But given his fatigue, and his great desire to get to the bottom of this whole ordeal, Finley simply nodded.

He told Diffenbaugh, the dean, and the man in the suit everything that had happened. Dean Longenecker collapsed into the nurse's stool. Professor Diffenbaugh clenched his jaw angrily. The man in the suit remained still and wordless. When Finley finished, the sky outside the window was pink.

Diffenbaugh paced in the room in front of the fireplace. "Here are the facts, based on your account. Via complex and illegal Understanding, your consciousness was Borrowed. It's how you were transported to that field you described."

Finley tilted his head.

"Borrowing was outlawed in the late 70s," the dean explained, "because, once that stem of Understanding was discovered, it was rapidly abused. Not to mention the side effects vastly outweigh the benefits."

"So, er, in my mind, I went to where? Olyphant's mind?"

This conversation was not helping with Finley's headache. He must have winced without realizing it, because the next thing he knew Diffenbaugh was touching his temple with his left hand, and with his right he pointed at the fluorescent lights in the ceiling.

The lights flickered, there was a tinge of neon blue sparks beneath the cylindrical bulbs, and Finley's headache was subdued. Just like that. Now the lighting in the room seemed at eighty or so percent.

"Essentially," the professor replied, turning on his heel and pacing some more. "Yes, you were in his mind."

"So, the next question is," Finley said, "*who* is he?"

Instead of replying, the dean and the professor looked at the man in the suit. He did not move from his spot. Instead, he lazily ran a hand through his wavy hair, proving he was not a statue after all.

"Perhaps this is where Professor Ambrose can weigh in," the dean said.

Finley recognized that name. He had seen it somewhere, fairly recently... His course schedule! This was Professor Ambrose? The man he would have to spend *two* periods a day with?

Ambrose stepped forward, and Finley gulped.

" 'James Olyphant?' " Ambrose said in a slow, crisp voice.

He unbuttoned his suit jacket and put his hands on his hips. He seemed to be masking a raw reaction to the mention of Olyphant's name...like his calmness was covering up something dark.

"There was an Olyphant incarcerated in the 80s by the surging community," Ambrose continued. "Man was a grifter, arrested after a heist gone wrong. Possible it's the same character. Olyphant's not a common name, is it? I'll look into it."

Finley had never heard such a unique voice. Ambrose

spoke with a sort of hum under his words, like wood chafing against wood. Subtle, noticeable, delicate.

"Professor here is also head of campus security," Diffenbaugh told Finley, like it was a reassurance. Finley looked at Ambrose and his stern face and important suit and knowing eyes and realized it had been a reassurance. Who in a sane state would cross this man?

"Okay, so, back to how I was knocked out," Finley said, scooting up into a sitting position. "There was this person, in a cloak, in my dorm room. I'm pretty sure she was in Olyphant's mind, too. She zapped me...with what felt like a *Taser*."

"It's another reason why Borrowing was outlawed," the dean said. "Requires a lot from the Root, meaning a lot of electricity. I'm betting it took her glove's *entire* charge to pull that stunt. Regardless, we have campus security scouring surveillance cameras now to see how your attacker got in and out of the Brighton grounds."

"Right," Diffenbaugh said, counting off with his fingers: "Finley was blindsided, knocked unconscious by Olyphant's accomplice, 'transported' to a field, where he—you—were asked to leave Brighton Prep, because we're supposedly lying to you and not forthright about things. Then, Olyphant mentioned Dissensions..."

Finley: "Something like, 'we're back.'"

"This is where my homework comes in," said Professor Diffenbaugh, fingering his bowtie. "I'll need to look into this immediately."

A knock came from the door.

"Time's up," Nurse Jasmine said. "He needs at least one hour of rest before he can leave."

Dean Longenecker stood, took Finley's hand again, and squeezed it. "I know this will be difficult, but try anyway: Forget about this whole nightmare and let us put the pieces together. And remember your promise. We will completely and fully understand if you want to—"

"I'm staying," he said, pulling his hand back.

He felt there was still a lot they weren't telling him, but he could not do anything about that now, so he put on a smile, waved to the departing faculty, and decided that he was going to enjoy the rest of the weekend—no matter what it took—and then, come Monday, when he and Professor Ambrose had their scheduled tutoring session, it would be as good a time as any to seek out the answers he felt he deserved.

Finley did not sleep a wink.

He stared at the teal retro clock next to the window for the entire hour of his mandated rest, and, the moment the second hand passed over twelve, he swung his feet over the bed and jogged out of the room. He found his way out of the hall and sidestepped past Nurse Jasmine, who ordered him to at least slow down and take it easy.

Outside, the sky was nearing dark, and the paved pathways that led from building to building were lit with tall lampposts. The exposed filaments in the bulbs glowed beautifully, and, mixed with the scent of the ocean and the cool sea breeze, Finley felt one hundred percent better already.

The Brighton populace was all migrating away from the grounds and heading down a wide sidewalk toward the beach, and Finley merged in with the procession—trying to look like he knew where he was going. A few senior-looking teenagers in the crowd were carrying tall, hand held flagpoles with banners at the end. The Brighton crest whipped in the wind majestically over everyone's head.

Finley could practically feel the energy aggregating around him. He still could not believe he was officially a part of this culture.

Everyone was talking in excited voices, and Finley assumed it was in keen anticipation for the annual bonfire...until he started paying attention to what people were actually saying:

"I heard the kid took one look at his course schedule and then passed out."

"Seriously!"

"Yeah, and get this—I don't even think he's a surger."

"Not a surger?"

"What's he doing here then!"

"I give him a week, tops."

"Nah, that's gracious. If he passed out after looking at his schedule, what makes you think he's gonna get all the way through an Ambrose lecture?"

Finley felt his neck prickle, and then redden. They were talking about him. *He* was the kid who looked at his schedule and then passed out and probably would not make it through an Ambrose lecture. That's not true, he meant to yell. I was attacked! In my dorm room!

But, who would believe him? Dean Longenecker had stressed that a breach of security had never occurred on the Brighton grounds. The incident had morphed into a lie, and that lie had morphed into a full-out rumor.

Finley's heart sunk into his stomach with a painful, heavy crash. Had the dean started this rumor? Had she wanted to preserve the integrity of the school's security? By that same token, it could have been Professor Ambrose, because it definitely was not Diffen—

"Fin! Wait up!"

Finley turned over his shoulder and saw the familiar form of his dorm mate, approaching rather quickly on his Lofstrand crutches. He was flanked by two girls, one who had long brown hair and braces, and the other who had a big smile, short yellow hair, and a slouch in her walk.

Finley was relieved his dorm mate had seen him. He was not looking forward to standing by himself at the beach—especially now that he was the new kid who had blacked out before he had even had a chance to put on his school uniform.

Had his dorm mate been the one who had started the rumors?

"Hey," Finley said back, stopping outside the sidewalk to wait for them. He joined them in stride, walking beside the girl with braces. "Thanks, for, uh…," Finley trailed off, unsure what he was thanking them for.

"I never introduced myself," Finley's dorm mate said, "I'm Miguel. This is Bridget"—the girl with the braces—"and this is Helena"—the girl with the short yellow hair. "We all sit together in English Lit, first period."

"Me too!" Finley said, excitedly. "With Professor Templeton?"

"The one and only," Bridget replied through her braces, trying not to have her words sound watery, but failing miserably. "You'll love her. She does a marvelous job of taking classic literature and relating it to us surgers, making it very much applicable to everyday life."

"Bridget wants to be Professor Templeton when she grows up," said Helena, her thick Michigan accent coming off strong, "because Professor Templeton is *awesome*." Only, awesome sounded more like *ough*-sum.

"You're just upset because she chose *me* to give our quarterly presentation first."

"Yes," Helena deadpanned. "I'm jealous you have to give a presentation first."

Finley chuckled. "Not too stoked about all the

catching-up I'll have to do."

"We'll help," Miguel offered earnestly. "What other classes do you have?"

Finley told them, and he was grateful to find that they all had the same schedule. If nothing else, he could follow them to every period—learning the campus layout in the process.

The sidewalk took a wide bend south and started to drop slightly as they neared the beach. Up ahead, they could see large scraps of wood piled against one another, forming what looked like a giant teepee on the sand.

"So, how you feeling?" said Miguel. "What did the nurse say? Was it just stress related? I get nose bleeds when I'm stressed."

"You get nose bleeds because you electrocute yourself," Helena said, laughing to herself.

That explained Miguel's singed hair. "Wait, why do you do that?" Finley asked, scrunching his eyebrows together.

"I *don't* electrocute myself," Miguel said, sounding like he had given this explanation before and it was merely a recital. "At least, not intentionally. Besides, we're not talking about me right now."

Finley cleared his dry throat. "Miguel, what exactly did you tell people?"

"About what?"

"About finding me in our dorm room."

Miguel laughed. "I'm an eighth grader, I don't really

'know people.' I just told Bridget and Helena, when we first spotted you."

Around them, the crowd of Brighton students had begun to chant. They were walking on sand now, in between rows of towering school flags. Tents were set up beyond the unlit bonfire, and Finley could smell hotdogs and funnel cakes and other types of food that were bad for you and left your stomach angry for the decisions you had made, yet strangely grateful for the delicious satisfaction only sugar can bring.

"Cool, yeah...," Finley said, scratching an itch behind his ear that wasn't there.

"What's wrong?" Helena asked, putting her hands in her back pockets. "Have you heard people talking?"

"Oh, just everyone," Finley replied, chuckling awkwardly. Before he could elaborate, the chanting grew to a near-deafening roar:

Brighton! Brighton!
Yours is tough, yours is hard,
But always we'll defend and guard!
Brighton! Brighton!
Hand in hand we'll march and fight,
Nary a corner a large enough plight.
Brighton! Brighton!
To seek the Root,
To chant and hoot,

To summon power,
To summon might,
To protect and learn
How to rightly FIGHT!
Brighton! Brighton!
Hand in hand we'll march and fight,
Until our enemies are out of sight!
Brighton!
Brighton!
Brighton!

The crowd fanned out and encircled the bonfire, everyone cheering and applauding loudly. The atmosphere was so lively and charged with exhilaration, Finley did not even have to try to forget about his worries and get caught up with the rush. He could stress about what people thought about him later. He could stress about that peculiar exchange he had with Olyphant tomorrow. He could stress about his classes when it was time to stress about those things.

Right now, he was on the beach, at a bonfire, at a surging school.

A boy and girl, who looked a little older than Finley, walked up to the pile of wood—holding a lit, flickering torch between them. They had perfect features, and appeared as if they should've been highlighted in Abercrombie and Fitch catalogues—a breed of annoying perfection. Finley watched them stride in unison, realizing they were fraternal twins. They both had the same blonde hair and blue eyes, and each wore an expression of utter disinterest.

"The Caverly twins," Miguel said, under his breath. "Only freshmen, but already school legends." He was speaking with genuine awe.

"They're strikers on the chargeball team," Helena said.

"First freshmen to ever make that position," Bridget added. "It's why they're lighting the fire."

Finley watched, with everyone else, as the Caverly twins reached the mound of wood and timber and kindling, and then dipped down simultaneously and deposited the flaming torch. It caught fire, illuminating powerfully, and everyone roared and cheered some more.

Now, with the snapping and popping fire in full swing, everyone started moving toward the ebbing and splashing ocean. Two members of the faculty stood at the shoreline, facing the waves, with their right hands outstretched. They both wore bulky, black gloves with exposed wires, and Finley had to stand on the tips of his toes to see what it was they were doing.

The crowd fell silent. The bonfire crackled and sizzled behind them.

Then, a wall of ocean water shot up into the air and hung, suspended, as images began to project on the saltwater and mist. Brighton students, wearing jerseys.

Competing in games. Battling in what looked like an intense, dangerous version of dodge ball, except, they were tossing and hurtling glowing spheres at the opposing team.

Around Finley, shouts of approval began to mount. Athlete profiles appeared next. The Caverly twins, Michael and Sarah. A beefy, senior-looking teenager named Doe who had, what appeared to be, calloused ears, like he was a mean, professional boxer. More names and faces flashed by, but everything was happening so fast that Finley was still caught up with the fact that the two professors were using Understanding so impressively…holding up the water like that…but where was the Root? Where was the electricity that they drawing their power from?

Those gloves?

Finley shook his head, a wide grin forming on his face. Beside him, Miguel, Bridget, and Helena were joining in with everyone else, clapping and shouting elatedly. Finley mimicked them, matching their level of enthusiasm.

He had so many questions. So much to learn. So much that still did not make sense. But, right then, in that moment, Finley simply clapped and hoorahed for the things he did not fully understand yet, and it was okay.

Chapter 5 | The Caverly Twins

The rest of the night, Finley, Miguel, Bridget and Helena mingled with the other eighth graders, who weren't hard to identify because they were all mostly keeping to themselves on the outskirts of the festivities—drinking coconut and pineapple punch and avoiding too much eye contact with one another.

In a dizzying flash Finley met the rest of his class, but he soon forgot just about everyone's name. He found comfort after confiding in this to Miguel, who told him not to worry, for they had almost positively forgotten his name, too.

With any luck his classmates had not associated Finley with those untrue, embarrassing rumors. But, well, how could they not? He was, after all, the only new addition to the eighth grade class.

At around half-past ten, a display of colorful and loud fireworks shot up over the ocean, and everyone screamed for joy at the night sky, and then Finley looked closer and realized they were *not* fireworks at all, but rather large plasma orbs being tossed into one another. Upon impact, the orbs exploded, and the neon guts and innards rained over the ocean, looking similar to the inner-workings of a lava lamp.

Finley gaped at the show, mesmerized, until everything faded, and then he followed everyone back up the path to their respective dorms—buzzed and enlivened chatter projecting the whole way.

Finley and Miguel bade goodnight to Bridget and Helena when the path split, and then the two boys, who were more tired then they would admit, headed straight for their beds and slept without changing. So tired were they that when their third dorm mate slipped in a little later, they were not roused.

The next day was Sunday, and it was about as slow and uneventful as Finley could have hoped for. It was the kind of off-set day he needed after his taxing first day on campus.

Miguel woke Finley from his slumber around 8:30 that morning, and the two of them brushed their teeth in the dual sinks before heading downstairs and walking to the Brighton mess hall.

On that morning, the food carts had pigs in blankets, waffles, steaming omelets, and chorizo with eggs. Finley took a hefty sample of everything and sat with Miguel and two other eighth graders. Lit bamboo tiki torches lined the outskirts of the covered patio, and the fruity fragrance wafted in the air.

"This is absolutely outrageous," one of the eighth graders was saying, a bespectacled kid with a map of freckles under his eyes. He crumpled up a piece of paper and tossed it aside, returning to his waffle, which was drowning in syrup.

Miguel sighed and said, his voice flat, "What is absolutely outrageous, Doug."

"That aptitude assessment! It says I'll be a Mender. Just because I'm book smart doesn't mean I want a job in surging medicine."

Finley took a bite of his breakfast. "What assessment?"

"You'll probably take yours tomorrow," Miguel said, setting his crutches against the table. "Every eighth grader has to. Determines what you're going to 'most likely' pursue in college. But everyone knows those assessments are a joke."

"Everyone but Doug," the other eighth grader said, sipping what smelled like hot chocolate. He twitched a little after he said this, and tried playing it off by taking another drink. His auburn, tangled hair was standing up in the front.

"Oh, great," Finley said, wiping his mouth with the back of his hand, "something else to look forward to."

"Don't sweat it," Miguel assured. "Like I said, means nothing."

"Maybe not to you guys," Doug said, pushing up his square-framed glasses dramatically. "But what if the assessment *is* right? I don't want to study Mending in college, that's like a death wish!"

"What's a death wish?" Helena asked as she and Bridget, breakfast trays in hand, plopped down at the table between Miguel and Doug. "Getting into a debate with you?"

"Ha. Ha." Doug took the last bite of his waffle and sighed through his nose. "Why couldn't I have had *Enhancer* suggested to me, like Parker here?"

The kid with the twitch looked away uncomfortably, unaware that a dab of whipped cream lay daintily on the tip of his nose. Bridget and Helena exchanged a quick giggle.

"I want to be a Gatherer," Parker muttered. "Not an Enhancer."

"An Enhancer," Finley repeated, sipping his freshly squeezed orange juice. "What do they do?"

"They enforce and uphold surging laws," Bridget answered, taking a bite out of her breakfast burrito, her long hair in a fancy bun that morning. "Pretty sure Ambrose was an Enhancer before his…er…'dismissal.'"

"Here we go," Doug said, his shoulders popping up and

down as he laughed silently. "This should be good. Let's hear it."

"Bridget did 'background checks' on all the faculty and staff," Miguel explained to Finley. "Wouldn't be surprised if she's done one on us. And you."

"It's why you could never be a Michigander," Helena said to Bridget, placing a soft, consoling hand on her back. "You're not trusting enough."

"First of all," Bridget said, holding up her finger importantly, "they're not 'background checks,' per se. Just simple research. Secondly, Michigan? Cold, gross, no thanks. Thirdly, what's so wrong with wanting to know a little bit about the folks we're going to be spending *five years* of our lives with!"

"How do you even find time for all this on top of homework?" Doug asked, resting his elbows on the table.

"I wanna hear what she knows about Professor Ambrose," said Finley. He was going to be spending a lot of time with Ambrose this semester in class and in his mandated tutoring sessions, so anything Bridget may have uncovered could be helpful.

"Well," Bridget said, tucking her hair behind her ears and leaning in. "It seems Professor Ambrose was one of the most skilled surgers on the Enhancer Force back in the 80s. His fighting and dueling was applauded all over the country. See, the problem with most surgers when they Enhance is that they're usually too obvious in their technique. Picking up heavy things and tossing them. Ramming their shoulders into eighteen wheelers. Winding up for big hits. Guess they get overly confident with all the strength they can tap into.

"But not Ambrose. No, instead of battling bad guys with all his energy invested in Enhancing, he would combine surging abilities and pull from his glove reserves sparingly. In one particularly awesome fight, there's a video of him Fueling and charging right at his foes, and at the tail end of his run he dishes out an Enhanced punch, essentially *multiplying* the impact."

"I read about that on Wikipedia," Parker said in a mousy voice, cowering a little when everyone looked his way. He added, because he was committed to his input now, "His technique was groundbreaking."

"Right." Doug relaxed his posture, sounding bored. "I read that too. But gimme the dirt on Ambrose."

"Well, apparently he was assigned to a pretty big investigation. There was a series of intense robberies back then, all over Washington D.C., and Ambrose and his partner were looking into the gang that was behind the heists. Well, after Ambrose's partner was killed, he sort of went…nuts. Grew impulsive, even erratic. It's why he was asked to step down and—"

"Teach." Helena shook her head, frowning skeptically. "You really think Brighton would let an ex-Enhancer with PTSD teach?"

"Apparently so," Bridget said, her voice low.

Finley perked up, intrigued by a particular detail Bridget had mentioned. "His partner was killed in a heist? Ambrose mentioned something about that, in the nurse's wing."

Everyone at the table sat up attentively, looking shocked that he had just corroborated Bridget's story. Even Bridget was all but cleaning her eyes, as if she had just seen something so unbelievable it prompted one to clean their eyes.

"He just flat-out told you about his firing?" said Miguel disbelievingly.

"Well, no," Finley said, setting his fork down and talking with his hands, "*but*, when Diffenbaugh and the dean were asking me about my attack in the dorm room, Ambrose drew a possible connection to, what he called, 'a heist gone wrong.'"

"Grasping at straws," Doug said in a tone of disappointment, "my least favorite pastime. C'mon, Parker"—he consulted his wristwatch—"we've got a lab report to finish. As much as I'd love to hear more about Ambrose's 'past,' we've got an hour or so of research left on thermodynamics and its correlation to surging. Joy." They both rose from their seats and waved goodbye before leaving for the library.

"Don't listen to him," Miguel said to Finley, noticing the embarrassed look in his eyes. "We think he was dropped as a kid. I don't think you're grasping at straws, and I want to hear what else Ambrose said."

Finley gave an appreciative smile, knowing that Miguel's interest was more in consolation than curiosity. Regardless, Finley was grateful, so he told them everything. How he was blindsided, knocked unconscious, transported to a strange field where a man with a walrus mustache told Finley he had to choose sides, and then there was his mysterious accomplice...the tall, slender form in the cloak and masquerade mask.

Finley concluded by telling them about the conversation in the nurse's wing. The Dissensions. Ambrose's face turning ice cold at the mention of Olyphant. Finley threw in the detail about the fizzy orange remedy for good measure.

"Whoa," Helena breathed. "Had quite the first day, didn't you?"

"So...a form of Understanding *transported you* somewhere else?" Bridget leaned forward, deep in thought. "That's interesting. And, this man, Olyphant—Ambrose said he was connected to those heists?"

"Said it was possible," Finley said, finishing the last bite of his breakfast and taking another drink of his juice. "But, it's the expression he had. Like he was hiding something."

"Professor Ambrose is one of the hardest people to read," Miguel said, eyebrows up. "You'll see. The fact that you were able to gauge anything other than apathy is a win for you."

"Maybe I should ask him about it tomorrow, during tutoring," Finley offered. "I mean, so far, Olyphant is the only one who has claimed to know what my abilities are. I'd kinda like to know if he's the bluffing type."

The table fell silent. Then,

"So, your abilities...the rumors are true?" said Helena, carefully. "You're *not* a surger?"

Miguel and Bridget snapped open their mouths, presumably to scold her for her bluntness, but Finley said, "No. I'm not a surger."

There, Finley thought. *It's out there for all the universe. I'm not a surger.*

He'd stated his words confidently. He wasn't afraid of this truth. Dean Longenecker believed he was something more, and so did Diffenbaugh. He would trust them until that proved to be insufficient.

Finley prayed that time never came.

"Hate to be the one that asks this," Helena said, visibly uncomfortable, "but, well, what are you doing here then?"

Once more, Miguel and Bridget shot her disgusted looks, to which Finley merely laughed inwardly and said, his words spoken with poise, "It's fine guys, really. Truth is, I don't know why I got accepted." He then recounted to them his test with Mr. Repairman on his parent's front patio.

Miguel, wearing a look of pure awe: "Y-You made fire

appear!"

"I...think?"

Bridget and Helena shook their heads in a wordless stupor.

" 'You think?' " Miguel looked around the table. Can you believe this! he was saying with his eyes. "Finley, that...*you made fire appear.*"

"The problem is, I don't know how I did it," he said, feeling—for some reason—relieved to be admitting this. He didn't realize that releasing his fears and anxieties and doubts could be this refreshing, like the very cracks and crevices in his soul were suddenly being sewn back together.

It also made him realize just how large a toll his pride and confidence had taken, and in such a short time.

"So, you guys haven't heard of the Dissensions before now?" he said, switching the subject back to more pressing matters.

"If anyone would have," Bridget said, skewering a sausage link with her fork, "it'd been Professor Diffenbaugh."

Finley nodded, figuring from the outset that this was the case. They asked a few more questions ("When you brought about fire, was there a tingling feeling? That's what happens when you surge, you know, almost like a pins and needles sensation." "Did being transported hurt?" "What did Olyphant look like?") and when Finley gave short, simple answers, they took the hint that he was ready to move on. Today was reserved for settling in. Tomorrow was for class and work, including setting aside time to investigate the mysterious James Olyphant—and the Dissensions of which he so passionately spoke.

They finished up their plates, walked to the outskirts of the mess hall together, and deposited their trays on top of the cylindrical trash bins. Miguel proposed they spend the rest of their morning on the beach, where they could check out a slew of items (like skimboards or volleyballs) on the pier at a community clubhouse named, fittingly, *Watt's Up*.

On the paved trail, Finley thought of something, and he turned to Bridget when Miguel and Helena started discussing the pros and cons of a 2-1 defense in chargeball when pitted against a reserve offense.

"So, you looked into all of the staff?" Finley whispered.

"Just about," Bridget said, flashing her braces in a grand smile.

"What have you found out about Wally, the campus driver?" he said, watching Bridget's face change from proud to curious.

"Hm," she replied. "Guess I haven't stalked—er, *looked into* him yet. Why?"

He told her about the moment he'd witnessed yesterday, when Dean Longenecker had inconspicuously slipped him a note, right before Professor Diffenbaugh had arrived at the dean's side of the car.

Bridget shrugged. "He kind of runs errands for the professors, aside from driving."

"Sure," Finley said, "but why choose that exact moment to pass along a note? Before Diffenbaugh's arrival? And why make it look so secretive?"

Bridget's face colored with realization. "She wanted you to see."

"You think?" Finley hadn't considered that. "Okay, so, why?"

"Although," Bridget said, scratching her arm, "could just be that, given everything that happened to you, that little exchange just *seems* suspicious. She was probably giving Wally your dorm room, so he could drop off your things."

"They wouldn't have already discussed that? On the drive over to pick me up?"

Bridget shrugged again. "I dunno. Either way, I'll see what I can find on him." She sounded eager and up to the challenge, though, given what she had found on Ambrose, it probably wouldn't be a challenge.

On the rest of their walk, Finley listened as Miguel, Helena, and Bridget told him the dos and don'ts of Brighton life. Don't ask to use the bathroom in Professor Guggenheim's class. Don't wander to the top floor of the clubhouse, which was reserved for seniors and members of the chargeball team. Always make sure your uniform is tucked in. Always abide by the curfew. Nikola Tesla and

Thomas Edison's ghosts haunt the grounds, so don't defame their names. Ever.

As they made their way down the sand, a few blurs of neon lights shot past them with a hum, heading to and fro about the shore. Near the water, a group of juniors were Lunging in the air—marking the spots in the sand where they landed, comparing their accomplishment with their peers. One teenager with especially long dreadlocks leapt a staggering sixty yards, his free flowing hair whipping in the breeze.

"Hope those glove things that they're drawing from are water resistant," Finley said, noticing that just about everyone on the beach was wearing them.

"Oh my gosh," Helena said, overexerting surprise. "I don't think they've considered that!"

Finley sniffed the sarcasm a mile away. "Right," he said, "guess they probably thought of that, when they were designed."

"If it makes you feel any better," Helena said, propping her arm on Finley's shoulder as they walked, "I said the same thing, the first time I saw them so close to the water."

"And we gave her an equally hard time about it," Miguel said, paying more attention to his crutch-assisted steps now that they were on the sand.

They ambled onto the pier, listening to the far off banter of their classmates, the crashing of waves, and the cawing of seagulls. Helena asked them if she should check out a boogie board or a skimboard, and Miguel suggested the latter, because that offered more opportunities for her to wipeout, which was pure entertainment, obviously, so there wasn't really a question.

Finley laughed along with Bridget, and then let his thoughts wander from him. He considered his parents, who were probably back at home, finishing up breakfast. His dad was undoubtedly watching the San Diego Chargers game now, and his mom was scolding him for yelling at the TV. Erin, Finley's sister, was probably still asleep—nursing what she called "party wounds."

Finley was suddenly overcome with guilt.

He felt guilty because his family was at home doing life together in the normal, usual way, with jobs and football games and the same old parties. It was a rinse and repeat cycle that offered no hope of change, whereas Finley's cycle had been broken. He was to be trained alongside the secret and mystical community of surgers. He supposedly possessed abilities outside the understanding of his mentors and peers. He was "meant for great things." And so how did he feel about the prospect of all this wonderful and unbelievable change?

Guilty, Finley thought, answering the voice that nagged in his head.

Last night, at the bonfire, he had decided to enjoy what was to come with his new lifestyle at Brighton Prep, even though he didn't have all the answers he wanted yet. But despite that resolve, he couldn't shake the guilt that had planted itself in the deepest recesses of his heart.

They're probably happy to have me out of the house, Finley mused in realization.

To his dad, he was the son who never made the effort to pursue athletics. To his mom, he was the child who drug dirty clothes into the house and was late for dinner. To his sister, he was just another person to fight with over the remote.

If Finley could hold onto that possibility—that his family was getting on a little better now that Finley was out of their hair—he just might be able to suppress the misplaced sense of guilt that gnawed at him and take an all-out plunge into what Brighton Preparatory School for Surgers had to offer.

They passed quite a few of their classmates on the pier. Some of them munched on frozen chocolate bars, others raced, in wetsuits, hoisting giant surfboards over their heads, and some simply read on the benches, keeping to themselves.

This isn't school. This is paradise.

They turned into Watt's Up, which sat at the end of the pier and overlooked the infinite ocean. It was a two-story structure with wide, open French doors and hanging China ball lanterns. Old arcade games sat to the left, a few booths and a register were off to the right, and a checkout station was set in the middle—where a large queue of students waited patiently, chatting about what they were going to rent that day.

Finley told Helena he'd wait in line with her while Miguel and Bridget made for the arcade games. Finley turned to Helena, a breath away from asking her which class she deemed the toughest, when a sly voice spoke beside him.

"You're Finley?"

He looked up, meeting Michael Caverly's intense blue eyes. He stood with his twin sister, Sarah, in the place in line directly ahead of him and Helena. The twins both wore expensive-looking wetsuits.

"Yeah," Finley replied, putting his hands in his pockets. "This is my friend, Helena—"

"You must be pretty annoyed with all those rumors, huh?" Sarah said, cutting him off.

Finley hesitated, unsure what she had meant. Was she implying that the rumors that had circulated about him passing out after seeing his course schedule were *untrue*? Or, was she being ironic?

Finley resorted to simply shrugging.

"I mean," Michael continued for his sister, folding his arms, "what a way to start off a new semester—having people think you're not built to be a surger."

"You *are* built to be a surger, aren't you?" Sarah asked.

Who talks like this? Finley thought, still unable to decipher their motives.

"I guess," Finley answered.

"So, what did happen then?" said Michael, moving forward with his sister as the line advanced. "If you didn't black out."

"I was attacked," Finley said, keeping his response vague, "someone wanted something I had."

Michael and Sarah exchanged a look.

"You were robbed?" Sarah asked, raising an eyebrow. "In the dorms?"

"Something like that." Finley held back sharing too many details. He felt that the whole ordeal with James Olyphant and the Dissensions was very much his problem, and the more people who knew, the more chance that panic was likely to spread. Best to just keep things to the point. Someone had, after all, tried to steal something.

Him.

"Knowing self-defense might have saved you some embarrassment," Michael eventually said, "but that's something you won't get into until your second semester as a freshman. Getting involved in the Games of Illumination, however, teaches you things a lot sooner." He faced forward when he finished saying this.

Finley furrowed his brow and glanced at Helena, whose mouth was slightly open. She was staring at the back of Michael's head with a longing look in her eyes.

"What do you mean?" Finley asked Michael. "I can learn how to fight if I join the team or whatever?"

Michael and Sarah snickered, then she turned over her shoulder and said, "You have to try out, you can't just 'join.'"

Try out. For the Games of Illumination. Finley didn't consider himself capable of faring well in sports—it's why he never bothered with any back home. And yet, he could keep his balance on a skateboard and a surfboard. That had to count for something. If this Olyphant character proved to be a threat...something truly dangerous and real in Finley's life...then equipping himself with some defensive know-how was imperative.

The line advanced some more.

"Are there any openings? On the team?" Finley asked eagerly.

"Sure," Michael replied, "on defense, in chargeball. It's really the only position eighth graders can play because it doesn't require a lot of surging." Sarah snickered after that last part.

Finley nodded, trying to seem calm, but inside his heart was racing. He didn't know the slightest thing about surging, he hadn't even had his first class, and sports were the furthest thing from his mind. But trying out for the games gave Finley a goal. Something to strive for, even if he had no clue how to go about striving for it properly. Where would he even start?

When he considered his course schedule, he remembered that he *did* have an extracurricular elective to choose, and this, he decided with a rush, would be it.

"Michael Caverly just said more to you in a few minutes," Helena said in a whisper, "than he has to the entire eighth grade class in two weeks!"

"At some point today," Finley whispered back, "I need you to teach me everything you know about chargeball."

"Sure," Helena said, her eyes going back and forth between Finley and Michael, who was now at the counter and filling out his name on a clipboard. "What do you wanna know?"

"How about the rules?"

Chapter 6 | Chargeball

"This!" Helena exclaimed, dragging her finger in the sand and creating a wide, lumpy oval, "is a chargeball pitch. And these"—she drew two divots on opposite ends of the field that looked like parenthesis—"are the goals." She then made an X in front of each goal, and five more Xs on either side of the pitch.

Six, Finley thought, studying the drawing. *So there are six players per team, including a goalie apiece.*

Miguel sat on the beach to Finley's direct left, his Lofstrand crutches in a pile at his feet. He was leaning on his elbows, watching Bridget attempt to stay upright longer than one second on the skimboard Helena had checked out. Miguel called out and critiqued her form while Finley and Helena discussed all things chargeball.

"Think of chargeball as being a combination of dodgeball and soccer, with some variations thrown in," Helena exclaimed, using her pinky finger to draw one last, long line that cut the field perfectly in half.

"Dodgeball and soccer," Finley repeated, nodding once, "got it."

She drew five small, evenly spaced circles on the line that split the pitch, with the fifth, center circle slightly larger than the rest. After tapping her chin and gathering her thoughts, she breathed out her nose and began with the basics:

"Now, first team to ten points wins. You score points by throwing the flashball—that's this larger circle here, in the middle—into the goal. But, you can't cross the intersect"—she rapped the sand with her knuckles, indicating the divot she'd drawn that separated the pitch into two halves—"or else you're out until someone from your team saves you."

"And, the way you get saved is if that someone catches the flashball?" Finley asked, cocking his head to the side to consider the drawing from another angle.

"No," Helena said, drawing little checkmarks next to the other four circles. "You get saved if the strikeball is caught. There are only ever four in play, and at the beginning of a match, the four strikers sprint from their respective starting points and try to grab as many of the strikeballs as they can."

"It's a free-for-all cluster," Miguel said, dropping his elbows and resting the back of his head on his interlocked hands. He sighed contentedly. "It's also the best part of the game."

"*Match*," Helena corrected instinctually.

"Whatever," Miguel said, closing his eyes.

"Okay. So the strikeballs are used to try and get people out." Finley said. He pointed at the remaining X on the sand drawing. "What about this guy? You have the goalie, the four strikers, and him."

"He *or* she," Helena said, to which Miguel snickered ("Usually a guy," he said in a whisper), "has the most important position: the charger. They function as a striker, too, tossing strikeballs and flashballs, and playing defense. But they also call out plays and improvise formations on the fly."

"Like a team captain?" Finley said, even though the position seemed much more than that.

"Team captain, sure, but play caller, defensive coordinator, and team manager as well, all bundled into one role." Helena wiped her hands and grabbed the bottle of sunscreen they had brought over from the clubhouse.

"Seems simple enough, I guess. Why did Michael tell me that defense didn't require any surging though?" Finley took the bottle from Helena when she offered it, and he set it between his legs on the ground.

"Finley," Helena said, rubbing her arms with the thick

white sunscreen, "technically, *no* position requires surging."

"Oh. Right."

He'd been thinking about this all wrong. He'd been thinking about chargeball as if he and his friends were playing in the school parking lot back in Huntington Beach. Playing this game as a *surger* meant Fueling to maneuver more quickly, Lunging to fly into the air and hurl strikeballs and flashballs from up above, and Enhancing to make one's throws faster.

Yup—I'd be annihilated if I tried playing without surging, Finley thought, plopping back onto the ground and staring up at the clear blue sky. He couldn't tap into any phase of surging, not yet, at least, so how was he possibly going to make the team?

Miguel sniffed, eyes still closed. "Michael probably meant that surging wasn't necessarily required to play in the way that swimming isn't required to surf. In other words, why try and kill yourself?"

"Yeah...," said Finley, trailing off.

"I mean, I kind of see what he meant," Helena said, rolling up her jean legs to her knees, and then applying sunscreen on her feet and shins, "better to be a goalie and not use surging, than to be on the frontlines and not use surging. Either way, though, there's a chance you'll get pelted with a strikeball."

"I'll be the laughingstock of Brighton if I try out for a position," Finley said, blowing his bangs out of his eyes.

"There goes that."

"I'm surprised you got more than two words outta the Caverly twins," Miguel said. "Since orientation, when I saw them first, they haven't associated with anyone younger than a junior."

"It's only because of those rumors," Finley assured, the shadows from passing seagulls rippling over his face. "Once things settle, they'll probably forget I even go here."

Helena stood and walked over to join Bridget at the shoreline. Finley sat up and watched as Helena held Bridget by the arm, keeping her balanced on the skimboard and towing her across the moist sand.

"Are there other sports?" Finley asked Miguel, who opened one eye. "I keep hearing about the Games of Illumination, but does that just reference chargeball?"

"Nah, there's Fueling relays, Enhancing spars, and other stuff," Miguel replied, "but chargeball is the most exciting thing to watch."

Well, if I can't learn self-defense in chargeball, maybe Ambrose or Diffenbaugh will teach me some techniques?

A one-on-one scenario presented fewer chances for being humiliated or embarrassed, so Finley decided to ask Diffenbaugh first, and then Ambrose, in their tutoring session.

Finley, Miguel, Bridget, and Helena spent the rest of that morning on the beach, doing absolutely nothing of importance, which was especially spectacular, in Finley's opinion. They ate burgers for lunch at Watt's Up, sitting in the booth closest to the French doors. Their classmates laughed and joked by the arcade games, and others ordered food from the diner—hands tenderly rubbing their growling stomachs.

While they ate, Bridget gave a thorough explanation for why skimboarding was pointless and dangerous and so *not* the best way to use your energy. When asked why she couldn't be pulled away to let Helena or Finley on, she simply slurped her bottled Coke and grunted.

After lunch, Finley and Miguel headed back to their dorm room so Finley could finally unpack and get settled in properly. They strode through the lounging area, where two or three of their peers were playing board games on the floor, and marched up the stairwell.

When they got to their room, Finley turned off the landing and made for his bed, immediately noticing the stack of books and supplies on his disheveled sheets.

"Christmas in September," Miguel said, noticing the "gifts."

"Wow," Finley said, picking up the textbook on top of the pile, which was entitled *The Root and Its Basic Theories*. "Some light reading, hm?"

"Wouldn't know," Miguel said, leaning his crutches against his bed frame and clambering to the top bunk. "I've just been grabbing the cliff notes from Bridget before we have to write a paper or a response." When he reached the mattress, he began tossing a few electronic appliances onto the floor, among which were a hairdryer, a set of old speakers, and what appeared to be a price scanner from a department store.

Finley returned to his mound of books. The other three titles were *The Surger's Take On Classic and Contemporary Literature: Volume 1*, *Electric Endeavors: A Comprehensive Look At The History Of Surging*, and *Control: Understanding Surging Attacks/Defenses In A Theoretical Context*.

Finley gulped. *It's okay*, he told himself. *I'll have Miguel, Bridget, and Helena to help catch me up.* He fought off the nibbling anxieties that were creeping and crawling inside of him, and then fixed his attention on the supplies that were set to the left of the books.

All the essentials were accounted for. Pencils, pens, a ruler, notebooks, a day planner, and even a calculator—despite the fact that he wasn't scheduled for mathematics this semester. He scooped everything into his arms, textbooks included, and cradled his new things over to the desks. Two were already taken, with papers and sticky notes cluttered about the surfaces, and two were up for the taking.

Finley thought of something as he began organizing his desk.

"Miguel," he said, opening the drawers and dropping his supplies in. They clanked loudly when they fell, like coins deposited into an empty piggybank. "Who are our other dorm mates?"

A moment later, Miguel plopped down onto the carpeted floor nimbly, using the bed frame to keep his balance. "I really should switch back to the lower bed." He collected the various electronic items from the ground, and then used his crutches to traipse over to the desks, which were arranged in front of the five-foot windows. "What's up?"

"Our other dorm mates," Finley repeated. "Who are they?"

"Parker, who you met at breakfast, sleeps above your bed. He's notorious for being the last one here at lights out, but the first one up in the mornings. Don't know how the little guy does it. And then there's Quinn—you won't meet him until next semester. He was suspended for fighting on like the first day of class. Dumb, right?"

Finley nodded in agreement, standing his textbooks up and arranging them on his desktop. "Who'd he get in a fight with—?"

"Gonna head to the study lab," Miguel interrupted, pivoting away from Finley, his random collection of electrical appliances hanging over his shoulder by their cords. "Working on this project…thing. Catch you at dinner?"

"Need help hauling that to—?"

"Nah, I got it." Miguel cleared his throat, staring at his shoes as he walked.

Finley took the hint, watching his dorm mate descend the stairwell with careful, practiced steps. Whatever Miguel needed his privacy for was Miguel's deal, and Finley wasn't in the business of prying.

He spent the next hour or so unpacking. He hung up his clothes in the shared closet, keeping his uniform near the front of the rack, giving it the easiest access. He took a few pictures of his family out of his backpack and wedged them beneath Parker's mattress. He tossed his other pairs of sneakers beneath the bed. He stored his bathroom necessities in the free shelf behind the mirror. He made his bed. He took a quick, hot shower.

Once he was finished, and only a couple hours remained before dinner, he made his way downstairs, where the same group of kids was still engaged in an intense board game. Some were yelling, making accusations about "bartering for the wrong resource," whatever that meant, so Finley ducked outside extra quickly.

The sun was offering heat, but not a sweltering heat, and it marked the sky with bleeding oranges and yellows like vibrant dyes spread before a clean surface. Finley whipped his bangs out of his eyes, striding up the sidewalk toward the campus buildings and greenway. He passed the girls' dormitories on his right, and he tried picking Helena and Bridget out of the small crowd that was gathered on the grass in the shadow of the building. They lazily passed a soccer ball back and forth, and every one of them appeared to be a senior, but it was too difficult to tell from where Finley stood, so he kept moving, eventually turning onto the exterior hallway. He followed the path counter-clockwise—the greenway on his left, classrooms to his right.

He could smell strong, peppered seasoning hanging in the air, drifting over from the direction of the mess hall, and he began to guess what the food carts would have in store for that evening.

Finley didn't know exactly where he was going, and was relieved to see a framed map of the campus grounds hanging on a nearby column. He wandered up to the map, hands in his pockets, but never had the opportunity to even casually glance at the directions.

A heated conversation ahead of him caused Finley to refocus his attention. He was close to the statue of the man clad in old clothes, hoisting a bulb in his frozen hand. It was from behind that very monument that the two voices were coming:

"...I mean, two weeks? *Two weeks!*"

"We did the best we could with what we were given."

"Now you're making excuses? You have any idea how insulting that is? Your excuses?"

"I'm sorry, but shouldn't we be doing this somewhere else?"

"Would the mess hall better suit you? Over crab legs?"

"You don't have to be so sarcastic."

"Give me better results, and I *won't* be driven to this point."

The second voice, lower still: "…could…caught…"

Finley backed up against the wall, looking around to see if anyone else was hearing this. Surprisingly, the only other people he could make out were a handful of eighth graders, playing Frisbee on the greenway a good distance away.

Finley held his breath, his heart beating like an engine in overdrive. He was pretty sure that second voice was Wally, the school driver. Though to whom was he talking? It didn't sound like Dean Longenecker. In fact, the whisper was so soft Finley couldn't tell if it was a male or female's voice.

"Look, what does it matter how long it took to get him here," Wally said, his voice now nervous. "He's here, isn't he?"

"…"

"…, and it will be here soon. I'll make sure the timing is right so that—"

"Finley?"

Finley felt his heart skip over five beats, and he almost yelped involuntarily. Professor Diffenbaugh had come up behind him and placed a hand on his shoulder. Finley flinched, but still had the wherewithal to sprint forward to the other side of the statue.

There was only Wally, and no one else in sight. He was

leaning up against the wall, acting as if he was searching for a key in a large key ring that he held in both hands. The only door around was the one that led into Rose Y. Hyde's office, but a sign on the door handle announced her operating hours excluded Sundays.

Wally feigned surprise, looking Finley up and down as Professor Diffenbaugh came up behind him.

"Everything all right?" Wally asked, looking back and forth between Finley and the professor.

"I was getting ready to ask the same thing," Diffenbaugh said, chuckling.

Finley steadied his breathing, trying to look unfazed by what he'd just overheard, especially because he was still trying to process all of it. "I...I was just trying to find the study lab."

Wally opened his mouth, but the professor was already on top of it.

"I'll show him," he said, to which Wally nodded.

"Here we go!" said Wally, picking out a random silver key and pinching it between his thumb and forefinger. He then Fueled out of sight, leaving neon pink particles in his wake, which fell like specks and splinters in sunlit water.

Finley swallowed, trying his best to discount the sudden dizziness that demanded his attention.

"Study lab's this way, Finley," Diffenbaugh said, leading him in the right direction. "Meeting someone there?"

Finley didn't say anything, his thoughts going off on a

dozen different threads, and he merely matched the professor's step. Before he could piece anything together, the professor brought him back to the moment.

"You're as pale as paper," he said, fidgeting with his wristwatch as they turned down the exterior hallway.

Finley could see the mess hall up ahead. "Isn't the saying, 'white as a ghost?'"

"Sure, yeah, but I like to give my audience what they want in a way they don't expect! Hence, my twist on the classic simile."

Finley attempted to smile, but he was too preoccupied.

"You know," Diffenbaugh said after a while. "For what it's worth, I was voted wittiest in my high school graduating class. Bet you never guessed that, huh?"

"Never," Finley said, trying to sound good-humored, but his response fell dry.

"Okay, you gonna tell me why you look so spooked?"

Finley wanted to more than anything, yet something was holding him back. Since he had arrived at Brighton Preparatory School for Surgers, he'd inadvertently sent the dean, campus security, and Professor Diffenbaugh on separate paths with a common goal: Find out why Finley was attacked, and who James Olyphant was. This obviously meant more work on top of their crammed school year agendas, something Finley wasn't proud of initiating.

And now he had a hunch—a particularly a strong

one—that something weird was going on with Wally. Two examples of odd, secretive behavior, one even involving Dean Longenecker. Could it be that this was all connected to yesterday's attack? Or was Bridget right when she had said that Finley was subconsciously exaggerating everything that remotely seemed suspicious because of said attack?

"Does this have to do with yesterday?" the professor asked as they passed the mess hall and then a second pathway that, a sign proclaimed, led to the faculty housing. When Finley didn't respond right away: "Finley?"

"Er, sorry," he responded, clearing his throat.

Was it worth the risk? Was it worth sharing these encounters Finley had had with Professor Diffenbaugh, which could either lead to more clues and questions, or be a complete and utter waste of everyone's time?

Finley and the professor stopped in front of the double doors that led into the study lab. "It's nothing," Finley muttered, flashing what he hoped was a confident-looking grin. "I was just feeling overwhelmed with the campus. Good thing you showed up, though."

Finley could see in the professor's eyes the disposition of an unconvinced adult, like when he'd tried convincing his parents he was too sick for school despite not even bearing a cough.

Unexpectedly, Professor Diffenbaugh beamed. "Took me at least three days to find my way around this place, so I get it. I was like a fish out of water."

Finley sighed theatrically and walked into the study lab.

"C'mon!" the professor called after him. "*That* one's a classic—straight out of the Canterbury Tales!"

Finley laughed to himself, navigating around the many square tables in the study lab. Each station had a large plasma globe set in the direct middle, a colorful source of pink and purple strands from which Brighton students could will. Most were seniors, practicing their Understanding. A sweaty hand pressed against a globe, a free hand pointed at some small inanimate object on a table—willing a coffee mug, pencil, or tattered copy of *The Rithmatist* to float.

He spotted Miguel at the back of the lab, sitting by himself at a table that sat directly beneath a stained glass skylight. Fractal patterns of sunlight fell through the yellows and greens and teals, draping Miguel and the plasma globe at his table in a glowing, ghostly, vat-like enclosure.

The hairdryer, speakers, and scanner gun that he had brought from their dorm room lay across the table in many pieces, a small pile of screws off to the side. Miguel ran his hands through his hair, noticed Finley approaching, and then hurriedly scooped everything together in an awkward fumble. He cursed to himself when he realized he had nowhere to hide everything.

"This doesn't happen to have anything to do with your singed hair, does it?" Finley said jokingly, sitting across from Miguel.

"Ha," he replied dully. Eventually, he came to his senses and straightened up. "It, uh, it dinnertime already?" He pantomimed checking a wristwatch that wasn't there.

"Not quite," Finley said, leaning forward and dropping his voice. "But we gotta find Bridget and Helena. Know where they might be?"

"Sure, yeah. What's up?"

"It's barely been a full day since I was attacked," said Finley, "and everything has already gotten more complicated. C'mon, I'll explain on the way."

Chapter 7 | The Root

Bridget and Helena weren't too hard to find, but by the time Finley and Miguel tracked them down at the chargeball pitch on the east side of the library, Finley was numb with amazement, and he had all but forgotten why it was he and Miguel were seeking out the girls.

The pitch was surrounded by stadium seating that rose three stories into the air, and the outer wall of the bleachers was backed by red and gray stonework, which enclosed the arena—giving it a mini-coliseum appearance. The retractable, sheet metal roof was half open, paving the way for the late afternoon sunlight, which blasted onto the turf at a slant.

Miguel led Finley up the stairs to where a group of their classmates was sitting, watching the practice unfold. Finley followed slowly because his head was craned back as far as it would go; he didn't want to miss a second of what was happening on the pitch. He bumped into Miguel twice.

The Caverly twins, a thickset teenager named Doe that Finley recognized from the video at the bonfire, and two other athletes, all took turns running up to a mark on the grass and hurtling a flashball at the goal, which was being defended by a tall, lanky girl with spiked hair.

Finley felt his jaw drop. The flashballs looked like the plasma globes from the study lab, and with the assistance of surging, were being shot out of the player's hands like cannonballs. When the goalie lithely dove and caught the flashballs, sprinkles of hot orange showered onto the ground.

"The goalie position might actually be the *last* thing you'd want to try out for if you can't surge," Helena said as Finley sat down between her and Bridget. Miguel sat on the aisle seat, next to Bridget, and leaned his Lofstrand crutches against the railing.

"You think?" Finley said sarcastically. "And how is she taking that kind of force!"

They watched the goalie maneuver around the space in front of the goal with finesse, and then leap out and snag the flashball, seemingly unfazed by the momentous brunt.

"She's timing her surge," Bridget explained, crossing her legs. "Right before the flashball hits her gloves, she's Enhancing to offset the impact."

"So basically Michael was duping me when he said defense doesn't require a lot of surging." Finley shook his head, gawking at the players as they now Lunged into the air five or six feet, and then chucked the shimmering flashballs toward the goal. Every other attempt would whip past the goalie, bouncing off the back net.

"He wasn't duping you when he said defense was an available position," Miguel noted, leaning his elbows on his legs and resting his chin on his fists. "She's only saving fifty percent of the attempts."

"*That's not good?*" Finley breathed, eyes widening. He thought what the goalie was managing to do was remarkable, especially given how fast the flashballs were shooting through the air.

"Surprisingly, no," Helena said, fixing her posture. "If we're going to have a prayer when the season starts, she needs to be saving about seventy-five percent during practices."

"Guys—why did no one pinch me when I was dreaming of trying out?" Finley asked, looking at Bridget, Miguel, and then lastly, at Helena.

She said, "Hey, you asked about the rules, so I told them to you."

"I woulda been *murdered* out there," Finley added, wincing as Helena pinched him in the arm unexpectedly.

"I owed you that, apparently," she explained nonchalantly.

On the pitch, Michael Caverly dropped his flashball and jogged over to the goalie, yelling in an aggravated tone. A tall, senior-looking teenager with broad shoulders and dark skin, held Michael back by the arm.

"That's the team's charger, holding Michael back," Bridget told Finley. "Name's Ross. He's probably refraining from scolding Michael because he has the skill set to back up his mouth."

The goalie took the verbal berating, her head hanging down. She began to fidget with the red strap around her waist. It seemed to be part of the uniform, which, at a quick glance, reminded Finley of a wetsuit. Yellow, tight fitting pants and shirts with sleeves that reached the palms. There was a small, octagon pack strapped to their backs, bursting with shiny neon swirls. It reminded Finley of the vest he wore any time he would play laser tag with his friends, though not as extraordinary. The laser tag attire had been the stuff of plastic and Duracell batteries.

This was surging battle gear.

"It's the power source they draw from," Helena said, following Finley's eyes. "In chargeball, it's best to keep your hands free. A glove would only constrain their throwing form."

"Do they charge those vests at halftime or something?" Finley asked.

He imagined that playing a high-octane sport like this would require a lot from the Root, though, truthfully, he still didn't understand the mechanics of willing power from electricity. The whole methodology was like trying to remember a dream you could only grasp bits of after being awoken suddenly in the nighttime.

It was frustrating.

"Depends," Miguel replied, leaning in front of Bridget to address Finley. "Part of the art of surging is *when* to call upon the Root. If you will nonstop, you'll use up your reserve in like ten minutes. But if you're intentional and selective, you can go an entire game on one energy pack."

"An entire *match*," Helena said, sounding annoyed. Miguel crossed his eyes and hung out his tongue mockingly before leaning back.

Finley chuckled, turning to the pitch again. He and his friends sat in silence for the rest of practice, rendered motion- and speechless by the moves and athletic prowess the players displayed. They worked on more fundamentals that afternoon: Lunging while having strikeballs tossed at them; dodging and sidestepping past an onslaught of attacks; adjusting/modifying their form while attempting a save.

When dinnertime rolled around, Finley groaned in disappointment at the practice's conclusion and was told by an excited Miguel, "You think their dress rehearsal is awesome? You just wait until show time!" "*Match*, Miguel—seriously, you're the worst." "It's called a 'metaphor,' get off my back." "Diffenbaugh's rubbing off on you…"

They followed the rest of their classmates out of the stadium, through the library, across the greenway, and into the covered patio mess hall. They ate jerk chicken sandwiches and drank mango and peach punch, while Finley, Miguel, and Helena recounted the entire practice. Bridget read from her eReader, sighing through her mouth every few minutes to be sure they knew she was bored by the conversation. When asked why she had bothered going to the practice with Helena in the first place, Bridget grunted in response and swiped her finger on the screen to turn the digital page.

Once they finished dinner, Dean Longenecker's voice came booming through the exterior loudspeakers:

"Two weeks into the semester and loving it! Hope everyone enjoyed their weekend break from classes, and I bet you still managed to get your assignments done." A collective moan filled the air. *"Good! Now, because it's Brighton's utmost priority to ensure your learning environment is the best it can be, we've decided to shift around some pieces and bolster our security!"*

That's when the whispers began. Finley suddenly felt his body temperature peak. He was the reason the school's security needed bolstering, and it was because of his attack in the dorm room. Miguel, Bridget, and Helena turned and looked at him—trying to be inconspicuous in the process.

A dozen men in World War II-looking chemical suits appeared on the fringes of the mess hall like a procession of apparitions in a murky graveyard. Finley's warm body heat was instantly subdued by a chill and goose bumps. The rosy, sunset sky outlined the tall forms as they closed in on the picnic tables. The ominous newcomers were silhouettes, and their facial expressions were stone.

Each of the men wore two gloves with a bulging array of wires and gears, a cache of electric power at his disposal. They stood now with feet shoulder width apart, hands clutched behind their backs.

"*No need to be alarmed,*" the dean said over the worried murmuring. "*They're here only to make certain that there aren't any gaps in our security. Every school mandates this kind of protocol occasionally.*"

Finley wondered how long it would take for people to connect the dots. He showed up on campus yesterday, became the "kid who passed out after seeing his schedule," and now this. Surely, with as popular as Michael and Sarah Caverly were, half the school knew the truth now since Finley had told the twins at Watt's Up.

"Freakin' sick," Miguel muttered, admiring the Enhancer Force with his mouth partially open.

"*By Professor Ambrose's suggestion, the surging community's finest will be a presence for—at least—the remaining duration of the semester.*" The whispering literally doubled in volume. "*Now, please give these men your full cooperation should they feel the need to pull you aside and question you about your goings-on at Brighton, and how that looks from a safety perspective.*

"Off to the dormitories with you, we've a got a full day of learning ahead of us! I, for one, am pumped for mid-term preparations, which aren't too far off!" The speakers popped, then there was semi-silence. The Enhancer Force fanned out, off to do whatever it was they did.

"C'mon," Miguel said, grabbing his crutches and getting up from their table. All around them their classmates were doing likewise. "I've got some more reading to put off."

They followed the crowd of their peers and swept, like a school of fish, down the path to the dorm houses. Bridget and Helena waved goodnight before breaking off with the rest of the girls. Finley and Miguel said they would see them at breakfast, and then trudged along with the boys further down the path. A few minutes later they stepped into the lounging area of their dorm house, and the small gathering of eighth graders and freshmen that was already inside fell instantly hush.

They were talking about me, Finley thought, pausing in place just past the threshold. *Whelp—that was fast.*

"You gonna tell us what happened?" Doug said, emerging from the throng and pushing up his glasses. His tone wasn't concerned or inquisitive. It was demanding. Expectant. He stood in front of Finley and Miguel, skinny arms folded across his chest.

"How 'bout you back off?" Miguel said, taking a crutch-assisted step forward.

"It's fine," Finley said, putting a hand on Miguel's

shoulder. To Doug: "What do you wanna know, dude?"

"I wanna know why an Enhancer Force was brought in the day after you show up." Behind Doug, a few kids voiced agreement. Finley saw Parker among them, keeping quiet with his eyes downcast. "We in danger or something?"

Finley almost had to literally hold his tongue to refrain from quipping. While he didn't appreciate Doug's attitude, he could understand the concern. Everything was going fine at Brighton until Finley McComb made his magnificent appearance.

Suddenly, Finley felt himself struggling for an appropriate response. Usually, he was okay faking confidence in the heat of confrontation. He had had no problem standing up to Dillon Trask the other day, behind the strip mall. But that had been because, on even the smallest level, he and Dillon were acquaintances. Friends, to an extent.

Here, in the lounging area at Brighton Preparatory School for Surgers, Finley faced a collection of eighth and ninth graders who knew nothing about him, and could possibly be resenting him for what was transpiring with the upgrade to campus security.

Finley swallowed. "I…it…"

Doug shook his head. "They're saying you're not even a surger." He dropped his hands and moved forward, standing at arm's distance from Finley now. "So what are you then, and why are you here?"

If Finley couldn't even answer that question, what could he say?

"It...I'm sorry."

Doug sniffed. "Whatever. Just try to keep your distance. It's bad enough we have to share the same dorm house. Wait until my folks here about this."

"I didn't mean for this to happen, all right?"

"Nah. You may not have, but it happened, didn't it? The Enhancer Force is here, which means we need protection from something, and you won't tell us what."

Tell them you were attacked! That you had no control over this! Finley balled his hands into fists, but said nothing. *It won't matter. He's made up his mind about me.*

"I hope that if something happens," Doug said, turning his back, "I'm a hundred yards away from you when it does. This is messed up, man."

He cut through the group of onlookers and took the stairwell to his dorm room. After a few beats, everyone dispersed and did the same, leaving Finley and Miguel in the lounging area by themselves.

"Let's go, Fin," Miguel said, crossing the ceramic tiled floor to the stairwell.

Finley unfurled his fists and walked behind Miguel. He kept quiet all the way up to their floor, and didn't even say anything after brushing his teeth and climbing into bed. Miguel and Parker tried making small talk with him, but he turned over and faced the darkened wall.

His first couple of days at Brighton had been all but disastrous, and he hadn't even attended a single class yet.

In the morning, Finley was the first one to wake up, though, in reality, he hadn't slept. He tossed and turned for the better part of the night, wondering how things could possibly get worse. At one point, in the neighborhood of 2:00 a.m., he had debated packing up his belongings and hitchhiking home. But, the thought of what might happen if the Enhancer Force mistook him for a stranger tiptoeing across the grounds was enough to keep him wrapped up in his comforter.

Finley put on his straight, starched khaki pants and blue shirt, and was relieved to see that the tie was a clip-on. He ran some water through his hair, put on his brown dress shoes, grabbed his textbooks and stuffed them into his backpack, and then headed downstairs.

The cool morning air rushed over him in a breeze, the sky was barely colored with the pinks and purples of sunrise, and the only sound came from Finley's footfalls and the infrequent seagull's caw.

Never even got a chance to tell Miguel, Bridget, and Helena about the conversation I overheard with Wally, Finley thought, grabbing his backpack straps. That's when he realized that he didn't care anymore—at least not for the moment. All he wanted was to get through his first day in one piece, and, as an added bonus, finally start to understand what he was capable of…find out what the heck he was doing at a surging preparatory school.

You made fire appear…that's gotta count for something.

Even though Finley still hadn't convinced himself he'd been responsible for that miracle, a flame *had* materialized from an empty lighter when he'd held it. Finley played back the moment in his head, trying to locate the exact spot in his emotional arch that had produced the extraordinary phenomenon.

Where had his mind been? What had he been thinking? *Probably: please, for the love of God, ignite!* Finley thought, turning up the exterior hallway and heading toward the mess hall. The lampposts were still turned on from the previous night, glowing at half power.

He walked up the short side path into the mess hall, which was devoid of students. The school cooks were setting out steaming trays of egg casseroles and sausage quiches in their respective food carts. Finley approached the nearest one, took a serving of bacon and cheese biscuits and a cold carton of milk, and ate by himself. In a few minutes he was done wolfing everything down, right as a few of his classmates were starting to appear and form lines. Yawns and lazy chatter filled the atmosphere, and a school staff member began lighting the tiki torches that encircled the mess hall.

Finley avoided everyone's eye lines, tossed his trash away, and sought out the campus map near the statue of the man proffering the bulb to the heavens. He found Professor Templeton's classroom in the legend, marked by a capitol E, which he assumed stood for English.

Finley sprinted across the greenway, wanting to be sure he was the first one there, this way he could be absolutely certain there was a desk in the back of the room up for the taking. The best shot he had at making it out alive today was to take the wallflower approach. Blend in. Stay out of the way.

He didn't know how it happened. Maybe he'd been staring at his shoes while he was sprinting. Maybe he just wasn't paying that much attention. Either way, one second he was on his feet, running, the next second he slammed into a body.

Finley grunted, toppling backward, but was able to remain upright. It was Professor Ambrose with whom Finley had collided. The man's sturdy frame hadn't faltered in the least bit. He didn't even appear surprised. He was standing next to an Enhancer who wore the dark, tactical jumpsuit as was customary to his field. Finley tried not to look daunted, but it was near impossible.

The Enhancer was tall—so much so that he had almost an entire foot on Ambrose. He wore his collar up, and there were two thin straps that connected to a combat mask covering his face. He had tight-fitted knee and elbow pads, and his gloves were skeletal, with bending and bowing appendages that moved in flawless sync with his fingers.

Finley steeled himself. "H-Hello, professor."

"Finley." Ambrose raised his eyebrows. "In a hurry? First period isn't for another thirty minutes."

"I know, I, um, just trying to give myself enough time since today's my first day, and, so yeah."

Ambrose and the Enhancer shared a look.

"All right then," the professor said, stepping back so Finley could proceed. "Don't let us stop you."

"Yeah, see you." Finley set forward with resolute eyes. He wasn't going to let them see how flustered he was.

Great start to the day, Finley scolded himself.

He wound around a park bench and beneath the shade of some palm trees. In no time, he arrived at Professor Templeton's door, turned the knob, and pushed forward—sighing with relief.

The classroom was large, and it had a beautiful vaulted ceiling. Skinny, rectangular windows reached from floor to crown molding, and a long table that seated twenty was set in the middle of the room. The professor's desk, which was currently unoccupied, sat in front of a giant chalkboard. There was a long list of authors on the board, among which were Hemmingway and Steinbeck.

Finley walked over to the seat at the table that was furthest from the front, took off his backpack, and sat down. Sunbeams shot through the windows in picturesque form, and Finley stared at the twirling dust as he pulled out his copy of *The Surgers Take On Classic and Contemporary Literature: Volume 1*.

It wasn't long before the rest of his classmates began to shuffle in, and Finley pretended that he was reading the introduction at the beginning of his textbook, when really all he was doing was scanning the words and letters. He even nodded, like he agreed with something he'd "read."

"Hey."

Finley looked up. Miguel and Bridget sat on either side of him. Helena was beside Bridget, and she took the next available chair.

"Doing all right?" she asked, leaning across Bridget slightly so as to keep her voice down.

"Yeah, no I'm fine," Finley lied. He smiled wanly. "Ready to get going."

Helena's lips formed a straight line as she leaned back in her chair—flattening her uniform skirt idly. Miguel and Bridget didn't pry, and instead opened their textbooks and fished for writing utensils in their bags.

Ready to get going, Finley repeated in his head.

Professor Templeton seemed to float as she whisked into the classroom, carrying a tall stack of old books and humming to herself jovially. She was a round, shorter woman with brown curly locks of hair and a fancy, flowing, elegant dress of teals and blues.

The professor carefully placed the books on her desktop and raised her hand, urging for silence. Simultaneously, she willed a collection of overhanging Edison bulbs to glow, and they faded on with gradual speed. Now ornaments of light hung from the rafters, and Finley and his classmates were swathed in ivory colored warmth.

Professor Templeton cleared her throat, smiling with an infectious smile. She said, " 'Writing is a form of therapy; sometimes I wonder how all those who do not write, compose, or paint can manage to escape the madness, melancholia, the panic and fear which is inherent in a human situation.' " She then held her hands behind her back, scanning the table of students. Eventually, a few hands rose into the air.

"Yes, Mr. Shipp," Professor Templeton said sweetly, calling on a boy with clean-cut hair and a gangly build.

"Graham Greene?" he said in a tensely tone. He dropped his hand back into his lap and squinted.

"Wonderful!" the professor replied, giving him a thumbs up. She paced around the long table of her pupils as she continued: "The beloved author could not have summed up writing more beautifully. It *is* a form of therapy, for peds and surgers alike. Open your textbooks, if you would, to page 89, where we'll begin a week-long segment on short stories—and how best to scribe them."

Okay. This I can do. Finley opened his textbook, pulled

out a pen and paper, and turned to the appropriate chapter. Professor Templeton asked them to read the chapter's preface aloud, going counterclockwise.

The woman who penned the text, a renowned grammatologist in the surging community who had won multiple accolades for her contributions, maintained that all fiction narratives bespoke an underlying thematic issue relevant to surgers. Corrupt tendencies of the wealthy. Unjust segregations within the Bolt Sovereign (the surger's government). Failed relationships. Costs of war. Hate. Love. And so on, and so forth. These were issues that overlapped and were very much intended for audiences that spanned the pedestrian/surger spectrum.

Finley scrawled down copious notes. He didn't want to miss a word. If this proved to be the only subject he could understand fully, he was going to excel at it—or die trying.

Their assignment was straightforward: Write a two thousand-word story with a simple theme. Professor Templeton admitted that no theme was "simple," per se, for that adjective could threaten to trivialize her class's understanding of thematic elements. But the point was to avoid over thinking.

A bell tolled. Finley looked up from his notes and realized an hour and a half had already passed. Just like that. His peers were scrambling to collect his or her things and rushing for the door.

Whew, Finley said inwardly. *One period down, four to go.*

He rose from his chair and walked in stride with Miguel, directly behind Bridget and Helena, who bounced story ideas off one another. ("Basically my characters fall in love, right before Jeremy—that's her lover's name—is summoned to war," Bridget was saying. "Awesome," Helena said, turning over her shoulder so Finley could see her roll her eyes.)

Professor Templeton waved them off as they stepped out of the classroom. With a few minutes to kill before Surging and Its Basic Historical Origins, they stopped at the mess hall and picked up some fruit smoothies. The sun was working its way up the sky, and it was proving to be one of the hottest days in September thus far.

Finley welcomed the heat. It had never felt so good. *I made it through a whole class!* he thought, ordering his drink. He smiled to Miguel, Bridget and Helena, telling them how amazing it felt outside. They regarded him like a madman, but were happy to see him in good spirits nonetheless.

Finley drank his frozen berry medley as they walked across the greenway to Diffenbaugh's classroom. Twice Finley scrunched his face in discomfort, trying not to think about the brain freeze his cold drink was causing, but trying to not think about it only made him think about it, which made it hurt more.

The history classroom was adjacent to the library—just like Professor Templeton's room—and it was cater-cornered from the large lecture hall where Professor

Guggenheim's Science of Surging class was held after lunch.

Finley found Diffenbaugh's classroom fairly similar to Templeton's. Same vaulted ceiling and cherry oak rafters. A vast chalkboard. A long table set for twenty in the center of the room. The one big difference was the clutter and disorder.

The shelves that lined the walls in between the windows were stuffed with tomes and bottled ships and weathered chests. Faded, beige maps hung from the ceiling like tapestries. There were old, rotary telephones. Dusty typewriters. A working stock ticker. Antique television sets. And other old things that smelled of must.

It was like a storage unit converted into a classroom.

Finley followed Miguel, Bridget, and Helena to the middle of the table, where they sat down in high-back chairs and began to pull out their textbooks. Fellow eighth graders ambled into the classroom, picking spots at the table until there were no more spots to pick. Strokes of neon pinks erupted into the room and halted dramatically in front of the chalkboard—fading and disintegrating around Professor Diffenbaugh, who now stood with his hands on his hips.

"Let's hurry and get settled now, shall we?" he projected over the sounds of the settling students. Diffenbaugh wore a bright yellow bowtie and a white, short-sleeved button-up shirt. "We've lots to cover this morning."

Finley hadn't even cracked his book open when a voice spoke, "Should you be sitting there?"

The classroom went silent.

Finley looked over his shoulder. Doug stood, his face serious, backpack hanging over his shoulder by one strap, hands pocketed in his khaki pants, glasses halfway down his nose.

Diffenbaugh said, "Mr. Horn? There a problem?"

"Yeah," said Doug, "there aren't any seats left. Shouldn't they be reserved for surgers?"

Whispers rippled out around Finley, who ground his teeth and gripped his led pencil.

"The seats are reserved for my students," Diffenbaugh said, walking to the table and leaning on it with his knuckles.

Doug snorted.

"Whatever," Finley said, not wanting to cause a scene. "I'll move."

"You most certainly will *not*," Diffenbaugh said firmly. "Mr. Horn, kindly pull a chair from the back. Tomorrow I'll make sure there are enough seats around the table, but until then, try and make do."

Doug did not argue.

But he did have a look in his eyes, and Finley knew the look. It wasn't hate, not yet—however, it was close, and it was strong. Doug pushed up his glasses.

He walked away dispassionately to fetch a spare chair, and Finley set his jaw. Things would be different now, he'd seen it happen time and time again. Someone inadvertently humiliates someone else, and that someone else never forgets. Ever.

Finley had made his first enemy.

Things would be different now indeed.

"In the interest of our newest addition to the class," said Diffenbaugh of Finley, as Doug dragged his chair over to a free corner at the table, "I thought it both necessary and, well, fun, to review the material we've covered so far."

The class groaned. Finley sunk in his chair, his neck and forehead warm with embarrassment.

"It would behoove you to summon a sponge-like mentality," the professor told Finley, who cracked open his textbook and hunched over it, "because you've got quite a lot to soak in!"

Finley winced at what felt like the burning and searing and menacing redness of a stovetop burner branding his body as his peers stared him down. He wanted to loosen his tie, but then, it was a clip-on.

"The Root," Professor Diffenbaugh announced, pushing off the table and turning to the chalkboard. There was a wooden arm set into the wall above the off-green surface. It, the wooden arm, lolled there helplessly, a conglomeration of mismatched nuts and pegs and pulleys and twine. Diffenbaugh pointed at an electrical pencil sharpener on his desk in a casual way, surging.

He willed power from this source, which shook the little sharpener and produced tiny sprays of hot yellows.

Through Understanding, Diffenbaugh brought the wooden arm on the wall to life. It twitched, then rose up, a piece of chalk wedged between its two lone fingers. The joints squeaked as they folded and bent.

It wrote, "The Root," on the chalkboard as fluidly as if a person had scrawled it, and Finley was well aware that his eyes were the size of dollar coins.

"It all starts with the Root," Diffenbaugh said. The wooden arm began drawing dates in list form. "In 1880, Thomas Edison pioneers methods and systems for distributing electricity. By 1887, his patented power stations have spread and multiplied, utilizing direct current—or DC, as his form of distribution.

"In that same year the War of Currents was waged, in which a man by the name of George Westinghouse promoted *alternating* current, also known as AC, as a means for transmitting electricity."

Finley's hand was already cramping, but he pushed onward and jotted down everything the professor said. He tried marshaling his notes in bullet points, but it quickly became a scribbled, stream-of-consciousness mess.

"Then," Diffenbaugh said, pacing in front of the wooden arm and chalkboard, which bore dates and now names of significance too, "it was in 1912 when Jane

Grossman discovered the Root. Anyone care to remind us *how* she discovered it?"

The wooden arm froze. The pencil sharpener stopped shaking.

Only a few timid hands rose, one of them belonging to Miguel. "Yes, Mr. Arroyo," the professor said, calling on Miguel.

"She was struck by lightning, right?" he said carefully, dropping his hand.

Professor Diffenbaugh nodded and grinned approvingly. "And she endured more than 15 million volts of electricity in the process. It is believed the experience tossed her over fifty yards through the air."

Finley stopped writing for a moment. *15 million volts of electricity? How could anyone survive that?*

Professor Diffenbaugh went on to explain that Jane Grossman, who had been on an anthropological assignment in a Polynesian jungle when she'd been struck, had to be nursed back to life. The tribe she had been staying with had to perform ritualistic healing dances and concoct remedies that contained mud and indigenous herbs and fly wings.

"When Jane Grossman 'came back,' " Diffenbaugh continued, his tone less informative and more serious. The wooden arm was not moving anymore. "She told of a vision, and how she'd been shown the Root."

He circled the table of students, eyes moving over them

as if he were examining a lineup. He was practically performing a soliloquy—playing up the dramatics of Jane Grossman's account. And it was working. Finley had stopped writing, totally and completely engrossed with the story.

"Inside every object that is either a distributor or recipient of electrical currents, the Root can be found, and it is an assortment of throbbing, oscillating, molecular 'bubbles.' It is the energy within the energy, the true and absolute makeup of energized matter.

"The Root is the soul of electricity."

Finley wrote that last part down. It all sounded so abstract, as if the professor was voicing ideas and theories, not facts. Yet surging *was* real, and that was a fact.

"Jane Grossman began to feel the yearning. The calling. The beckoning, she would later write, of the Root. From the safari car she rode into the village on, to the box radio in her tent."

Professor Diffenbaugh pointed his forefinger at a vintage fan on his desk, giving the pencil sharpener a break, and the wooden arm began writing on the board once more. Consequently, the metal fan vibrated and spewed colorful neon yellows of light. Finley found that he merely accepted this particular side effect of surging now.

"You know the feeling," the professor said, sitting on the edge of his desk and folding his arms. "Like a beating heart, like a subtle pulse—every time you walk by an electrical socket or use an appliance."

Finley sighed. He'd never experienced that before.

"Sure, anyone can understand the Root in theory," Diffenbaugh said, scanning the table. "But not everyone can *feel* it. Not everyone can tap into it and summon its power."

I can't feel it, Finley thought. *And I can't tap into it.*

He set his pencil down, disheartened.

Doug's right—I'm no surger...

Chapter 8 | <u>The Calling</u>

"So glad *that's* over!"

Miguel shouldered his backpack and rose from the table while Finley was still collecting his notes from the lecture. The clamor of students talking and gathering materials echoed in Professor's Diffenbaugh's classroom. Everyone sounded excited that another period was in the past.

No one more so than Finley.

They'd been given their first real assignment of the semester; everything up until then had been required reading, Bridget explained. The class was to work in pairs, and, to everyone's surprise, Diffenbaugh let them choose his or her partner.

Finley and Miguel would have to write a two thousand word paper on Jane Grossman's inception of the art of surging. Professor Diffenbaugh listened to the litany of complaints from his students as he handed out their topics at random, and he promised them only "fun and challenging and exciting nights of research and writing are ahead of you!"

"I think we should use our free period to get a head start on this," Bridget offered as they left the classroom. Finley glanced over his shoulder as they passed over the threshold, and he saw the professor exchanging words with Doug Horn in front of the sprawling chalkboard.

Doug looked over and made eye contact with Finley, who swallowed and followed his friends across the greenway. Sunlight tingled over them and gave Finley goose flesh as the air-conditioned classroom was now behind them. Students leaned against palm trees and chatted, whereas others jogged in various directions—apparently late for something.

"How does Professor Diffenbaugh do it?" Finley asked, walking beside Helena. Behind him, Miguel snorted.

"Do what? Create the most painful and exhausting assignment known to man?"

"Utilize Understanding so effortlessly," Finley said. Ahead of them, a groundskeeper had Lunged into the air and landed on the roof of the study lab, customary whisks of lights trailing at his feet. He began cleaning the skylight with a long brush.

"What do you mean?" asked Bridget.

"He just taught! Went through his entire spiel without looking at that wooden arm thing." Finley could not see how this wasn't something to marvel at. "It's like it had a life of its own, writing whatever the professor said. It was like no big deal for him."

"Some people can master certain phases of surging better than others," Helena answered simply. "Few people are good at *all* of them."

"What about the Games of Illumination?" Finley turned to her, furrowing his brow. "Like chargeball. You have to be good at everything, don't you? Least that's what I got from watching our team practice."

"Think about those kids back at your school," Bridget said, "before you came here. You know, the ones who are athletic, good looking, *and* book smart."

"Some people are just lucky," Helena agreed. "Some people got it all. And those 'some people' are annoying and should live on their own planet so the rest of us can feel relevant."

"Aw," Miguel said, sounding pouty, "but I like Earth just fine and don't wanna leave."

Some people got it all, and some don't have any *of it*, Finley thought bitterly, reflecting on his situation.

It was hard to be optimistic the more he learned of surging because he was also learning about how he was so very unlike everyone here at Brighton Prep. No amount of being told how "special" he was by the faculty could squelch that feeling of isolation and sheer out-of-placeness.

"When did you guys find out that, um, you were able to, er, *sense* the Root?" Finley stopped underneath the shade of three palm trees, and Miguel, Bridget, and Helena mimicked.

"It's different for everyone," Bridget told him. "I was walking to the end of my street, trying to catch the bus to my dad's house in San Diego. The bus had started to leave before I got there, and, the next thing I know, my MP3 player is rattling in my overnight bag, giving off this tingling heat. Then, I'm suddenly zooming into the street—faster than I've ever been able to run! It was like this dizzying blur.

"The next day, some reps from the Bolt Sovereign were at my dad's house, having tea with us and explaining how I had been 'called' to be a surger."

"But the real question is," Miguel said, leaning on his crutches, "were you able to catch your bus that day?"

Bridget rolled her eyes. "Anyway, you're typically called at age thirteen, and whatever phase of surging you experience first is usually what you'll end up mastering."

That made Finley wonder something. Because of Miguel's condition, whatever it was that constrained him to Lofstrand crutches, did that mean Lunging and Fueling were out of the question?

"I was in an accident," Helena said, running a hand

through her choppy, golden hair lazily. "Got cut up on my arm pretty bad. So, I'm sitting there, in the living room, waiting for the ambulance with my mom and dad, when the lights begin to flicker, and the TV starts shaking, and then, my cuts closed up."

"Whoa," Finley exhaled, picturing Helena on that day holding up her arm as her gashes and cuts Mended themselves. Her parents must have freaked out.

"I know," she said in agreement, "I'm *dreading* Mending school, if that theory holds up about what phase we end up excelling at."

"Let me set the scene for you guys," Miguel said, talking animatedly. "Me, a young man, grasping a video game controller intensely, navigating my avatar soldier through the Nicaraguan jungle, on a search and rescue mission, my automatic rifle poised and ready."

Helena snort-laughed. "You were playing *video games* when you were called?"

"The sweat was dripping from both my brow and my soldier's," Miguel continued, louder, "I could literally feel the sticky jungle heat against my skin—"

"*Practically*," Bridget corrected.

"I TURNED BEHIND A BUSH," Miguel said, all but yelling, "and then, from the depths of a manmade, thatched hideout, the enemy sprang forth and stabbed me in the back!"—Miguel resumed a normal level voice now—"It scared me so much that the console and TV shot into the air and crashed into my bedroom ceiling."

Bridget and Helena burst out laughing, and Finley joined them when he figured out what had happened. Miguel, through Understanding, had sent all of his things flying into the air because the video game startled him.

"I'm proud of how my calling came," Miguel said, his face an expression of satisfaction.

"Bet your parents weren't," Helena said, her laughter fading into sporadic hiccups. "What a mess!"

"A beautiful, magical, life changing mess," stated Miguel, his eyebrows raised. "And don't you forget it."

"Trust me, we won't."

As the rest of the laughing lightened, Finley began to wonder what *his* calling would have been like. Probably not as exhilarating as Bridget's or as epic as Helena's, or even as exciting as Miguel's.

Had he already had his equivalent to a calling? Because Finley was different from them, that would mean his experience would be its own sort of event. Right?

The lighter? With Mr. Repairman, on my parent's doorstep? Finley tapped his backpack straps, eyes distant.

"So how about Doug making a scene back in class?" Helena said, interrupting Finley's thoughts. "He just got on my you-know-what list."

"I'm not worried about it," Finley lied, right as the warning bell rang, reminding those who didn't have a free period only two minutes were left before the start of the next set of classes.

"Man, forget going to the study lab to get a head start on this project," Miguel said. "Let's go down to the pier. We can write after dinner."

"I second that!" Helena declared. Bridget opened her mouth, but opted not to argue.

"Hate that I can't join you guys," said Finley, brushing his untidy bangs out of his eyes. "I've got tutoring with Professor Ambrose."

"Brutal," Miguel replied. "Well, fill us in at lunch!"

They made plans to meet Finley at 12:15 outside Ambrose's classroom, which was a standalone, octagon-shaped building that sat beside the mess hall. They wished him luck, broke off, and Finley walked up the exterior hall to his destination—thanking the universe that this was only a forty-five minute period.

It's not that he was scared, or even intimidated, really, it's just that, given how Professor Diffenbaugh's class had gone, he longed for some window or opportunity to breathe and collect his thoughts.

Finley knocked when he reached the door, but after a full minute, when still no response came, he turned the knob and walked inside.

The room's eight slanted walls were windowless, and the large space was dim and cold and felt like a chamber. Unlike Diffenbaugh and Templeton's rooms, this one had traditional individual desks. Each desktop had a small lamp, and only a few of them were turned on, creating the eerie muted luminance that permeated the atmosphere.

Finley walked down the aisle toward the front of the empty classroom, wondering when Professor Ambrose would make his appearance. Had he gotten his times mixed up? Was his tutoring session *after* lunch? But no, because he remembered that it took up his free period, which was what Miguel and Bridget and Helena were enjoying at that moment.

The professor's desk was small and clean, with sharpened pencils arranged from longest to shortest beside a half-full French press and leather-bound journal. Finley ran his finger over the desk's surface—like the room, it too was cold.

"Professor Ambrose?"

No answer.

There did not appear to be any doors that led to an office or an adjoining building. Finley took off his backpack and dropped it to his feet, then plopped into the nearest desk. He scratched his right hand, looking around the classroom curiously.

That's when he noticed the cubes. Two of them. The size of coolers. They were both made of four panes of glass, and they sat on display against one of the walls. They each contained an old, twisted, bent tree branch—suspended in air as if frozen in amber.

Finley got up from his desk, walked over to the display

and, upon a closer look, realized that the cubes were acting as tables. On one there sat a lantern, on the other a plastic flashlight.

Professor Ambrose still had not come.

Finley got on one knee and leaned closer, examining the branches, which seemed both sad and stunning, in their stagnate and white and almost *glowing* ways. The images offered him a frisson of seeing such unexpected beauty.

Entranced though he was, Finley eventually stood back up and returned to the desk he had chosen earlier. *Where is the professor?* Finley thought. It easily had been over ten minutes since he arrived, and no Ambrose in sight.

Ten minutes turned into twenty.

A half hour.

The lunch bell rang outside when forty-five minutes had expired, and Finley rose to his feet—befuddled yet eager to leave Ambrose's mausoleum-esque room. He pulled his backpack on and sprinted outside, fresh air and heat washing over him.

That had been strange, for lack of a better word. Forty-five long minutes elapsed. No professor. He hadn't even bothered to send a note or leave something on his door, indicating that he would be unable to attend their session.

He probably got caught up with something, Finley decided, walking in circles in front of the building at a leaden pace. *Maybe the Enhancer Force needed his expertise on something.*

"Look, guys, he's in one piece!"

Finley stopped and turned as Miguel, Bridget, and Helena approached. When they reached him, he moved in step alongside Miguel toward the mess hall.

"So, how'd it go?" Helena asked in front of him.

"Er, well, it technically didn't go."

"Huh?"

"Professor Ambrose, he...he never showed up."

"What?" "What?" "What?"

"Yeah, I basically just sat there the whole time in his classroom, which is pretty creepy, as classrooms go, the more I think about it. It's so cold and lifeless."

"Wait until you hear him teach."

They ate lunch and came up with theories about why Professor Ambrose had gone M.I.A. Bridget and Helena shared in Finley's conclusion, figuring the most realistic scenario involved the professor getting sidetracked in a meeting with the Enhancer Force. Miguel tried convincing them that Ambrose had been attacked by the same person who had knocked Finley unconscious, and that the professor was now lying—blacked out—in his office, and it was their duty to go and revive him.

Bridget scolded him, telling Miguel that wasn't something to joke about, but they all exchanged worried glimpses because it wasn't too far fetched.

Finley tried assuring them that the professor was fine, and that lightning didn't strike twice, after all. Yet he had a hard time believing his own words...

The fourth period bell echoed across the Brighton campus. Finley and the gang rose from their seats and assembled their belongings. They left the mess hall and strode together with a newfound sense of apprehension hanging between them, but they ultimately decided *not* to go and check on Ambrose because he was the last person at the school who could be unexpectedly bested. (Though, really, Finley was afraid of what they might find in the professor's office if their deepest fears ended up being a reality.)

The Science of Surging professor, Emmerich Guggenheim, was an elderly man with a mustache that had twisted ends. He taught in the lecture hall, which easily sat up to a hundred people. He wore brown pants with a matching brown jacket—the kind with off colored elbow patches.

Finley, Miguel, Bridget, and Helena took the desks near the bottom of the boomerang-shaped seating. The rows worked up behind them in tiers, and, though Miguel made a case for sitting in the back ("Then the professor can't see us when we doze off!"), Finley said he needed to be close enough to the board to ensure his notes were as precise and accurate as possible.

This class proved to be the dullest so far, and Finley deeply and terribly wished he'd heeded Miguel's suggestion to sit in the back, though being so close to Professor Guggenheim and his pulpit didn't stop Miguel's head from rocking up and down every so often as he battled post-lunch exhaustion.

Guggenheim navigated them through various "lists." He listed, in his charming and fatherly voice, the stages of potential power in each appliance that possessed the Root. From remote control cars to laptops, and everything in between. He wrote down complicated and multilayered equations next to each object on which he lectured, and this illustrated both the input and output of electrical force.

Finley was keeping up, for the most part, until the equations Guggenheim wrote on the dry erase board began to contain letters.

Then, the headache came, and it was all Finley could do to concentrate the rest of the time.

Professor Guggenheim detailed that evening's reading assignment on the board, and then dismissed them a few minutes early. Finley stuffed his textbook, pen, and notebook into his bag and nudged Miguel awake. He wiped his mouth and sprang into action, blinking his eyes and fumbling with his things.

Finley followed Bridget and Helena toward one of the lecture hall's side doors, and they paused to let a queue of their peers exit first, which gave Miguel a chance to catch up to them.

"Mr. McComb," came a deep, muffled intonation.

Finley started. The same Enhancer whom Professor Ambrose had been chatting with earlier that day was now standing in the doorway, his dark combat mask reflecting the overheard fluorescent lights.

Bridget and Helena parted, clearly not wanting anything to do with the frightening form that towered before them. Now the Enhancer had a clear line of sight to Finley, who gulped.

"Is there a problem?" Professor Guggenheim asked from the stage directly behind Finley.

"I've come to collect Mr. McComb," the Enhancer said, marching into the lecture hall. His heavy boots sounded as if they were crunching over puny broken fragments, or snow, even.

"You have?" said Professor Guggenheim.

"You have?" said Finley.

"Come," the Enhancer said in a surly voice, his gloved hand outstretched.

Finley looked at Bridget and Helena, hoping they'd intervene for some reason. They didn't, so he looked over his shoulder at the professor, and then at Miguel, and then when the moment became awkward, Finley resigned and obeyed.

The Enhancer about-faced and left the lecture hall with Finley in tow. They moved across the greenway in the afternoon sunlight, passing students who watched on with a mixture of fear and awe. *If Doug is around*, Finley thought, *he's probably hoping I'm getting escorted out of here...*

...Wait—am I?

"Sir?" Finley said, his mouth and throat suddenly dry. "Are you...where are we going?"

The tall Enhancer looked down at him, but did not reply.

Chapter 9 | <u>Control</u>

"Uh, sir?" Finley repeated, stalling on the grass and holding his backpack straps. *This can't be how it ends...I didn't even go a full day!*

The Enhancer seemed impassive, even though his facial expression was unreadable behind his combat mask. He hesitated, then said, "We're going to your next class." His deep and resounding voice was calm.

"Oh. Right." Finley felt his chest relax as he let out a long breath.

The Enhancer turned up the greenway and continued toward Professor Ambrose's octagon classroom. Finley jogged to catch up, his backpack bouncing up and down on his shoulders.

"Am I in trouble? Why do I need an escort?"

"Not in trouble."

"Okay, so, am I in danger?"

"No danger. Not yet."

That wasn't foreboding or anything.

"We're randomly selecting students to escort and question," the Enhancer said, not looking down at Finley as he spoke, as if he were merely sharing this statement with the universe.

Finley had a difficult time believing his being chosen was "random." "Okay," he said, as they stepped off the grass and onto the paved sidewalk in front of Ambrose's classroom. They both stopped and stood, facing one another, and Finley tried to be unafraid in the presence of this giant, uniformed, masked Enhancer, but fear blustered through his other emotions and won.

"You've been here how many days?" the Enhancer asked.

"Er, three—if you count today."

"Upon your arrival, did you notice anything strange?"

"That's tough because, well, *everything* here seems strange, doesn't it? Up until last Friday I put surging in the same category as the Easter bunny!"

The Enhancer did not laugh; he continued with his questions.

"How about your interactions with the staff? Have you ever felt threatened?"

Finley made a face. It was a mixture of surprise and

amusement, though both reactions almost instantly faded as he thought of someone. Wally, the school driver. Finley had seen the dean slip him a note circumspectly. That had been strange. Finley had overheard Wally talking to someone in whispers, referencing something about an "it" appearing soon. That too had been strange.

Was this worth mentioning?

"Mr. McComb?"

"Sorry, I...," Finley began, looking around, like he was ashamed of what he was considering and everyone could see his thoughts. But no one was around. Professor Guggenheim had dismissed the Science of Surging early, so the rest of Brighton was still tucked away behind the walls of the extensive campus.

You wouldn't bring this up to Diffenbaugh, Finley scolded himself, *so would you* really *tell a practical stranger?*

"Um, the driver," Finley found himself saying. The Enhancer put his hands on his hips, staring down through his thick mask at Finley.

"Wally Grondahl?"

"He..." *What are you doing! What if your suspicions, whatever they are, end up being wrong!* "Yeah, he, um, I overheard him talking to someone secretly about 'results' and 'making excuses.' When I went around the corner to see who was with him, no one was there. He was standing by himself. Also, he mentioned something 'appearing' soon."

The words came spewing out of Finley like water and pressure bursting forth from a geyser. He couldn't stop, nor could he tell how the Enhancer was receiving all of this. He was relieved then when the Enhancer said, "I see. We'll keep a close eye on him. You did the right thing."

And the Enhancer was gone. The class bell rang.

Juniors flooded out of Ambrose's classroom and jostled past Finley, who sifted around his peers and made it to the fringes of the exodus in time to see Miguel, Bridget, and Helena approaching.

"Dude," Miguel said, sounding out of breath. "What was that about?"

Finley, while staring at the grassy floor: "He...he wanted to know if I'd seen anything strange since I arrived."

"You mean other than that Olyphant man in the field when you were knocked unconscious?" Helena shook her head, sighing. "I'm sure they're following their procedures and all, but don't they realize if any of us saw anything we would have already reported it? They should be focusing on security!"

Finley was starting to notice that whenever Helena was worked up or under duress, her native Michigan accent mounted.

"I think that's the point," said Bridget. "They're not just here to fill in security gaps, like Dean Longenecker told us. They're investigating..."

And Finley just handed the Enhancer Force a possible player in all this. Or, he could have created for them a massive waste of time and resources: If this was their only lead, would they pursue it doggedly? Would Wally be brought in for questioning? He'd know it was Finley who had said something—their moment next to the statue had been an awkward one, and not easily forgettable.

"Let's go inside and grab some desks in the back," Helena said, looking over her shoulder. "I don't want to be stuck in the front during one of Ambrose's *stirring* lectures."

Finley followed his friends inside.

You did the right thing. The Enhancer's words. They echoed in his thoughts like the trickling vibrations that lingered and hung in the air after the school bell tolled. He could hammer that sentiment all day long—that he truly *had* done the right thing—but a twinge of guilt still pricked at his insides like a deeply burrowed splinter.

Finley sat in the desk behind Helena and next to Miguel, putting Bridget cater-cornered from him, next to Helena. He, Finley, set his backpack in the metal tray beneath his desk and leaned forward. The two Plexiglas cubes were still there, at the front of the classroom, and so was the flashlight and lantern. The tree branches inside were almost completely imperceptible from this distance.

As the rest of the class began to file inside, Finley realized that Professor Ambrose was already at his desk beside the dry erase board—penning something down on a long sheet paper, taking an occasional sip of coffee.

The French press on his desktop was empty.

The last student entered, shutting the door behind her. She took the last available seat to the professor's left. Then, it was still. The stillness bespoke of something reverential or obeisant, like Finley and his classmates were in the presence of someone more than a professor or scholar.

This man, this Ambrose—with his suit and tie and brawny build—was a warrior.

The professor rose.

He stalked up and down the aisles. Finley tried to make eye contact with him, as if to say, Where were you earlier?, but the professor was looking over everyone's heads.

"Control," he said. You could hear a pin drop. "The fundamental element of surging." He was next to Finley's desk now. "We have learned that the Root is alive. It's wild. It must be tamed."

Finley swallowed, and he was sure he could hear Miguel doing the same.

"We have also learned that the Root is comparable to a tempest," the professor continued, moving along the walls now. "What do we know about storms? That they can't be controlled or predicted. So, if the Root is like a storm, and it is terrible and unpredictable and impulsive, how can we possibly tame it?"

For the first time that day, no hands rose into the air. Finley wasn't sure if it was because no one knew the answer, of if everyone was too afraid to participate. Then, a familiar voice confidently spoke: "The only true way to control something is to become a part of it."

Finley turned his head, along with the rest of the class. Doug Horn sat in the front row, pushing up his glasses and directing his pointed stare at the professor. "That's why, at the end of the day, you can't really control people. Sure, you can 'force' someone to do anything with a gun to their head, but you wouldn't be changing their mindset or beliefs, would you? They'd just do whatever you'd say because they wouldn't want you to pull the trigger.

"Now, if you could 'control' them, you'd be doing more than just forcing them into something. 'Control' would be to…to *change* them."

Everyone was stunned. They all turned to the professor, who unbuttoned his suit jacket and folded his arms across his chest. Even he appeared to be impressed.

"Well put," the professor said evenly. "So, from a pragmatic standpoint, how do we control, or, 'change,' the Root? How do we take hold of it?"

"We stop thinking about it in abstract terms," Doug answered simply and importantly.

"Enlighten us," Ambrose said.

"Well, coming to terms with the fact that the Root is real, that it's tangible, will help us move toward understanding its capabilities and limits."

Finley jotted down everything that Doug said. He wasn't talking like a shy, apprehensive eighth grader, but rather like a learned understudy.

"It's why many people are unable to master all of the phases of surging," Doug said, a hint of disgust in his voice. "It's so hard for them to fully grasp the *idea* of becoming a surger, that it hinders them from ever reaching their full potential. The second you accept that the Root is real and alive and waiting to be willed, the sky's the limit."

"You may be treading on philosophical waters now, Mr. Horn," Professor Ambrose said, returning to his desk. He didn't sit down.

"So?"

A few people gasped.

"So what?" Doug sounded like he was keeping some chuckles at bay.

Finley could hardly accept this was the same kid who was complaining about his aptitude test the day before. Here was a darkly smug and confident and well-spoken eighth grader who wasn't afraid of challenging Brighton's finest.

"Philosophy is just as essential to surging as the fundamentals."

"I'm not maintaining that it's *not*, Mr. Horn," the professor said, and that's when the lamps on the desks began to flicker, for a moment, and then that moment passed. Doug seemed to sink into his chair a little. "But it's important to have a grasp on the fundamentals before we can successfully segue into antecedent conditions, causes, and finalities as pertaining to surgers. Understood?"

Doug nodded, and, instinctually, so did the rest of the class.

"Mr. Horn raises some good points," Ambrose said, turning to his board and writing, in red, "CONTROL," and "BALANCE." "And he has teed up for us a second element necessary to surging. Balance. If you studied about driving until you were blue in the face, but opted out of driving lessons, how do you think you would fare on the freeway on your first try, Mr. McComb?"

Finley's heart skipped a beat. "Er, not well?" he managed to squeak, to which the class laughed.

"No, not well at all," the professor said in agreement. "Likewise, if you bypassed the driver's manual and focused only on the mechanics of controlling a motor vehicle, how well do you think you'd be able to interpret traffic signs and warnings and guidelines?"

Finley gulped. "Not well, either?" More laughter.

"Right again." The professor paced in front of the whiteboard. "You see, like driving, surging requires balance. Open your textbooks. Go to chapter thirteen, on page four hundred and twenty-two. Outline and expounded upon the key points to Lunging. At the end of the week, you'll present your conclusions and then get your first stab at Lunging."

Whispers of enthusiasm spread around Finley. *Great*, he thought. *I'd better figure out what I am, and what I can do, by Friday.*

"All right, all right, settle down," Ambrose said over the hushed commotion. "Start reading, or I'll make us read aloud—popcorn style. Everyone hates popcorn."

Miguel snorted, then said to Finley out of the corner of his mouth: "He's never had popcorn with hot sauce."

When the bell sounded that afternoon, signaling the completion of the final period, Finley expected noisemakers to go off and confetti to fall. The whole classroom exploded into a jumble of kids cramming things into backpacks and bodies rushing for the exit. When textbooks slammed shut it was like thunderclaps resounding amidst a storm. When feet bustled out the door it was like a stampede of prey evading predators.

Finley made to follow Miguel outside, but he hesitated near the doorway. He glanced over his shoulder at Professor Ambrose, who was putting papers into his briefcase.

"I'll see you guys in a minute," Finley told Miguel.

"Huh?" Miguel's face bore puzzlement as he leaned on his Lofstrand crutches between Bridget and Helena. Finley didn't explain, but simply pulled the door closed and turned toward the professor. The door failed to shut all the way, allowing a sliver of sunlight to penetrate the gloomy atmosphere.

There was a long spell of silence. Then,

"Mr. McComb, and how was your first day?"

Don't be afraid. Don't be afraid. Just talk to him, like he's anyone else.

"Mr. McComb?" The professor finally looked up, his hand hovering over the briefcase buckles. Finley was a heartbeat away from spinning on his heel and leaving the frigid classroom, but his stance remained—his shoes firmly planted on the cement ground.

"My first day was good," Finley said weakly. The professor made a noise, like a grunt, and then resumed stashing his materials away.

"I mean, my first day kinda sucked." Finley added this in a solid and annoyed tone.

"Beg your pardon?"

Finley took off his backpack and tossed it onto the floor before striding across the classroom and facing the professor in front of his black, metal desk.

"It sucked because I don't know what I'm doing here," Finley said, sensing the red in his cheeks before the warmth came. "And because I was attacked, and because I'm the reason security has to be altered, and because *you* didn't show up for tutoring, when I was supposed to finally get my answers! It sucked because everyone here is a surger, learning about the art of surging, and I'm just along for the ride, apparently, because I CAN'T SURGE!"

Finley was panting. He saw something change in Ambrose's eyes then, as if every expression he wore was simply a mask, and now, for the first time, the professor was offering Finley a glimpse into how he really, truly looked at things.

"Have a seat, Finley," Professor Ambrose said. It was the first instance in which he had called Finley by his first name.

"Not until you tell me what's going on!" Finley thundered. "Why was I brought to Brighton? Why did Olyphant insist I was 'on the wrong side'? What are the 'Dissensions'? Why are you keeping these things from me!"

Finley wasn't sure how he had let himself get so worked up, but the next thing he knew the tingle and burn of approaching tears came upon him. Professor Ambrose walked around his desk, took Finley by the shoulder gently, and sat him down in the nearest chair.

"You know, you lasted longer than I would have," the professor said when the first tear appeared below Finley's left eye. Ambrose's voice was uncharacteristically kind. "Transitioning into the surging community is tough, no doubt about it. But coming here late into the semester, and without knowing what it is you're really capable of, well, not even a solid arrester can remedy that."

"Please...," Finley said, sniffing. "Tell me what I am." To his surprise, the professor got to one knee beside Finley's desk and, once they were eyelevel, Ambrose cleared his throat.

"Here's what we've been led to believe," the professor said, his lazy eye drifting a bit. "You possess a special ability that was previously thought to be a myth. You can *recharge*, Finley. Or so the school's been led to think, anyway."

"W-What does that mean?"

"Here, look," the professor stood and walked back to his desk, yanking open a drawer.

Finley heard the clinking and clanking of objects bumping into each other. Eventually, Ambrose found what he was looking for: a AA battery. He showed it to Finley, held between his thumb and forefinger.

"A dead battery," the professor said.

Then, he turned and pulled the clock off the wall next to the whiteboard and swapped the good battery for the bad one he had just retrieved from his desk. He walked back over to Finley and set the now dead, still clock in his lap.

"Use Understanding," the professor said, matter-of-factly. "Make that clock tick."

"But, t-that's impossible," Finley said, holding the white clock in his now trembling hands. "The Root is in electricity, in power. This battery is—"

"Stop telling me why it won't work," Ambrose said, though it sounded like he was smiling as he said this. When Finley checked, there wasn't even a hint of a grin on the man's face.

Finley rose to his feet. He didn't know why, but it felt right to try this while standing. *I was standing when I lit Mr. Repairman's lighter*, he thought. Finley gripped the clock in both hands, holding it at arm's length, level with his face, like it was a mirror, and then he set his jaw.

C'mon...I don't know what I'm supposed to be doing or thinking, but please just work. Work!

Behind him, the professor sat on the edge of his metal desk, watching closely, which only made Finley more nervous and distressed.

The only true way to control something is to become a part of it, Finley recited Doug's words in his head. *So...I need to become part of this old battery...part of this clock... But how? The Root's not here—it can't be!*

Finley could feel his arms start to shake. Blood was rushing to his head. *C'mon! I* will *you to work!* Nothing happened, just as he figured. He tried and thought and prayed and wished.

Nothing.

He could hear the soft wind pushing its way inside through the partially closed door. What little sunlight was present now spilled over Finley's shoes, like it was urging and encouraging him to try harder. So he did. And again, nothing. Then, he did the only sensible thing: He gave up.

That is when the second hand clicked, sounding like the majestic strum of a harp's string, and Finley's spirits sparked and flew.

The clock, for the moment, was working.

INTERLOGUE

The old man who tinkered with gadgets and devices found himself alone, in a room with no windows and one bed and sparse light. There was a black and white periodical lying face-up on the ground by the bed, and it was the first thing that came into focus as the old man regained consciousness.

The date on the headline read August 31st, 2014.

The old man scrambled out from underneath the loan sheet on the bed and collapsed to his knees on the hard ground, holding the front page to his face to be absolutely sure his fading eyes were seeing the right date. They were. August 31st, 2014.

"Let me out of here!" the old man bellowed, leaping to his feet awkwardly and feeling along the wall for a door against which he could bang his fists. There was none. It was simply the walls, ceiling, floor, and bed.

And the old man and the newspaper.

"Please!"

"My wife, she's ill!"

"She needs me!"

"What are you doing to me! Why have you locked me up!"

These were among the desperate words of the old man as he rammed his shoulder into various spots in the wall, flailed his arms about, screamed some more, and kicked the metal bed frame. This shot a sharp pain through his toes and up his foot and leg.

He kicked the bed frame a second time.

Then, sobbing wildly, he gave up and fell on the bed. The sheets smelled of dust and antique things kept in the backs of attics. The old man sobbed harder. It did no good.

His throat was dry.

His foot was numb.

His stomach grumbled and throbbed and it cursed the old man, who hadn't eaten in a long while.

Had he really been here, locked up and deprived of life and light, for that long? That couldn't be—it was impossible! He had just been at his desk in his study, poring over delinquent bills and restructuring his and his wife's finances...

...No. That was not right.

The old man's tears stopped as he sucked in his breath. He'd been searching. For the legendary Root. He'd been searching for a miracle. There had been a candle, on his desk, and a bizarre movement of shadows.

Then the flame had *popped!* away.

"And now I'm here," the old man said aloud, his voice sounding both frail and terror-stricken. But *where* was here? And, more importantly, when?

It had been March 1st, 1987 that odd night in his study, nearly twenty-five years ago.

{book ii}

Chapter 10 | <u>On Lunging</u>

Finley McComb slumped back into his desk in Professor Ambrose's classroom. He still held onto the clock with the dead battery. The second hand *ticked* and *tocked* and it was music—no, a concerto!—to his ears.

Now he understood.

You see, for Finley, it wasn't about control. It wasn't about concentrating on how he could utilize an appliance or power source. It wasn't about focusing on one command or another until his teeth chattered and his temples pulsed.

It was about letting go.

It was about letting the power of the Root manifest itself inside of him, and allowing its force...whatever that was...to take over.

Stop, Finley mouthed—which was both what he meant to say, and what he didn't. The clock's second hand froze. His thoughts and intentions, it seemed, were in perfect sync without something else. What? The Root?

Finley was terrified and amazed, afraid and invigorated.

"In its physical state," Ambrose said, startling Finley. He had forgotten the professor was there. "The Root is a collection of microscopic bubbles literally bulging with energy. Once a surger draws from this cache, the bubbles burst—releasing their power to be willed as the surger pleases.

"You, on the other hand, can will power even after the Root is extinguished."

"I don't…how is that possible?"

"Well, the only theory Brighton has been able to formulate is that the minute residues—leftovers, if you will—that remain after the Root is drawn from are *precisely* what you are able to fix on. It's like being able to feast and sustain on the juice left over in a can of fruit."

"I still don't get it. So, I can't surge with working appliances or electricity, like everyone else?"

"Now *that* we won't know until you try, will we?"

The professor got up from his desk and pulled out a glove from one of his inner suit jacket pockets. Its wires were red and its gears brass. Ambrose gestured for Finley to hold out his right hand, which he did reluctantly. The professor slipped on the glove and then motioned for

Finley to follow him to the other side of the classroom.

Here, in one of the many dark corners, sat an overstuffed bookshelf teeming with encyclopedias and tomes and references.

"Use Understanding," Ambrose said as Finley approached the shelf. "Move a book, any one of them."

"Um...," said Finley, regarding the large glove on his hand.

The tool seemed futuristic, like it belonged in a science fiction blockbuster. It also felt awkward and loose on his hand. Ambrose flicked on a tiny switch on the glove beside the pinky finger, and Finley felt his hand vibrating as the gears hummed.

"It's like any other power source," the professor explained, putting a hand on Finley's shoulder. "It's like that clock back there."

Okay, Finley thought.

It was quite overwhelming for him to have gone nearly three days while experiencing surging in a theoretical and observational way, and now he was actually practicing and carrying out application. Suddenly, things felt as if they were moving too fast.

This is insane, Finley thought, making a fist with his gloved hand. *Rise,* he mouthed, fixating his eyes on one particular book with a cracked spine. It remained motionless. Finley was intentional about avoiding thoughts of the controlling nature. *Let go. Let the book come to you.*

The book did not even flinch.

Nothing happened, except that Finley eventually sighed with frustration.

"How interesting," Professor Ambrose said, tapping his chin.

He left Finley by the shelf and moved toward his desk, where he pulled some notes out of his briefcase and leafed through the handful. Ambrose then began to mumble to himself.

"Professor?" Finley joined him at his metal desk.

"Those in our history who have claimed to be able to recharge never mentioned possessing the conventional abilities of a surger."

"Um...meaning you guys don't know if they could do both?" Finley took off the glove, which proved to weigh a lot less than he'd imagined. He set it on the professor's desk next to the empty French press, which smelled strongly of fresh grinds and a touch of honey.

"Yes."

"Sir, why has this been some kind of big secret?"

Ambrose paused what he was doing and met Finley's eyes.

"I'm sorry about that," was all the professor said at first. Then, after chewing on the inside of his cheek in contemplation, he added, "We still aren't entirely sure what this means, how or why it makes you so valuable to James Olyphant, and why he went through all of the trouble to corner you."

"Sure, okay. But did you guys really expect that I would be okay fumbling my way through Brighton? That reading about surging would be enough for me, while everyone else trained?"

"Honestly, no, I didn't suspect that would be okay." Professor Ambrose blinked, clearly thinking through his words before he spoke: "Look, Dean Longenecker is a strong and capable administrator. It was her call to have you simply immersed into the program. She wanted to be unquestionably certain you could recharge before we looped you in.

"But then, you were attacked in the dorm house. Then James Olyphant revealed himself."

Finley tilted his head. "Meaning?"

"Meaning I have no qualms whatsoever telling you everything we know, even if I am breaking my promise to the dean. It's what you deserve."

So everyone here just figured I'd be fine without knowing anything! Finley could sense the beginnings of a migraine approaching. What Professor Ambrose was saying about the dean made Finley reflect on what she had told him, in Wally's car:

I want you to make me a promise, the dean had said. If things start to get too intense for you, if your classes and studies seem to suffocate you, promise me you'll come find me. There's no shame in walking away.

It seemed that she was setting him up to leave. If Dean Longenecker wanted to help Finley and keep him at Brighton, wouldn't she have sat him down in a room on that first day and detailed *every single thing* the school knew about him and his apparent ability to recharge?

What's with all the secrets? Finley said inwardly, thinking next of the note the dean had slipped Wally. *What else aren't they telling me?*

"My," the professor said, interrupting Finley's thoughts. He, Ambrose, was looking at his wristwatch. "It's already half past six. You best run along for dinner." He went back to collecting everything in his briefcase.

Finley wanted to ask more, but he knew Ambrose was already stretching himself by telling him what he had. Finley thanked the professor for his help, grabbed his backpack, but stopped in front of the exit when Ambrose called his name.

"Yes, professor?"

"When I surge, there's a unique sensation that overcomes me," Ambrose said, clicking his briefcase shut. "Some refer to it as a pins and needles feeling."

"So I've heard."

"You don't feel that when you recharge?"

"No. I do feel something, though."

"What?"

"Don't really know how to explain it. It's like I do and think things before I realized I wanted to do or think them." Finley laughed at himself. "Wow, that sounded really stupid out loud."

"No. It didn't. See you around, Mr. McComb."

Finley opened his mouth, but the professor had taken his briefcase off the desk and Fueled passed him and out of the classroom—stripes of hot pinks trailing behind him like the fading imprints in the sky after the northern lights.

Finley could tell his friends were itching with a lot of questions, but they did their absolute best to give him space, which he appreciated. At dinner, they didn't ask Finley what he and Professor Ambrose had discussed, but instead recounted their day and made a game plan for tackling their homework and assigned reading.

It's not that Finley was purposefully avoiding telling them his new discovery, it's just that every time he wanted to bring it up, he found himself smiling dumbly and unable to adequately articulate the news.

I can recharge! Maybe I do belong here!

Now it was as if there was beauty to be found in every single thing around Finley McComb. Hours of catch-up reading ahead of him? Great! Two thousand word research paper due in a few days? Can't wait! (He was even enjoying the grilled fish platter that was prepared for dinner—his mother would have been proud.)

At last Finley had been presented with real and

authentic motivation. The Root may look and feel differently to him—it may not be a source of gifts in the same way it was to Miguel, Bridget, and Helena—but it was there for Finley all the same.

So it was, when he finally brought himself to tell them what he had learned, that his friends broke library protocol and shouted excitedly.

"Finley!"

"That's so cool!"

"You'll have to show us!"

The librarian, an elderly man with no hair on his head and bushy eyebrows, held his forefinger against his lips petulantly—signaling for them to keep their voices down. He happened to be walking by their table at that exact moment, lugging a squeaky book cart behind him.

They had migrated to the library after dinner to begin researching their history papers for Diffenbaugh's class, but all they'd managed to do thus far was write their names and the date on the top of their respective papers.

Now, with this news of Finley's ability, it would be much longer before they gained traction with their assignment.

"Professor Ambrose said recharging was something previously thought to be a myth?" Bridget asked, lowering her voice when the librarian glared over his shoulder at them. It seemed all the old man was doing was prowling the aisles and tables, waiting for someone to speak above a whisper.

"Yeah," answered Finley.

"Makes sense," Helena said, "I mean, because I've never heard of recharging."

"What *doesn't* make sense is why they were keeping this from you." Miguel put his pencil down, took off his clip-on tie, and set it next to his open textbook on the table.

"Totally agree," said Finley. "Ambrose said Dean Longenecker had her reasons, but what could those reasons possibly be?"

"They couldn't have really believed you would just skate through classes blindfolded, completely ignorant to all of this," Bridget said, looking thoughtful. "How did they expect you to learn anything?"

Finley snorted. "What's crazy is that I would still be as lost as ever if I hadn't essentially demanded answers from Professor Ambrose."

"Good point," Helena said, inclining forward. "And who would've thought the professor would have just given in like that? He must really disagree with the dean in her wanting to keep everything under wraps."

"All I know is I'm glad I can move forward," Finley declared, leaning back in his chair. "We still don't know why the dean's being all secretive, we still don't know who James Olyphant is—or why he cornered me—but now I have an identity. Now I feel like I actually belong in this place."

"You've always belonged here, Finley," Bridget assured him, her voice soft. "You were recruited, just like us."

"And now I know why," Finley replied, smiling. "Now I get to work on Lunging with you guys."

"And suffer through the rigmarole of a Diffenbaugh assignment," Bridget added.

" 'Rigmarole?' " Miguel rolled his eyes. "Really, Bridget?"

"It was probably on her daily word calendar," Helena said, listlessly turning a page in her textbook.

"I don't have a daily word calendar, thank you," Bridget stated stiffly. "It is incumbent upon the both of you to keep up with Professor Templeton's reading goals. Then you could keep up with me."

"That's extra credit bull," Miguel said, waving his hand dismissively. "I'll spend my free time having a life."

"I just wish that 'having a life' included a daily shower for you," Bridget quipped. Miguel touched his arm with his pinky finger and made a singing noise with his tongue. Finley laughed at their banter, taking pleasure in the moment.

The wonderful, current state of his journey at Brighton made it so that he saw humor in just about anything. He could smile more easily; find the silver lining in the toughest of places. Sure, he was still lost on a lot of things, but there was a tiny glint of light in that darkness. Learning about his recharging ability was that light.

Miguel, Bridget, and Helena were that light, too.

The rest of the week flew like a sped-up film, and it was all Finley could do to keep his head above the thrashing waters of information and homework that sought to drown him violently.

Finley was grateful for his friends more than he ever imagined he would be. Sure, they helped one another with research and findings, but they also suffered and vented with him. He was positive he would go crazy if not for the times at breakfast, lunch, and dinner where they could complain and curse their professors for the mind-numbing assignments they created.

Every day that week Professor Diffenbaugh would check on Finley after Surging and Its Basic Historical Origins. How are things, Fin? Picked an extracurricular activity yet? Staying on top of your reading? Blown fuse, you've had quite the busy first week, haven't you!

Finley deeply appreciated that the professor cared enough to pull him aside.

Professor Ambrose, on the other hand, was pretending as if he and Finley had never talked or been introduced. In his class he resumed calling on Finley as "Mr. McComb," and he seemed annoyed with each instance in which Finley would raise his hand and ask a question.

And he still hadn't shown up for a single tutoring session.

Finley was hurt, of course, but by Thursday he was so

overwhelmed with papers and readings that he just used this block of time as a study period. The only thing constant during those "tutoring sessions" was the flashlight and the lantern sitting atop the Plexiglas cubes.

Was it something I said? Finley thought, trying to remember exactly how his last conversation with the professor had ended. Ambrose had asked Finley about the feeling associated with recharging, and, when Finley had given his response, the professor seemed perturbed...

By Friday, the Enhancer Force was starting to make a stronger presence of themselves on the Brighton Prep campus.

At that point it was normal for Finley and his friends to see an Enhancer coming out of a bathroom stall and sharing the sink with them. It wasn't a surprise to see one or two at the front of the lecture hall, flanking Professor Guggenheim as he attempted to break down the molecular structure of a Root bubble. It wasn't a shock, then, to hear that the Enhancer Force would be implementing strict security measures on the first day of the Games of Illumination Saturday afternoon.

"It wouldn't be so big of a deal if they weren't so terrifying!" Bridget said beside Finley as they made their way to their final class of the day: Control with Professor Ambrose.

"I'm sorry," Miguel said in front of them, "but they look *badass.*"

"I can't argue with the man," Finley said in response to Bridget's disgusted face.

Even Helena, who strode in front of Bridget to Miguel's right, agreed with a nod.

They filed into Ambrose's classroom and took up post at what had become their usual spot. Today was the day one of their many papers were due, but it was also the day they would be practicing Lunging.

Professor Ambrose was at the front of the octagon classroom, pouring coffee from his French press into an enamelware mug. He then sipped the hot contents, engrossed in paper grading.

"Still hasn't shown up to your tutoring sessions?" Miguel whispered, motioning to the professor with a flick of his head.

Finley shrugged. "It's whatever. Gives me a chance to work on my short story for lit."

Miguel leaned back in his chair as the rest of the class began to tread inside. Seats filled. Chatter diminished. The organic, immediate silence of Professor Ambrose's period initiated once the last desk was occupied and the door creaked shut.

Then, like a switch was turned or a button pressed, the professor was on his feet. He paced in front of his whiteboard, which was filled—from edge to edge, top to bottom—with advanced diagrams and intricate dueling stances, most likely left from his previous class.

It was a good while before Ambrose said anything.

"Glad to see everyone in good spirits." He didn't sound glad. "You can leave your response papers on my desk at the end of class. Follow me onto the greenway, bring your gloves. Time to work on Lunging."

Then, he walked up the center aisle and pushed open the door with his shoulder. He didn't wait to be followed. In fact, it wasn't until the door was almost shut again before everyone got to their feet wordlessly and marched outside.

"Guys!" Finley hissed desperately as he and Miguel, Bridget, and Helena trailed out last. "I need something to recharge!"

"You don't have a glove?" Miguel asked next to him, grunting when he accidentally overextended his crutches.

"Obviously not," Helena said, pulling out her cell phone and handing it to Finley. "Here. Use this—it's practically dead anyway."

Finley exhaled with relief and stuck the bedazzled cell phone into his back pocket. "You're the best."

"Did Professor Ambrose explain how you should gauge your Root capacity?" Bridget asked as they wound past some palm trees and started toward the area on the greenway where the rest of their class had amassed.

Finley cocked his head. "What are you talking about?"

"She makes it sound like going to the dentist or something," Miguel joked, to which Bridget shot him an irritable glare. "Anytime we surge we have to figure out how much of the Root is inside the specific power source we're drawing from. Then, we can learn what our limits will be in that moment."

"That's why gloves were so revolutionary," Helena said, putting hers on. It, like her cell phone, was bedazzled in spots. "Unlike smaller objects, such as MP3 players or toasters, which will only give you enough juice for a few surges, a glove—after it's charged—can last a full day."

"Crap," Finley cursed as they joined the circle their peers had formed around the professor. *Ambrose forgot to mention that detail.* And yet, if recharging relied on the "leftovers" of the Root, how could Finley possibly expect to assess what his limits were?

"This everyone?" the professor asked, turning around and looking each student in the face quickly. "Good. Lunging is the easiest form of surging. It's why I've been given the blessed task of instructing it to eighth graders."

Finley's classmates nudged each other and whispered excitedly. This was the moment they'd all been waiting for. Three weeks into the semester and it was finally time to surge.

Or, in Finley's case, recharge.

"Line up, shoulder to shoulder, over there," the professor instructed, pointing to the east corner of the greenway.

The eager crowed obeyed without question, and as they

moved, Finley found himself separated from Miguel, Bridget, and Helena. Finley instead ended up standing between a mousy girl with dyed black hair, and Doug Horn.

"This should be fun," said Doug hollowly, yanking off his clip-on tie, stuffing it into his front pocket, and undoing the top button on his shirt. He wore a glove that went halfway up his arm, rows of exposed wires and copper strands threading in an out of the tight-fitted fabric.

"Where's your glove, Finley?" Doug asked, a smirk appearing on his face.

"Don't need one," he answered confidently, leaving his tie on.

Doug did not appear convinced, but he wasn't given an opportunity to remark because Professor Ambrose was talking and giving more instructions. The late afternoon sun beat down behind him, forcing everyone to squint or shield their eyes.

"Studies have shown that first year students don't excel when they're put on the spot," Ambrose said, his hands on his hips. "That working in pairs is more ideal, more comfortable. Those studies are a joke, which is precisely why you'll be Lunging individually—one by one."

Everyone groaned.

"You should not be comfortable when you Lunge," the professor continued. "Surging is a gift. It's all about aiding you when you're in a tight spot, or when you're trying to help someone less fortunate than you. What's comfortable about that?"

To Finley's left, Doug sighed as if he was bored.

"Now." Ambrose strode up and down the line of his students. "Lunging, much like Fueling, is about seeing where you intend to go, and how you intend to get there. But don't dwell on that aspect of it too much, just like you wouldn't overanalyze getting up from the kitchen table to get a glass of water. Make sense?"

Some people nodded, but most people—Finley included—did nothing in response. Sure, what the professor was saying sounded simple enough, but Finley knew that it wouldn't be until they applied these principles that things would start to click.

"How about we just start," the professor said, like he was reading Finley's thoughts. He pointed at the girl next to Finley, who gasped dramatically. She looked to her left and right frantically, but when neither Finley nor the boy on the other side moved, she dropped her head in a defeated manner and stepped forward.

The greenway plunged into stillness. There was only the sea breeze, passing through palm leafs, and the distant roar of the ocean waves. Finley's hands moistened and practically dripped with perspiration. He could tell the girl in front of them would have rather subjected herself to the flu shot over standing here amidst her peers.

She was a harsh contrast to the sunny lawn, with its

paradise-like landscape of newly trimmed grass, potted beach flowers, ceramic tile walkways, and exterior halls. The girl wore black eyeliner, black lipstick, and black fingernail polish in direct equivalence with her dyed hair.

Finley didn't think someone could make Brighton's uniform so gothic. It seemed she wasn't wearing the same skirt, shirt, and tie as Bridget and Helena.

"Ms. Woods," the professor said, standing aside and holding out a flattened hand. "We'll start in small chunks. Fifteen yards, please."

The girl nodded, sucked in a long breath, pulled her gloved fist back like she was winding up for a punch, bent her knees a little, and…

…Lunged.

She looked weightless for all of two seconds. The earth was beneath her. The spot of grass she'd previously been standing on swirled and twisted, as if a leaf blower was blasting the ground. She arched as high as six feet into the air, her long locks of dark hair rippling behind her, and then she landed awkwardly—stumbling over her feet and almost losing complete balance.

Yet she had done it. She had Lunged. Fifteen yards and some odd change were behind her, where the rest of the class cheered and applauded and yelled, "Nice! Go Lauren!" Finley was stunned for a moment, but he eventually clapped along with everyone else.

"Nice work," Ambrose called out to her when the last

trickle of neon greens washed away in the sunlight. Finley rubbed his eyes. "Landing will come with practice, but your launch was rather impressive." Even from this distance it was obvious she was blushing.

Doug volunteered himself next, and he wasted no time.

Unlike Lauren, he took a running start before planting his right foot onto the grass and leaving the ground. His arch was masterful and expertly executed, and the neon green streak emanating from his glove looked like long exposure light photography.

He landed softly beside Lauren. More applauding, even some oohs and ahs.

"Good, very good." Professor Ambrose waited for another volunteer, but no one came forth. Who was about to follow *that* act? And when the professor's eyes fell on Finley, he was sure there was another student standing behind him, and that Ambrose was merely looking straight through him.

But, of course, no one was standing behind Finley.

"Sir?" he said, as if to imply there had been a mistake. There were a few chuckles. Then hushed words exchanged. What's he doing? Where's his glove? He can't surge, remember?

"Why don't you give it a shot," Ambrose said.

Finley started praying for a fracas to break out. Maybe a fire alarm. Anything to end class early and save him from what was sure to be an embarrassing and humiliating act.

No such distraction ensued.

Fine, it's fine. Finley broke from the line of his classmates and stood a foot or two ahead of them. *Focus on the phone in your pocket. The Root is there, around you, it's waiting.*

Finley could feel the muscles in his cheek begin to twitch. His heartbeat pounded in his ears, drowning out all other noises. He'd been able to revive Mr. Repairman's electric lighter. He'd willed Professor Ambrose's dead clock to life. These were both seemingly complex acts of Understanding.

So why did Lunging—what Ambrose had referred to as the easiest form of surging—feel like the hardest thing in the world next to picking up a car or holding ones breath for an hour.

Because now you have an audience…

Finley breathed through his nose and mouth. He blinked slowly, letting his vision go slightly out of focus. *Don't think about the professor. Don't think about everyone watching you.*

He let his posture go lax. His hands—which were in nervous, tight fists—unfurled. He could feel Helena's cell phone in his pocket, lying in the snug and innocent way of inanimate objects.

Don't try to control the Root, Finley ordered himself. *Let it come to you.*

Let go.

And so he did.

Chapter 11 | <u>Finley's Glove</u>

Standing there in the sun in the presence of Professor Ambrose, his friends, and his peers, Finley McComb should have experienced the apex of jitters and anxieties. He should have crumbled to his knees with embarrassment—face red, confidence crushed.

Instead, he felt the strongest presence of the Root he'd ever felt. He allowed himself to be free, which meant touching his hands to the grass, blinking once, breathing, and then letting the Root in Helena's dead cell phone battery course through his veins.

He felt a wave of tremors, then, he Lunged.

Not fifteen yards.

Fifty.

He was almost flying. The wind pounded in his ears.

The rush of falling unexpectedly stirred inside his stomach, like butterflies were thumping their wings inside him. Six, seven, eight feet in the air! His Brighton shirt and pants flapped. His tie flew over his shoulder. The earth appeared so far and distant below his shoes. This wasn't almost flying...this *was* flying.

And that's when he landed carefully, near the edge of grass and pavement—right next to the statue of the man with the bulb in the exterior hall. He grunted, expecting harder impact, but it was as if he'd only jumped a foot in the air.

At first, his classmates were silent. Unmoving. Watchful. But then they burst into shouts and stormed across the greenway. They encircled him. Patted his arms and shoulders. How did you do that! Ohm's Law, and with no glove on! You were flying, man! Miguel punched him in the side playfully, a wide grin across his face. Bridget and Helena took turns hugging him from the side, saying, "You did it!" and "That was *awesome*!"

"Nicely done, Mr. McComb," the professor said, walking up to them.

The crowd parted, and Finley, who felt like laughing and yelling and hurrahing, turned from his peers and faced Ambrose. The commotion fizzled. Lauren and Doug rejoined the group. Doug looked repulsed to the core.

"But next time," Ambrose went on, "try not to show off so much."

Finley's face dropped, and he felt very small.

"Yes, sir," he muttered.

The atmosphere had quickly switched to an awkward one. Finley chewed on his tongue and stared at his shoes, well aware that everyone was glancing back and forth between him and the professor.

"That's all for today," Ambrose finally said. "We'll pick right back up on Monday. Take the rest of the day to celebrate Mr. McComb's accomplishment." He spun around and stalked back to his octagon classroom beside the mess hall.

No one seemed to know how to react. Even Doug, who looked pleased with himself after Finley's scolding, appeared addle-brained. He took off his glove, pushed his glasses up his nose, and was the first one to break away.

"That was really cool, man," Parker told Finley under his breath before jogging after Doug. A few more of Finley's classmates praised him before heading off to collect their things in Ambrose's room.

But the compliments fell flat. The professor had completely sucked the wind out of his sails. No, Finley hadn't meant to show off. He didn't even realize he'd tripled Doug and Lauren's distance until after he'd landed and turned around.

So was chiding him in front of the entire class really necessary?

"C'mon, Fin," Miguel said. Helena looped her arm

around Finley's, and Bridget clapped him on the back consolingly. Together, they walked back to the classroom to turn in their papers and retrieve their backpacks.

"Maybe he was afraid the dean would see you recharging," Bridget said, sipping her tiki torch—a frozen drink containing pineapple, coconut, and spicy Mexican chocolate. "You know, because he technically wasn't supposed to say anything."

They sat in a booth inside the loud and bustling Watt's Up. Apparently, the pier was the place to be on Fridays after classes were done. The beeping and jangling of arcade games reverberated in one corner, the rental desk had a line out the door of kids waiting to check out surfboards before the sun was down, and the restaurant side had its own crowd of burger and smoothie-seeking students. "Mrs. Wilson" by the Honeybells was playing through the hanging, overhead speakers.

Finley, Miguel, Bridget, and Helena had chosen a booth past the register and kitchen, near a tall window. Outside, the Pacific Ocean was sparkling like frosted glass beneath the almost-sunset, seagulls gliding over the surface with the cloudless sky as their backdrop.

"Yeah, but unless Finley was planning on telling Dean Longenecker that Ambrose was the one who taught him about recharging, how would she have known?" Miguel said, stealing a sip of Bridget's tiki torch when she wasn't looking.

"I can deal with him thinking I was trying to show off or something," Finley said, taking a seasoned French fry from the community basket they had ordered. "But I wanna know why he still hasn't shown up to any of our tutoring sessions."

"Given everything that's going on here, on campus," Helena said, scratching her elbow. "He could have legitimate reasons for not being there. Maybe it's the only time he can meet with the Enhancer Force?"

"Okay, fine," Finley said between chews. "So why not tell me then?"

Helena shrugged. Suddenly, the side of the booth she and Finley shared started to vibrate. Finley started, but it was only a second or two before he realized he still had Helena's phone in his pocket. He pulled it out and handed it to her.

"It's my mom," Helena said, rolling her eyes. She scanned the text message. "Uh oh, Michigan lost to Michigan State yesterday. Dad's probably lost his mind."

"Nothing like pointless rivalries to dampen your day!" Miguel said, raising his water into the air before drinking it.

"'Pointless?'" Helena sounded aghast.

"And cue the Michigan pride speech." Miguel winked and took another sip.

"I thought you said your phone was dead?" Finley took

her phone and pressed the home button, his eyes darting to the top of the screen, which read 27% low. "There's still some battery life!"

"Yeah, so?" Helena took her phone back. "I said it was *practically* dead. Same difference, all right?"

"No—not at all...," Finley said, trailing off as his thoughts raced in circles.

"Yo, earth to Fin!" Miguel said, snapping his fingers. "Care to fill us in on what's going on upstairs?"

"It's just..." Finley sat back, eyes narrowing. "Professor Ambrose gave me a completely dead battery to work with on Monday when he was testing out my recharging abilities. That's how I was able to use Understanding on that clock, because the battery was fried. Then, when he let me borrow his glove to try and use it a few moments later, nothing happened."

"Cool!" said an invigorated Bridget. "So this proves you can will from dead *and* active power sources after all. That's what you did today in class, after all."

"But then why couldn't I surge in Ambrose's classroom, when I used his glove?" Finley folded his arms across his chest, unconvinced of Bridget's claim. "This doesn't make sense."

"Neither does a professor hanging out in Watt's Up," Miguel said, his left eyebrow arched.

"Huh?"

They all turned and saw Professor Diffenbaugh entering

the clubhouse, scanning the interior with a determined face. When his eyes fell on Finley, he lit up, waved to them, and bounced over.

"Knew I'd find you here!" said the professor, standing at their table.

"Er, hi, professor," Finley said, trying to sound pleased. Instead, he came across surprised, which he was. "Want a fry?"

"Bah, you're too kind," he replied, untying his yellow bowtie. "I have a faculty dinner in a little bit. Don't want to spoil the mahi-mahi. Anyway, I wanted to bring you this."

He set a metallic silver glove on the table. It had slips covering the three middle fingers, which left the thumb and pinky exposed, similar to an archer's glove. Its wires were coiled and swirled around the palm, looping back and merging with a holster around the wrist.

"Look, here," the professor said, pulling two AA batteries out of his pocket and slipping them into the holster. He then added, his voice filled with fervor: "You can lock dead batteries into this canister. I'm already on the lookout for some extras, so I'll have those for you in class on Monday."

Finley, who was at a loss for words, picked up the glove and tried it on. It was a perfect fit. His fingers bent and moved smoothly, unhindered by the wires and metal.

"So, um, if Finley's glove is just a holster for dead

batteries, are all the wires and stuff necessary?" Miguel asked, leaning forward and examining Finley's glove.

"Well, no, I don't suppose they are," Professor Diffenbaugh admitted. "But, it would look a lot less *cool*, don't you think?"

"Man's got a point," Miguel replied, taking Bridget's tiki torch and drinking it again. She slapped him in the arm and took it back immediately.

"Professor," Finley said, pulling off the glove. "Thanks, this, this is awesome. But, so, does that mean everyone knows I can recharge now?"

Diffenbaugh smiled, blinking softly. "You really have no idea how good it sounds to hear you talking about your ability so openly. Now that you've figured out what you're capable of, I promise we'll be forthright with any developments and details we find surrounding your skills. This is the beginning of something very, very special, Finley." And then the professor took his leave.

"See there?" Miguel said, watching Diffenbaugh leave. "He has no idea Ambrose told you about recharging."

Finley held the glove Professor Diffenbaugh made in his hands, turning it over and bobbing it up and down. He was trying to distract himself from a sudden, nagging pierce of guilt.

Now that you've figured out what you're capable of, Professor Diffenbaugh had said, under the impression that Finley had discovered his recharging powers all on his own.

But, that of course was not the case. He had stomped up to Ambrose's desk and screamed for answers to be given to him.

So was that Dean Longenecker's plan from the beginning? For Finley to find the answers in himself and *by* himself? He'd once been told of a how a parent bird intentionally lets its offspring break forth from its egg under its own, weak, fragile strength. The parent will watch, but the parent will not assist.

"Guys," Finley said, setting his glove on the table. "You think I made a mistake?"

Miguel chuckled. "What are you talking about?"

But Finley did not have a chance to elaborate. A chanting had started at the back of Watt's Up, and it was working its way around the entire clubhouse and spreading fast:

"Brighton! Brighton! Yours is tough, yours is hard, but always we'll defend and guard!"

Finley, Miguel, Bridget, and Helena all sat up and looked over just in time to see the chargeball team marching down the stairs from their upper level lounge. The team all waved as they made their way down the steps—all, as in, all *but* the Caverly twins.

"Those two actually looked annoyed," Bridget noted to their table beneath the mounting chants.

"And why shouldn't they be?" Helena said. "If our goalie performs tomorrow like she did in practice, they're going to be scrambling around and playing defense the whole time. That's not the best game plan for playing N.S.A."

" 'N.S.A.?' " Finley asked after the entire team had left and was disappearing down the pier.

"North Sacramento Academy," Miguel explained. "They're supposedly Brighton's biggest rivalry, and they always bring a fast-paced offense to the match."

"How do you guys know so much about chargeball?" Finley asked, grabbing a few more fries from the basket. "Didn't you three just learn about surging this past summer?"

"Nah." Miguel grabbed the ketchup bottle and replenished the dipping supply in the corner of the basket. "Both my parents are surgers. Watching the National Games of Illumination every four years is a big deal at our house."

"Aunt from my mom's side is a surger, but my parents are peds," Helena said, and clarified when Finley scrunched his eyebrows together: "peds, as in, pedestrians."

"How about you, Bridget?" asked Finley. She was finishing off her tiki torch, and she wiped her mouth with a napkin when she was done.

"First surger in my family," she said proudly. "Or, so far as I know. Guess I could have a distant relative that's keeping their gifts a secret."

This gave Finley pause. Did he have an aunt or cousin

or grandparent surger? Was there someone in his bloodline that was a part of the surging community? Impossible. It was hard to keep anything under the radar in the McComb household. Something that big would have come out years ago...

The four of them lounged for a little while longer at the booth, and then, at Helena's suggestion, they left Watt's Up and walked across the pier toward the beach. They sat on the sand in the shadow of the white lifeguard fort, talking about everything from Doug's face after Finley inadvertently upstaged his Lunge, to how many different bowties Professor Diffenbaugh must have owned.

When the sun touched down and the ocean split it in half, they got to their feet, wiped the sand from their pants and skirts, and meandered back to the dorm houses. The three-tone bell chimed from the lifeguard fort, announcing to the surfers that the beach would be closing soon.

Friday was almost over, which meant a whole week had passed since Finley was enrolled at Brighton Preparatory School for Surgers. He heard Miguel and Helena arguing beside him, each claiming to know the best brand of gloves money could buy. Bridget was trying to settle the debate, but she could hardly get a word in.

Finley smiled. These were his friends, this was his school. He took in a breath, and the sea air tickled his nose. He listened to the three of them quarrel all the way back to the dorm houses, neither side of the debate conceiting defeat when it was time to split into their separate buildings.

"You'll see," Miguel said to Finley as they walked up the stairwell to the fourth floor. "Ballast makes the best gloves. Helena's *so* wrong."

Yet Finley didn't have a dog in this fight. He had his own, special glove.

He had a glove Professor Diffenbaugh had made, and that, in his opinion, could not be beat.

"You know what I love about Saturdays?" Miguel said, walking out of the bathroom after his morning shower, his Lofstrand crutches squeaking quietly with every step.

"What?" Finley rubbed his eyes and yawned from his bed. Above him, on the top bunk, Parker stirred.

"That it's not Monday, Tuesday, Wednesday, Thursday or Friday," replied Miguel happily, his wet hair dripping onto the hardwood floor. He didn't appear to have been very thorough in drying himself because there were more than a few wet spots on his T-shirt and jeans.

But Miguel didn't seem to mind. It was Saturday, after all.

Finley and Parker took turns showering and brushing their teeth, and when they were finished dressing, the three of them headed downstairs together, just as a sophomore came barreling into the lounging area—pointing his thumb over his shoulder.

"You guys gotta come see this!" he shouted, turning on his heel and racing back outside before Finley, Miguel, and Parker could react. They sped-walked outside, and Miguel did his best to move quickly with his crutches.

But they didn't have to go far to see what all the commotion was about.

Across the pathway, in front of the girl dorm houses, a freshman boy in a tank top and gym shorts hung six feet in the air—stuck in some kind of semitranslucent net. Nearly half of the school was standing around, pointing up and either laughing or gasping.

"Plasma trap," Parker said to Finley and Miguel as they got closer.

The freshman was yelling and demanding to be brought down. He wiggled and shook his outstretched hands and legs, which actually shook his restraint, but ultimately did no more than that.

The plasma trap, as Parker had called it, seemed to encase the girls' two dorm houses in a dome, though it was only visible in certain points where the sunlight struck it through thin clouds. The trap looked as if it was constructed of the same makeup as jellyfish. The surface glowed and throbbed, with tiny particles and strands periodically flashing in purples and blues.

"Should we help him?" Finley asked, staring up at the freshman, who now began to swear.

"How?" Miguel chuckled. "That thing is programmed to entrap anyone who has a *thing*. I'm not going any closer than this."

It was only a few seconds later until Dean Longenecker appeared, flanked between two Enhancers. A handful of the crowd dispersed, but most stuck around to see what would happen—Finley, Miguel, and Parker included.

"Third time in two years, Mr. Lees," the dean said, crossing her arms and sticking out her hip.

The Enhancers worked together to set up a three-legged device beneath the dangling freshman. A soft hissing noise rang out—like air escaping a tire—and the plasma trap was diffused.

One of the Enhancers used Understanding, pointing their glove at the freshman and catching him before he toppled to the grass. The Enhancer eased the boy onto the ground gently.

"Detention for a week," the dean proclaimed, grabbing him by his arm and towing him away. "*And* I'm phoning your parents this time!"

Finley turned back to the Enhancers. One was collapsing the tripod-like contraption, and the other was punching numbers into a scanner—probably resetting the plasma trap. They shared a few words among themselves, their masks making it impossible to hear or read their lips. Then, they left.

"Let's get some breakfast," Miguel said, turning on his

crutches. Finley nodded, noticing that Parker had already slipped away unannounced.

The mess hall was alive and rowdy. The many food carts were already backed up with orders. The scent of English muffins and oatmeal hung in the air. Finley and Miguel found and joined Bridget and Helena in the back of one of the queues.

"You guys see Jourdan on your way over?" Helena asked, amused.

"Ha-larious," Miguel said, shaking his head.

"Does it hurt?" Finley said, concerned. "The plasma trap?"

"Nothing more than your pride," Bridget replied. "Or so I'd imagine."

"Don't feel too bad for him, Fin," Miguel said as they inched closer down the line toward the food cart. "Didn't you hear the dean? This is the *third* time he's gotten caught in that trap."

"He's dating one of the junior girls," Helena explained. "Except that, every time this happens, I hear that she pretends they're broken up."

" 'Love is a complex web of lies and hurt,' " Miguel said, feigning tenderness. "That's a line from my poem, for Templeton's class. Be jealous, Bridget. Be very, very jealous."

"You're something to aspire to, Miguel," Bridget deadpanned. "By the way, you know we're supposed to be working on short stories, and *not* poems, right?"

Miguel paled. "Eff…"

They eventually collected their breakfasts, and then went onto the greenway where they gathered on the ground beneath some palm trees to eat. They munched on their oatmeal and muffins, and talked about which weekend assignment they should put off until Sunday night.

A few announcements boomed across the campus over the loudspeakers. The study lab wouldn't be open until after the Games of Illumination were over. Lunch would be served at the concession stands. The spars, relays, and javelin throws would commence in one hour, and the chargeball match was set for 1:00pm.

"Which means," Miguel said, licking his spoon clean. "The buses should be arriving right about now."

Finley, confused: "Buses?"

"N.S.A.," Helena said, her face lighting up. "Miguel's right. Their team bus is probably already pulling up. C'mon!"

Chapter 12 | <u>The Games Of Illumination</u>

Finley followed Miguel, Bridget, and Helena across the greenway, into the library, and through the tunnel that led to the chargeball pitch. Beside the stadium they found four black and blue buses. There were Pegasuses with bolts of lightning in their mouths painted on the vehicles' sides. *North Sacramento Academy* was scripted in fancy calligraphy above the mythological creature.

But there was no one around, which meant that—

"—they're already on the field, warming up," Miguel said, pivoting on his crutches and leading them into the stadium. They turned up the steps behind the bleachers and came out on the other side, now standing by the south goal.

Finley's heart jumped. The field had the Brighton crest

painted in the center—the white and yellow bulb, voltage symbol, fuse, and fork of lightning wonderfully contrasted on the green grass. There were also white and yellow banners hanging from the retractable roof, boasting past championships. "Children Of The Night" by Survivor reverberated through the stadium speakers.

On one side of the field, Brighton's chargeball team stretched and ran drills, and on the other side, N.S.A.'s team did the same. Theirs were jerseys of black and blue, much like the colors on the buses outside the stadium.

Students were already spilling into the bleachers, trying to claim the best seats even though the games weren't set to begin for another forty-five minutes.

"Let's go," said Helena, waving for them to proceed along with her. "I want to make sure we get good midfield seats."

They strode past the goal and took the lower path beside the fence that kept spectators off the pitch. As they walked, they sized up N.S.A.'s athletes, who didn't seem any less capable of winning the chargeball match than Brighton. They had a stocky senior guy for a goalie with a bright pink mohawk. Two of their strikers were junior girls, and the other two were boys: one a senior, one a sophomore.

And their charger was the meanest looking teenager Finley had ever seen. He stood out from the rest of the team because his jersey was a different shade of blue, and, instead of black, his secondary color was gray. His nose was bent, like it had taken a major drubbing all his life, and his black hair was crazed and disheveled.

Finley made eye contact with him for only a second, and he felt like his blood had turned to ice as a result.

"Here, this is good," Bridget said, pointing out a spot three rows back from midfield. A group of sophomore girls had taken up the first two rows, giggling and checking out the boys from N.S.A.

Finley sat between Helena and Miguel, and Bridget took the aisle seat. They started evaluating the visiting school as the stretching and drills ceased. Now, the practice throws began. N.S.A.'s charger had his team passing the flashball back and forth while they stormed toward the goal and took turns shooting. Their goalie was fast and aware; out of every shot taken, only about twenty percent made it past him.

"Once the games get closer to starting," Miguel told Finley as they turned and watched their own team practice. The Caverly twins were yelling at one of their teammates. "The chargeball teams will sit in designated sections on the sidelines. They'll watch the competitions with everyone else before taking the field for their match."

Finley nodded, watching flashballs and strikeballs whip through the air. Even now, as he was beginning to have a grasp on the Root, and what it meant to surge, Finley could still not imagine how much concentration and skill went into chargeball.

They have to Fuel, then Lunge, then Enhance their throws to have the best shot at making a goal! Finley thought, closing his mouth as soon as he realized it had fallen open in awe. *Fueling, Lunging, Enhancing...*

"What about Understanding?" Finley asked, turning to his friends. "I mean, couldn't they adjust the course of their throw? Curve the flashball's path *around* the goalie?"

"It's the only phase of surging considered illegal in chargeball," Miguel replied, his voice carrying disappointment. "Aside from catching offside players and enforcing the ten-second rule, the refs make sure none of the throws are altered by Understanding."

"Ten second rule," Finley repeated. "Missed that one."

"No team can hold onto a flashball or strikeball longer than ten seconds," said a sly, pompous voice. Doug and Parker sat in the spot directly behind Finley, who turned around to see who had spoken.

"See," Doug continued, talking as if he were explaining the ABCs to an adolescent. "The ten second rule ensures that both sides are taking shots as frequently as possible. Maintains a consistent pace throughout."

"Cool. Got it. Thanks." Finley turned around, clenching his jaw.

"No one asked you, *Douglas*," said Miguel, keeping his eyes on the pitch and not bothering to look over his shoulder.

"Hey, he asked," Doug replied defensively, holding up his hands.

"Yeah?" Helena snapped, spinning her heard around and scowling. "And who asked you to be a Grade A jerk?"

"Whoa! Name calling, really?" Doug raised his eyebrows. "There a reason you guys are acting so snappy?"

"You already forget about how you called me out in front of Professor Diffenbaugh's entire class?" Finley said, turning back around to face Doug. Beside him, Parker twitched. He was fixated on the pitch, trying not to look uncomfortable.

"What?" Doug pretended to think for a second, then, "Oh, that!"

"Yeah, *that*."

"So…was I wrong? Is this not Brighton Preparatory School for *Surgers*?"

Finley could feel his face warming up.

Doug sniffed. "You weren't wearing a glove, on the greenway, when we were practicing Lunges. Therefore, you weren't surging. So what *were* you doing?"

"Are you writing an article on Finley for the school paper?" Bridget asked, glancing back at Doug.

"We don't have a school paper."

"So leave Finley alone, or get out of here," she said through clamped teeth. Finley, Miguel, and Helena almost flinched with surprise at Bridget's quick, uncharacteristic retort.

"Look, there's Brendan and David," Parker said after a long silence. "Let's go sit with them." His right eye twitched, and then he got to his feet and left before Doug could respond.

"Whatever you're hiding from the rest of us," Doug said to Finley in a whisper, standing up. "I know it has something to do with the Enhancer Force being here. Your little fan club may be okay with you putting this school in danger, but I'm not."

Then he walked off, disappearing into the influx of students that poured into the stadium. Miguel and Helena busted out laughing.

Helena said, "W-Writing an article?"

" 'So leave Finley alone or get out of here!' " Miguel did his best to imitate Bridget, but all his voice did was grow more nasally and whiny.

Finley eventually joined in their laughter, but Bridget simply pursed her lips and grunted. "He started it," she said.

"Well, then, I guess you finished it, huh?" Finley exclaimed. "Thanks."

It was close to 9:30 a.m. when a series of horns replaced the contemporary music in the loudspeakers. The fanfare played loudly, the packed stadium hushed, and the two chargeball teams on the pitch went to their respective sidelines. Finley looked around. It seemed the whole place was at capacity—no empty seat to be found. Even the small visitor's section across from them was full, N.S.A. students scrunched together shoulder-to-shoulder clad in black and blue.

Dean Longenecker Fueled onto the middle of the pitch from nowhere, and she was instantly met with earsplitting cheers. She wore a white business skirt and jacket, and her red hair was down and flowing past her shoulders.

"Good morning, all!" she said into a microphone, sending her boisterous voice out into the stadium. "Who's ready for another season of games?"

More deafening shouts. A group behind Finley had even begun chanting *Brighton! Brighton! Brighton!*

"Please join me in welcoming our guests," the dean continued, "Northern Sacramento Academy."

This time, deep boos and scattered taunting spread around the bleachers, and the dean had to raise her voice to reel everyone back in—even though her words were amplified through the loudspeakers.

"Okay, okay," she said. "We only strive for the highest level of sportsmanship here at Brighton. Show the respect N.S.A is due. Now, if you would, rise for our national anthem."

Finley got to his feet along with everyone else. A pretty senior girl Fueled onto the pitch and stopped beside the dean—neon pink streaks marking her path for a moment, then leaking into the grass and disappearing.

The senior girl took the microphone from Dean

Longenecker, cleared her throat, and sang a cappella: "Oh say can you see..."

Finley, his hand above his heart, mouthed the lyrics. He scanned the bleachers, soaking in the atmosphere. His father had only taken him to a couple of professional sporting events before. Although, it's not that he felt he missed out, Finley just never had a desire to go sit in the uncomfortable plastic seats and watch his father's favorite team lose, which meant relentless yelling from Mr. McComb. Then, on the ride home, his father would ask him, voice hoarse, where he'd like to eat, and they wouldn't be able to agree on a place, so they would just end up back home, eating leftovers and drinking Brita filtered water.

"And the rocket's red glare, the bombs bursting in air..."

Finley looked up, at the top tier of bleachers, and froze. Above the sea of faces, in the announcer booth, he saw a slender form wearing a gray cloak and a purple masquerade mask.

It was James Olyphant's accomplice. The person who had struck him unconscious in the dorm room. The masked figure stood behind the glass, hands clasped in front of them.

"...that our flag was still there."

Finley nudged Miguel with his elbow, then said under his breath, "Miguel, look!" He pointed up at the glass-encased announcer booth, but the person was gone, as if they had evaporated.

What? Miguel mouthed, squinting up at the booth.

"And the home of the brave!" the senior girl finished.

Joyous clapping and roars exploded from the bleachers, and then a flurry of lantern bugs were released from a cage somewhere in the stadium. The insects soared into the air and vanished beyond the roof.

Dean Longenecker escorted the senior off the pitch, and a smooth male voice announced the first competition: sparring. It would start with the featherweights.

"*Guys!*" Finley said as they sat back down. "I just saw the person who attacked me in my dorm room!"

Miguel, Bridget, and Helena leaned in, their eyes wide as tennis balls.

"What?"

"Where!"

"Are you absolutely sure?"

"In the announcer booth," Finley said, bouncing his right leg up and down like he was ready to spring to his feet and bolt at a moment's notice. "We have to warn the dean!"

But after he'd said this, no one gave an immediate response.

"Didn't you hear me? My attacker is in the stadium!"

"Finley," Helena said, gazing at the booth. "That's where the faculty watches the games."

"So? I know what I saw!"

"If your attacker was up there, the entire Brighton staff would have seen something," said Bridget. She sighed, like she had just given someone heartbreaking news.

Finley wasn't buying it. "My attacker's up there! Maybe they found someway to slip in and out unnoticed."

"Why? To stand in front of the window and taunt you?" Miguel asked. "I believe you saw something—"

"Just not what I *think* I saw?" Finley interrupted, laughing through his nose.

"It doesn't make sense," Helena said in agreement with Miguel. "Think about it, if your attacker was in the announcer booth, up to no good, why be so obvious about it? Why go to that effort just to be seen?"

"I have no idea," Finley answered. "Which is why we need to alert the dean!"

"Maybe someone already has…," Miguel said distantly. He motioned to the side of the stadium, where the concessions were.

An Enhancer was talking into a walkie-talkie, pacing back and forth in front of the smoothie stand. Then, the Enhancer was joined by four of his comrades, and the five of them jogged away hurriedly.

"There. Looks like it's been reported." Miguel's posture relaxed, but Finley was not comforted. "I'm sure they'll handle it, Fin."

"What if they got called away for something completely unrelated?" Finley offered, looking back at the announcer booth.

The reflection made it so that he could only see someone when they walked right up to the glass. At that moment, Professor Ambrose was standing with Professor Templeton. They each had a drink between them, and Templeton laughed at something Ambrose had said.

There seemed to be no urgency to their conversation.

"Something's not right," Finley said. He made to stand up, but Helena put a hand on his shoulder, keeping him down.

"I hate to be the one who says this, but…" Helena dropped her hand before nervously averting her eyes toward the pitch.

A circular yellow mat had been laid out on top of the turf, and two junior boys from Brighton and N.S.A. were talking with their respective coaches before the spar began. The announcer read off their names energetically over the loudspeakers.

"You 'hate to be the one who says this but' *what?*" said Finley, giving her a sideways glare.

"I dunno," said Helena awkwardly. "I just…if we tell the dean, the Enhancer Force will halt the games and evacuate the stadium. Which, is the right thing and all, but only, if, er…"

"Only if I *actually* saw my attacker up there." Finley couldn't believe his ears. *I know what I saw—why are they being so difficult!*

Miguel came to Helena's defense: "We're not saying you didn't see them."

"We just want to, er, be sure," Bridget concluded.

"Right. Whatever." Finley hunched forward, resting his chin atop his fist. "I'd hate to interrupt the precious games for you guys if there's a threat to the school."

He kept his unblinking stare fixed on the announcer booth, even though the first spar had begun. He stole a look every so often, but tried not to watch for too long. The students who sparred wore loose pants and a tight shirt beneath their pulsating energy packs.

Brighton's fighter had just dodged a Fueled spin kick, and, while ducking, he divvied out an Enhanced punch to the chest, which sent N.S.A.'s fighter sliding across the mat.

The stadium shook with chants and applauds.

Miguel and Helena high-fived, and even Bridget was clapping. Finley wanted badly to join in with the enthusiasm, but he was too distracted. He was too unnerved.

I know I saw you, and I know you're out there...

"Quite the spar this is turning out to be!" the announcer said, chuckling in a cheesy way. "Our own Devin Sarvaunt is really asserting himself as a highly-capable fighter. *Oh!* Look at that high wrist block!"

Now both of Finley's legs were bouncing. Between the mystery of his attacker's whereabouts and the intensity of the spar, plus the raucous multitude of spectators, Finley felt like his heart was going to lunge straight out of his throat.

As the games progressed, his stress climbed.

The spars each ended in dramatic fashion, with Brighton ultimately having only one more victory over N.S.A. Then, the games switched to the relays. Blurs of burning pink rushed around the pitch as the two schools competed for the best times. The speed and quickness of it all made Finley incredibly dizzy.

"And *that's* unfortunate," said the announcer dully. "N.S.A. finishes with an overall best time at one minute and forty six seconds."

The stadium filled with heckling and boos.

Next, came the javelin throws—or a surger's take on it, anyway. The handful of competitors from Brighton and N.S.A. lined up on a curved mark on the pitch, and they each held a long, spear-like pole in their throwing hands. A plasma net appeared in front of the goal on the other side of the pitch, a shot rang out, and the group of students threw his or her javelin with an Enhanced effort.

The javelins cut through the air like orange missiles, puncturing the plasma net with potent force. Not a single javelin made it all the way through the floating, glowing obstruction, but they had poked through to an extent—some more than others. And this was a measure of how the competitors performed. The ones whose javelin had gotten the furthest through, obviously received the most points, and she (a Brighton student) and the next three would advance to the semifinal round. The other four were eliminated.

"Talk about holding nothing back!" said the announcer, after the points were awarded and the javelins were retrieved. Miguel fist pumped, then urged Finley to get excited.

"That was impressive," Finley said, confessing his investment in the games, but he quickly resumed staring at the announcer booth. No sign of his masked attacker. Just the dean, peering through binoculars at the pitch.

After the semifinals eliminated two more, leaving only Brighton athletes, the final round became trivial, and so double points were added to the home team's total.

"Getting it done!" the announcer boomed, as the two Brighton girls on the pitch hugged and celebrated. The two N.S.A. competitors walked back to their sideline with their heads hanging. "Now we'll take a thirty minute recess as the pitch is cleared for chargeball!"

Helena and Bridget stood and stretched. The aisles were almost instantly packed and congested as students headed for the concession stands.

The perfect time for something to go wrong, Finley thought, on edge. *When everyone's scrunched together like this and unable to run...*

"Wanna get a hotdog?" Miguel asked Finley, picking

his Lofstrand crutches up off the floor.

Finley shrugged. "Still full from breakfast." He could sense his friends exchanging glances among themselves, but he refused to say anything more.

Helena sidestepped past him and patted his shoulder. "We'll bring you back something," she said, and then she and Bridget and Miguel headed into the procession of students flocking toward the concession stands.

Finley rose to his feet and rolled his head. He put one foot on the seat in front of him, pocketed his hands, and narrowed his eyes—focused on the booth above the bleachers. If not for the clogged aisles, Finley wouldn't have hesitated leaving the stands and poking around the stadium himself.

But that would be foolhardy. It was possible his attacker had revealed his or herself to draw Finley away from the games, get him alone and ensure he was vulnerable. Finley shuddered at the thought.

Why did his experience at Brighton Preparatory School for Surgers have to be like this? It wasn't enough that he was pulled from his normal life and thrust into the surging community. No, it had to happen in dramatic fashion. If Finley wasn't getting knocked out in his dorm room and being "transported" to a field, he was overhearing weird conversations by the school driver. He was causing Brighton Prep to bolster security and bring in the Enhancer Force. He was bumbling his way into learning about his recharging abilities.

Finley almost wished he'd never been recruited, but he caught himself.

Surging is a gift, Professor Ambrose had said in class yesterday. It's about helping those who are less fortunate than you.

In other words, it was about helping "pedestrians"—Helena's name for non-surgers. So, when put that way, Finley felt the weight of a great responsibility. His parents and sister back in Huntington Beach were peds, after all.

I'm at Brighton for a reason. Finley blinked, then sat back down. *I'm not going to feel sorry for myself just because things get tough—just because I don't have all the answers I think I deserve. And I'm not going to jeopardize my safety by feeding my curiosity.*

And so he looked away from the announcer's booth. Once the chargeball match was over, he'd report what he'd seen to Dean Longenecker and Professor Ambrose. Then, when security strapped down even more, Finley would suffer the hate and ridicule he was sure to receive from his peers.

"Hope you like deep-fried Snickers bars," Miguel said, sitting beside Finley and taking off his crutches. Bridget and Helena walked up behind him, each carrying an armful of spectacularly scented junk food.

"My favorite," Finley said, helping the girls out with the snacks. Once everyone was settled in on their row, they munched on nachos, pretzels, churros, and what Miguel called a "high voltage"—the deep-fried Snickers bar.

"You see anything else suspicious?" Bridget asked Finley after he passed her the tray of nachos.

"No," he answered, slurping his tiki torch through a green straw. "You guys might be right, could've just been a trick of the light."

"Did you mean for that to rhyme?" Helena asked, poking him in the arm.

"Yeah, it's straight out of my poem for lit," he replied sarcastically, turning to Miguel with a jeering grin.

"Oh you're *so* funny, guy," Miguel said, chewing on his churro with a straight face.

Only a few minutes later, and the stadium workers had finished carting everything off from the previous games. Now, both chargeball teams were back on the pitch, running drills on separate sides.

Ross, Brighton's charger, was standing near their goalpost, chatting with a brown haired lady who wore white pants and a yellow track jacket. She was holding a clipboard in one hand, and with the other pointing across the pitch.

"Who's Ross talking with?" said Finley, taking another sip from his tiki torch.

"That's Coach Tenenbaum," Bridget replied. "We'll have her next year for Phys. Ed."

"Hate to miss out on all the laps you guys are going to have run." Miguel nudged his crutches with his foot.

"Well, okay, no, that was a lie."

The seats in the stadium were full again, the aisles were clear, and the announcer's animated voice was thundering through the loudspeakers. A group of students across the pitch had started the wave, and it moved in a full circle around the stands.

"Brighton! Get on your feet and make some noise for your team!"

Finley and his friends stood up and cheered with the rest of their school. On the right side of the pitch, Michael and Sarah Caverly were hopping on the balls of their feet, rolling their shoulders back. The strong, muscled senior named Doe was flapping his arms up and down—motioning for louder yells and screams. The spiked-hair goalie was adjusting her gloves, and Ross and the fourth striker, a sophomore girl with pale skin and small lips, performed their last set of stretches on the turf.

"Calling the shots at charger, Ross Heinlein!" The crowd received this by chanting and hurrahing, and Ross waved politely.

"Give it up for Joyce Gray, our goalie!" There were less applauds, but not much less. Joyce paced in the goal, like a caged animal prowling behind bars.

"And your strikers, Doe Bradley, Valeria Kaufmann, and Michael and Sarah Caverly!" This was the biggest reception yet. Finley could feel the stands shaking around him and beneath his Vans. White and yellow streamers shot out of canons and slowly drifted down over the bleachers.

"*Let the match begin!*"

Chapter 13 | <u>The Electric Ghost</u>

Finley, Miguel, Bridget, and Helena remained standing. From the looks of it, no one in the stadium was sitting. Everyone had chosen to stay on their feet, which only carried the atmosphere to more electrifying heights.

Finley watched as both teams took to designated spots on the field. They all bent over and touched the ground, like they were getting into the starting position for running track. The two referees appeared, wearing striped shirts and solid-colored pants. They set the four strikeballs on the line in the middle of the field, and the slightly bigger flashball in the center.

The cheering grew louder and louder.

The match hadn't even begun and Finley was glued to the pitch. The referees stepped back, inspected both sides of the field, and made sure everyone was in his or her correct position.

A gunshot rang out, and the match commenced.

Both sides sprang forward and Fueled toward the line, but N.S.A. somehow managed to retrieve all five balls. They slid on the grass before they hit the line, like a hitter stealing second base in baseball. This maneuver put them closer to the ground than Brighton's team, and, as such, they were in better position to snatch away the balls.

Ross shouted orders. His strikers backpedaled, but it was only a split second later that Valeria Kaufmann took a strikeball to the ankle. She moaned and toppled over, completely caught off guard by the instantaneous attack.

"Ooh, quick strike from N.S.A., and Valeria is out!" the announcer said.

The strikeball that had hit her rolled on the ground, and Ross scooped it up instinctually. He ordered his team to fan out, to keep moving. Valeria limped to the sideline, where Nurse Jasmine was waiting to Mend her injury.

"I DON'T KNOW WHAT I'VE BEEN TOLD!" the stadium bellowed. "BUT N.S.A.'S ABOUT TO FOLD!"

Both goalies bobbed and weaved like boxers in a corner. N.S.A.'s charger called out a play, and they executed it masterfully: one striker dove sideways and Enhanced, pelting Joyce—Brighton's goalie—in the arm. This distraction gave N.S.A. a brief window in which to throw the flashball. It zoomed right past Brighton's entire team and hit the back of the net.

The stadium grew quiet. Just like that, N.S.A. was on the board.

"N.S.A. goal made by Elliot Pynchon," the announcer droned. "Brighton, zero. N.S.A., one."

The referees warned N.S.A. about excessive celebration. They were running around their side of the field as if they'd just scored the game-winning goal. The flashball and strikeballs were collected and reset.

"That's so stupid!" Helena said, punching her fist into her palm. "Joyce should know that anytime a goalie's targeted like that it's a diversion because goalies can't get out!"

"It's fine, it's fine," Miguel said beside Finley. "That only ever works once. Now that they got that out of the way, it's one less 'trick' in N.S.A.'s arsenal."

"Both teams are in position," the announcer said, the shouting and applauding returning in the stands. "Ready for the next set."

A second gunshot went off, and Brighton and N.S.A. were at it again. This time, Ross sent out only Doe and Sarah, who both grabbed the flashball and a strikeball apiece. Doe flipped the flashball over his head, and, as it crested in the air, Michael Lunged up and caught it. Then, while he was airborne, he fast-pitched with Enhanced strength.

The goalie was ready. He Fueled to the corner of the

goal and caught the flashball just in time. The whole stadium let out a breath.

Michael landed, and instantly had to roll to avoid two shots taken from N.S.A.'s strikers. The strikeballs missed, bouncing off the turf and sending shards of dirt and grass into the air like landmines exploding.

Sarah, one strikeball still in hand, Fueled toward the free strikeballs and grabbed the one closest to her so that she now held two. She spun and chucked both as hard as her Enhanced form would allow. The attack hit *two* unsuspecting strikers from N.S.A. and sent them flying back into the air.

The stadium ruptured with shrieks of approval.

"*Sarah Caverly!*" the announcer said between laughs. "*Blasting* her way through N.S.A.'s team!"

Brighton's opponent was down to four players, including the charger and the goalie, who passed one of the strikers the flashball he'd caught nearly seconds earlier. N.S.A. now had four balls, leaving Brighton with only one strikeball.

Ross ran up beside Doe, who had taken the strikeball that had been targeted at Michael. "Right wing strike, right wing strike!" he shouted, pointing for Michael and Sarah to edge toward the line while he and Doe passed the strikeball between them.

N.S.A. took the bait, sending their two remaining strikers forward with their hands wound back. Only, they didn't take a shot at the Caverly twins. Instead, they threw the three strikeballs at the ground with Enhanced force, sending up more sprays of grass and dirt chunks. This had essentially created a curtain of debris, and it forced Brighton back a step or two.

That's when the flashball came hurtling through the falling dirt, whipping right past Joyce and into the goal.

"Wow," said Finley. It was now two to zero, and the stadium had lost its life. Slowly, students were sitting back down.

"Second goal by Elliot Pynchon," said the announcer, trying to sound unimpressed. "Too bad style points don't exist." This garnered a few scattered chuckles, but that was all. N.S.A.'s team slid on their knees and shouted victoriously.

"Third set upcoming." The announcer played "Eye Of The Tiger" as Brighton and N.S.A. prepared for the next phase of the match. Finley set down his drink beside his sneakers and leaned in next to Miguel.

"Is Brighton usually this bad?" he asked. They watched as Valeria shouted words of encouragement from the sideline. N.S.A.'s strikers were being tended to by their school nurse.

"It's still early, no need to panic." Miguel didn't really sound sure of himself.

"First one to ten goals, remember?" said Helena. "Still *plenty* of time."

Finley nodded. The third set started after another gunshot fired, and this time Brighton was able to retrieve all but one strikeball. Ross singled out N.S.A.'s charger, counted down from five, and they threw all three strikeballs when Ross had yelled, "TWO!" The N.S.A. charger was able to dodge and Fuel out of the way in time to miss the first two attempts, but Doe's strikeball smacked him right in the center of the chest, catapulting him twenty yards back. After the charger got back up, he swore—his face ashen from the pain. Finley grimaced, suddenly thankful he was only a spectator.

N.S.A. was down to two strikers and the goalie. The crowd was quickly getting back into the match.

"OH N.S.A.! OH N.S.A.!" the stadium screamed, using the melody from "When The Saints Go Marching In." "OH N.S.A. IT'S NOT YOUR DAY!" Finley laughed, following the example of the fans and singing along.

"YOU CAN'T KEEP UP...WITH OUR PACE! SO JUST SAVE FACE AND LEAVE THIS PLACE!"

More shots were exchanged on the pitch in a frenzied mess, and at one point Ross even Lunged up and caught a strikeball midflight. This sent the striker who had thrown it to the sideline, cursing loudly, and Valeria back into the match.

N.S.A. was down to their goalie and one striker. The junior girl squared her body, keeping Brighton in front of her at all times. Her best chance was to catch a strikeball and get her team back into the fold one at a time.

The flashball zipped back and forth from side to side as both teams attempted to make goals. Joyce made four consecutive saves. Her confidence was building, and she even let a smile slip after her fifth save. She passed the flashball to Michael, who passed it to Doe, who Fueled to the edge of the line and spun threw it with all his might.

N.S.A.'s goalie slid forward, meeting the impact of the flashball, and, in one fluid motion, Enhanced and tossed the ball to his teammate, who was ready for this "alley-oop." She snatched the flashball and without hesitation Enhanced—building on the momentum the ball already had when the goalie threw it.

This doubled the speed of the initial Enhanced pitch, and Joyce wasn't ready for it. The flashball smacked into her, bounced off her arm, and flew into the left corner of the net. With only one striker, N.S.A. had managed to score yet again—going up three points to none.

The visitor's section of the stadium was dancing and jumping on their seats.

"Just when I think this sport can't surprise me anymore." Finley shook his head, marveling at the brilliantly conceived maneuver from N.S.A. "Why doesn't our team do anything fancy like that?"

"C'mon, Fin," Miguel said, waving his hand. "We don't need to rely on gimmicks."

"Those 'gimmicks' have N.S.A. up three to nothing," Bridget pointed out, tossing a chip into her mouth. "If they score another unanswered goal, this place is going to go berserk."

"It's probably why the Enhancer Force was brought in all along," said Helena, folding her arms angrily. "They knew we'd suck this bad, and that riot control would be an issue."

Finley chuckled to himself. He couldn't process why they were taking this sport so seriously, but then, wasn't it his own father who painted his face and wore another grown man's jersey?

"Fourth set almost underway." The announcer's energy had disappeared; he had resorted to stating facts now. "Brighton, getting into position with their entire team in place. N.S.A. is down to one striker. That doesn't seem to be a factor as they are now in a commanding lead."

The stadium broke out into another wave, with only partial participation this time. The result was that it looked like some of the students were getting up to leave at coincidental moments, but then deciding to sit at the last second. Finley had to admit it was a tad pathetic.

"What happens when it's only down to N.S.A.'s goalie?" he asked Helena.

"Brighton will get to send a player of their choice to the line for one free shot," she answered, taking Finley's tiki torch off the ground and sipping it. "Then, the set will end, and N.S.A. will get all their players back—if we make the free goal or not."

"It's a popular strategy in the bigs," Miguel said. "Knock out the whole team, then call on your best thrower."

"Could be our chance to get a goal!" Finley said hopefully.

"You've seen their goalkeeper, right?" Helena retorted, bitterness spraying out with her words. "In fact, N.S.A. is probably going to call a dead seahorse!"

"Which," Finley said, taking his drink back. "Means...what, exactly?"

"Look," Miguel said, pointing at the pitch after another gunshot blasted—signaling the fourth set. N.S.A.'s only striker Fueled forward and stopped at the line. Then, she took an intentional step onto Brighton's side. A whistle blew. She was out.

"They did that on *purpose*?" Finley couldn't understand why that was a good decision for N.S.A.

"The way their goalkeeper is making saves," Helena said, her tone filled with annoyance. "It's worth the risk to get their whole team back onto the pitch."

"Bold move from N.S.A.," the announcer intoned as Brighton's team huddled up, most likely discussing who was going to attempt their free shot. Michael Caverly eventually broke from the huddle first, jogging toward the line with the flashball cradled in his right arm. The crowd was on its feet once more.

"Michael Caverly up to the line. Last season he set a school record with a thirty-nine completion percentage at the line. Can he get Brighton on the board for the first time this afternoon?"

"Sure hope so," Bridget said, answering the announcer's rhetorical question. "For our safety, anyway. He misses this shot, and you can go ahead and cue the pitchforks and torches."

Michael grasped the flashball in one hand. He got into a comfortable stance and exhaled through his mouth. Everyone in the bleachers seemed to be holding their breaths—save for the visitor's section. Here, N.S.A. was shouting and trying to cut into Michael's concentration. If it was working, Michael did a good job not showing it.

He put one foot behind him, bent his knees, and Lunged.

The goalkeeper squared his body with Michael.

Time slowed down.

All Finley could hear was his own heartbeat now.

Michael Enhanced, and then he threw the flashball.

And that's when the chaos began. Not the chaos that Bridget had feared should Brighton's team lose, but a different kind of chaos. The ground shook. Students screamed. Michael's flashball hit the back of N.S.A.'s net, but no one noticed. The pitch started to split, like canvas tearing. Michael landed awkwardly, and then he and both teams retreated for the sidelines.

"What's happening!" Finley screamed over the pandemonium. He grabbed onto Miguel's arm to keep him from falling. Bridget and Helena helped, but it was hard for any of them to keep upright.

A giant, colossal beast surfaced from underground—ripping through the turf and snapping at the stands. It screeched the screech of high pitches and ear shattering resonance, and it was awful.

"EVACUATE! EVACUATE!" Dean Longenecker's crazed voice said, echoing through the loudspeakers. But she didn't have to vocalize this command. The aisles between the bleachers were already swarming with evacuees.

The beast was huge and towering. It was the size of an eighteen-wheeler, and it looked like a mix between a rabid canine and a scaly goblin. There were black, hardened shells growing out of its joints, as if this creature had natural padding and protection.

It ran around the pitch, biting at students with its jagged muzzle. It was ferocious, wild. Parts of its hunched body glowed in the way that Finley had seen the plasma net do earlier that morning. It rammed into one of the goals with its shoulder, flinging the metal-framed net into the sands. It toppled onto some unsuspecting students, pinning them against the bleachers.

Finley saw blood.

The creature howled, getting onto its thick hind legs.

"This way!" Helena yanked Finley forward, and together, they helped Miguel over the bleachers as opposed to fighting for the aisle. Right when Finley had started to wonder where the Enhancer Force was, the violent demon of a beast rose into the air.

Finley's eyes fell on the pitch, where Professor Ambrose and three Enhancers were pointing gloved hands at the monster. Then, a heartbeat or two later, they stepped back and jerked their hands down—sending the still biting and drooling beast headfirst into the turf.

It's neck audibly snapped, and it lay unmoving.

The stadium was still again, for a moment, but quite a few students across the stands had begun sobbing in fear. Finley, Miguel, Bridget, and Helena stopped moving, and finally dropped back down onto the seats.

On the grass, next to the wide hole in the ground, the monster lay dead.

"Guys," Finley breathed after a few seconds. "Everyone okay?"

His friends merely nodded. Professor Ambrose conversed with the Enhancers on the pitch, and then they spread out—hopping over the fence and organizing a quick exit for the students.

Finley and Helena would eventually stand up first, but, before they did, Miguel said, his hands shaking: "What the hell was that?"

***

A few dozen students had sustained cuts on their arms and legs, as well as a handful of broken bones, but that proved to be the extent of the injuries. Those who needed to be Mended were taken to the nurse's wing, but the rest of the student body was corralled into their respective dorm houses. Here, everyone would wait until dinnertime while the staff worked with the Enhancer Force to sort out the madness.

Most of the eighth graders and freshmen, who shared one dorm house, were talking in the lounging area, dreaming up fantastic theories about what it was exactly they had witnessed.

Finley would have much rather been with his peers than in his room, but he had a strong feeling Doug would publicly pin this ordeal on him. Finley had neither the stomach nor the patience for this type of interaction, so he and Miguel went straight through the lounging area and up the stairwell to the fourth floor.

They were both surprised to find Parker there, sitting on his bunk bed and starring at a comic book. He didn't appear to be reading because his eyes didn't move across the strips.

"I'm telling you," Miguel said, sitting in one of the desk chairs and taking off his Lofstrand crutches. "I've never heard of something like that. Ever. Not even in the surging community."

"Could someone have released it?" Finley paced around the hardwood floor, folding his arms.

"We don't even know what 'it' is, dude," Miguel replied.

"Here. Pull out your laptop," Finley said. "Let's see if we can—"

"It was an electric ghost," Parker said in his small voice. Finley and Miguel turned to him, each wearing the same puzzled expression. "My dad hunts them."

Miguel snorted. "*Okay*. Anyway, Finley, I really think that—"

"Wait." Finley held up his hand. "I want to hear Parker's explanation."

Parker dropped his comic book. He didn't look scared, but more apathetic than anything else.

"An electric ghost," he said, informatively, "is a shell of a former person. Someone who starts willing power from the Root, but never surgers. They're just essentially accumulating and harboring all of this energy. Then, they become addicted. Dependent. They start to...change. Mutate into what you saw back there."

"Sounds like a tall tale to me," Miguel said skeptically.

"Did you or did you not just see one?" Parker replied, to which Miguel said nothing. "They mostly stay beneath the earth, in tunnels or sewers. They abhor sunlight."

"So what would have to happen to cause one to come up like that and start attacking?" Finley asked, intrigued.

"Not sure. Bet my dad will be brought in for consultation"—Miguel started to laugh, but then caught himself and pretended to cough—"Anyway, you probably never heard of them because the Bolt Sovereign likes to keep electric ghosts out of the public eye. Dad says that if people started to see those drastic side effects of the Root, it would call into question the safety of surging as a whole."

"Tall tales *and* conspiracy theories," Miguel said, clapping once. "What else you got for us?"

"You can think what you want to think," Parker snapped.

"Thanks," Miguel said casually. "I'll do that."

"Would you cool it?" Finley scolded Miguel. "Why is what he's suggesting so impossible? We all just saw a...a...a *thing* attacking our stadium!"

"And Parker's basically saying that that 'thing' was once a human," Miguel argued, throwing up his hands. "Sorry, but I have a hard time buying that."

Parker: "Okay, so, what *was* it then?"

"I dunno!" Miguel rubbed his forehead. "I dunno, all right?"

There was partial silence then. Faint banter from the lounging area drifted upstairs. Finley eventually walked over to his bed and dropped down onto his blankets. He sighed, then said into his pillow, "What's going to happen now?"

"School's probably already phoning our parents," said Miguel.

"This'll be all over the news," Parker added. "I bet you *half* of our classmates get pulled out of the semester for this."

Finley rolled over. His mom, dad, and sister all smiled down at him from a family picture wedged underneath Parker's mattress. Today it had officially been a week since he was home last. It was a shame that now, when he was finally settling in at Brighton, he would have to gather his things together and prepare for a return journey to Huntington Beach. No way his parents would keep him in school after hearing about something like this, even *if* having a surger in the family was the coolest thing to happen to the McCombs in...well, ever.

Your safety is far more important than staying at a surging prep school! he could hear his mom saying.

"I can't go back to a regular school," Finley said to no one in particular. "I just can't."

"I hear that," said Miguel, exhaling depressingly.

They didn't talk for the rest of that afternoon.

Miguel would eventually dig through his backpack and procure his notebooks. He scrawled away quietly at a desk—either doodling languidly, or making progress with one of their assigned papers. Parker returned to his comic book, and the sound of pages turning periodically came from his bunk.

Finley slept. He slept in the deep, calming way of boys dreaming with abandon, where problems weren't so scary or terrible that they couldn't be handled after succumbing to sleep and its healing touch.

At 6:00 p.m., Miguel shook Finley awake and told him they were allowed to head over to the mess hall for dinner. Parker had already left the dorm house with the majority of the eighth graders.

There was an eerie, morose vibe in and around the covered patio that evening. The tiki torches surrounding the mess hall burned with their usual calming fragrance, but on that day, the flickering flames seemed like an omen. It was as if the fire and the shadows and the sunset all existed to give warning of greater things to come—greater, even, than an electric ghost wreaking havoc during the Games of Illumination.

"It wouldn't be fair to you if we withheld even the smallest piece of information," Dean Longenecker said, walking around the tables.

The rest of the Brighton staff stood on the grass next to the mess hall beside a gathering of masked and uniformed Enhancers. Finley sat with Miguel, Bridget, and Helena and two other eighth graders—including Lauren Woods, from Professor Ambrose's class.

"What we know is little, at this point," the dean continued, passing by Finley's table. They made eye contact, but only for a second. "That creature apparently burrowed itself beneath the stadium months earlier, and it had been, er, 'hibernating' ever since. We don't know what it is exactly, or what caused it to emerge, but the Bolt Sovereign is launching a full investigation into the matter.

"That being said, it pains me to say this, but chargeball and the rest of the Games of Illumination have been suspended indefinitely."

There were a few sporadic mumbles and groans, but the general consensus seemed to be that this had been expected. Across the table from Finley, Helena closed her eyes and palmed her face with both hands.

"Please just bear with us as we get to the bottom of all this," the dean urged. "It is the priority of the Bolt Sovereign, as well as Brighton Preparatory School for Surgers, to keep our students—the bright future of the surging community—safe.

"As it stands now, we mean to continue on with classes and providing the highest level of education. What that will take, however, is a temporary lockdown."

More whispers, louder this time.

"I'll need your full cooperation," the dean went on. "Starting tomorrow, and for the duration of the weekend, the beach and pier will be off limits. Curfews will be earlier. No one is to stray from the campus grounds. The stadium is strictly prohibited. You will walk to and from the dorm houses with escorts."

Even though Dean Longenecker's decree bore necessity

and importance, there were still waves of disapproving shouts and questioning.

"Hear me when I say this will all blow over." Dean Longenecker held up her hand, imploring the mess hall to fall quiet. "Sometimes bad things just happen, leaving us confused and hurt. This is the true test of one's character: how we're able to respond. I, for one, want to be able to endure bad things, don't you?

"Don't you want to come together and be a culture that endures? That fights? That *survives?*"

Finley couldn't be one hundred percent sure, but he thought Dean Longenecker met his eyes after she'd said that last part. But, if she had, the moment had passed quickly, because before he knew it the dean was finishing with, "I'm not shutting down the school, but if your parents decide to pull you out I won't be making a case for any of you to stay."

What's that supposed to mean? Finley mused, and then Dean Longenecker took her leave, and slowly everyone rose and formed lines for dinner. Finley noticed, with anxiety in his stomach, that the first person the dean approached when she left the mess hall was Wally Grondahl.

"Mark my words, there's a clue somewhere in here that we're missing," said Bridget in a hushed voice, leaning over the table and wagging her pencil.

After breakfast the next day, Finley and his friends had all agreed to meet in the library to "work on their homework." He and Miguel sat across from Bridget and Helena in one of the corner tables. The library, for the most part, was empty.

This was what they had been hoping for.

"We've been over it a thousand times, Bridge!" Miguel moaned, dropping his head onto the table and banging it softly.

"Did you just call me a bridge?"

"Hey, we shorten Fin's name sometimes," Miguel replied, keeping his face down. "I thought I'd work on a nickname for you too. Welcome."

"*Anyway*," Bridget said, sliding a piece of paper forward and turning it upside down so that Finley and Miguel could examine it as it was intended to be viewed. "It" turned out to be a timeline that Bridget had drawn with her pencil.

"I find that having a visual aid helps me process my thoughts," she said, rapping the page with her pencil's eraser. "Let's review: Finley shows up on campus last Saturday, witnesses a weird exchange between Wally the driver and Dean Longenecker, then gets attacked in his dorm room. *Then*, he's transported to a field where a James Olyphant tells him he better join the dark side because the Dissensions are coming.

"Shortly after that Finley finds out about his recharging

abilities from Professor Ambrose, who, by the way, is a no-show to every scheduled tutoring session. And then yesterday Finley catches a glimpse of the creepy, masked, cloaked figure staring down at him from the announcer booth, and, well, we all know what happened next."

Finley picked up Bridget's timeline with his right hand, and with his left he tapped his cheek thoughtfully. Helena pulled a bag of chips out of her purse and opened it noisily. After only one bite, the librarian walked by with his rickety cart and snatched the bag out of Helena's hand in passing. He dropped it onto the stack of books he was wheeling across the library, *hmph*ing triumphantly.

"Seriously?" Helena said, appalled.

"It will certainly be interesting to see how the Bolt Sovereign addresses this creature *thing* that was living under our school," Bridget said, throwing open a large book and thumbing through the pages. "I can't find any mention of it in these reference volumes."

"Check with Parker," Miguel suggested dryly. "He seems to have this one pegged."

"Wait...," Finley said, straightening up. "I forgot to tell you guys about something."

Miguel perked up. "What?"

"I overheard Wally talking to someone, over by the statue in the exterior hall," he said, taking Bridget's pencil and adding a few words to the line labeled "Sunday." "He seemed on edge, and the person he was chatting with was demanding results and sounded frustrated.

"Also, he said something to the effect of, 'it will be here any day.'"

Miguel, Bridget, and Helena exchanged quick glances.

"*It?*" Bridget repeated, wrinkling her forehead. "Could be anything. Did you get a look at Wally's friend?"

"No. When I walked around the statue, it was only him. Tell me that's not pretty incriminating though, right? He could've been referring to the monster at the Games of Illumination!"

Bridget took her timeline back, and Helena leaned over and inspected it with her, like the answers to all these questions were just waiting to be discovered in the sequence of events.

"I've put off digging into Wally's past for too long," Bridget mumbled to herself, setting the paper down and writing something.

"You guys remember how that Enhancer walked me from Science of Surging to Control?" Finley asked, and everyone nodded. "Well, I ended up telling him about that exchange, too."

Helena turned her head at a slant. "And? What did he say?"

"Nothing, really. I guess I wasn't expecting much though."

"This is all just so baffling." Bridget set her pencil down and leaned back. "I can't help but think everything comes back to Olyphant, you know? Wally's suspicious behavior. That monster wrecking our stadium. I have this feeling we're in the middle of some dangerous storm…"

"In the middle?" Finley said, turning to Miguel, Helena, and then Bridget. "Or in the beginning?"

Chapter 14 | <u>Professor Ambrose's Challenge</u>

Surprisingly, Finley's parents never arrived at Brighton Prep to pull him from school and drag him home to Huntington Beach. He never got a phone call, email, or letter, which either meant they were still comfortable with their son under the protection of the Enhancer Force, or they had never been informed of what had happened with the electric ghost. Finley was thankful to still be with his friends, but he knew there was a chance that his family could show up at any moment to collect him.

No news is good news, Finley reflected, which is why he ultimately decided not to reach out to his parents concerning the monster attack...

With Halloween at a fast approach, and the fall semester more than halfway over, Brighton's spirits should have been soaring in the clouds. But, given that the Games of Illumination were on hold—the big event the student body looked forward to every other Saturday—it was hard to embrace the upcoming festivities and semester break.

For Finley and his fellow eighth graders, classes only grew more and more difficult with each passing day. The last half of September and first chunk of October proved to be painfully slow weeks, with one assignment piling on top of the next.

Miguel was convinced the professors were punishing them for the disaster that had occurred during the chargeball match, like it had been a student's doing. Bridget and Helena calmed him down, saying that was ridiculous, but Finley wasn't so sure.

"Hey," he said between classes one day, "tell me Diffenbaugh's research papers don't feel like punishment!"

"Egg sack lee!" Miguel said, to which Finley, Bridget, and Helena all scrunched their eyebrows together.

"I was drawing out the word for emphasis," he explained. Finley and the girls merely shrugged in response as they all continued across the greenway to their next period.

A couple weeks prior, Finley had barely made it past quarterly finals, with his worst grade coming out of Professor's Guggenheim's class. But, as he considered his situation, a pass *was* a pass—regardless of how ugly the red 76 looked atop his test.

Now, Finley was hearing that quarterlies were only the appetizers. Final exams were the main course, so to speak. This was where the professors would get an accurate look at what their students were retaining. Or *weren't* retaining. This was where their progress would truly be measured.

At breakfast one Tuesday in mid-October, a representative from the Bolt Sovereign came to Brighton and spoke to the students about the monster attack.

"Thank you all for giving up your stadium these past few weeks," the older woman said in a dour tone. She wore an ostentatious suit with pressed pants, and a two-toned patch was stitched onto her jacket above the heart. She also had on a thick, four-fingered glove with only one wire running from the tip of the forefinger to the wrist. It was sleek and shiny, most likely made of alloy.

"Our officials have been working tirelessly to uncover the truth about this awful, tragic occurrence." She held her hands in front of her stiffly. "Rest assured knowing that progress is being made. I'm glad to see that the majority of Brighton's student body has remained intact throughout these trials. That clearly speaks to the trust your parents have in President Moonan and the Bolt Sovereign, and our ability to act and protect."

Then, she left, and chatter resumed in the mess hall.

"So…what exactly is the update?" Finley said, looking around his table. "She basically just threw a bunch of words at us."

"As is the Bolt Sovereign way," Miguel said, cutting into his omelet. "The B.S. feeding us BS. You guys see what I did there?"

Finley looked around the mess hall. Everyone appeared to have had no problem swallowing what the representative had fed him or her. Some of his classmates were already joking and cutting up. They had no qualms with the lack of information surrounding the monster's attack.

Finley thought of Parker. The more time that passed without any real updates from the Bolt Sovereign and its supposed ongoing investigation, the more he was inclined to lean toward Parker's theories.

It would call into question the safety of surging as a whole, Parker had said of the electric ghost. Meaning, it would jeopardize the ideal attached to surging. Surging, which was meant for good, which was meant to help those less fortunate.

Something like this would shake the surging community to the core, Finley thought, pushing the scrambled eggs on his plate to the side with his fork.

"We heard about what you did in Ambrose's class," a voice suddenly said.

Finley looked up. Michael and Sarah Caverly were standing over Miguel, who was frozen mid-bite in shock.

"I...what are you talking about?" Finley said, turning to Bridget and Helena for help. They looked just as thrown off as he was.

Michael flattened his school tie against his chest. "You're modest. Gonna have to squelch that characteristic if you ever plan on being a real competitor."

Where is this going? Finley thought, laughing aloud. "I'm not trying to be modest, I just really don't know what you're—"

"Your Lunge, on the greenway," Sarah said, sounding bored. "Furthest anyone's ever gone on their first try, and with just a cell phone battery to work with."

"Oh. That." Finley flushed.

Since that afternoon back in September, Professor Ambrose hadn't mandated another practice session. Finley had gotten the impression that the episode at the chargeball match had thrown a wrench into every professor's lesson plan because that following Monday—and every period since—only lectures and readings had taken place in class.

It was a grueling, taxing way to go about learning—especially with something as exciting and involving as surging.

"Not sure what you guys want from me," Finley admitted.

"Be our goalkeeper," Michael said bluntly. A piece of Miguel's omelet dropped from his fork and into his lap.

Finley chuckled awkwardly. "Um…what?"

"Hate to interrupt," Helena said after she found her

voice. "The Games of Illumination were suspended. There hasn't been a chargeball match in weeks. But, then, you probably knew that."

"Coach Tenenbaum put in for an appeal last week," Sarah said, her eyes remaining on Finley. "If all goes well, we'll travel to Long Beach for our first away match. There's still time to save face for the season."

"Wait. *This* Saturday?" Finley coughed into his fist, like the prospect of all this was physically choking. "That's in three days!"

"Four, if you count today." Michael combed back his wavy hair with his hand.

"I...t-that...," Finley stammered, incapable of processing the possibility that he could be a part of Brighton's chargeball team.

"Three unanswered goals is unacceptable," Sarah said, crossing her arms. "Especially to N.S.A. We need to make a change on defense. A *drastic* change."

"That's definitely what you'd be doing if you put me in front of the net," Finley said, his palms clammy. "But I'm positive it wouldn't be a change for the better."

"I guess we'll see about that," Michael said. "We're resuming practice today, in the field behind the girls' dorm house. 5:15. Hope to see you there."

The Caverly twins sauntered off, joining a table on the other side of the mess hall that consisted mostly of seniors.

"Guys," Finley said to Miguel, Bridget, and Helena. "I

haven't recharged since that day in Ambrose's class. I'm gonna make an idiot of myself!"

Bridget set her napkin onto her empty plate. "I guess it's time to pull out the glove Professor Diffenbaugh made you!"

Finley skipped his scheduled tutoring session with Professor Ambrose at Miguel's suggestion. ("It's been over a month and he still hasn't shown!" Miguel had said. "You think he's gonna notice if you're not there for the next couple of days?") It didn't take much to convince Finley. If the professor showed no interest in his tutelage, why should he?

So, instead of sitting in Ambrose's cold classroom for a solid forty-five minutes, Finley and his friends chose to spend their free period in a corner of the greenway, where they would focus on building Finley's recharging chops.

"Here, use these," Miguel said, handing him two AA batteries. "Pulled them out of the remote control from the lounging area in our dorm house. That thing's been dead for days."

"Thanks." Finley took the batteries and snapped them into place on his glove.

Bridget and Helena sat on the grass with their backs against a palm tree. They had three large books lying open in front of them, though only Bridget seemed to be consulting the texts. Helena was blowing her bangs out of her eyes idly.

"So, what should I work on first?" Finley asked, walking up to the girls.

"Definitely Enhancing," Helena replied. "That's a given, if you plan on surviving the brunt of a flashball hit that is."

"Yeah let's do that," Finley said quickly.

An image flashed in his mind's eye of a striker hurtling a flashball at Finley, who attempted to save it, except that when the ball made contact with his gloves, his hands ripped free from his wrists bloodily.

Finley gulped.

"Says here that Enhancing, in theory, is just like what Professor Ambrose said about Lunging and Fueling." Bridget turned a page. "Meaning, all you're doing is picturing to yourself how Enhanced strength can aid your situation, and then doing it."

"Sure, okay. Seems simple enough."

"Wait." Bridget held up a finger. "There's also a warning here. This instructor writes that 'if the surger is not especially specific about his or her timing, there could be painful consequences.' She then goes on to use an example of lifting a heavy object, and what would happen if the surger stopped drawing from the Root a second before they meant to."

"Said heavy object would collapse and crush them,"

Miguel said, leaning on his crutches. "You catch all that, Fin?"

"Yeah, no pressure or anything." That was a flat out lie: Finley didn't just feel pressure, but rather an *all-encompassing* pressure.

What am I doing here? he said inwardly, walking away from the palm tree and pacing.

Bridget: "Finley? Is this too overwhelming?" She closed the book closest to her. "We're not going to think less of you or something if you don't want to go through with all this."

"She won't," Miguel said. "But I will."

"I'm fine, I think." Finley stood still and faced his friends. "I think I need to do this, you know? If nothing else, this will be the start of me exploring my recharging abilities."

"That's the spirit," Helena said, rising to her feet. She pulled a hardback novel out of her bag and tossed it to him. "Now how about you show us something."

Finley, after he caught the book, said, "What am I supposed to do with this?"

"Tear it in half with Enhancing," she responded, and added, when Finley made a startled face, "it's a hand-me-down romance. I've started it like three hundred times. It won't be missed."

Finley thought, *Okay then*, and shrugged.

He closed his eyes.

He sought to feel the Root in the batteries strapped to his wrist. He could sense his friends watching him closely. He cleared his mind, or did his best to, and then tried picturing himself pulling the hardback book apart. First, he imagined the novel was made of construction paper—that it could be easily torn. Next, he mouthed *Let go, Finley*, and waited.

His arms jerked.

Both his hands tingled—not *just* his gloved one.

Then, he pulled.

The book didn't simply tear, it *shredded*, as if someone had cut it haphazardly with a chainsaw. Finley opened his eyes. Paper and cover chunks fell around him and his friends like confetti.

"You did it!" Bridget screamed, but then her voice caught in her throat and she gasped. When Miguel and Helena saw what she was looking at, they too sucked in a breath.

"What?" Finley demanded, as the swirling paper and debris finally settled. He looked down, and that's when the pain hit him. A vicious, fierce pain he had never known.

Both his arms hung like limp, lifeless sweater sleeves.

When he Enhanced, he had exerted too much too quick, and he'd dislocated his arms.

"Ouch," Miguel said, and it was the last thing Finley heard before he blacked out.

***

When Finley regained consciousness, it was still light outside, and he was lying in a familiar room. Nurse Jasmine was at his bedside, wiping his forehead with a dripping rag. That's when Finley remembered what had happened, and he immediately lifted his arms into the air and wiggled his fingers.

Relief sunk in. There wasn't even a hint of pain. He dropped his arms down and chuckled despite himself. *There's gotta be a first for everything, right?* The nurse stood from her stool and took the rag to the sink, ringing it out.

A couple of Brighton groundskeepers passed by the window outside, carrying armfuls of pumpkins and gourds and other fall décor. Inside, the recovery room was already decorated for the season. There was a banner with paper cutout ghosts and leaves hanging above the bed. A cauldron overflowing with candy sat beside the terracotta fireplace, and there was a witch's broom in the corner by the wastebasket.

Finley could hear voices outside the door. It sounded like Miguel, Bridget, and Helena. Finley checked the clock above the nurse's head. It was almost 3:30 p.m., which meant he had missed lunch and the Science of Surging.

His stomach grumbled.

"I should just move my stuff in," Finley said jokingly, leaning up into a sitting position.

"Why? You plan on making this a habit?" Nurse Jasmine said, draping the damp rag over the faucet to dry before turning around. "There's a reason Enhancing is reserved for your junior year, Mr. McComb."

Finley sighed. "Am I in trouble then?"

"Don't be silly!" Professor Diffenbaugh marched inside unexpectedly, and before the door closed, Finley caught his friends standing in the hall—frantically trying to look inside. "It's perfectly normal for you to want to explore your powers and limits."

Finley caught the nurse's face dropping at the appearance of the professor. "Get some lunch," she said to Finley. "And, I know you're going to disregard this, but don't do any heavy lifting or physically taxing activities for twenty-four hours."

Nurse Jasmine left. Once more, when the door opened and closed, Miguel, Bridget, and Helena peeked in to check on Finley.

"How are you feeling?" Diffenbaugh asked, sitting on the stool by Finley's bedside. He had a rolled-up newspaper in his hand, which he used to poke Finley in the arm with.

"Embarrassed more than anything, really."

"Don't be." The professor chuckled and folded his arms. "I don't think there were too many witnesses. Why *were* you practicing Enhancing though? Curiosity?"

"Michael and Sarah Caverly asked me to try out for

goalkeeper. Ridiculous, right?"

Professor Diffenbaugh's smile vanished. Finley was certain the scolding was about to begin.

"Finley that's *fantastic!*"

"It is?"

"Of course! Why do you think I've been asking about your extracurricular activity? The best way to master surging is through application. It's how all the great surgers in our history got to where they were."

Finley felt reinvigorated. "I used your glove," he said, grinning. "To hold some dead batteries."

"And you were apparently *very* successful in recharging."

They both laughed. There was a loud *bump!* outside the recovery room, followed by muffled yelling. Finley swung his feet around and stood up, saying, "Guys—you can come inside, you know."

There was a beat of silence, then the door burst opened and Finley's friends spilled into the room.

"How are you doing?"

"I'm sorry we pressured you into that!"

"Helena got a picture on her phone. Your arms looked *so cool* dangling like that!"

Professor Diffenbaugh stepped aside so they could clap Finley on the back and see how he was doing. The professor then pulled four slips of paper out of his pocket and jotted something down with a pen.

"Here," Diffenbaugh said, handing out the slips. "You

guys will need these excuses for being late to Control. Finley, make sure you stop by the mess hall and grab a box lunch to take into Ambrose's class."

Finley nodded, folding his slip. "Thanks, professor."

Diffenbaugh winked, then left.

"So, what did he say?" Bridget asked, sitting on the edge of the bed. "You're not in trouble, right?"

"Nope," Finley replied happily. "In fact, he's glad I'm trying out for the team."

"He is?" Miguel stepped over toward the sink with his crutches and leaned against the counter. "So, that means you're still planning to?"

"I mean, I dunno...," said Finley. He moved toward the window and gazed out at the greenway. Groundskeepers lunged up and hung orange and black streamers from palm trees. "I think that I'll have more regrets if I don't go this evening, than if I do."

Helena said, "At least you'll know you tried. I mean, this is a pretty big deal. No one would wanna miss out on this!"

"It's the fans that I'm really worried about," Finley said teasingly, turning away from the window. He led his friends out of the recovery room, and they walked down the hall single file. "If, by some cosmic intervention, I do make the team, I'm going to be playing under a microscope."

"Whatever," Miguel and Helena said, almost

simultaneously.

"Who wouldn't want to be playing for passionate fans?" Miguel demanded.

Bridget rolled her eyes at the ceiling. "Yes. Passionate. *That's* the word for it."

As they headed for the exit, they passed by Nurse Jasmine's office. The door was ajar. Out of his peripheral, Finley spotted the nurse waving her hands animatedly as she whisper-yelled at Professor Diffenbaugh. She was obviously not happy about how he had handled Finley's accident.

The professor, who heard Finley and his friends chatting as they traipsed through the hall, reached over and shut the door. Finley knew Diffenbaugh was weathering this reproach on his behalf, and it made him appreciate the professor all the more.

After grabbing Finley's box lunch at the mess hall and scurrying down the exterior hall toward Ambrose's classroom, they ended up being a total of fifteen minutes late to Control.

Professor Ambrose, who was in the middle of a lecture, was not happy when Finley, Miguel, Bridget, and Helena slipped inside. He received their excuse slips with pursed lips, and hardly even regarded Professor Diffenbaugh's words.

Ambrose waved them off to their seats curtly and continued to address his room full of students:

"As I was saying. Lunging can be very useful during a duel. It gives the surger a whole new slew of defensive and offensive maneuvers. Take the launching kick, for example."

In one fast, graceful move, the professor pointed at a lamp on one of the student's desk. The light flickered and transferred energy from the Root to the professor, who used Understanding to pull a dry erase marker from his desktop. The writing utensil soared through the air, and Ambrose caught in stride as he moved toward the board—drawing with fast, wide strokes.

I'll never be able to Understand that well, Finley thought to himself. *He just snatched that marker from his desk like he had a hidden magnet!*

"This is a launching kick."

The professor stepped aside when he was finished. What he had drawn depicted two fighters sparring. One figure was standing with their back bent a ways, arms spread out, while the other figure was off the ground with both feet pressed against the first figure's chest. There was a long, curved arrow drawn across the board, which showed the trajectory of the fighter after he had Lunged off of his opponent's chest.

"All you're essentially doing is using your attacker as a launching pad for a Lunge," the professor said, capping his marker. "But the move takes quite a bit of practice. You have to time the initial leap off the ground *perfectly* with when you pull your legs back and aim at your attacker's torso.

"Make sense? Good. I'll need two volunteers then."

It was like a giant vacuum had sucked all the air out of the classroom. One big, giant, collective gasp.

"C'mon. Surging's about taking risks." Professor Ambrose's eyes fell on Finley. "Isn't that right, Mr. McComb?"

Finley meant to say, *Yes, sir*, or even nod. But when everyone turned and looked at him, he was forced into a panic. He knew exactly where this was going.

"I'll take that as a yes. You're our first volunteer. Who's my second?"

Finley didn't have to look across the room to see whose hand had shot into the air. He'd known before the moment had happened. Doug Horn was the professor's second volunteer.

"Good." Ambrose walked down the center aisle, heading for the exit. "To the greenway. Leave your things here."

There were murmurs of perturbation, but by the time the professor pushed open the door, nearly half the class was already on his or her feet. Finley moved his tongue across the roof of his mouth, trying to distract himself from the stares he received as his peers passed by his desk and headed outside.

"What do you look so nervous for?" Miguel asked, standing up and putting his crutches on. "Just go out there and do your thing."

"I've already been humiliated once today." Finley bristled after he said this. "Don't know that I can take much more." He finally stood with reluctance and followed his friends out of the classroom.

Decorative bales of hay lay scattered about everywhere, and the occasional scarecrow was staked into the ground—its drooping, outspread arms quavering creepily in the brush of sudden winds.

Professor Ambrose's class had collected together near the center of the greenway, practically equidistant from the encircling exterior hall. The late afternoon sun leaked onto the grass through scattered clouds. It was mostly a beautiful, Californian day.

Finley felt his spine tingle.

The more he recharged, the more confident he got. Understanding had taken focus. Enhancing had proven tricky and, Finley had learned, came with consequences when not performed correctly. Yet Lunging had come natural, which was all a launching kick was—according to the professor, anyway.

Finley brushed past his classmates and joined Ambrose and Doug, who stood in front of the crowd expectantly.

"Here's how this will go down," the professor said,

loosening his tie. "Each of you will take a shot at a launching kick. I'll be your target. Start a few yards off, and I would suggest a running start."

Finley could feel his nerves instantly softened. They were to attempt this move on the professor, *not* each other. That immediately took a load of pressure off.

Until Doug Horn cleared his throat.

Ambrose, after turning to Doug, said, "Yes, Mr. Horn?"

"Would it not be more beneficial for me and Finley to try the launching kick on each other?"

Finley's fingers wrapped in on themselves as he formed two shaky fists. The crowd began to speak softly in an excited manner. Professor Ambrose didn't reply instantly. He looked back and forth between his two students. Doug was already pulling his glove out of his pocket and putting it on unhurriedly.

"I see no harm in that," Ambrose finally said. Finley bit down on his teeth and scraped them together. "Start about twenty-five yards apart, facing one another. On my signal, charge."

The whispering crowd grew louder then. Finley yanked Diffenbaugh's glove out of his pocket and jammed it on while he stomped off and took position.

I'm fed up with this! I'm fed up with taking your comments and glares and stupid mouth! He narrowed his eyes and stared Doug down. *This ends right here and right now.*

"Ready." Professor Ambrose joined the rest of his

class.

Across the greenway, Doug Horn clenched his gloved fist and bent his knees. Finley did the same, praying inwardly that enough of the Root residues were left in the dead AA batteries strapped to his wrist.

"Set."

This ends today...

"*Go!*"

Finley took off running as fast as he could. He wasn't sure what he was going to do exactly when he reached Doug, but he just knew he had to get to him. The rest would surely figure itself out. That was the thing about Finley when he got pushed over the edge—acting came first, then thinking.

When they were mere feet apart, Finley leapt into the air and brought his knees against his chest. He had beaten Doug to this action, and Finley was about to ram his sneakers into his body, but the unthinkable happened.

Doug Fuel-slid underneath Finley. A streak of hot pink light whisked beneath his airborne feet. Finley tumbled to the ground awkwardly, somehow managing a halfway decent land, but by then a force had hit him in the back and propelled him forward strenuously.

Doug had spun around and issued a launching kick into Finley's back.

He experienced his first whiplash that afternoon, and it was the most raw and surprising and hideous sensation he could ever recall. Finley eventually landed on the grass some great distance away and rolled over half a dozen times before the momentum finally wore off.

He could taste the bitterness of bile on his tongue as he lay there, and, though he probably had enough strength to lean his head up, or at least moan a little, he chose to remain still, and the sunlight felt hotter than it probably was that October afternoon.

Chapter 15 | <u>Stems</u>

Nurse Jasmine was furious.

Professor Ambrose carried Finley to her wing and set him down on the bed in the recovery room he'd grown accustomed to. The nurse yelled and paced and told Finley he could not be serious right now—he could not *seriously* be hurt again. She condemned him to the recovery room for the rest of the day, and even said she would seek Dean Longenecker's approval to keep him overnight.

Finley wanted to argue. He wanted to blame Professor Ambrose, who hadn't batted an eye when he had consented to that "exercise" in his class. He wanted to tell the nurse the many reasons why he couldn't be kept in the recovery room, and trying out for goalkeeper was at the top of his list.

But Finley couldn't call upon the strength required to talk. His neck was impossibly sore, and he'd left his pride out on the greenway. So he simply let Ambrose prop his head up with a pillow while enduring Nurse Jasmine's reprimanding.

After the nurse had calmed down and started to sort through her medicine cabinet, Professor Ambrose squeezed Finley's arm with an apathetic gaze. That was all he did before he left. Finley tried not to dwell on the fact that Ambrose was practically the reason he was injured; that, after the professor had told Finley he could recharge, their interactions together had been as mere acquaintances; that the professor hadn't attended a single tutoring session.

The nurse slipped her hand under Finley's neck. He closed his eyes. He could feel the skin warming beneath Nurse Jasmine's touch as she Mended him. The pain was gone. It was quiet. Then, while Finley's eyelids were still shut, the nurse told him dinner would be brought over in a little bit, and two Enhancers were stationed in her wing, so he shouldn't try sneaking off. He should rest, difficult as that sounded.

So Finley kept his eyes sealed, and he slept.

He woke up twice. Once to eat the dinner that was provided to him in bed, and then to use the restroom. It was night by that point. Finley walked down the hallway in his socks, and eventually found his way to the restroom at the other end of the wing.

He splashed water onto his face and regarded his reflection. He couldn't believe that one day he was happy and discovering his true purpose in the surging community with his recharging abilities, and then he was running for his life when a ferocious monster wrought chaos on the Brighton stadium. One moment the Caverly twins were practically begging him to try out for the chargeball team, and then Doug Horn was humiliating him in painful fashion.

It was time to start expecting the unexpected.

Finley sighed. He cupped his hands, let the running water sit in his palms, and then he took a drink. When he brought his head back up, he saw the cloaked figure in the masquerade mask standing behind him.

Finley whipped around.

No one was there.

The water pouring from the faucet suddenly sounded louder. He reached behind his back and cut it off. His heart thumped. His mouth was dry despite having been quenched with water seconds ago.

You're just imagining things, Finley assured himself.

He refused to let himself be shaken. It was probably just the medicine Nurse Jasmine had given him. Yes, that had to be it…only, now that Finley thought about it, the nurse *hadn't* given him anything. She'd just Mended him, then let him rest.

Finley kept his back against the wall as he sidestepped

across the bathroom. He grabbed hold of the door handle, turned it, and then paused.

There was small, brass key on the tiled floor—right where he thought he'd seen his masked attacker standing. Finley looked around. He was definitely the only one in the restroom.

So, cautiously, he reached down and picked up the key, which was chinked and deceptively heavy. Then, he slipped out the door and ran to his room—the pitter-patter of his feet the only sound in the nurse's wing.

Once he was under his covers, the key still in hand, his nerves still shaken from seeing his attacker in the mirror, Finley had a sudden revelation.

"Professor Diffenbaugh?"

Finley knocked again. It was early, but he was sure the professor was up. The next morning, after his stay in the recovery room, Finley had wasted no time checking out and racing to his dorm. There, he showered and changed and brushed his teeth—careful not to wake Miguel or Parker in the process.

Now, wearing a fresh Brighton uniform with his backpack slung over his shoulder, Finley rapped on the door labeled B. Diffenbaugh in the faculty housing building.

He had lied to the Enhancer guarding the main, gated

entrance. But then, it was the only way he could get inside. When the Enhancer found that Professor Ambrose *hadn't* summoned him to his office, he was sure to be irate.

Finley could deal with that, and his conscience, later. Right now he needed Diffenbaugh.

"Professor!"

Finally, Finley heard the sound of a deadbolt unlocking, and the door swung open. The professor stood over the threshold with his bowtie draping around his neck. The top two buttons of his shirt were undone. He had a newspaper in one hand, and a steaming mug of coffee in the other.

"Finley? Is everything okay?" He looked over his shoulder, consulting a clock on the wall inside his quarters. "It's not even seven yet."

"May I come in, professor?"

Diffenbaugh did not even hesitate. "Of course, of course."

He stepped aside, and Finley walked forward. Unlike his classroom, Professor Diffenbaugh's on-campus apartment was immaculate. The open floor concept adjoined the living room, kitchen, and dining room into one. The furniture was matching, and had muted colors. The sliding glass doors were spotless, devoid of a single smudge, and the distant ocean looked picture perfect.

Finley walked along the wall, where a few framed photographs were hanging.

"Is this you?" Finley asked, stopping at one picture that showed a young teenager with short hair and a big smile shaking hands with an elderly man. They stood in front of a flag that bore a strange, hexagon pattern Finley didn't recognize.

"Which one?" the professor replied, setting his coffee and newspaper down on the breakfast table.

"Ha. Very funny." Finley set his backpack on the couch.

"That was taken almost a decade ago," Diffenbaugh said distantly. He walked up behind Finley and admired the photograph. "Man's name is Alan Gibbs. Taught me everything I know about surging, and life. He raised me, after my parents were killed."

Finley stumbled over a response. "Oh, I…didn't. I'm sorry."

"For what?" The professor smiled, then led Finley away from the wall and to the breakfast table. "They died when I was young, and I've had a long time to heal."

"Right, yeah." Finley suddenly felt as if he was imposing.

"Get you some breakfast?" Professor Diffenbaugh pulled a skillet out of his cupboard and put it on the stovetop before Finley could answer. "The cooks on campus don't have anything on my omelets."

Finley laughed. "Sure, thanks. That sounds great."

"Feeling any better?" he asked, spraying the skillet's

black surface with olive oil. "Between your Enhancing 'accident' and run-in with Doug in Ambrose's class, you had quite an eventful day yesterday!"

"Yeah, um, that's actually why I'm here," Finley said, popping his knuckles.

"Am I supposed to talk you out of beating the crap outta Doug?" The professor cracked two eggs into a bowl and began to whisk them. "Because that is one thing I'm comfortable turning a blind eye toward."

"I appreciate the permission," Finley said, smiling. "But, as satisfying as that sounds, I know I shouldn't risk suspension over something like that. Finding out about Brighton is the best thing that has ever happened to me. I wouldn't trade it for anything."

Professor Diffenbaugh beamed to himself like a proud parent. "That makes you a better person than me, Finley McComb." He poured the egg yoke onto the skillet, and it sizzled loudly.

Finley flushed. He didn't believe there was anything extraordinary about avoiding a brawl with Doug Horn. Sure, it would feel fantastic to put him in his place, but at the expense of what? He'd end up like his fourth dorm mate, Quinn—shipped out of Brighton and suspended for an entire semester.

"Okay, so what's up then?"

Finley took a seat at the breakfast table. "I saw my attacker. The one who was in the field, with James

Olyphant."

Diffenbaugh turned from his eggs, his jaw set. "You *what*? When? Where?"

"Twice. Once, in the announcer's booth at the chargeball pitch, right before that monster destroyed our stadium. And then again, last night. I saw the figure in the restroom, for a split second. But when I spun around, they were gone…

"…Am I crazy, professor?"

Finley could see the tension leaving Diffenbaugh's face, but he still looked intense. After an extended moment, he returned to his eggs and said, "No, Finley. Of course you're not crazy."

"Well, I'm not so sure." Finley leaned his head back. "Anyway, those two instances got me thinking last night, thinking about Understanding."

"What about it?"

"Well, you know how Dean Longenecker said Borrowing—the way Olyphant transported me out of Brighton—was outlawed? She referred to it as a stem of Understanding. 'A' stem, meaning, maybe, that there are others?"

Professor Diffenbaugh was silent for a moment. A moment that became so long Finley wondered if the professor had heard him. Then,

"Advanced surging is the stuff of universities and graduate programs," he said, salting and peppering the omelet. Next, he pulled some sliced ham out of the refrigerator and placed it in the egg. "Most students don't start to wonder at the potential of Understanding until they're seniors. I've got to say, I'm impressed."

"Wait, so, I'm right?" he said, perking up. "There *are* other stems?"

"Dozens, Finley." The professor grabbed a green plate from the dishwasher and set it beside the stove.

"Okay, so, these visions then, of my attacker," Finley said quickly, standing up. "Could it be that Olyphant is putting them there? In my head? Like he's trying to scare me out of here?"

"It's definitely possible." Professor Diffenbaugh slid the finished omelet onto the green plate and put it on the table. "Understanding can empower a surger like no other phase. I've seen men vanish into thin air, only to discover that they had reappeared miles away. There are some, even, who use it for *mind control*."

"And that's all legal?!" Finley questioned, sitting back and down and accepting a fork from the professor.

"No, absolutely not," he replied gravely, taking the chair across from Finley. "Understanding was contained by the Bolt Sovereign and regulated into one form: telekinesis. The Enhancer Force's top priority is ensuring no surger tampers with and abuses Understanding. This kind of stuff has started wars."

Finley was speechless. There were still so many things

he didn't know about the culture of which he was now a member. He used the side of his fork to cut a bite-sized portion out of his breakfast. That's when he noticed that his omelet was shaped like a fish.

"Sorry," Professor Diffenbaugh said, following Finley's eyes. "Had a niece stay with me one summer. Been making animal-shaped meals ever since."

But that wasn't why Finley had stiffened. He had just thought of something. That night, back in his home in Huntington Beach, when his family had been eating fish and Mr. Repairman had paid them a visit.

Finley swallowed.

"What is it?" Professor Diffenbaugh inclined forward. "Finley?"

"Mind control," he said, looking up from his plate. "Have you seen it done before?"

The professor nodded, his face stone cold. "It's a terrible thing. Bears one of the largest punishments in the surging community, second only to murder. When a person has their mind manipulated, the surger using Understanding can have his subject say or do whatever he or she pleases. It's disgusting."

"And, and would there be anyway to indentify that someone is being controlled?"

"Yes," Diffenbaugh replied. "There would an out-of-sync rhythm to the subject's actions. It would be subtle, but the astute observer would notice it immediately."

An out-of-sync rhythm, Finley thought, his left hand trembling beneath the breakfast table. *As in, when my family was talking, and their words didn't match their mouths…*

"Finley." The professor reached across and grabbed his arm gently. "If you've ever seen this done, you *have* to report it to the Enhancers. It's breaking the law."

Finley could hear his heartbeat resonating in his head like bombs igniting in rapid succession. Should he tell Professor Diffenbaugh about what he saw? He was, after all, the person in whom he trusted the most at Brighton Preparatory School for Surgers. More so, he realized, than even his friends.

And yet…

And yet James Olyphant's words.

You're being lied to, he'd said. And you're on the wrong side.

Had Brighton knowingly broken surging laws to collect Finley McComb? If what Professor Diffenbaugh was saying about Understanding and mind control was true, then that's *exactly* what the school had done.

Was…was Olyphant right? Am I on the wrong side? Finley couldn't believe that, he just couldn't. He had looked into Diffenbaugh's eyes many times. Felt the assurance, the safety. Even Ambrose, who had distanced himself from Finley, had told him everything he'd known about recharging.

Or *had* it been everything?

Finley felt like he was right smack in the middle of some psychological thriller. He was the sane patient in the ward, and every doctor and nurse was lying to him and keeping him incarcerated. Keeping him in the dark.

In under a minute, his appetite had disappeared.

He couldn't tell Professor Diffenbaugh what he'd just discovered about Mr. Repairman—Brighton's appointed recruiter. Not yet, at least. He decided right then that he wouldn't mention the key he'd found last night, either.

"W-What have you been able to uncover about Olyphant?" Finley said weakly, setting his fork down. "And the Dissensions?"

"I'm afraid there's been no progress on that front," the professor said, sounding troubled. "Believe me, I've poured countless hours into research and digging, but I'm getting nowhere. Whoever this guy is, if he wanted to send a message, he did a poor job relaying it."

"And, Professor Ambrose? Thought he said he had a lead with that name."

Diffenbaugh looked crestfallen. "Ended up being a dead end, or so he claims. Apparently, the name *was* just a coincidence—converse to what he initially thought."

"Oh."

Finley tried remaining calm, but because his head was zipping off in so many various directions, he was sure he looked flustered. Blessedly, Diffenbaugh misinterpreted his mood.

"I know you want your attacker behind bars," he said. "It's not fair for anyone to have their conscious Borrowed—especially a young, bright surger such as yourself. We *will* get to the bottom of this. I promise. I'll mention to the Enhancer Captain that you're seeing visions. Could end up being a clue."

Finley meant to nod, but he failed to bring his chin up for the second half of the gesture. *Idiot! Stop looking so guilty!*

An alarm sounded from a back room. The professor checked the clock on the wall again. "Time to feed my iguana, and *you* better get to class."

Finley, despite his unease, actually let out a chuckle. "You have an iguana?"

The professor got to his feet and buttoned the rest of his shirt. Then, he set to work on his bowtie. "Yeah—you interested in taking her home over the break? Need to find a sitter."

Finley blanked on an appropriate response. "Er…"

"I'm kidding," he said, walking with Finley into the living room. He grabbed his backpack and then headed for the front door with Diffenbaugh in his wake. "I'd never entrust Tesla into the care of a teenager. Not even you."

Finley couldn't help but smile. He wanted to go back to trusting the professor without the slightest semblance of doubt or suspicion, but this new light shed on Understanding and mind control—and how it had unquestionably been used on his family to see to his placement at Brighton—put Finley in a tough spot.

He told himself that the first opportunity he got, he would write his family a letter to see how they were doing. An email or a phone call could be risky, as those avenues were easier to monitor. Finley had seen enough movies to know that.

"I'm sure there's a lot of pressure that comes with being 'special,' " the professor said, stopping Finley by the shoulder, "now that you know you can recharge. But, despite all that, there are things you can choose to shelve for a later day."

"What do you mean?"

"You're thirteen, Finley," Diffenbaugh said, finishing his bowtie and then putting his hands in his pockets. "You should be stressing about finals. Chasing after crushes. Heck, skip a class or two! Just don't tell anyone I condone that sort of behavior, okay?"

Finley breathed out through his nose, and then shrugged. "I want to be that kid, but how can I when I'm constantly looking over my shoulder?"

He could see an adjustment in the professor's eyes as they turned glassy. He regarded Finley, who stood outside his quarters in the morning sunlight.

"You're right, Finley." Diffenbaugh's tone was sharp, cutting into the air. "We haven't been doing enough. For that, I'm sorry. But I'm *not* going to make excuses anymore, and I want you to believe me when I say I *will* get to the bottom of everything. I *will* find out who James Olyphant is, and what his motives are."

Finley almost had to take a step back. The vigor in which the professor spoke with was highly uncharacteristic. He nodded once, then slammed his door shut, leaving Finley more startled than reassured.

He turned and headed for the mess hall, fingering the key in his right pocket and wondering if things would ever be normal for him at Brighton.

"Seems old," Miguel said, examining the key over breakfast.

"Excellent deduction, Sherlock," said Helena, leaning over and getting a look.

"You said you found this in the restroom?" Bridget took a bite out of her egg and sausage burrito.

"It was lying in the spot where I *swear* I saw my masked attacker standing." Finley took the key back quickly and stowed it in his wallet. Next, he took a drink of his pulpy orange juice and said, after wiping his mouth with the back of his arm: "And, as crazy as you guys might find this, I'm starting to rethink the whole Olyphant's-the-bad-guy thing."

Miguel pretended to choke on his breakfast. "I'm sorry—*what?*"

Finley lowered his voice and told them about what he learned of Understanding and mind control. He then switched to telling them about how his family had exhibited the very side effects of which Professor Diffenbaugh spoke.

"Intense," Helena said, checking over her shoulder for eavesdroppers.

In fact, she wasn't the only one who now seemed on edge and alert. Both Miguel and Bridget were glancing out of the corner of their eyes every so often.

"With final exams around the corner," Finley said, "I can't lose sleep over this kind of stuff. I just want to get through the semester."

"Even if this school ends up being responsible for illegal recruiting practices?" Bridget said, almost shouting. She calmed herself with quick breaths.

"Look, I say we use the upcoming holiday break to put our heads together," Finley suggested. "We take that time to do what Brighton and the Bolt Sovereign have failed to do—figure out who James Olyphant is. If this school *is* at fault for infringing on Understanding regulations, there's no telling what else. We may be on our own here."

"So does 'putting our heads together' require being in the library?" Miguel asked, his singed hair bobbling as he looked around the table. "Because I have no intentions of being in the library during holiday break thank you."

Bridget threw a crumpled napkin at him, and it hit him

right in the middle of the forehead. Finley was the first to laugh, and then, because of the infectious way of laughter, the whole table joined in. For a moment, albeit a short one, they weren't troubled, and they simply laughed until there were tears.

Chapter 16 | The Garden Of Glass And Ice

Halloween came on a warm, but crisp day, and, before Finley realized it, it had passed.

You see, while Brighton Preparatory School for Surgers held its annual costume party and corn maze in the greenway, Finley had been stuck in the library with most of his fellow eighth graders—prepping for an elaborate test Professor Ambrose had suddenly scheduled for the following day.

With a collective poor showing of midterm results from the eighth grade class, every subsequent test and assignment meant a lot more. There was no way any of them could afford to skip a much needed study period, partake in the Halloween festivities, and anticipate skating through the Control test.

Ergo, Finley missed Halloween.

What made matters worse was a particularly awkward exchange Finley had with the Caverly twins on the Thursday before the chargeball team's first away match since the Games of Illumination were reinstated.

"Think you can no-show to a tryout and then just talk to us?" Sarah said, bumping into his shoulder with hers as she and Michael walked away.

Finley chased after them down the exterior hall. "I told you! The nurse kept me in the recovery room for the whole night!"

"Did she board up the window, too?" Michael sneered.

Finley stopped. "You expected me to sneak out of the nurse's wing?"

But the Caverly twins had turned onto the greenway and were out of earshot. Finley was forced to collect his pride—which felt like it was lying around him in scattered fragments—and walk off to his next class.

Michael and Sarah didn't speak to him the rest of the year.

With the hardest stretch of the semester behind them, Finley and his friends were surprised to find that they had gotten into a rhythm of sorts. When it came to Literature for the Surger, they evenly separated the required readings among the four of them, and then came to the table and shared their notes. For homework in Surging and Its Basic Historical Origins, they met in the study lab and did their research with a joint effort.

The Science of Surging presented its own challenges, as most assignments were done in class with Professor Guggenheim's supervision.

"Don't you see how beautiful the equations are?" the professor would say, twisting his mustache from behind his pulpit as his class slaved away on tedious problems. "Only until you can break down the structure of the Root's components will you be able to fully wield the gifts that a surger is capable of! *That's* beauty!"

"But I don't *wanna* break down the structure of the Root's components," Miguel said after class as they walked away from the lecture hall.

Finley held his friend's books as he adjusted his Lofstrand crutches. When he heard Helena and Bridget start to talk about some cute boy from their class, Finley lowered his voice and said to Miguel: "Hey, so, I've been wondering about something."

"Yeah? What's up?"

"Sorry if I'm out of line for asking this," Finley said, slipping Miguel's books into his backpack for him. "But, well, why can't you just Mend your injury?"

Miguel smiled. "Not out of line, trust me. Mending only works on minor injuries. Cuts, maybe a broken bone, stuff like that. Plus, there's a certain window of time that you have to Mend before it won't work properly, at which point you have to just let your body do the healing."

Finley nodded. "Gotcha. So, does that you mean you can't Lunge or Fuel?"

"Well, let's see." Miguel stopped unexpectedly, causing Bridget to run into his back. He slipped his hands out of his crutches and handed them to Finley before he could argue. Then, Miguel put on his glove and, with beautiful flair, he Fueled in a figure eight across the greenway—shedding the neon pink specks in his trail.

He stopped where he'd started, wobbling so that Finley and Helena had to reach out and keep him upright.

"Miguel that was awesome!" Helena said as Miguel leaned on his crutches.

Finley thumped his friend on the arm. "Dude, you just Fueled better than most freshmen!"

"I started to practice on the day I found out I was going to Brighton," Miguel admitted, as they continued strolling across the grass. "Apparently my body operates like normal when I'm surging. But then, when I stop, it's back to the crutches."

Helena offered to help him take his glove off, but Miguel said he wanted to keep it on until they got to their next class. She said, Okay, and they began guessing at what the school cooks would have in store for dinner that evening.

The next few weeks rolled by in lethargic fashion, and Finley surprisingly came to a place where things happened as he expected them to, with no more bombshells, like

Ambrose being absent from tutoring, and Doug gloating loudly to his friends about his fancy launching kick, which—did you hear?—had put Finley in the nurse's wing for an entire night!

Ignoring Doug became harder and harder, but Finley had no other choice. He instead channeled his energy into things he could control, such as recharging.

During the weeks leading up to Thanksgiving, Finley had acquired a bucket-sized portion of dead batteries, and he used them to practice recharging behind the boys' dorm houses. The only thing that made it difficult to concentrate when he Lunged over palm trees and across the grass was that he always had an audience.

The Enhancer Force never let a student out of their sight.

Their presence seemed to have multiplied since they were first introduced after Finley's attack. They watched, from a distance, as students ambled to classes. They were there, standing like statues beside the tiki torches on the outskirts of the mess hall. They sat in corners of the study lab. They peered around shelves in the library.

Always they watched, always they observed. Though their being on the Brighton campus was meant to instill a sense of safety, all the Enforcers were doing, really, was creating atmospheric fear...

Sometimes, because the masked and uniformed surgers were so stealth, Finley would forget they were in the same classroom he was in, and he would jump in his desk when he caught them staring at him.

On Thanksgiving eve, a particularly cloudy Wednesday, the female representative from the Bolt Sovereign returned, only, she addressed the school in a more impersonal way this time:

"I am pleased to announce that the Bolt Sovereign has uncovered the truth about the monster debacle," she said emotionlessly, her voice cackling through the speakers in the mess hall.

Finley and his friends stopped eating their dinner to listen.

"As you know," she continued, "the surging community has worked closely with the pedestrian government over the last century to approve sanctions—sanctions that sectioned off land for us. Well, because of a clerical error, there was an 'overlap' in land distribution.

"It seems Brighton was built on top of an underground government laboratory, and what you students witnessed was an experiment gone wrong."

Finley almost laughed out loud. Bridget shook her head. Helena rolled her eyes and returned to her meal. Miguel mouthed, *Sure*, and then took a drink.

"The lab existed covertly because of its top secret operations," the representative stated, like she was reading from a script, "and it will now be moving to a different location."

Experiment gone wrong? Finley thought to himself, mouth agape in disbelief.

"So we're to believe that a preparatory school was coexisting with a secret lab," Bridget said, twirling her fork into the spaghetti on her plate. "And not once, until now, did either parties notice?"

Finley looked away from his table, and he spotted Parker standing in a queue in front of the smoothie cart. Their eyes met. Parker seemed to say with his expression, *Now* do you believe me?

Finley swallowed, then went back to his dinner.

Thanksgiving day finally arrived, and Finley slept in until 10:00 a.m. When he emerged from beneath his covers, he found Miguel sitting upright on his bed—unscrewing the back plate to a megaphone. Once Miguel heard Finley stirring, he swept everything under his covers and climbed down his ladder, where his Lofstrand crutches stood propped up against the wall.

"Only a couple more weeks until Quinn gets back," said Miguel, walking toward Finley. "Then I'll have to give up the top bunk."

Finley yawned. "Why?"

"Technically it was assigned to him," Miguel answered, leaning on his crutches. "I only took it when he was suspended. Ready to go grab breakfast?"

"Hope you guys have been stretching your stomachs," Parker said, walking out of the restroom with a towel wrapped around his lower half.

"I really hope you're going to explain yourself," Miguel replied, his eyebrows up.

"You know," Parker said in his tiny voice. His auburn hair was dripping wet. "Before Thanksgiving you're supposed to eat a whole lot, to stretch your stomach. That way you can stuff your face." He twitched, and then, before either Miguel or Finley could respond, he retreated to the closet to put on his clothes.

"If that's the case I've been preparing for this day for a *long* time," Miguel declared merrily.

Finley laughed from his bed, then swung his feet around and headed into the bathroom to brush his teeth.

They would end up spending most of the day on the beach, since Brighton had reopened it, and Finley ran up and down the shore and Lunged into the air—catching the football passes that Miguel spiraled over the sand and water.

Bridget and Helena cheered them on, but teased Finley when he would drop a pass. He challenged them, betting that they couldn't do a better job because they were girls, after all. Helena stood up, dusted the sand off her shorts, and ordered Miguel to chuck the football.

Reluctantly he complied, and Helena darted across the sand. She ended up catching the football with one hand, and she didn't have to surge.

"As you were, boys," she said, tossing the football back

to Finley.

He and Miguel decided it was time to head to Watt's Up for lunch.

Night fell, and after Finley and his friends all washed up for dinner, they met outside the girls' dorm houses and walked to the mess hall together. They found the round tables draped in linen, and sparkling dishware was set with folded napkins. The tiki torches burned with the abounding smell of amber and assorted spices, and orange LED lights hung from the patio ceiling.

Finley and his peers marveled at the décor as they found seats and chatted eagerly.

Roasted turkey was served with mashed red potatoes, sweet corn, stuffing, deviled eggs, and four different potato salads. There was such an abundance of food that Finley was able to help himself to thirds. Everything tasted fabulous, as if the foods had been cooked for royalty.

Finley caught Miguel loosening his belt after his fourth helping, and he contemplated doing the same thing. But, when Finley grabbed his buckle circumspectly, he met Helena's eyes across the table, and she gave him the most disturbed gaze. He jerked his hand up, laughing awkwardly and forcibly at something Bridget said.

Dean Longenecker, who was sitting with the rest of the faculty at a long table in the center of the mess hall, tapped her fork against her glass and stood. Next, she pointed her gloved hand at the ceiling, which slightly brightened the

LED lights—enough so that she was certain all could see her.

"With a meal like this, what's *not* to be thankful for?" she said, to which the mess hall responded with laughter and applause. "Enjoy these next few days, because classes will resume in full force on Monday!"

The laughing and applauding tapered off.

"I did want to take this opportunity," the dean continued, "while I have you all gathered here, to remind you that our Christmas banquet and dance is set for the second Sunday of December. One of my favorite events that we host here at Brighton, so I hope you're all as stoked as I am."

Christmas banquet and dance? Finley thought fretfully. He hadn't considered dating since...well, since Melanie Plum back in Huntington Beach. It was not that taking a girl to a school dance was the equivalent to dating her, but Finley figured it would take the same amount of courage to ask in both scenarios.

"Dances are stupid," Miguel said beside Finley. Then, to Bridget and Helena: "Be our dates?"

"Ppff," Helena said, crossing her legs under the table. "You two want us to go with you, you had better find a more creative way to ask us."

"We're *girls*, you know," Bridget added.

Finley and Miguel glanced at each other out of the sides of their eyes. For the first time in a long while, neither of them knew what to say.

That following Monday, the campus had been transformed, as if overnight.

The palm trees were draped in multicolored lights. Fake snow covered the campus roofs. The greenway had been turned into an exhibit, showcasing massive glass sculptures. There was a rearing reindeer. A life-size light bulb. A bolt of lightning jutting up from the ground. A glistening pine tree.

It was the stuff of theme parks or art galleries. Finley could not believe how much detail and effort had been put into the decorations. There was even a small patch of ice built into the ground, wide enough for figure skating, and Finley was told that advanced design beneath the installation kept the ice chilled and frozen; coolers ran on individual generators around the clock.

But there was something more unbelievable, even, than all of the Christmas displays: Bridget and Helena had avoided Finley and Miguel since the Thanksgiving dinner.

"You know what they're doing, don't you?" Miguel asked at breakfast Monday morning. They sat with three other boys from their grade because Bridget and Helena had chosen to eat with Lauren Woods and a couple freshmen girls.

"They're playing tricks with our minds," Miguel

continued, wolfing down his French toast. "It's what they do."

"So, why don't we just find a way to ask them that's...," Finley said, struggling to say the last part: "...that's *romantic.*"

"Finley. Whoa." Miguel dropped his fork. "We're busy men. How are we supposed to find time for that?"

Finley shrugged. He glanced over at Bridget and Helena's table. They were whispering to the girls at their table, even though they were far enough away that no one in Finley's group stood a chance overhearing them. He felt his face blush, so he pivoted in his seat and looked in the complete opposite direction.

In their first class of the day, Literature for the Surger, Finley and Miguel found as much tension as there had been in the mess hall. Bridget and Helena didn't save them seats. They were sitting at the front of the long table, talking with their hands cupped over their mouths. When Finley and Miguel tried getting their attention, they looked over their heads as if they hadn't heard them.

This went on for days.

Finley and Miguel noticed a steep decline in their schoolwork productivity. It was harder to stay focused in the library without Bridget there to keep them on task, and their discussions lacked Helena's witty remarks, which consequently made the hours seem longer. Even the librarian, who was accustomed to staying near their table so he could reproach Helena for being obnoxious, seemed vexed by the girls' absence.

Finally, on the morning of the dance, Finley stormed out of his dorm room in his gym shorts and T-shirt, marched down the stairs and through the lounging area, and stalked across the paved path that separated the boys' and girls' housing.

He stopped on the grass when he heard the hum of the plasma trap, and cried out: "Bridget! Helena! You guys there?"

A couple of faces appeared in different level windows. Thankfully, one of them was Bridget's. A moment later, she walked out the main door with Helena.

"Finley?"

"Is everything okay?"

"Look," he said, improvising. "I know Miguel said dances are lame, but, well, I mean, I guess I sorta agree with him. But that's not the point. Er, I know they're important to you two. Dances, that is—"

"Fin, you're rambling," Helena interrupted.

"Right. Yeah. So, you guys—I mean, *girls*—mean a lot to me. But, you've become, like, my best friends, you know? I guess what I'm asking is will you go to the dance with us, as friends? No pressure."

Bridget and Helena were silent for a full minute.

"That's probably as good a romantic gesture as we're gonna get out of these two," Bridget said to Helena, who folded her arms.

"Yeah, but shouldn't Miguel be here too?" she asked. "Oh—nope, there he is."

They all looked over and saw Miguel, standing in the threshold of the boys' dorm house. When he noticed them watching him, he yawned theatrically and pretended to stare at the morning clouds.

"We see you, Miguel," Bridget called out to him. He feigned surprise, then shouted back.

"Huh? Oh, hey guys!"

"Fine," Helena said to Finley, drawing his attention back in. "Be here at six to pick us up."

Finley smiled with relief. "You got it." And then he walked back to his dorm house with his chin up and a spring in his step.

That evening, while Finley and Miguel got ready for the banquet and dance, they borrowed some of Parker's hair gel and attempted to de-wrinkle their pants and shirts with the iron in the dorm room closet.

Parker, who had been asked to the dance by Lauren, intervened when Miguel's sleeve began to smoke. He then insisted on ironing both Miguel and Finley's clothes.

"Dude gets asked out by a girl *and* knows how to iron," Miguel said, watching with awe. "I might've underestimated you."

Parker twitched and kept silent.

Once they all deemed each other presentable, they walked down the stairwell and headed for the girls' dormitories. They were early, which Finley said was probably a good thing. Almost singly, girls began to trickle out of the two houses with sparkling dresses and their hair in bows—off to meet their dates. Finley tried not to stare.

He almost didn't recognize Bridget and Helena when they finally appeared with Lauren, who was perhaps the most different-looking of the three. They all had on lacy dresses (Bridget's and Lauren's had sleeves) and wore lightly applied makeup on their faces.

"Whoa," Miguel said. Bridget flushed, but Helena elbowed her—urging her to remain nonchalant and confident.

"You, uh, you look really nice," Finley told Helena, who looped her arm around his. She whipped her bangs out of her eyes coolly, but Finley was sure he could see the restraint of a smile.

They walked in front of Parker and Lauren, but behind Miguel and Bridget, who were laughing at something one of them had said.

"Your cologne is, um, *strong*," Helena noted.

"Huh? Oh, that's probably Miguel's you're smelling. He all but brushed his teeth with the stuff."

Helena giggled.

They merged onto the greenway with the rest of their

peers. Tables set for six were placed around and among the glass sculptures, and Finley and Helena followed Miguel and Bridget to the one beside the rearing reindeer.

"This is all so pretty," Lauren said, as Parker pulled out her seat for her so she could sit down. Finley was positive those five words were the most Lauren had ever spoken around him. With her gothic persona stripped, Lauren was practically a different person.

"Ahem," Helena said out of the side of her mouth. Finley started, then jumped into action—mimicking Parker and pulling out his date's wooden chair.

There was a snow globe in the middle of the table, surrounded by candles in mason jars and snowflake coasters. A server wearing a red vest over a ruffled shirt appeared, pouring chilled water into their glasses.

This puts mom's charity dinners to shame! Finley mused, wondering of what the dinner would consist. There were track lights on the ground next to every sculpture, shooting up a warm glow. The result was that the glass seemed to shine from within.

"Sir, the wine list please," Miguel said seriously. The server arched an eyebrow, then moved on to the next table.

"Worth a shot," Miguel said, shrugging.

Somewhere, on the other side of the greenway, carolers had begun singing "O Holy Night." Finley watched Parker and Lauren, and when they had started talking amongst themselves, he leaned over and said, so only Miguel,

Bridget, and Helena could hear: "Winter break starts in one week, guys."

"Which means we'll all be heading home to collect the gifts the fat man leaves under the tree." Miguel put his hands behind his head.

"Which *means*, it's time to get serious," Finley continued in a low voice. "It's time to dig our heels in and get to work. We have to figure out who James Olyphant is."

"You know," said Helena, flattening out a crease in her dress. "As rad as all of that sounds, could we maybe talk about it *after* dinner?"

"O-Oh," Finley stammered. "Of course, I just…" He stopped himself short. Finley understood how much the banquet meant to Bridget and Helena, but was it really so significant that they couldn't discuss their game plan—even leisurely?

"I've got to tinkle," Helena said suddenly. "Bridget, Lauren. Join me?" All three girls got up and left without another word, leaving Finley and Miguel to drink their waters distractedly.

"You think I said anything wrong?" Finley asked Miguel.

"Hm? When?"

"To Helena. Just now."

Miguel didn't have an answer for him, so they both turned to Parker, who held his glass importantly and shook his head.

Finley: "What?"

"You guys are blowing it," he replied, sloshing his drink around like it was more than simply water.

Miguel scoffed. "Who, us?"

"Have you complimented their dresses?"

Silence.

"Have you told them how pretty they look tonight?"

No response. Finley meant to say that he had, but he was too slow.

"Have you thanked them for doing you the honor of being your date?"

Miguel opened his mouth, but Parker was faster still:

"You tell them you're looking forward to dancing?"

Miguel cleared his throat. "Listen, Caesar, you—"

"Caesar's the dog whisperer," Parker interrupted. "I think you mean Dr. Phil."

"Whatever," Miguel said, waving his hand. "Me and Fin are doing just fine, you hear?"

Parker twitched, then sipped his water. "Loud and clear."

"Aren't you supposed to be the shy one?" Finley asked Parker, who was examining his cuticles under the candlelight.

The girls returned to the table, and only Parker stood up until they were all seated. Finley and Miguel, when they realized the missed cue, got to their feet frantically—but by then Bridget and Helena had already sat down.

Bridget asked, "Going somewhere?"

"Nah, just stretching for the dance," Miguel said smoothly as he and Finley plopped back onto their chairs. "Which, by the way, is going to be one awesome dance."

Bridget looked unconvinced.

Finley turned to Helena as the server returned with menus printed on parchment. They each took one, thanked the server, but Finley immediately set his down on the plate and said, "So, Helena, um, Michigan. It's probably mad cold up there right now, huh?"

Helena kept her eyes fixed on the menu. "Mhm."

"You miss it? The cold?" He folded his hands on the table. "I mean, this is your first winter away from home, right?"

Because Finley's tone gradually turned more genuine, Helena became more receptive. "I mean, sorta. Me and my folks used to fly down to Florida every Christmas."

"Just you and your parents? So you don't have any siblings?"

"No." Helena put her menu on the table. The carolers started "Joy To The World." "They talked about adoption, but it never went anywhere."

"I've got an older sister. Erin. Pretty sure she hasn't noticed yet that I haven't been home for months."

"Really? You guys fight a lot then?"

"No, but I kinda wish we did," Finley said, scooting his chair closer to Helena's. "At least that would be interaction. Erin's got her own thing going, and I'm just someone who shares the same roof as her and has the same last name."

Helena smiled flirtatiously. "Is that a pity party I hear coming on?"

"Yeah right," Finley said, eyes rolling. "Trust me—you don't know Erin."

"I believe you," she said.

A moment passed between them.

"So, what are you gonna order?" Finley asked, picking his menu back up. "Lobster or steak?"

"I was thinking both," she answered.

Finley laughed. When he went for his water and took a sip, he felt a hand touch his shoulder. It was Professor Diffenbaugh.

"Hey, everyone," he said to the table, smiling a toothy smile. "Mind if I borrow Finley for a moment?" No one answered, most likely because they all wondered if he was in trouble.

"Uh, I'll be right back," Finley told Helena, slipping out from his chair and following the professor to the exterior hall. They had to sidestep around passing servers and banquet attendants.

"Sir?" Finley said when they reached the statue of the man with the bulb. "Everything all right?"

"Yes, absolutely," Diffenbaugh said, unbuttoning his formal suit jacket. "I just wanted you to be the first to know that the Enhancer Force is making its first arrest in regards to your attack."

Finley felt a rush of blood go straight to his head. "They are? Who is it?"

"Wally Grondahl—the campus driver."

"I...what were they able to find?" Finley hoped his arrest wasn't based solely on the suspicions he'd relayed to the Enhancer.

"Supposedly, a lot." The professor gave the impression that he was restraining. Holding back. Keeping something in check. His anger, no doubt. "He's in cahoots with someone on the Brighton staff, and the two of them may even have been responsible for the electric ghost's attack, too. They found an offshore account under his name, and he's been receiving large sums of cash over the course of the entire semester..."

The rest of the professor's sentence drowned out, and three words rang in Finley's head: the electric ghost. Diffenbaugh just referred to the monster in the way Parker had, which most likely meant he too believed in the theories of willing and suppressing the Root. The professor noticed, whether by silence or a facial expression, that Finley was shuffling through his thoughts.

"Finley?"

"You don't think it was an 'experiment gone wrong' then?"

"Pardon my language," Diffenbaugh said, dropping his

voice to a whisper. "But *hell* no. If the Bolt Sovereign has only one thing in common with ped government, it's this: secrets. I wouldn't be surprised if these incidents were common, and, likewise, *commonly* written off."

Finley could feel a chill, and then goose bumps spread up his arms. "Has the Enhancer Force figured out who Wally was working with?" *Dean Longenecker?* he thought to himself and almost said out loud.

"No," the professor replied. He stuffed his hands into his pant pockets. "But it won't take much effort on the Bolt Sovereign's part to get Wally to crack."

Finley sure hoped he'd been right in telling the Enhancer what he had. Either Wally *was* involved in some elaborate plan with James Olyphant and had helped arrange Finley's attack, or the Brighton driver was innocent—and mere hours away from wrongful imprisonment.

And it will be here soon, Wally had said behind the statue. I'll make sure the timing is right.

If he hadn't been referring to the electric ghost's attack, then what? And there was still the mystery of *whom* Wally had been talking with, and where they had vanished to when Finley had come around the corner.

"I'm sorry to have put a damper on your night," Diffenbaugh said, pulling out his right hand and placing it on Finley's shoulder. "I just thought you deserved to know. The dean's probably going to keep this quiet—I'm not even sure I'm supposed to be telling you."

"Thanks," Finley said.

"You go and enjoy the rest of your night," the professor encouraged, winking. "Nice job with your date, by the way."

Finley flushed. "What! No, she's not...we're friends."

Diffenbaugh chuckled. "Hey, you know? That's a good place to start."

Finley wasn't sure what the professor was implying, but he wasn't in the right place to argue further. His thoughts were careening and sloshing and tossing around in his head, as if stuffed into a blender that was turned up to full blast.

If Wally Grondahl and Dean Longenecker were somehow involved in James Olyphant's schemes, it would mean that the dean had been lying to everyone's face. Her bringing in the Enhancer Force had been part of the show. Her urging Finley to leave everything up to the authorities had been an act. Her concern, her promise to get to the bottom of it all—lies.

Yet, in the midst of it all, two questions shone through—bolded, italicized, and underlined:

Why were the driver and the dean working with Olyphant? What was the purpose of bringing Finley to Brighton, only to have him told that the school was lying to him and that he needed to leave? Would it not have been easier to intercept Finley *before* he was on campus?

Something wasn't adding up.

Finley half waved to Diffenbaugh before turning around and heading back to his table. Before he got too far, however, he heard the professor calling out to a passing campus groundskeeper.

"Hey! You know, it's been over a *month* since I put in for that request," Professor Diffenbaugh said irritably. "How hard is it to change a couple of locks?"

Finley stopped in his tracks.

"We're working on it," the female groundskeeper said impatiently. "The holiday décor always sets us back—"

"My spare apartment key gets stolen," the professor said, "and you guys are more worried about hanging mistletoe?"

Finley's heart rate almost tripled. The key he'd found, in the boys bathroom in the nurse's wing. Coincidence?

The groundskeeper shifted her weight. "We'll send someone over first thing next week—"

"Yeah, all right," the professor said sarcastically, buttoning his formal suit jacket and tugging at the bottom. "Sorry—I'm not angry with you, but I've been hearing that for weeks." He then turned and swept back onto the greenway.

Finley stood in the shadow of the glass pine tree sculpture, wondering what he should do about the key. There was a good chance that it was not the one to the professor's quarters, but, then, there was also a good chance that it *was*.

There's no way things can get any weirder, Finley said inwardly, walking back to his table—his mind inundated with yet another confusing layer.

Chapter 17 | The Gatherer

When Finley returned to his table, there was a medium rare steak on his plate, as well as steaming mixed vegetables and a fluffy roll.

"Miguel ordered for you," Helena said as Finley took his seat.

"Was I really gone that long?" he asked, laying his napkin across his lap.

Helena nodded.

"Yeah," she replied. "Everything cool?"

"I'll explain later."

Parker and Lauren were in their own world, feeding each other bites of their respective meals and laughing when Lauren dropped a steamed carrot onto Parker's lap. Miguel and Bridget, however, watched Finley worriedly.

"Really," he assured them. "Everything's fine. Let's eat and then—"

"Don't gotta tell me twice," Miguel interrupted, tucking his napkin into the top of his shirt like a bib and cutting into his fish.

Finley chuckled, but it wasn't a natural response. It was a front. He was distracted by Wally's impending arrest, what the implications could be if he was guilty of involvement with Olyphant, and Professor Diffenbaugh's stolen key.

Finley must have been staring off into space because Helena nudged him gently. He smiled at her, then took his roll and lathered it in butter.

The rest of the night proved to be quite entertaining, with ice-skating immediately following dinner. Most of the girls sat this out, stating they weren't dressed properly, and instead sipped hot cocoa with mini marshmallows and whipped cream.

Finley and his friends partook in the ice-skating, but purely as spectators. See, only a handful of their classmates were actually able to stay on their skates longer than thirty seconds, which resulted in comic gold. Somehow, seeing freshmen attempt to Fuel on the ice and then fail miserably and painfully never got old. At one point, a junior tried Fueling and then Lunging, but he slipped before he left the ice—eventually landing on his head on the grass a dozen yards off.

Dean Longenecker stepped in and banned surging from the rink.

Once they got bored, Finley, Miguel, Bridget, and Helena walked over to the makeshift dance floor, which was set up beside a grouping of palm trees. It took a lot of coaxing to get Miguel to join them under the lights, but once he loosened up, it was impossible to get him to stop his butt-waggling frisk.

"Forever Young" came on, and Finley said he was thirsty, but Helena gave him a sharp look, so, he forced a nod, put his hands on her hips, and attempted to slow dance with her next to Bridget and Miguel—who looked like he'd rather be in any other situation than the one in which he found himself.

"Is this really so bad?" Helena asked, her hands on Finley's shoulders.

"No," Finley said, his voice sounding nasally, as if puberty had just hit him. He cleared his throat and repeated, "No, no. This is great."

"You look uncomfortable."

"I'm not. Promise."

"Then you're distracted?"

Finley didn't say yes or no.

"It's about what Professor Diffenbaugh said, isn't it?"

"I'm sorry! It's just, he said the Enhancer Force is going to make its first arrest!"

"They are?" Helena appeared interested, not upset.

"Well, who is it?"

"The school driver. Wally."

Helena considered this, but gave no response. What she did do, however, was step closer to Finley as they danced. He opened his mouth to ask her what she thought, but opted to remain silent the rest of their dance.

The song ended. Students clapped. Professor Diffenbaugh, who was playing the role of D.J., announced there would be one final song before the festivities ended.

Finley and Helena broke apart. A half grin appeared on the side of her face, and she leaned in to say something, but caught herself at the last second.

Finley said, "Thanks for dancing with me."

Helena said, "Anytime."

And the two of them walked over to the hot chocolate station, where Miguel and Bridget were already waiting.

Because Monday marked the last day before the start of finals, every professor conducted light lessons or focused on reviews.

Professor Templeton read to the class for nearly the entire period. The novel she had selected was written by a former colleague, she explained elatedly, and it was entitled *Once The Surger Fell*.

It was dramatic fiction, and it bored Finley into a trance, though he did appreciate the mental break. Somewhat.

" 'Oh Tiffany, sweet Tiffany,' " the professor read, in a state of hysterical rapture. She held the trade paperback in her hands and paced before the long table. " 'If I could but possess only one phase of surging, it would be to Mend. For you see, if you choose to take Mr. Gouker's hand in marriage, I will be forced to Mend my broken heart all the days, all the days, all the hard aching days!' "

Miguel made a gagging noise, but quickly turned it into a fake sneeze once every girl shot him a furious glare.

Professor Diffenbaugh gave his Surging and Its Basic Historical Origins class a free study period. He sat at his desk and read from the newspaper while Finley and his peers scrambled to cram any important dates or figures that might make an appearance come finals time. The professor offered to field any last minute questions, but all anyone did was concentrate on memorization.

I bet there's a way to use Understanding *that gives a surger photographic memory*, Finley thought, scratching his chin. And in that brief window of contemplation, Bridget snapped her fingers at Finley urgently and pointed to the text they were all reading.

During lunch, when Finley was finally able to tell Miguel, Bridget, and Helena how his talk with Professor Diffenbaugh had gone at the Christmas banquet, the mess hall went unexpectedly silent.

Everyone was staring past the line of tiki torches, where two Enhancers were towing a surprisingly willing Wally

Grondahl across the greenway. He glanced over at the tables, caught Finley's eye line, blinked once, and then was taken out of sight.

Finley felt something in the pit of his stomach. It bestirred itself at the sight of the school driver. Regret. Regret for having said something to the Enhancer, for turning Wally in based on a hunch.

Professor Diffenbaugh said they had a lot on him, Finley told himself as he returned to his tacos. *I did the right thing.*

So why did he feel so guilty?

In the Science of Surging, Finley could barely focus. Professor Guggenheim had reserved the entire class for open questions. Finley knew he was most likely missing valuable material anytime one of his peers raised his or her hand because the professor responded by either writing an equation on the board, or directing the asker to the appropriate page in the textbook. Yet Finley couldn't erase the image in his mind of Wally Grondahl being escorted across the campus…his face bearing the resolve of dread, and not necessarily guilt…

This led Finley to wonder what the Enhancer Force intended to do with Wally once he was incarcerated. Would it be like those crime films? Cold, blue room with dim lighting. A single table. A good cop, a bad cop.

Or would Wally be…tortured?

Finley was quiet on the walk to Control. His friends did not notice because they were busy lamenting about the difficulties they were sure to face in Guggenheim's test come Wednesday.

"I have a friend back in Riverside who can opt out of his science final if he memorizes the periodic table!" Miguel said, pouting. "Why can't we do that?"

"You can't remember to shower every morning," Helena gibed. "What makes you think you could remember one hundred and eighteen elements?"

"Oh ha, ha."

When they walked into Ambrose's octagon classroom, they were shocked to see someone *other* than the professor standing in front of the dry erase board. It was a man in his late forties, wearing a prospector's outfit—down to the suspenders and knee-high boots. There were even bits of dirt and dross on his thick beard, and the ruffled bandana that was wrapped around his neck was torn and stained.

The man plucked at his black beard as Finley and the rest of the class were seated. Parker, who was one of the last ones inside the classroom, set his bag down and walked right up to the man, exchanging a few words with him.

"All right, let's get settled." Ambrose stomped through the door and walked down the center aisle to his desk—his suit jacket whipping like a flag. Parker went back to his seat.

"Since this class will be taking its Control final on Thursday," the professor continued, pouring himself a cup of coffee from his French press. "I think it's safe to assume you all will *not* retain any new material these next few days."

Finley folded his hands and set them on his desktop, curiously watching the man, who now hooked his thumbs around his suspender straps. He was beaming at the students in a rather goofy manner.

"I thought it might be enlightening to have a surger come and speak about his career," Ambrose said without color, putting the French press down and sipping his black coffee. "Special thanks to Parker Tenbrook for lending us his father for the afternoon."

So this is Parker's dad, Finley thought, *the one who supposedly hunts electric ghosts.*

Mr. Tenbrook tipped his dusty cavalry hat at the classroom, and then stepped forward. He scanned the rows and desks, his eyes twinkling. Finley started to feel uncomfortable after a whole minute had elapsed, but Parker's father finally clapped his hands and spoke.

"Wow, there's a lot of synergy here. Can you guys feel it? It's practically palpable!" His voice was hard and tough, like battle-worn leather.

Finley shared a perplexed look with Miguel.

"You may not feel it yet," Mr. Tenbrook said again, "but you'll learn to. Now! Who wants to raise their hand and tell me what career most interests them?"

Because of the leap in topics, it took a few seconds for the class to catch up. One of Finley's classmates, a boy named Brendan, put his hand in the air.

"Might be cool to be an Enhancer," he said after he was called on.

"Good, good," Mr. Tenbrook replied happily. "They've a lot of responsibilities, those Enhancers. Keepers of the peace. Who else?"

Lauren Woods raised her hand. "Cadaver Observer," she said emotionlessly.

"Okay, okay," Mr. Tenbrook chuckled. "Tough job, that is. In charge of examining those whose lives were taken by surging. Anyone else?"

Someone said Mender, and then another student said Archivist—a job where the main goal was filing and organizing historical texts and lore. After a couple more job titles were thrown out, Mr. Tenbrook took off his hat and tossed it onto Ambrose's desk. The professor was grading papers, and idly slid the hat aside so he could resume.

"These are all great, truly *great* careers," Mr. Tenbrook said, holding up a finger. "But you've forgotten one. Probably the most thrilling and rewarding job in all of the surging community!

"Gatherer."

There were no murmurs or whispers of agreement, which probably meant Finley wasn't the only one who hadn't heard of this profession.

"A Gatherer," Mr. Tenbrook went on, "gathers! I

travel all across the world in pursuit of lost things. Strange things. Terrifying things. *Wonderful* things. Your very own Professor Ambrose here currently has two of my findings present!"

He marched over to the side of the classroom, where the two see-through cubes displayed the twisted tree branches.

Mr. Tenbrook said, "These were cut from a lightning-struck willow. See, trees that have been scorched in an electric storm are said to possess the highest quantity of the Root."

"But no one has been able to effectively extract the Root from lightning-struck trees," Doug said coolly. In the desk next to him, Parker looked aghast by his friend's outburst.

"Well, um, *no*," Mr. Tenbrook admitted, walking back to the front of the classroom. "But we've been working on that for years, and I strongly believe we're getting close!"

Mr. Tenbrook tried to not sound unsettled or thrown off as he continued to detail his job tasks and duties. He told them that one of the more difficult hurdles to jump was corralling enough funding for each of his team's expeditions.

He then shared a few war stories, including one ridiculous anecdote that had him and a colleague pinned in a cave on an island off the east coast. They were hiding for their lives from a band of bloodthirsty surger pirates, and, had it not been for Mr. Tenbrook's quick suggestion to create a diversion using Understanding and dynamite and a shark tooth, he and his colleague would probably still be trapped.

He finished his presentation and bowed, which was met with scattered clapping. Miguel twirled his finger next to his temple and mouthed to Finley, *Crazy!* Mr. Tenbrook said he would be happy to take any questions, but there were none.

After the bell rung, Finley collected his backpack and followed his friends outside. It seemed that every single one of their classmates was whispering about how that period had been a waste of study time.

"I mean, I can see Diffenbaugh doing something like that," said Helena, exasperated. "But *Ambrose?* What was the point?"

"Gatherers sound about as necessary as Ghostbusters," Miguel added.

Finley kept his opinions to himself as they headed down the exterior hall, passing by the miniature Christmas trees that lined the path. Finley stopped when he heard Mr. Tenbrook's voice projecting from outside Ambrose's classroom.

"I'll meet up with you guys later," Finley said unexpectedly, spinning around and jogging back to meet Parker's father. Miguel, Bridget, and Helena were too stunned to respond.

Finley arrived just as Professor Ambrose was thanking Mr. Tenbrook and heading back into his classroom.

"Ah! Mr. McComb!" he said delightedly, sticking out a hand.

Finley completed the salutation, shaking his hand and grinning widely. "Hello, sir."

"How do you think that went?" he asked eagerly. "Parker said everyone seemed *enthralled*!"

"Y-Yes," Finley stuttered, hastening to say the right thing. "I'm all enthralled out."

Mr. Tenbrook chortled even though Finley rolled his eyes at himself. He took Finley by the shoulder gently and led him onto the greenway. "My son's told me a lot about you. I'm ecstatic you two are such good friends."

Finley was humbled, and couldn't muster up a good reply.

"You know," said Mr. Tenbrook. They stopped by the glass light bulb sculpture. "The whole surging community is buzzing about you, Finley."

"T-They are?"

"Ohm's Law, son! Hasn't anyone told you how special recharging is? Before you came along, that ability was the stuff of legends." He took off his hat and held it before him. Then, he leaned in and added, "And, if not for those legends, it'd be like recharging never existed…"

"Yeah, well, that's kind of funny," Finley said frankly. "Because even though recharging is 'legendary,' I'm not getting much help from Brighton, to be honest. I'm just sort of fumbling my way through everything."

"Well, I don't suspect you'd get much help here—or anywhere, for that matter."

"Why?"

"No one's ever been able to recharge until you, remember?" Mr. Tenbrook said, smiling. "Who would know how to train you properly? Who would be able to field your questions? Critique your technique?"

Finley sighed at the rhetorical questions.

"I'm sure the professors are still running around behind closed doors, trying to figure out how recharging works exactly." Finely detected a lot of amusement in Mr. Tenbrook's voice, and even a bit of sarcasm.

"Comforting."

Mr. Tenbrook chortled again. "I wouldn't lose too much sleep over it, Finley. Even if you never get your big explanation that elucidates your unique abilities, you're going to make a fine young man."

Except that I'm at Brighton, Finley thought, frustrated. *A fine 'young man' is not good enough. I want to a fine surger.*

"So!" Mr. Tenbrook put his hat back on. "Did you come back to discuss more on the roles of a Gatherer? That profession suits you, by the way."

"Um, right," Finley said clumsily. "No, actually, but I did have a question."

"Shoot."

"It's about electric ghosts."

Mr. Tenbrook's eyes darkened. He stroked his full beard, looking distant.

"Sir? Do you really believe in them?"

"Yes," Mr. Tenbrook said, unabashedly, "they exist. Surgers, stockpiling the Root in their system to quench feelings of ecstasy."

"You think it's what attacked our stadium?"

Mr. Tenbrook looked around, like he was scoping out for eavesdroppers.

"I do," he whispered, nodding.

"Okay, so, why would a surger junkie be living underneath Brighton's stadium?" Finley asked. "And why would it have come out and gone crazy like that?"

"All questions I've been wrestling with since Parker texted me about the incident," he replied, his voice even lower. Finley had to read his lips. "My guess? It was a political move. Scare something like that out into the open, and it sheds a whole new light on surging."

"Unless the Bolt Sovereign keeps it in the dark," Finley said, referring to how the representative had succinctly explained the situation as an "experiment gone wrong."

"Precisely. Something they've been doing for many, many years." Mr. Tenbrook shot a glance over his shoulder. "I think it's why they—whoever arranged for the attack to happen—made Brighton the stage. What better way to grab hold of a community's attention than to put children at risk?"

It was an excellent point. Although, if the parents of Finley's peers were just as easily convinced as their children, this whole thing had probably blown over by now. Finley shivered at the thought.

"Probably shouldn't be discussing these things here, Fin—" Mr. Tenbrook started to say, but Finley cut him off:

"Why?" he demanded. "Are we not allowed to have opinions or theories in the surging community? That a crime?"

Mr. Tenbrook looked like he had just endured a bee sting. He tipped his hat at Finley, thanked him for their talk, and then headed for the administration building to sign out. Finley watched him go, flipping his head to the side to move his bangs. When he and the professor had talked about the electric ghost at the Christmas banquet, Diffenbaugh wasn't cautious with his words. What was Parker's father so worried about then?

After dinner, clouds rolled in, and, while there was no rain or thunder, it still felt like a storm was imminent. The moonlight was weak, and there was a chill in the air that hung with persistence.

Finley and Miguel were on their way to meet Bridget and Helena at the pier, when Doug Horn walked up beside them casually. His glasses and the semidarkness shrouded his eyes.

"Yo, Fin," Doug said, patting Finley on the back. "How's your back?"

"Did you need something?" Miguel said, interceding. "Or were you just planning on reasserting yourself as the school ass? Trust me, you put the 'ass' in re*ass*erting."

"You write your own material?" Doug asked, chuckling. "If not, fire your writer immediately."

"What do you need, man?" Finley said, halting where the paved path met the sand. He faced Doug with an uninterested stare.

The waves roared in the distance. Even though the beach was closed after dark, the pier was still open, and the lampposts—which were wrapped in garland—glowed against the dim blue sky.

Doug pushed up his glasses with his middle finger.

"Gonna be a cold night," he said. "I think they're calling for a storm."

"Enjoyed the company," Finley said sarcastically, and then he turned with Miguel and headed across the sand. Two Enhancers were pacing across the beach on either side of the pier, shining powerful searchlights over the shore.

"No, Fin, wait," Doug said, chasing after them.

"I'm good," Finley replied, not breaking his stride. Doug eventually jogged passed them and stopped between

Finley and the pier entrance.

"Please. I wanted to say sorry," said Doug, his hands up. Miguel laughed.

"A little late for that," he said, and Finley found that he had been thinking the same thing.

"Right, I know," Doug continued. "I guess I kinda pulled a fast one on you back in Ambrose's class, huh?"

Finley didn't answer.

"Which," Doug said, pulling his black glove out of his pocket, "is why I want to give you a fair shot."

"*What?*" Finley was sure he hadn't heard Doug correctly, or that, if he had, Doug was being facetious.

"I want to give you a fair shot," Doug repeated. "A rematch, if you wanna call it that."

By this point, a very small group of passersby had heard the word "rematch," and, because they assumed a fight—or something of that nature—was in store, they started to loiter around the pier entrance discreetly.

"No chance," Miguel said, leaning on his crutches. "Fin's got nothing to prove to you."

Finley startled himself by thinking, *No, I do have something to prove.* He absentmindedly felt around his waist, unsure if he had left his glove back at their dorm, and was darkly delighted when he felt his right pocket bulging.

Without indecision, Finley slowly pulled out the glove Professor Diffenbaugh had made him. There was a D battery strapped to the holster with electric tape, and the metallic, malleable material on his glove was starting to show wear.

Finley put his glove on his right hand.

"What are you doing, Fin?" Miguel hissed in his ear.

"That's the spirit," Doug said in his cocky way. "Twenty-five yards apart then? Just like in class?"

"Don't do this," Miguel begged, but Finley was already brushing past his friend and marching into position.

More students began to congregate. If Finley was going to humble Doug once and for all, they had better get started before the patrolling Enhancers decided to investigate the commotion.

I shouldn't risk suspension, Finley had told Professor Diffenbaugh when they were discussing putting Doug in his place. *But what's the harm in this? Friendly competition, that's all this is… And besides, Diffenbaugh practically gave me a free pass.*

"On three," Doug called over, "we'll see who can get in the first launching kick."

Finley clenched his gloved hand. The material folded against his will, feeling both smooth and coarse in his palm. The wires bent, and the battery glistened in the faint lighting.

"One!"

It seemed like the full eighth grade class had assembled for this "duel."

"Two!"

A few people actually shouted along with Doug. Finley's heart was beating louder than he'd ever heard it. He caught Miguel, out of the corner of his eye—watching on with a fear-filled gaze. Everything had happened so quickly, and, conversely, was moving so slowly now...

...*Three.*

Finley let go. He made himself available to the Root residues that resided in the dead D battery in his glove. He ran with his head down, sneakers kicking up sand.

Let the Root come to you, Finley ordered himself.

Doug was mere feet away.

Only a few breaths until they would meet.

Who would jump first?

The beach was silent.

Doug *froze*. Finley left the ground. He brought up his knees, he aimed his feet. Doug squinted, bracing for impact. He was Enhancing! Finley could see droplets of neon orange falling from his glove. This was his move—brace against Finley's launching kick.

It doesn't matter! Finley told himself in the split-second he was airborne. *He's going to pay!*

Finley's feet met Doug's chest, and then, in a blink, Finley pictured himself Lunging off of Doug's torso. What happened next was excruciatingly anticlimactic. Finley was able to successfully push off of Doug's chest, but he didn't Lunge. All he did was fall backwards and land on his butt a few inches back.

The pier went nuts with laughter.

Doug, who looked more surprised than anyone, joined in.

"No, no," Finley said, rushing to his feet.

He gripped his glove and mouthed, *Let go*, and then tried Lunging into the air over Doug. While he did manage to get off of the ground, it was no surge. He toppled forward, and Doug even had to catch him from falling over his own feet.

More laughter.

What's happening! Finley yelled inwardly. Was the battery not "dead" enough? Did it still have a faint charge? That shouldn't have mattered, though—he had surged with Helena's cell phone.

"Fin, c'mon," Miguel said, walking over to his friend's rescue.

"Back off," Finley snapped, and then he pushed Miguel, who almost fell. Thankfully, he was able to right himself with his Lofstrand crutches, and no further damage was done.

"I *can* surge!" Finley boomed.

"Then prove it," Doug said, his laughter abating. "Or was that time in Ambrose's class a fluke?"

Finley spun. He didn't know what was coming over him. It was like his actions were racing ahead of him...set free from the restraint of his conscience. Now, while he still wasn't able to surge, what he *did* do was throw Doug a fast punch to the mouth.

Miguel gasped. Doug's glasses slid over his head and plopped onto the beach.

Then, Professor Ambrose and an Enhancer appeared.

The crowd on the pier scattered. Finley panted, looking around in disbelief. Miguel watched him, like he was examining a monster behind protective glass. He shook his head, then left Finley alone with the professor, the Enhancer, and a bleeding Doug.

"Mr. McComb!" Ambrose thundered, grabbing him by the shoulder and yanking him back. The Enhancer tended to Doug, who had tears streaming down his cheeks. "Just what do you think you're doing!"

Finley's whole body was leaking perspiration. The back of his T-shirt felt soaked. "I...he..."

"That's the same student," the Enhancer said, after he'd Mended Doug's nose and sent him off to the dorm houses. He strode toward Finley and the professor, and his combat mask appeared particularly menacing in the limited moonlight.

"That's the same student who lied to me and snuck into the faculty housing," the Enhancer continued, arms folded.

No, no...this can't be happening right now.

"That true?" Professor Ambrose said, pulling Finley's glove off and confiscating it. "Did you lie to the Enhancer Force?"

Finley was sure the muscles in his mouth had

deteriorated, but he still found the strength to say, "Y-Yes...but—"

"If you're so easily misled," Ambrose said, turning to the Enhancer. "Perhaps your ability to perform your Enhancing duties should be called into question."

The Enhancer dropped his hands at his side, and Finley was sure he was about to witness a surger brawl. But the professor sighed and rounded on Finley again.

"Nevertheless, two offenses like this are inexcusable."

Finley nodded, bracing for his detention sentence.

"Suspension," Ambrose said coldly. Finley's ears started to ring. "Go straight to your dorm and pack your things. You leave for home first thing in the morning."

"Professor..."

Finley was stunned. He couldn't believe that in all of five minutes his entire world had come to a screeching, humiliating halt. The Enhancer, whose body language suggested he was satisfied with this ruling, tightened his gloves.

"Don't bother, Finley," Ambrose said, loosening his tie. "I don't know what you were thinking, but you've managed to dig yourself a big hole. Dean Longenecker will be by later to confirm your punishment, and she'll give you a slip your parents will have to sign—"

"You can't send me away!" Finley bellowed, words spilling off his tongue before he could think them through. "I can surge! *I swear!* I saw the neon lights, when Doug

Enhanced, which means the battery in my glove is probably just—!"

"Dorm. Now." Professor Ambrose pointed up the path without another word.

Finley's eyes watered. There was literally nothing he could say or do. What had been done, had been done. He was being sent away from Brighton. He was leaving his new home and going back to his old one.

He wouldn't even partake in finals, which, for the first time, sounded heartbreaking.

Chapter 18 | Home For The Holidays

Finley McComb read and then reread the slip Dean Longenecker had given him to pass along to his parents. This letter was not handwritten, like his last one:

Dear Mr. and Mrs. McComb:

We regret to inform you that your son, Finley Jacob McComb, has been suspended from Brighton Preparatory School for Surgers on one count of lying to the Enhancer Force, and on one count of striking a student. We have a no-tolerance policy toward this type of behavior, and we thank you in advance for understanding Brighton's longstanding disciplinary standards.

Finley will not only miss the last week of the fall semester, but he will not be allowed to return until after the first quarter of the spring semester. If he plans to stay on course with the rest of his eighth grade class, Finley will have to take his final exams at the end of February. He will also be required to fill his extracurricular activity slot with mandatory tutoring—all to ensure he is successfully caught-up on the material he's sure to miss in his absence.

Enclosed you'll find Finley's grades, with four zeros in place of the four final exams he is missing this week. Please sign below and return via USPS.

Thank you again for your cooperation in this matter, and we truly hope Finley returns with a fresh, renewed attitude.

Dean Margaret Longenecker
Brighton Preparatory School for Surgers
Est. 1956

Finley felt like crumpling the letter and tossing it out the window. He refrained, however, and instead stuffed it back into its envelope. The bus was empty, exactly like it had been on Finley's journey to Brighton. The driver was different. A young lady with highlights in her hair. She wore it in a bun and chewed gum and didn't talk to Finley.

He didn't mind, though. In fact, he appreciated it. He had plenty to consider and think about, which, sure, was wallowing, but what else could Finley do but wallow? The previous night had been nightmarish.

After his suspension sentence, he'd taken the long walk back to his dorm house. The lounging area had been empty. In his shared room, both Miguel and Parker were on their bunk beds. Unsurprisingly, Parker kept to himself. He didn't even ask why Finley was packing his things. Miguel refused to look Finley in the eye. He meant to apologize for shoving him on the beach, but the words never came. He was too embarrassed, and Miguel was idly disassembling a Nintendo Gameboy anyway.

So Finley packed in the quiet of his dorm room.

The next morning, Dean Longenecker showed up a little bit before seven. The dawn sky was dark and blue with clouds aplenty. Finley was standing by the window, staring through his soft reflection, when she had called his name. He'd been up for hours, unable to get a full night's sleep.

Let's go, Mr. McComb.

Finley followed her down the stairs wordlessly.

The same woodie that had picked up Finley from the beach months ago, was waiting outside the dorm house to take him away. An older man with a lot of wrinkles and tar-black sunglasses sat in the driver's seat in place of Wally Grondahl. He didn't get out to help Finley with his bag.

Take this to your parents, the dean said after she handed him an envelope. She wore a puffy jacket over her suit. It reminded Finley how cold it was on that December day. He couldn't feel much.

Okay, Finley muttered.

I'm sorry your semester has to end like this.

Me too.

Be safe, Finley, she said in an uncharacteristically gloomy voice. I hope to see you in a few weeks.

Finley climbed into the backseat, and the woodie lurched forward after he had shut the door. They cruised down a path that hugged the outer campus limits, and, thus, Finley wasn't able to take one last look at the greenway—or the rest of the Brighton grounds, for that matter.

A transit bus waited at the front gates. Finley got out of the woodie, threw his backpack on, and stepped up onto the bus. He took the furthest seat in the back, where he was now, holding the envelope addressed to his parents. He was unsure how they'd react to all this, considering Finley had managed to avoid detention for almost two years now. Suspension was a whole new ballgame, sure to have its own fireworks display.

The ride home was long, and there were four separate occasions where Finley contemplated putting his headphones on and listening to music. But all he did was lean his cheek against the cool window and watch the

Pacific Coast Highway speed by. His stomach grumbled and longed for breakfast; Finley regretted not eating anything before leaving the school. But how would he have gone about that? Should he have asked the bus driver to keep the engine running while he went back to the mess hall to snatch a breakfast burrito? Should he have mentioned receiving a "last meal" to Dean Longenecker before they said their goodbyes?

I could really go for one of Diffenbaugh's omelets right now, Finley thought, making him realize that he hadn't gotten a chance to see the professor prior to his departure. He pushed off the glass window and felt around the top pocket of his backpack, which was on the floor between his shoes. He felt the key protruding through the fabric. Since he'd found it, he hadn't gotten an opportunity to investigate the key's purpose, and, there was still the peculiar way in which Finley had discovered it that raised questions.

It was as if someone had taken pieces from dozens of different puzzles and presented them to Finley in the hopes that he could solve it. Yet even *if* the pieces had been from the same puzzle, he had no reference picture.

And so there Finley was, in the back of a giant bus, riding back to Huntington Beach with nothing but pieces to his name:

Who was James Olyphant, and what were the Dissensions?

Why was Finley's masked attacker following him around like an apparition?

Was Wally, the school driver, really connected to Olyphant's schemes—and, by that same token, Dean Longenecker as well?

What had been the point of the electric ghost's assault? Was it an element to some bigger plan? If so, what had it really accomplished other than destroying the Brighton stadium and terrifying the student body?

And, most importantly, why had Finley been unable to recharge on the beach last night—when he'd needed to more than ever?

Finley closed his eyes, forcing his thoughts away. He didn't mean to fall asleep. In fact, if he had made a conscious effort to try and doze off, he might not have been able to. Either way, the next thing he knew he was swimming in blackness, submerged in slumber, and then he was jerking forward as the transit bus shrieked to a stop. He blinked his eyes and sat up, looking out the window.

He was home.

Dinner that night was awkward, at best.

Finley's parents were delighted to have him home, sure, and they fired round after round of questions at him about Brighton, his abilities, his professors, and how his first semester as a surger had been. At one point, Mr. McComb even asked Finley to pass him the mashed potatoes by using Understanding.

That was when things turned awkward. Finley had to explain to his parents that, not only could he *not* surge in the traditional sense, but he had also temporarily "lost his touch."

I plan on going to my room to work on my recharging after dinner, Finley told them. He almost had to yell over Nat King Cole's rendition of "O Tannenbaum," which blasted from the living room.

Were classes just that overwhelming? his mother asked, reaching over the table and taking Finley's hand.

He didn't want to talk about it. He asked where Erin, his sister, was.

Out, Mr. McComb replied without further explanation. Could you pass the gravy?

After dinner Finley scoured the house for all of the remote controls and appliances. Only a handful of them ran on batteries, and only one of them was dead: the clicker for the Christmas lights on the tree. Finley took it to his bedroom, which looked exactly as he had left it— save the made bed.

He shut the door, walked over to the window and closed the blinds, and then put the clicker in his back pocket.

All right, Finley thought, rubbing his hands together. *Baby steps.*

First, he tried Enhancing and tearing a hardback book in two. His attempt lasted long enough for his wrists to get sore and tingly. When he couldn't surge in that phase, he tried Fueling across the room from wall to wall. No result. All he was doing was sprinting back and forth, and he felt quite foolish in the process. That, coupled with his stomps knocking over action figures and skateboard figurines from his dresser, meant this ended a lot quicker than it started.

Lastly, he tried Understanding. He pointed his open hand at one of the smallest things in his room: the key he had found at Brighton. It, the key, sat on his desktop beside some paper wads and comic books.

Let go. Finley bit his teeth down. *Come to me!*

The key never moved. Finley pulled the clicker out of his pocket and threw it against the wall. The back plate snapped off and the dead AAA battery slid across the floor.

The next two weeks were depressing, slow, and downright brutal. Finley stayed at home, mostly, and only went outside when the mail arrived. He had never given Miguel, Bridget, or Helena his phone number or email address, so he figured if they were going to try and get a hold of him, Bridget would be the one to suggest getting his home address from the administration's office.

He never received a letter, not even from Diffenbaugh—who Finley figured would be the only professor to reach out to him and offer consolation.

Bitterness and resentment began to manifest inside Finley's heart.

Christmas Eve brought several aunts and uncles and cousins to the McComb household. Finley learned that only his mother, father, and sister knew he'd been called to a surger's life. Everyone else was told boarding school, which meant Finley was cornered multiple times by concerned relatives.

How are you holding up?

Boarding school, that's just *awful*.

What did you do?

Your mom and dad must hate having you out of the house.

Finley tried smiling the questions off, and merely drank his eggnog and scratched beneath the itchy parts of his Christmas sweater. When Mr. McComb called a toast in the living room for Erin, who had just decided to accept a scholarship from the University of California, Berkeley, Finley grabbed his skateboard and slipped outside.

It was cold, somewhere around the mid forties, so he didn't stay out too long, but the crisp air and ashen moonlight provided good, temporal therapy. He practiced his kickflip, which was rusty. He fell twice and cut his hand once.

After New Year's Day, Finley told his parents about his suspension. Initially, they were very upset, especially at the fact that he'd waited nearly two weeks to tell them. Mrs.

McComb kept saying she hoped Finley had learned his lesson, and Mr. McComb found some creative way to contrast Finley to his sister, who had just selected her collegiate destination, remember? *She* had great things ahead of *her*.

Finley took the verbal scourging with patience, and, instead of grounding him, Finley's parents decided he had to go to work with Mr. McComb Monday through Friday—all the way up until he was allowed to return to Brighton at the end of February.

You can't be serious! Finley cried, blindsided by this drastic punishment.

It'll do you good, his father replied.

Finley begged to differ. His father worked as an accountant for Brakenick & Speid, and, as far as Finley was concerned, it was the dullest and most uninteresting job ever conceived. He'd gone once, when he was younger, on take-your-kid-to-work day, and Finley had been bored beyond belief.

But he argued to no avail because his parents had made up their minds. And so the next two months were all but written in stone for Finley McComb, who couldn't believe things had gone from so wonderful to so terrible so quickly.

February 6th was a cold Thursday, and Finley spent it

like every day since the start of the New Year: in his father's office, beneath the window, sitting on the floor with his back against the wall, listening to his iPod. Since his first night back in Huntington Beach, he'd completely given up on trying to recharge. Finley knew more failed attempts would only add insult to his slew of injuries.

Maybe the Bolt Sovereign has some way of restricting any surging outside the sanctioned communities? Finley thought desperately, staring at one of the many Thomas Kinkade paintings in Mr. McComb's office. "Surging restrictions" were obviously not the answer to his problem because his inability to recharge had started on the Brighton campus.

Finley leaned his head back and turned up his music.

After 4:30 p.m., Finley and his father left the office and drove home, and in the car Mr. McComb said that he would be dropping off Finley because he was meeting some colleagues at their favorite bar to watch the Thursday night football game. Finley nodded.

When they pulled up in front of their house, Mrs. McComb was on the lawn—gathering the Christmas décor that they traditionally left out well after the holiday season passed. Finley waved goodbye to his father and strode toward the front door, brooding. He was sure his mother was going to request his assistance, but she instead set the box of Christmas gnomes down and said, There's someone here to see you, son.

Finley looked up. What?

They're inside, said Mrs. McComb.

Finley felt like someone had just jumpstarted his heart. *Professor Diffenbaugh? Miguel, Bridget, and Helena?* He didn't wait for further details. He sprinted across the grass, pulled open the front door, and practically tripped into the living room.

It was the last person he expected to see.

Chapter 19 | <u>Orion Heights</u>

Professor Ambrose rose from the leather couch and set his coffee mug on the ottoman next to scattered home and gardening magazines.

"Hi, Finley," said the professor.

Finley didn't respond.

Ambrose unbuttoned his suit jacket and put his hands on his hips. His lazy eye seemed especially noticeable that day.

"I know you must be extremely frustrated right now."

"What gave that away?" Finley scoffed.

The professor sighed. "Right. Look, no one understands how patient you've been more than me. I want to offer thanks for that."

Finley folded his arms. "You came here to *thank* me?"

He also wanted to say that he had been the furthest thing from patient, but he was sure his expression was conveying that message already.

"That's one reason." The professor checked his wristwatch. "I also came to pick you up."

Finley dropped his hands. "But my suspension isn't up for another two weeks?"

"I'm not taking you to Brighton. Not yet, at least. Go pack your things, I'll explain everything in due time."

Finley remained planted on the spot in the living room threshold. More than a month had elapsed with absolutely no communication from Brighton Prep or his friends.

Now Professor Ambrose is showing up out of the blue and he expects me to drop everything and simply tag along?

He wanted to leave with the professor more than anything. He wanted his new life back. His recharging abilities. His classes. His dorm room. His friends! But the bitterness and resentment that had formed in his heart took precedence and power over his other emotions.

"You're angry, I get it," Ambrose said, reading Finley's thoughts. "And I know you feel in the dark about a lot of things. But that's all going to change today. You have my word."

Finley didn't have to try and believe the professor. He just did. Ambrose was, after all, the only one who had taken the time to actually explain to Finley what recharging was. That had meant a lot.

"Where are we going?" Finley asked.

"Orion Heights," the professor replied, walking across the living room to face Finley. "It's the largest surging community in Southern California. We have to hurry, there are people waiting for us."

"Does Dean Longenecker know you're here?" Finley didn't know why that mattered, and he figured the answer was no, but he asked anyway.

"She does not," Ambrose said. "Now go pack your things."

It hit Finley at that moment. It was over. It was *finally* over. His suspension. His absence from Brighton. His seclusion. He felt fresh life breathed into him and he could have shouted for joy. Instead, he hugged Professor Ambrose, who wasn't expecting the gesture.

"I've been packed for *weeks*," Finley admitted into the professor's shoulder.

After Finley grabbed his stuffed backpack and kissed his mom on the cheek, she told him he had better not pull another stunt like the one he had in December because his parents wouldn't stand for a second suspension, and his going to Brighton Preparatory School for Surgers was a privilege, and he should not soon forget that.

Professor Ambrose thanked Mrs. McComb for the coffee, and for allowing her son into his care. Apparently the professor had written Finley's parents a couple of days earlier, explaining how important it was for their son to accompany Ambrose into Orion Heights. His mother and father had differed on the matter, which explained why Mr. McComb had dropped off Finley and essentially fled the scene.

Finley was reminded of Mr. Repairman, who had used Understanding illegally to get him out of Huntington Beach and to the Brighton campus.

"You didn't, um, use mind control to convince my parents, right?" Finley asked, riding in the passenger seat of Ambrose's black 1966 Plymouth Barracuda. An old, scentless four-leaf clover air freshener hung from the rear view mirror.

"Of course not," the professor replied, taking a left at the light.

"Did you know that the school allowed that? Allowed Mr. Repairman to warp my parents minds with illegal Understanding?"

"No, but given what Dean Longenecker and the school think you can do, it doesn't surprise me that they pulled out all the stops to get you to Brighton."

"Huh? 'Think' I can do?"

Professor Ambrose gripped the steering wheel. He didn't say anything for the next ten minutes. Finley knew the professor would follow through on his word and answer his questions, so he waited.

They passed through a few stoplights heading toward the coast, and, every single time they approached the next traffic signal, it turned green in their favor. Then, the professor turned up the street that led to the beach, and he eventually eased off the acceleration and parked beside an abandoned mall.

"Are we here?"

"Yes," the professor replied, taking the key out of the ignition. "Don't forget your backpack."

Confused, Finley did as told, and then he followed Ambrose across the deserted parking lot and to the entrance. The faded paint on the department store walls promised the best deals in all of Huntington Beach.

The professor said, "Stay close. Don't wander."

Finley promised, and then they walked through the door together. But they weren't inside. They hadn't entered the abandoned mall. Apparently that had all been some magical mirage, because Finley found himself at the edge of a wide forest. There were hundreds of pine trees spread out before them, with small houses and cabins built around the branches above the ground. It instantly reminded Finley of where he and his family often camped, in the woods in the Pacific Northwest—minus all of the stunning tree houses.

Finley looked over his shoulder. Where there should have been the cement department store wall, there was instead the semi-translucent barrier of a plasma trap. It warbled and pulsed, daring Finley to touch it. He tilted his head back, trying to see where the plasma trap ended. It eventually curved in the sky, giving the illusion of a gigantic snow globe.

That was when Finley noticed the stars. Although it was close to full evening, the sun was still out, so it should have been impossible to see any hint of stars and their constellations. Yet Finley could see them, glowing in the pink and blue sky.

"I...I don't understand..."

"The dome keeps the community hidden," the professor explained, pocketing his hands. "It's a fusion of holographic technology and the same framework that goes into a plasma trap."

"No, no—the stars."

Finley's neck was starting to hurt, but he didn't drop his gaze. The stars were beautifully sprinkled all along the firmament's canvas, like thousands of drops of spilled paint.

"Amazing, isn't it?" Ambrose joined Finley in admiring the hybrid night and day sky. "Designed by some of the finest astronomers in the surging community. They took the technology in the dome and expounded upon it—using the glass to assemble a highly advanced telescope, which provides a view of space that cuts through the sun's light."

Finley was mesmerized.

"C'mon," the professor said. "We're late."

He led Finley, who had to force himself to stop staring, deep into the woods. Men and women Fueled up and down the trails, heading for their destinations without pause. Finley heard hushed voices coming from the branches, and when he looked up, he caught glimpses of people Lunging through the air from tree house to tree house.

"Does everyone always…er, sneak?"

"No," Ambrose said, ducking under a low hanging branch. "The ground is usually bustling with surgers, but lately people keep to themselves in the trees."

"I see that…," Finley said. *But why?* "Where are they getting the electricity to surge out here?"

"There's an underground network of wires that draws from surrounding power stations," Ambrose explained. "Every pine tree has strips of electricity strapped onto its bark." Finley started to notice what the professor was referring to. Nearly every tree they walked past had small, thin, metallic tubes wrapped around the trunks.

Aside from hearing whispers and catching the occasional flash of neon colors when a passerby surged, Finley didn't see much. They even walked through an empty marketplace, with shops and stores toting signs that declared early closings. There were a few Enhancers out and about, patrolling the pine needle covered trails.

This wasn't exactly what Finley had expected out of the surging community. He pictured tall skyscrapers and industrial streets that flourished with advanced technology and futuristic transportation, not a few acres of woods with scattered tree houses and an empty marketplace.

The professor stopped when they had reached the opposite end of the heights.

"This way."

Professor Ambrose pointed to a rope ladder hanging from the nearest pine tree. The passage led up to a four-story tree house. Finley clambered up the ladder first, his full bag bouncing on his back. After he'd climbed only a half a dozen rungs, a pair of hands lifted him up the rest of the way and through the open hatch.

Finley was deposited into one of the corners of the room, and after he stood up and dusted off his jeans, he screamed.

He was in the company of three people: an attractive young woman in cargo pants and an aviator's jacket; a man with dark skin and a hi-top fade haircut; and...and a creature that looked like it had once been a man.

Finley panted, backing up against the tree house wall and shouting, "Whoa! Whoa!"

"Finley, please calm down," the creature implored in a deep, soothing voice. It held up its thick hands non-threateningly.

On the whole, it looked mostly human, except that the skin on its face was pulled and stretched back, and its features were both deformed and exaggerated. There were long scars that started beneath its beady eyes and ran down its cheeks and neck—disappearing below its tight T-shirt. Above its neck and around various spots of its head there were protruding growths, as if large balls had been crammed underneath its skin for safekeeping. The creature was also very tall and broad shouldered, and awkwardly proportioned from head to toe.

"Here, here, this usually helps." It pulled a pair of wide sunglasses out of its jean pocket and put them on. Professor Ambrose appeared through the tree house hatch a second later.

Finley chuckled uncomfortably, as the sunglasses did little to cover the creature's appearance.

"Better?" asked the creature.

Finley took two, slow breaths. "Uh, sure, yeah."

"How many times I gotta tell you the sunglasses do nothing?" said the man with the hi-top fade haircut. He wore a bright pink windbreaker and acid-washed jeans and looked like he was stuck in the year 1991.

"Your opinions are your own, Victor," the creature said importantly. "Just like your choice in fashion."

Victor opened his mouth to counter quip, but the creature turned on the ball of its foot and greeted the professor with a handshake.

"You're late, Josiah."

"I even tried Remi's trick with the traffic lights," Professor Ambrose said, pulling out a chair from the small table in the middle of the room and sitting down.

"You did!" The young woman with the aviator jacket sat across from the professor. Her face was lit up. "And?"

Ambrose stared at her for a moment. "*And* we were still late, Remi."

"Oh. Right."

"Can I offer you a drink, Finley?" the creature asked, its hands held behind its back. "We have water and tea, and, with just the right amount of sugar, *sweet* tea as well." He spoke clearly and properly, like a butler might have.

"I..." Finley cleared his throat.

"You can stop standing on your tiptoes, kid," Victor said, unzipping his windbreaker and hanging it beside the window.

Finley looked down. He was still backed up against the wall—his palms flat and plastered to the wood. He slowly peeled himself away, looking down at his sneakers awkwardly.

"Water's fine," he said. "Thank you."

The creature nodded, and then disappeared up the spiral staircase on the opposite end of the room.

"Here you can sit next to me," Remi said in one swoop, offering Finley the chair beside her and the professor.

Finley took off his backpack, left it in the corner, and accepted the seat. He flipped his bangs out of his eyes and glanced around the tree house. The windows had the drapes pulled down shut, and three lit lanterns hung from the rafters. The walls were littered with swaths of burlap, and, when Finley looked closely, he saw names and dates written on the fabric.

There were also some old nautical charts that hung between the windows, a few Polaroids, and, strangely, a mounted deer head with great antlers.

"Tumble likes to hunt," Victor told Finley, taking the last available chair. He added, after motioning toward the ceiling: "You should see his room. Man's got issues. Stuffed squirrel and all kinds of other junk."

Tumble, as it turned out, was the creature's name. He returned via the spiral staircase and handed Finley iced water in a mason jar.

"Dinner will be ready in an hour," said Tumble, pushing up his sunglasses. "I've got venison and potato soup slow cooking on the roof."

At the mention of a meal, Finley's senses seemed to suddenly kick in, and he could smell the strong aroma of roasted meat and spices. His stomach roared, and he took a drink of his water.

"What's taking him so long?" Victor asked the professor, who had pulled a folder out and laid it on the table. He was thumbing through documents and pictures.

"You know Delaware," Ambrose replied, stopping on one of the pages and tapping it absentmindedly.

Finley stole a glimpse of Tumble, except that his glimpse turned into a stare. After a few beats, the creature noticed and did his version of a smile. It was wry and twisted, and his chipped, yellowing teeth peeked out from behind his scarred lips.

"Never seen an opala before, have you?" asked Tumble.

"Er..."

"Course he hasn't," said Remi, continuing politely: "most surgers go their whole lives without seeing you guys."

"And...what exactly is an 'opala?'"

"An addict," Tumble said, walking across the room and shutting the hatch. "Or rather, an *ex*-addict. I was a hopeless dependant. Used to will from the Root for *hours* on end without ever surging. Until Josiah here came along. Saved my life, he did."

Finley turned to the professor, who was still reading from the texts on the table.

"So you were basically turning into an electric ghost?" Finley asked Tumble, who folded his arms and leaned against the spiral staircase.

"That would have in fact been my outcome if not for the professor's intercession."

Finley was totally speechless. The Bolt Sovereign was apparently in the business of brushing off electric ghosts and deeming them fantastical material for campfire stories. Yet not only had Finley witnessed and survived an electric ghost's attack at Brighton, but now he was in the presence of a man who was living, breathing proof of the Root's destructive side effects.

"We never properly introduced ourselves," said Remi, breaking up Finley's thoughts. "I'm Remi Ambrose—Josiah's younger sister."

"I'm Victor Sims." He leaned back in his chair leisurely, placing both hands behind his head.

"And I'm Tumble." Tumble remained by the stairwell, enwrapped in shadows. Finley waved to them all, and then turned to Professor Ambrose, who was still poring over his documents.

"Professor?" Finley said, scooting his chair in. "Will you please tell me why you brought me here? Will you please tell me what's going on?"

Ambrose looked up, sighed through his nose, and then closed his folder.

"I was hoping Delaware would be here by now, but I suppose we can go ahead and get started without him. You've waited long enough, haven't you?"

Finley blinked. He straightened up in his chair, trying to mentally brace himself for whatever Ambrose had in store. *I know you feel in the dark about a lot of things,* the professor had said.

But that's all going to change today...

The professor pulled out his glove, put it on his right hand, and turned on the small switch above the thumb—starting the flow of electricity from which he could surge.

He then took an old quarter out of his other pocket and tossed it into the air above the table. Using Understanding, Ambrose held the quarter in suspension, and the usual spray of neon yellows sparked and popped around the professor's glove.

"Tell us what you saw, Finley," Ambrose said. He stopped surging and Finley caught the quarter.

"Huh?" He looked to Remi, Victor, and then Tumble for help. But they remained silent in expectation of Finley's answer. "I saw you surging. You used Understanding to float this quarter." He set it on the table heads side up.

Victor dropped his hands and leaned forward. "What else, kid?" He didn't sound impatient, but rather curious. Excitedly curious. "What else did you see?"

"I mean, there were the neon colors too. Around your glove."

The room was quiet. Victor let out a soundless gasp. Remi's bottom lip had begun to quiver, and her eyes were watering. Professor Ambrose, who was always so reserved with his emotions, was actually *smiling*. He turned off his glove as Tumble walked over to the table.

"Are you...are you sure?" he asked, his voice laced with awe.

"What's the big deal?" Finley chuckled uneasily. "That always happens when someone surgers—"

"What color?"

Finley furrowed his brow.

Remi repeated the question. "What color was it?"

"Yellow. It's always yellow when someone uses Understanding, just like it's always green when someone Lunges."

Remi wiped her eyes, and Victor started laughing.

"Can't believe we doubted you, man!" he said to the professor, his laughter bordering on hysterical. "*Blown fuse*, this is crazy."

"Okay now you can start explaining what I'm missing," Finley said, his patience waning.

"Peds can't see the colors associated with surging," Ambrose said, pulling off his glove. "And neither can surgers."

Finley cocked his head. "What?"

"The visual aftereffects of willing power from the Root are impossible to witness with the naked eye," Tumble exclaimed, pacing around the hatch. "In fact, up until the development of powerful microscopes, the neon colors you described, Finley, only existed in a theoretical context."

"You're saying that this whole time I've been seeing things no one else has?" Finley stood up slowly. "The colors…the streaks of light…*no one can see that?!*"

Professor Ambrose reached across the table and grabbed Finley's arm tenderly.

"I want you to pay attention to what I'm about to say," he said, guiding Finley back into his chair.

Finley nodded, and he tried to hide the dizziness he was starting to feel.

"That night, when you were suspended, you mentioned seeing the neon colors," Ambrose said, talking quickly. "That's when everything became clear, and I was able to put the pieces together over the ensuing weeks.

"You can't recharge, Finley. Truth is, no one can. Once the Root is completely extracted from a source of electricity, it's gone. There are no 'residues' or 'leftovers,' like I'd previously been led to believe—like Dean Longenecker and Brighton Prep *still* believe. Like James Olyphant believes, too.

"But to believe in recharging is to believe a lie."

Finley meant to drink from his jar of water, but he couldn't make himself move.

"Recharging has only ever existed in surging lore to protect a kekoa's identity." Ambrose lowered his voice and pointed. "*You're* a kekoa, Finley. You have the ability to will power from a supreme source of energy. Unlimited energy. Transcendent energy… *natural* energy…

"…Your strength is found in the sunlight."

Finley's vision was starting to blur. He remained silent for a moment, then reached forward and drank his water. It chilled his mouth and throat as it poured over his tongue. He couldn't think of anything to say, so he took another long sip.

"Every time you've surged, it's been in sunlight,"

Ambrose continued. "That day, in my classroom, when you were able to Understand. Then, when you Lunged for the first time, or when you hurt yourself Enhancing."

And that night, on the beach, when Doug Horn had confronted him. The moon, which bears the sun's reflection, had been hidden behind the clouds. *That's* why he'd been unable to perform a launching kick.

When I let go, Finley thought, his eyes widening, *I'm letting the Root in the sun—not from some dead batteries—flow through me! I've been focusing on the wrong thing...*

"A kekoa is basically an enigma," Tumble spoke in a hushed tone.

"One whose calling is to draw from the Root that lies in the olden power, *not* the limited power of man's invention." Remi took off her aviator's jacket, like all this talk was making her warm. "You're a surger whose ability predates the creation of electricity and Jane Grossman's historical calling. Your kind has been lost in the fog of time for centuries."

Finley took a third drink, finishing his water. "I'm gonna need a refill," he croaked.

"Right now you're at the epicenter of a great tug-of-war," Victor explained, pulling in Finley's attention. "And you, kid, are the rope. The Bolt Sovereign and Brighton Prep are working in conjunction with one another, claiming that you—Finley McComb, recharger extraordinaire—belong to them."

"Meanwhile," Remi said, taking lead again, "James Olyphant finds out about you and tries to scare you onto his side, making threats about the Dissensions."

"You guys were able to find out who Olyphant is?" Finley asked the professor eagerly.

Ambrose nodded. "I've known all along, Finley. He's a radical, a maniac. Olyphant's part of a minority that believe surgers should be free to explore every potential stem of Understanding, regardless of the laws and guidelines set in place by the government.

"The Dissensions were a great political war waged between the radicals and the Bolt Sovereign years ago in Washington D.C., and, when things turned violent in the courts, James Olyphant and his disciples were locked away."

The professor went on to explain that the incident had managed to stay mostly out of the press's attention. The Bolt Sovereign staged a few petty crimes, like bank robberies, and pinned it on Olyphant—justifying his incarceration. The last thing they needed was for Olyphant to become some sort of martyr or ideal, which could have potentially resurrected the Dissensions and instigated copycats.

The professor folded his hands together on the tabletop. "I kept all of this from the dean because, well, technically it never happened. Only those close to the situation know what really transpired, know why Olyphant was really imprisoned."

Finley should have been taking notes. There was so much being explained that he felt like he was back inside a Brighton classroom.

"So, Olyphant escapes prison," Finely said, working through the information, "finds out I can 'recharge,' and then decides to give me a sales pitch. I can't believe I'm saying this, but why didn't he just kidnap me? Force me to be his pawn or something?"

"James Olyphant may be a radical," Tumble said, walking over and standing between Remi and Finley's chairs. "But the man *did* claim to have morals. We're convinced that's why he Borrowed your conscious: to merely offer you the proposal. After that, the choice was yours."

"But just because he claims to have some morals," Victor said, "doesn't mean the man can't get restless."

Finley somehow caught the reference immediately. "The electric ghost, at the Games of Illumination."

"He set that monster loose in the hopes that Brighton would halt the semester and send everyone home," Ambrose said in agreement. "At least that's what we've concluded. He probably figured that once you were back in Huntington Beach, stripped away from the surging lifestyle you'd grown to love, you might have gotten…desperate."

"He doesn't know me then," Finley said through gritted

teeth.

He remembered that Saturday, when all his peers had been screaming in fear and running for their lives. To think that Olyphant had orchestrated that on his behalf was overwhelmingly sickening.

"Of course, there's still a small chance he had nothing to do with the attack." Ambrose exhaled a long sigh. "Delaware still believes the electric ghost was an act of some unrelated, brazen politicking."

"Yeah," Victor snorted, "but Delaware's drunk most of the time, so…"

"It was Olyphant," said Remi assuredly, her voice grave. "We all know what he's capable of, and, if you think about it, he's trying to knock out two birds with one stone here—shake up the Bolt Sovereign, *and* attempt to get an early semester dismissal out of Brighton Prep."

And, not to mention Finley saw his masked attacker in the faculty booth—mere hours before the electric ghost emerged. To tie this back to Olyphant, Finley didn't need much more proof than that.

He pushed off of the table, slid his chair back, and walked to the nearest window. Finley pulled down on the drapes, and the spring reacted. He slowly guided the cloth up with his hand, opening it just enough to see the full moon above the pine treetops. The view was like a painting hanging in the most prestigious of galleries.

My strength is found in sunlight.

The moon seemed to glow more radiantly than Finley had ever seen it do. It must have been the dome, blowing up the moon's features and details. White light shone in the sky, bleeding through the pine trees and appearing to set the night on fire in a soft, pale, beautiful blaze.

Finley turned around. The moonlight spilled onto his backside. He clenched his fists at his side for a moment, thought to himself, *Let go*, and then unfurled his hands. He felt a wave of tremors...he felt the Root being released from the light at his back...he felt the power to surge entering his body...

He channeled Understanding. He channeled it *effortlessly*.

The table in the middle of the tree house began to rise, floating nearly three feet above the floor. Finley was so surprised he could surge after going so long without being able to that he flinched, lost his focus, and the table crashed down—stubbing Victor's foot in the process.

Remi clapped her hands together, and Ambrose and Tumble shared a laugh. Victor favored his foot, cursing under his breath. Finley apologized profusely.

"I can't believe I'm actually standing in the same room as a kekoa," Tumble said, lifting his sunglasses and wiping his eyes.

Remi whistled. "Wow. If James Olyphant knew what you really are, Finley, he'd be doing a whole lot more to get you on his side."

"S-So, I'm the only one?" Finley asked, reclaiming his chair. His hands were shaking beyond the point of control.

"No way to tell, really," Ambrose responded.

"How were you guys able to find out about my true ability then?" Finley said, scratching his arm. "I mean, if kekoas are so rare, and they've always claimed to be able to recharge to keep their identities hidden?"

Right then, the tree house hatch flung open, and Mr. Tenbrook's head appeared through the floor.

"Sorry I'm late!" Parker's father boomed, climbing up the rest of the way and dropping his rucksack onto the ground. "The problem with secret hideouts is there so damn secret and hard to find! *Ooph*—sorry, didn't see Finley there. What have I missed?"

Chapter 20 | What The Tide Brought In

Once Tumble brought down a chair for Mr. Tenbrook, dinner was served. Finley had offered to help pass out the bowls and spoons, but Tumble insisted he remained seated, stating that the most important topic of the night hadn't yet been discussed.

Professor Ambrose reopened his folder while Finley devoured the warm, spicy soup that was set before him.

"This turned up on Brighton's shore yesterday." He slid a photograph across the tabletop so Finley could see. Finley wiped his mouth and took the photo, studying it beneath the lantern light.

It was an argosy. An old Spanish merchant ship with a

damaged frame and tattered sails. It looked like it had traversed through multiple hurricanes. How it was still floating on the water was a mystery.

"Dean Longenecker sent everyone home shortly after it appeared," Remi said, taking dainty sips of her soup with a wooden spoon. "She didn't want to take any chances."

"Bolt Sovereign was notified immediately, of course," said Mr. Tenbrook, drinking from a tankard. It was alcohol of cloying bitterness. "They got the whole campus sealed off. Think the ship is some kind of act of terrorism. Bah!"

"So what is it?" Finley handed the photograph back to Ambrose. The broken, ramshackle vessel was making him uneasy.

"It's a harbinger," said Victor simply, combing the sides of his head with a brush. "A mark of bad fortune."

Finley snorted, and he almost spewed out a mouthful of squishy potatoes in the process. He chuckled, wiped his mouth, finished swallowing, and then turned to the professor. "What is it *really*?"

"I'm afraid Victor is mostly right," Ambrose said, frowning, and then absently popping his knuckles. "There are many adages in the surging community, like in any culture, and our sayings and proverbs have a through-line. A consistency."

Remi quoted, " 'The surger wills for good; to those whose intent is ill, may their headrests be of stone, and their dreams cargo on the black vessel."

Victor pulled up his shirt, revealing a tattoo. It was swirly calligraphy over his left rib. " 'Virtue bears the diadem of lights…evil mans the fleet of black flags."

" 'The surger is built of fortitude and patience,' " Tumble said ominously, pushing his sunglasses up his bent nose. "But the hasty and impetuous bring the curse of the black ship upon their lives." The opala then ran his hands over his short, patchy, disheveled hair.

"All right, so, this 'black ship' is like a metaphor?" Finley said, moving his now empty bowl aside.

"Well, that's all it *used* to be." The professor held up the photograph again.

Finley thought of how empty the trails had been when he and Ambrose had first entered Orion Heights. The marketplace had closed early. The Enhancer Force had been out in patrols. Was this why? Because some wrecked, broken ship had mysteriously appeared? Everyone was hiding because they were afraid—because they thought this was an omen?

Dean Longenecker wouldn't send us home after the electric ghost's attack, Finley reflected. *But now she does? Surgers must really take this black ship thing seriously…*

"Shouldn't we be talking to Diffenbaugh about all this?" Finley offered. Brighton's history professor would probably go frothy in the mouth at the thought of digging into old legends and surger mythology.

"Not sure where he stands yet," said Ambrose, taking his first sip of the soup.

Finley turned to Remi. "What's he talking about?"

"Well, there's James Olyphant and his radicals," she explained, pinning a loose strand of hair behind her ear. "There's the Bolt Sovereign. And then there's us."

Finley wasn't following. "Okay...so, you five are the good guys?"

"I'd be all right with that title if it weren't for Tumble's inclusion," Victor joked, raising his jar of water and drinking it. Mr. Tenbrook laughed, and then hiccupped.

Tumble adjusted his sunglasses and then squatted beside Finley's chair to get eyelevel. "We're outliers, Finley. Mere clandestine observers...until there is a need for us to do more than observe."

"Cool. You're kinda like the freemasons!" Finley looked around the table, but everyone seemed to disagree with his comparison. Even Mr. Tenbrook had gone expressionless. "Only, except that you're not. Anyway, so what makes you think Professor Diffenbaugh can't be trusted?"

"Never said he couldn't be," Ambrose responded.

"We have to play this close to the chest, Finley," Tumble said, standing up and walking toward the same window Finley had been in front of earlier. Tumble grabbed the drapes and tugged, shutting out the view. "If we're too quick to deem the professor likeminded, and we end up being wrong about him, there could be consequences."

Tumble went on to explain that, while being outliers didn't necessarily involve illegal practices, having the Bolt Sovereign watching their every move would still be a blow to their research and operations. Prematurely inviting Professor Diffenbaugh—or anyone, for that matter—into the fold was to take a needless risk.

That was when Finley remembered something. "At the Christmas banquet, the professor talked about the electric ghost! That means he doesn't buy into the lies the government is using to cover up the attack!"

"While that is a good sign," Tumble admitted, still facing the window even though the drapes were pulled. "We still need to be sure about Diffenbaugh. This is only his first year at Brighton Prep, you know."

That made sense. The professor looked like the youngest member of the faculty. Finley would not have been surprised if Brighton Prep was his first job out of college. Whenever that time came when Ambrose and his fellow outliers could trust Professor Diffenbaugh, Finley was certain they would be gaining a smart, capable ally.

"All right, so, this black ship." Finley wanted to ask what it had to do with him, but he didn't want to sound presumptuous.

"I'll field this one!" Mr. Tenbrook hit the table with his fist, got up from his chair, and retrieved his rucksack.

When he returned to the table he took off his hat and pulled something out of his bag. It was a piece of parchment inside a protective seal, and the edges of the old paper were crinkled and cracked, and Finley wondered if it was part of some antique map, the kinds in adventure movies with stolen treasure and artifacts.

"A couple of months ago, a colleague and I were on an archeological dig in the Polynesian jungles." Mr. Tenbrook placed the sealed parchment on the tabletop beside the photograph of the black ship. "For years, Gatherers have been searching for the exact spot where Jane Grossman had her historical calling—the place where surging was born. The ground where she was standing is said to be sacred."

"Don't get all spiritual on us, Del," said Victor, reclining back and putting his feet on the table. Tumble scolded him for getting his shoes near the food.

"Regardless of your beliefs, you can't deny the…the *power* in the air…," said Mr. Tenbrook, his eyes glassy. "Those jungles are alive with energy. It's unlike any place I've ever been."

Finley reached over and took the sealed parchment, which had faded runes and symbols on it. The parchment was very light—lighter, almost, than a dollar bill or scrap of tissue paper, and Finley was positive that if he wasn't careful the material could damage under his fingers.

"Have you been able to translate it?" Remi asked,

looking over Finley's shoulder.

"Yes."

Tumble went around and looked over Finley's other shoulder. "And? What does it say?"

"It's a prophecy," said Mr. Tenbrook. He took a long swig from his ale. "It foretells the coming of a new age for kekoas. A new age marked by the arrival..." He trailed off, then burped involuntarily.

"The arrival of what?" Victor asked, tilting his head, his hi-top fade haircut highlighted beneath the lanterns and his furrowed brow deepened by shadows.

"That's where the page cuts off," replied Mr. Tenbrook, hooking his thumbs around his suspender straps. Finley looked at the runes closely, and then turned the parchment upside down, like this would help him understand the text.

A new age for kekoas. Meaning more people would be called in the way Finley had? More people would be granted the gifts of a kekoa? There would be others who could leverage the sunlight as a source for surging? As prophecies go, this one was pretty vague.

Finley chuckled inwardly. *There's always a prophecy.* He handed the sealed parchment back to Parker's father.

"You think *that*"—Remi gestured to the sealed text—"is referring to the arrival of the black ship?"

Both Ambrose and Mr. Tenbrook nodded.

"It could lead to more knowledge about kekoas," the professor said, "and Finley's destiny."

"Bit of a stretch, wouldn't you say?" Victor swung his feet around, planted them on the floor, and stood up.

"Only one way to find out then," said the professor. He looked from Victor to Finley, and Ambrose's look was avid, challenging, and excited. Remi gave Finley a sideways glance. Tumble folded his arms, and held his chin by this thumb. Victor sat back down slowly.

Finley laughed uncomfortably, but then he understood.

"You want me to break into Brighton and go onto that ship."

Finley stood beneath the ghostly moon, his backpack hanging by his shoulders and his hands in his jean pockets. He was on the south side of Orion Heights, waiting alone by the edge of a small pond. The stars were so bright and sharp that they bounced off the still water in alluring reflections.

He heard footsteps, and a second later Ambrose, Tumble, and Victor materialized from the shadows.

After dinner, the professor and the outliers had wasted no time setting their plan into motion. Victor needed quite a bit of convincing to get on board, arguing that the last thing they needed to do was send a minor onto a ghost ship because of a wild hunch regarding some decades-old text.

In the end, though, Ambrose had raised enough points

to back up their mission.

"Isn't there a chance this is some kind of a trap?" Finley had asked when the professor and his sister, Remi, had cleared a space on the wall in the tree house to hang a map of the Brighton grounds.

"I'm with Solar Power," said Victor. "Olyphant could've set this whole thing up! Solar Power's my new nickname for you, by the way." He winked at Finley.

"Impossible," Mr. Tenbrook said, and then he went on to pull more sealed parchment out of his rucksack and laid them all on the table in a configuration. Finley was stunned: There were collections of odd symbols, charcoal rubbings, and ancient constellations.

"I'm the only member of the Gatherer's Guild who has access to these texts and relics," Mr. Tenbrook continued. "There is no way Olyphant would have known to conceive a trap *specifically* with the black ship in mind. If anything, he's probably just as frightened as the rest of the surging community."

"And that's another thing," Finley said. He could feel perspiration starting to form all over his hands. "Didn't we just get done talking about how this black ship is like a symbol for doom and bad things? Now you want *me*—the youngest and least experienced one here—to go exploring its cabins?"

Ambrose took a red pen and started drawing arrows on the map. "Start thinking about it in the same way you would recharging."

"What, as a lie?"

"Precisely," Mr. Tenbrook said, taking a sip from his tankard, and, upon realizing it was empty, frowning disappointedly.

The professor drew two divots around the space on the map that depicted the shore. "What better way to conceal a kekoa's forthcoming opulence than to disguise it in an omen?"

"Why do it out in the open then?" Victor had disputed further. "If this is supposed to be a sign for kekoas, who have remained hidden in history all these years, why call a lot of attention to it?"

"That's it!" Remi said, standing on the tips of her toes and brightening the lanterns. "This black ship appeared to *draw out* the kekoa from hiding, whomever he or she may be."

Everyone turned to Finley, and he smiled a tense, toothy smile. Then he remembered. "Oh, right, that's me. Gonna have to get used to that title."

"But who?" Victor said to Remi. "Who would go through the trouble of orchestrating all this business with the black ship?"

Finley knew what the response was going to be before the professor turned to Victor. "If we're right about this, it will be up to Finely to figure that out…"

And if you're wrong? Finley thought, his throat getting

dry. *And it is a trap? What then?*

On the water's edge, beneath the moon- and starlight, Finley turned to meet the approaching outliers. Professor Ambrose was still in his suit, though he'd left his tie behind. Tumble wore a thick jacket with a hood pulled over his head, and Victor's brightly colored windbreaker ruffled noisily as his arms swung back and forth.

"Let's move," said Ambrose, and they led Finley around the pond and back into the heart of the woods. Owls hooted in the distance, but other than that and the groups' quiet footfalls, no other sounds came from the forest of pine trees.

They ducked beneath a large, fallen trunk, and the overgrowth of moss grazed Finley's head. He took a second to wipe his hair, and then he continued along with the others.

The professor said, "Here's the plan."

Earlier, in the tree house, when Ambrose had finished drawing arrows and making barley-legible annotations on the map, he capped his red pen, channeled Understanding by surging from some appliance in the upper rooms, and moved the table out of the way with a flick of his hand. Now, with the space cleared, Finley, Remi, Victor, Tumble, and Mr. Tenbrook could gather around and study the map.

"The entire campus is shut off to the public," Ambrose had said, pointing to the major entrances on the map, beside which he had drawn tiny Xs. "The Bolt Sovereign has stationed the Enhancer Force along the outer perimeter of the grounds."

Tumble pointed to the portion of the map that represented the Pacific Ocean. "Easy solution, we come in from behind the black ship via the ocean."

"The government has sealed off ocean access with buoys and alarms," the professor replied, shaking his head. "We get within fifty yards and the entire Enhancer Force is swarming over us."

"Which leaves the beach," said Remi, putting her hazel hair in a ponytail. The rest of the group agreed, and Finley even found himself nodding along with them.

"The north and south sides of Brighton's shore have been sealed with barbed wire fencing," the professor said, folding his arms behind his back, like he was getting into a military stance. "We will cut across the beach about a mile out, and then, in coordination with Victor and Tumble—who will set a diversion into play, drawing the Enhancer Force's attention—we can break into the quarantined portion of the beach unnoticed."

"At which point," Mr. Tenbrook said, unfolding a small blueprint and tacking it to the wall next to the map, "Josiah can set this up, and hopefully buy you some time, Mr. McComb."

Finley leaned forward, examining the intricate drawing. It was a complicated, comprehensive design of a tripod, plate, and a—"Plasma trap?" Finley said to Mr. Tenbrook.

"I've seen one of these, outside the girls dorm houses."

"Except this one has been modified," said Mr. Tenbrook, his eyes wide and proud, his grin broadening from ear to ear. "Works just like the dome, using holographic technology to project a false image."

"The only problem is," Ambrose said, taking the red pen, uncapping it, and writing 00:54 on the blueprint. "The Enhancer Force has taken many security measures, including one that will notify them should any technology be used within the Brighton grounds. You'll have exactly fifty-four seconds after I turn on the hologram, Finley, to find whatever you're supposed to find on that ship."

"No pressure…," Finley said, trying to make light of the situation, only, his voice sounded weak and muffled, like he'd spoken from within a closed room.

"You should go with him." Remi put her hand behind Finley's back while she addressed her brother. "Someone has to, just in case."

"This is Finley's task," Ambrose said, "and I'll be close should something go wrong."

Should something go wrong. The words echoed in Finley's head as he waited, crouching under some branches, pine needles smothered beneath his Vans, for Tumble to signal him over.

This is crazy! Finley thought, holding up against the bark of a pine tree to keep his balance. He half expected his sister, Erin, to come stomping into his bedroom and wake him from a lucid dream, for his mother to call him down to breakfast, for his father to remind him he had to go to work with him again as part of his punishment for getting suspended.

But Finley was not dreaming, he wasn't going to be pinched awake, because he *was* standing in an actual surging community, he was about to break into Brighton Prep, and he was hours away from venturing onto some black ship in search of answers regarding a supposed kekoa prophecy.

A kekoa...I'm a kekoa.

Over the last couple of months Finley had gone from thinking he had no right being at Brighton Preparatory School for Surgers, to thinking he could recharge, to believing he had lost that ability, to learning that he could actually surge, except his source of power wasn't electricity. It was the sun.

Your kind has been lost in the fog of time for centuries. So Remi had said earlier, of kekoas, and then Finley had tested their words and was actually able to draw from the moonlight and Understand.

Finley shook his head, disbelieving it all even though he thought he was past that and ready to accept this was his destiny now.

"You don't have to do this," Remi had said, in the tree house, when Ambrose finished informing the group of their instructions. She put her hands on Finley's shoulders and hunched down, looking him straight in the eyes. "You deserved to know what you really are…what you can really do…but you have absolutely no obligation to help us."

"James Olyphant had me knocked unconscious," Finley replied. "Dean Longenecker had my family's mind messed with just to get me to Brighton. You better believe I'm helping you guys."

"Don't just do this because of some burning desire to get back at everyone," Remi said, blinking softly.

"I'm not," Finley promised. "I want to find out if there are answers on that ship. I want to be someone—*a kekoa!*—and I want to have a destiny, just like you guys."

"Yo, Solar Power," Victor said from across the room, putting on his windbreaker. "Who's to say we're not just feeding you lies and trying to manipulate you too?"

Finley held Remi's gaze.

"Guess I don't know for sure," he said. "But if I'm wrong in trusting you guys, I'll learn from my mistake. Seems like that's all I've been doing since I came to Brighton anyway."

Remi smiled. "You're so strong and patient for your age, Finley," she said, pulling him into a hug.

"Not sure about that," Finley said back, chuckling. "I am, after all, only thirteen, and pretty good at making terrible choices."

"I don't believe that last part for a second," said Remi after she pulled away.

Finley flipped his bangs out of his eyes, surprised at how good it felt to hear her say something that simple. Remi had known him for all of two hours. How could she possibly know Finley enough to judge his character? Unless, her brother had talked about him?

Finley looked past Remi to Professor Ambrose, and he was pretty sure he caught him smiling. That marked twice in one night. The fact that Finley had just discovered he was a legendary kekoa paled in comparison to *that* phenomena.

Someone whistled. Finley shook off his thoughts and stood up, peeking around the pine tree. Tumble stood by Orion Heights's exit some fifty yards off, and the opala whistled a second time—signaling that the coast was clear. Finley darted across the trail and met Tumble by the double doors, and together they walked outside. Ambrose and Victor were waiting by a row of parking meters, and, there was a spate of angry words being exchanged between them.

"You know, sure, I was okay going along with everything," Victor was saying, "but this is just going too far!"

"It was Finley's idea—"

"He's just a kid, Josiah!"

Finley immediately figured out what the point of their disagreement was. As their meeting was adjourning in the tree house, and Mr. Tenbrook and Remi were getting ready to leave and retrieve the hologram device that the professor would use on the beach, Finley had an idea. Tumble had left already to make a few phone calls, and Victor had been upstairs using the restroom.

"Guys, wait!" he'd said, stopping Mr. Tenbrook and Remi as they were beginning to head down the hatch. "What's going to happen if you get caught by the Enhancer Force? What's going to happen if something goes wrong, and we can't get away with this?"

Professor Ambrose, who was rolling up the map, shrugged. "I don't know. The lot of us would probably face lifetime incarceration."

"And me? What would happen to me?"

Mr. Tenbrook had one foot down the ladder. "Your suspension would most likely be extended to the end of the semester. You could even get expelled."

"Yeah, well, expulsion sounds a heck of a lot better than prison time," Finley said, walking up to the professor with his arms outstretched. "There's no way I'm gonna let you guys risk this much for me."

"Finley." Professor Ambrose tucked the rolled-up map under his arm. "Listen. You've no idea how unbelievably incredible your gift is. A kekoa's power source is virtually unending. It's why your kind has stayed in the shadows for so long. If people knew what you could do they would try to control you—or worse, harm you.

"But this prophecy could in fact lead to a new era for

kekoas. Maybe it's time for your kind to come out of the shadows, and into the light…where you belong."

Finley nodded, and didn't voice a single disagreement. "I hear you, I know you're trying to help, and I won't let you risk your freedom for me."

Remi pinched the bridge of her nose and sighed. "Finley, you're not doing this on your own. We've no other choice—"

"Yes we do." Finley grinned. "The worst-case scenario for me is expulsion, meaning the worst-case scenario for *any* Brighton student caught sneaking onto the grounds is expulsion."

Professor Ambrose's expression became knowing as he figured out where Finley was headed. "You want to ask your friends to help you break in."

Remi gasped. "Josiah, we can't do that. We can't just sit back and—"

"Why not?" said Mr. Tenbrook, stroking his beard. "We're essentially sitting back while Finley sneaks onto the black ship, aren't we?"

Finley nodded, looking back at the professor, who didn't say a word for a very long time, and instead stared at Finley while he contemplated his decision. Finley could practically hear the professor working through his thoughts as the he stood there, unmoving, map under his arm, head and shoulders blackened by lantern shadows.

The professor blinked, and Finley thought they had

arrived at a stalemate.

Only...

"This ain't right!" Victor said, almost shouting, as they walked toward a blue van behind Ambrose's Barracuda in the sprawling mall parking lot. Tumble opened the side door and climbed in, and then Finley joined him—shutting the door securely.

"It was Finley's idea," the professor repeated, getting into the passenger seat. Victor climbed into the driver's seat, slammed the door shut, but didn't pull his keys out just yet. "If we're asking him to brave the unknown on that black ship, the least we can do is honor his request."

" 'The least we can do!' " Victor rolled his eyes. "He's a kid! No offense, Solar Power."

"None taken."

Tumble put on his seatbelt, and Finley mimicked.

"Victor, your concern is admirable," said Tumble, "but your persistence is uncomely."

"I'm 'bout to *come* back there and—!"

"All right enough." The professor held up his hand, and Finley had to bite his tongue to ward off the wave of laughter threatening to burst from his throat.

"Victor. Drive." Ambrose put on his seatbelt. "The decision's final and the arrangements have been made. We're heading to Long Beach to pick up Mr. Miguel Arroyo first."

Victor muttered obscenities under his breath, jammed

the key into the ignition, turned it clockwise, and the engine coughed to life. The next thing Finley knew they were speeding out of Huntington Beach, swerving around cars, getting honked at, and then jerking forward without warning—like a magnificent force had just sucked their van from one spot to the next, and Finley's head hurt, such as it did when he rode roller coasters.

"W-What happened!" he demanded when the speed eased a little and they were back to eighty miles per hour. He panted, his breath lost for a second, and then rubbed his temples.

"Victor just Fueled," Tumble said, yawning. "With the van."

"You can do that!" Finley exclaimed, amazed.

"Victor can."

Finley leaned back in the seat, impressed beyond measure. Though, considering what he had learned in the past two hours, *nothing* should have come as a surprise anymore.

A couple of minutes later and they were cruising through a neighborhood, and then Finley started to pay attention to the houses, trying to guess which one was Miguel's. He heard the professor, in the front seat, giving Victor directions.

The van stopped in front of a corner house, and Finley saw his best friend standing on the lawn with his Lofstrand crutches, looking both impatient and annoyed. He had a bag slung over his left shoulder, and he was wearing black pants, a black turtleneck, and a black beanie.

Finley almost immediately swung open the side door. "Miguel!"

"Ugh, *finally*. My crutches were getting tired."

"That doesn't make any sense."

"Listen, when you've lived with crutches as long as I have, they become extensions of your body."

"Weird, but okay." Finley got down and approached Miguel. "So, um, about that time I pushed you on the beach."

"Water under the bridge, amigo," Miguel said calmly. Slowly, a smile appeared on his round face.

Finley heaved a sigh of relief, then tilted his head. " 'Amigo?' "

"Trying to embrace my roots lately."

"Then don't you mean *agua* under the bridge?"

Miguel deadpanned. "Help me into the van, gringo."

They drove south next, and when Victor merged onto the 405 freeway, he Fueled again—whipping in and out of lanes dangerously. Finley thought it was reckless, but, when Victor would meticulously navigate behind eighteen-wheelers and cut in and out of lanes with finesse, the tension started to escape his body.

Victor knew what he was doing.

In the backseat, Miguel asked if anyone would be so kind as to fill him in on why they were breaking into

Brighton, and why it was so important for Finley to explore the black ship, which, in case anyone had forgotten, was the whole reason the school was closed in the first place.

In the driver's seat, Victor shook his head. "*This* is who you got helping you, Solar Power?"

Professor Ambrose asked for patience; they were almost to Escondido, where Bridget lived, and Helena was staying with her while the Bolt Sovereign sorted out the ordeal at Brighton Prep. To placate the giddy Miguel, Tumble pulled a peppermint out of his jacket pocket and handed it to him over the seat. Unsurprisingly, it worked, and Miguel sucked the peppermint happily and asked everyone who their favorite professional chargeball team was.

A few minutes elapsed and they were pulling into an apartment complex. Bridget and Helena, also dressed in black, stood behind the building management headquarters. The van screeched to a stop, Finley opened the side door once more, and Helena bolted past Bridget and hugged Finley unexpectedly.

"Finley!" she said. "You're alive!"

"Ha, ha," Finley replied as she broke away. "Of course I am."

Bridget, beaming, joined them and side hugged Finley. "It's so good to see you, Fin!"

"*Ahem*," Miguel said from the backseat. "Sorry, but

we're kind of on the clock here ladies."

They both rolled their eyes, but clambered inside and joined their friend in the back of the van. Victor took a U-turn, exited the complex, and sped toward the Pacific Coast Highway en route to Brighton Preparatory School for Surgers.

"So what's up, Finley?" Bridget whispered, tapping him on the shoulder. "Professor Ambrose said you need our help, that we're going to sneak into Brighton. What's going on?"

Finley turned around, his face determined and his eyes alight. "You guys are *not* going to believe this."

Chapter 21 | <u>The Black Ship</u>

It was well past midnight when Victor Sims pulled the blue van off the road and onto the beach, and the tires blasted and sprayed sand into the air as the vehicle zoomed ahead under the star-flecked sky.

"Good thing I didn't eat anything before we left," Miguel commented, holding onto the handlebar above the side window with both hands.

Finley had just finished telling his friends everything. He was a kekoa, someone who could surge by willing from the Root found in sunlight.

"Wait, so you're like solar power?" Miguel had asked, to which Victor said he'd already claimed that nickname, and Miguel should just find another one. Bridget and

Helena were having a difficult time believing kekoas actually existed, and they were so taken aback by Finley's account that they demanded an example of his surging.

So, Finley concentrated on the moonlight that poured in from his side of the window, forced himself to relax and let go, and then used Understanding to pull Miguel's beanie over his face.

The girls laughed and applauded, shaking their heads. Miguel didn't find the demonstration as funny and awe-inspiring as Bridget and Helena, so he changed the subject by calling out to the professor and asking if they were there yet.

Finley went on to explain what Parker's father, Mr. Tenbrook, had found on his archeological dig, what the prophecy could potentially mean, and why he had to go onto the black ship to see for himself.

"This is so *awesome*," said Helena. "I was so glad to get away from school, but now I can't wait to break in!"

"I'm still not convinced this isn't some trap," said Bridget, crossing her legs and folding her arms. "What if Finley's actually put in real, grave danger?"

"We will be monitoring you four closely," said the professor. He pulled a digital tablet out of the center console and flicked it on. A map appeared, tracking the van's movement. "The second I so much as get a *bad feeling*, I'm moving in. You can pull up here, Victor."

The van decelerated and came to a stop.

"You girls stay put," said Ambrose, unbuckling his seatbelt. "Victor's going to double back and then take you two to the stadium, where Tumble here will give you instructions on the diversion."

Finley opened the door, hopped out, waited for Miguel to slide out of the seat, and then he helped his friend down.

"Please be careful," Bridget implored.

"Get into trouble," said Helena, winking.

Finley and Miguel waved. Tumble lifted up his sunglasses and said, his voice soft, like wind, "I must echo what your friend Bridget has said. Do be careful, you two."

Professor Ambrose walked around to where they were standing. He had a large duffle bag hanging from his shoulder. He signaled to Victor, shut the side door for Tumble, and then led Finley and Miguel down the beach as the van drove off.

"Dude," Miguel whispered, elbowing Finley. "Did you see that guy's face?"

Finley opened his mouth to explain that Tumble was an opala, but Ambrose cut him off too quickly:

"We've got about half a mile's walk," the professor said. Miguel groaned. "Once the quarantined portion of the beach is in sight, we'll stop so I can show you how to set up the hologram device."

"Normally I'd say *wicked!* or *sick!* at the mention of a

hologram device," said Miguel. "But then, there's that half a mile walk ahead of us, so…"

Finley laughed and clapped his friend on the back. They trekked in silence for a few minutes, keeping pace with Miguel. The ocean waves were tame that night, and Finley was grateful. He figured he'd have to get into the water at some point, and the less intimidating it seemed the better.

"Professor?" Finley said, when a couple of quiet minutes had passed. "You never told me why you didn't show up for my tutoring."

Miguel coughed and looked away, pretending to admire the Pacific Ocean as they moved across the shore. Finley tried reading Ambrose's body language, but, like so often, the professor was utterly unreadable.

Then, after a while, he spoke: "Finley, I'm sorry. I do owe you an explanation for that. Since the recruiter Brighton employees first mentioned the possibility of a young recharger living in California, I was skeptical. First of all, the ability to recharge hasn't existed outside of legends since, well, ever. Secondly, I wasn't too fond of being tasked with educating you on an ability I wasn't even sure was real."

"So you thought if you just didn't show up I'd, what, go away?" Finley's ears were starting to grow red with heat.

"I thought if I showed up, even once, I'd be embracing something that hadn't been vetted." The professor looked straight ahead, staying the course, and he didn't falter even though Finley's words were getting louder.

"But *you're* the one who told me about recharging!" Finley boomed, and, if not for the urgency of their mission, he would've stopped on the spot and demanded they talk through this.

Ambrose sighed, switching the duffle bag from his right shoulder to his left. "There was a time when I had been convinced by my peers. But even after that afternoon—when you were able to surge in my classroom—I felt like something was still off. It was the way you described feeling while channeling Understanding...plus, I couldn't understand why there were absolutely no other accounts in history of other surgers being able to recharge outside of myth—"

"Is that why you let Doug make a fool of me in your Control class?" Finley said, hating himself for sounding so bratty, but feeling good at the same time for letting that off of his chest. "You were hoping that, when I had surged in your classroom, it was just a fluke?"

"Fin, he said he was sorry," Miguel said beside him.

"That incident on the greenway, with Mr. Horn..." The professor sounded like he was embarrassed, or worse, ashamed. "I should have never condoned that. I honestly didn't see him besting you. Gangly, punk kid, isn't he?"

Finley laughed, but then caught himself. "Look, at this point it doesn't matter whether or not you believed I could recharge. Obviously I can't. No one can. But I don't get why Dean Longenecker made you—or the rest of the staff—promise not to tell me about recharging."

There's absolutely no shame in walking away, the dean had said on Finley's first day. *It's like she was setting me up for failure!* Finley mused. *Why would she do that?*

No one said anything for a while, and when at last Finley mustered up the courage to continue the conversation and say all was fine, the professor held up his hand for them to stop. Up ahead, the glow of construction lights marked their destination. The black ship was barely visible, and Finley already felt chills coming on.

Miguel moaned dramatically, thanking the professor for letting them stop.

"Now listen close," said Ambrose in a hushed tone, dropping the large bag and unzipping it. "There are only four components to the hologram device, okay? First, set up the tripod and make absolutely sure it's level. Use the bubble near the top for accuracy."

"Gonna be really hard getting it level on the sand, isn't it?" asked Miguel, leaning on his crutches.

"Find a way to make it work. It has to be level to function properly. Next, attach this plate." Professor Ambrose held up the piece he was referring to, and he showed them both how it slid in. "Tighten the knob on the side, and then clip on the projector. That's this device right here. It might take the two of you to lift it, so work together, and work quickly.

"Lastly, take this pewter key and insert it into the hole above the hazard warning and turn it *counter* clockwise, you got that? Counter clockwise, Miguel, I can't stress that enough."

"All right, all right, I got it professor." Miguel looked over Finley's shoulder and squinted in the direction of the ship.

"Since all the electricity is being monitored by the Enhancer Force inside the grounds," Ambrose said, pausing while he took one last item out of the duffle bag. It was the oil lamp, from his classroom—the one Finley had seen sitting atop one of the glass cubes. "Use this after the girls trigger the diversion. You'll need light to see."

"Just what exactly is the diversion?" said Miguel, his left eyebrow arched. "You know, so we're all on the same page here."

A tiny alarm beeped inside one of Ambrose's pocket. He reached inside, turned it off, zipped the duffle bag up, and rose to his feet. "Bridget and Helena are in place, which means you two only have a few minutes."

Finley grabbed the duffle bag and was instantly surprised by its great weight. He hoisted the strap up and over his shoulder, and swallowed multiple times to wet his dry mouth. There was absolutely no turning back now, and he knew it.

"Professor," Finley muttered, attempting to not sound

afraid. "I...what am I supposed to do when I get on the black ship. What am I even looking for?"

"You're a kekoa." Ambrose put his hand on Finley's shoulder. "Only you will know what to do." And then, presumably drawing from the battery in his digital watch, the professor Fueled out of sight.

"And then there were two," Miguel said, turning up the beach and striding toward the construction lights. "C'mon, Fin. We still gotta figure out how we're going to get over that fence without surging."

As they approached the barrier, they kept to the shadows, and Finley quietly set the bag onto the sand when they'd gotten about as close as they could without being seen. On the other side of the barbed wire fence, a group of about ten Enhancers with dual gloves was standing guard with their backs to the black ship.

Finley gulped. The black ship. It was monstrous. A huge, decaying frame of wood that should have sunk to the bottom of the ocean long ago. And yet it was on Brighton's shore, waiting, like a storm kept in a jar. But eventually the glass would shatter when the rain and wind and lighting broke free...

The Bolt Sovereign thought it was a terrorist move. Professor Ambrose and the outliers believed it had to do with the prophecy Mr. Tenbrook had found. There was still a small chance Olyphant could be behind this, and that it was a trap.

What did Finley believe?

"Look, there's a gate," Miguel said, pointing. Finley followed his gesture and saw what he was referring to. There was a small wire door in the middle of the fence, but it was padlocked.

"Let me see that bag," Miguel whispered.

Finley reached down and scooped it up, cradling it in his arms while his friend searched the compartments. In one of the inner pockets, Miguel discovered an allen key set, a flathead screwdriver, and a wrench.

"Bingo," he said, pocketing the tools.

Finley thought of all the times he'd seen Miguel disassembling random objects and appliances, and he smiled. "You've been training your whole life for this moment," he teased.

"Whatever," Miguel said, brushing off the remark. He clearly caught the reference, but did not bother addressing it.

"So what's up with that, Miguel?" Finley asked, setting the duffle bag down on the sand and remaining squatted.

"What do you mean?"

"Always taking things apart. Just a hobby, or what?"

Miguel leaned on his crutches, quietly staring off into the distance. His bushy, tousled hair waved in the breeze, like clumps of dry seaweed tumbling along the shore.

Miguel said nothing for a long, extended moment, and then,

"When I was six, I got hurt. The doctors said my leg mobility would be limited the rest of my life. But I didn't believe them. Not even then, as a kid. I thought there just had to be a way I could get one hundred percent better.

"Last summer, some Brighton reps came over to our house and explained that I'd had a surger's calling."

Finley chuckled, remembering the story of how his friend's TV and video game console flew into the air and smashed into the ceiling. Miguel had had his calling when he'd channeled Understanding.

"The Brighton reps told me and my parents how special this was for me," Miguel continued, "you know, because of my handicap. They told me I would be forevermore defined as a surger, and nothing else. So, they left some packets of information, along with a DVD that explained surging, its five phases, and other random stuff."

As Finley began to wonder what all of this had to do with Miguel's interest in disassembling electronics, his friend was cut short: All the construction lights flashed, then dimmed, then were fully extinguished, as if all their fuses had blown.

Finley and Miguel gasped. To the east, over the slopes and beside the school stadium, mini explosions erupted.

The Enhancer Force screamed and shouted orders to one another in a great big scramble. In the darkness, in the starry sky, a display of colorful discharges ignited like a fireworks display, and the Enhancers abandoned their posts and raced off of the shore toward the mayhem.

"What is that!" Finley muttered to Miguel.

"It's the girls," he said, laughing to himself. "They're tossing flashballs and strikeballs into the air, and then using Understanding to rip them apart!"

"Like at the bonfire...," Finley said, as he and Miguel started rushing toward the gate. "That's exactly what we saw that night, above the ocean."

A genius diversion!

When they reached the wire door, Miguel wasted no time getting to work. He examined the padlock, and even bobbed it in his hand like he was guessing at its weight. After a second or two of inspection, he began his task of picking it open.

Finley watched, his heartbeat thumping in his ears. Behind them, Bridget and Helena were still performing their brilliant diversion, but Finley knew it wouldn't be long before they had to clear out of there and—

CLICK!

"We're in," said Miguel, simply.

He stepped aside with his crutches so Finley could swing open the gate. Finley hesitated, shocked with how easily his best friend had managed to get them inside.

"Today, chosen one!" Miguel urged, stomping his foot.

"Okay, okay."

Finley jogged through, the duffle bag bumping against his back heavily. He pointedly averted his eyes away from the black ship, and just kept the eerie vessel in his peripheral.

He skidded to a stop on the portion of beach that was directly in the shadow of the sails. Carefully, Finley took off the bag, set it down, and began to set up the tripod as Miguel caught up. Halfway through assembling the legs, Finley took the oil lamp and put it on the ground—turning it on with a long-nosed lighter he'd found in one of the bag's pockets. His arms were shaking, and he could sense his vision threatening to blur, so he yelled at himself inwardly: *Stay calm, you can do this.*

The oil lamp glowed, offering much needed assistance.

The flashballs and strikeballs stopped exploding, and the remaining lights faded above the stadium, morphing and gelling like molecules beneath a microscope until they were no more.

"The girls are done," Miguel said, "and hopefully headed off to safety." He reached down and jammed the pewter key into the hologram device while the contraption was still on the ground in the duffle bag.

"Help me lift it into place," said Finley, of the holograph device, "and then I gotta jet. You okay leveling it by yourself?"

Miguel nodded in response, and, even though he had a tricky time aiding Finley while standing with his Lofstrand crutches, Miguel still managed to support him just enough to snap the machine into place on top of the tripod.

Miguel breathed in and out quickly. "G-Good, now go, Finley!"

Finley scooped up the oil lamp and snatched some coiled up rope from the bag—all while Miguel fidgeted with the hologram device's legs, trying to get it perfectly level, such as Professor Ambrose had stressed it needed to be.

But Finley was too quick, too hasty. As he spun around and made for the black ship, his right foot caught one of the tripod's legs, and it immediately tipped off balance. Finley tripped, cursing loudly at his mistake, and it was enough to draw the attention of some Enhancers, who were apparently still close to the beach. Voices raised in the distance the second after the device crashed onto the sand.

"No!" Finley said, spinning around. "I'm so stupid!"

"Go, Fin, I got it!" Miguel threw off his crutches and slid to his knees.

Three or four shadowy forms were running toward their direction, and Finley knew it was too late. The construction lights hadn't turned back on yet, so maybe, if they were quick enough, they could at least get away before being indentified and—

Miguel turned the pewter key, the device clicked on and rumbled, and then it shot a distorted, sideways image at the black ship *of* the black ship. But Miguel obviously knew what he was doing, because he then fixed his attention on the approaching Enhancers, threw up his hands, surged with the device, channeled Understanding, and *tossed* the unsuspecting officers fifty yards back.

They flailed and cussed, crashing down a few moments later. The hologram device hummed weakly, now drained of most of its power, and it eventually turned off of its own accord.

"You...you just...," said Finley, frozen with amazement.

"Yeah, now will you go already!"

Finley thanked his best friend, turned back toward the enormous black ship, and headed forward. He waded through the cold water until it was up to his knees, and then he hesitated—a moment of fear and uncertainty taking over him.

The holes and chinks in the ship were like dark eyes and smiles, evil faces cut from the shadows—straight from the places underneath beds that you never dared look. Finley shivered, holding up the oil lamp, and the faces were gone.

"Go on, Fin! We're running out of time!"

He sloshed forward and lowered his oil lamp, but that's when the blinding neon lights shimmered through the cracks of the black ship's frame. Startled, Finley lost his grip, and the oil lamp slipped from his fingers and into the ocean water, where it was instantly extinguished. The water lapped at his waist.

"Hurry, Fin! They're coming!"

Finley took the coiled up rope and glanced up through the holes in the sails at the moon. It was the same moon hanging over his family's house in Huntington Beach. It was the same moon glowing outside his sister's window. It was the same moon that had made him believe he was a kekoa.

From this day forward, Finley realized, throwing the rope over his shoulder. He could hear the Enhancers circling around Miguel and taking him into their custody.

From this day forward the moon- and sunlight will be there to help me. He crouched down a little. *So as long as there is light, I have nothing to fear.*

The moonlight fell over him like a cleanse, and Finley breathed out through his mouth, said *Let go* in his heart, and allowed the Root to flow into his system. He surged like no other surger could at Brighton Prep, and he Lunged up into the darkened sky just as the Enhancer's had begun to splash into the ocean behind him.

Finley soared, as if he were wispy fabric caught in the wind, bearing little to no weight, and the rush of energy he'd summoned from the light had him laughing and howling as he arched over the black ship's railing.

He braced himself for the land, but when his feet hit the deck, he crashed straight through and tumbled onto the floor in a ball—shards of splintered wood raining down on him.

Chapter 22 | <u>The Great A'alona, Thunderlight!</u>

When the rubble and debris finally settled around Finley, he grunted and forced himself to stand. The joints in his knees popped, and there was a painful crick in his neck. As far as he could tell, he hadn't broken any bones after the fall, and he was grateful for the lucky break. Those seemed to be in short supply.

He did find a few cuts around his elbow. *Knowing how to Mend would've come in handy*, he noted, wiping the specks of blood off his skin.

The first level of the ship was dark and still, and it seemed to be keeping out the sounds from outside even though there were numerous holes and passages of air. Finley turned in a full circle, taking in his surroundings, and that's when he saw the large, native tiki mask at the far end of the deck hanging from a pillar. It was colored in strips of red and green, and Finley approached it cautiously.

"H-Hello?" he called out, tightening his fists.

The mask was fairly large, about four feet in length and two feet in width. Its mouth was wide and curled in an expression of mirth, and straight teeth came down behind the lips. Its eyes were perfectly cut circles, lines of tribal paint accenting its brow.

Is this what I'm supposed to find? Finely thought, leaning closer to examine the tiki mask when he was an arm's length away from it. *Am I supposed to take it back to Mr. Tenbrook?*

He reached out with his hands slowly, licking his lips and preparing to unhook the tiki mask from its hanger, when a boisterous, broad voice let out a declaration inside Finley's head, causing him to fall backwards and nearly trip over an old crate.

Finley McComb what *are* you doing! There was an accent to the man's voice that Finley could not place, but that was certainly the least of his concerns. How this person had managed to get inside his head was the more pressing question.

"W-Who is that!" Finley blurted out, scrambling to his feet.

He rushed across the lower deck toward one of the windows so he could have access to the moonlight should he need to defend himself. Outside, something caught his eye and claimed his attention: a few members of the Enhancer Force were still apprehending Miguel, and two others were in pursuit of Finley...but, they were moving extraordinarily slow, and so was everything else...the waves, some passing seagulls...

I've bought us some time, you see, the deep voice said. It was a soft kind of deep, full of wisdom and age and the quality of a king or lord. The voice was knowing.

Finley turned around and opened his mouth to respond, but he stopped. Six hot, bright, neon colors were emanating around the tiki mask like an aura. There was green, pink, blue, orange, yellow, and white.

Finley blinked a few times, struggling to adjust to the powerful, multicolored luminance.

The lights, Finley thought, stepping forward with his arm raised to shield the brightness. *They're a surger's lights.*

Yes indeed, Finley! They are associated with the great gifts.

Green is to Lunging, pink is to Fueling, blue is to Mending, orange is to Enhancing, and yellow is to Understanding.

The glow around the tiki masked dimmed significantly, and Finley lowered his hands. The tiki mask was beautiful, it always had been, and Finley admired it like one admires mountains and canyons. Finley was not afraid.

But there's a sixth light, he thought, pointing. *Neon white.*

Finley could almost hear the person, the being, smiling in his mind. **Finley McComb, what do you think of all** this?

All of what?

All of the news about you being a kekoa! You've been called to a great responsibility, hiki nō?

So they're telling me... Finley took a chance and stuck out his hand, grazing his thumb over the tiki mask's surface. It was warm, like the top of a microwave after it has been in use.

Who are you?

I am the Great A'alona! said the tiki mask, and Finley dropped his hand. **My tribe called me Thunderlight, Lord of Kekoas. Try staying humble with *that* kind of a title! Ha!**

You're a kekoa? Finley thought, excitement beginning to swirl up his soul. *You're here to teach me then? To show me how to use my gifts properly?*

A'alona sighed. **If only, Finley McComb. Perhaps that opportunity will present itself on another occasion. I only have enough time this evening to tell you a few things, so pay attention, as they're very *important* things, hiki nō?**

Finley nodded eagerly, taking a step closer to the mask.

I have been gone for many centuries now, A'alona said, and the aura of neon lights began to pulse in rhythm with his voice. **But my spirit will always remain so long as at least *one* kekoa is called every generation. This is more difficult than it sounds, unfortunately,**

because our kind has been at risk since the early days. We're perceived as being too powerful, Finley McComb, and, well, rightfully so, hiki nō? We're not like ordinary surgers, who came to be long after kekoas were born.

Having access to sunlight over electricity is a threat to surgers, Finley thought, understanding. *Manmade power is limited, it can run out. The sunlight is, well, the sunlight.*

Somewhere around the mid 1800s, our kind was almost wiped off the face of the Earth. We were erased from history. A'alona's voice was thick with sorrow. But there was a certain kekoa from Spain who had managed to escape, and, thus, prevent genocide.

Finley looked around the lower deck, his eyes widening. *This was his ship?*

This was his home, A'alona corrected. With every other kekoa slaughtered, I lost my omnipresent state and became concentrated into one spirit. I found Joaquin Ortega, on the sea, and he was lost and scared and angry.

But with time, he found hope and purpose. He dedicated his life to seeking evil and thwarting it. To protecting the innocent. To finding out who was behind the slaughter of our people.

Finley heard a clatter. Above them, on the top deck, an Enhancer was closing in. Their footsteps were slow, with about ten long seconds between each.

The legacy of the kekoa has remained for this reason, hiki nō? To move toward the fire instead of seeking shelter. To pick up those who have fallen. To save the world from consuming darkness, when all light seems to have been snuffed out.

Who was the kekoa before me? Finley asked, looking back and forth between the ceiling and A'alona's tiki mask. *Are they still alive? Maybe they can help me!*

Silence. The Great A'alona breathed out, as if releasing time's oldest and heaviest sigh. **That is why you've been called, Finley McComb. The kekoa before you is very much alive and well, but he has found the darkness and he has gone rogue. His name is Damian d'Halcourt, and he is the Great Man̲o. He's found a way to surge using electricity, too, and I strongly believe he will try to find you and seek your help to—**

The hatch door flung open, and bits of wood fell down into the lower deck, but the shards fell in slow motion.

Seek my help to what?

Find the third, final way to surge.

Finley knew his time was running out, so he decided to mention that last part to Mr. Tenbrook and the other outliers. If he only had a few more precious moments with A'alona, he would make them count.

What's that neon white represent? he asked, beads of perspiration running down his forehead. He didn't realize he was sweating until the droplets spilled over his eyes and burned.

The lost phase of surging, Finley McComb. Bursting. It is the most powerful, and it will help you defeat Damian d'Halcourt.

There was a large thud. The Enhancer was coming. The conversation was about to be over, and Finley didn't know when he'd see the Great A'alona again.

I lost contact with Damian years ago, so it will be up to you to find him. A'alona's lights were fading. **You have to stop him, Finley McComb. If he can successfully surge using *three* sources of the Root, he will be unstoppable.**

You must find him. You must stop him.

A gloved hand gripped Finley's shoulder and spun him around in real time, without the slosh of drawn-out movement. Finely looked up, expecting to see an angry Enhancer.

But it wasn't a member of the Enhancer Force.

It was Olyphant's masked, cloaked accomplice. She lifted Finley into the air by his throat and threw him across the deck. Finley fell on his arm, and the distinct noise of a bone snapping rang out.

Finley screamed and writhed in pain, barely listening as his attacker spoke:

"When James finds out what you are," she said, her voice familiar sounding, "things are going to change. I saw you Lunge onto this ship. I saw you surge when all the electricity within a mile radius had been extinguished. Where's your glove? Where's the dead battery or drained power source you're supposedly recharging? Hm?"

She stomped across the deck toward Finley's wiggling form—her cloak flapping and her masquerade mask catching the moon's reflection as she passed through beams of light.

Finley felt like his arm was lifeless. Dismembered. Had no blood flowing through it. He bit his teeth and clamped down, trying to focus on something other than the pain. His attacker helped, kicking him in the ribs.

Finley heard something else crack.

He screamed again, louder this time.

"It's a lie, isn't it? Recharging?" Finley's attacker laughed. "You find your ability to surge in other ways. *Remarkable!* When James hears about this."

So that's all she'd really witnessed? She made no mention of Finley's conversation with the Great A'alona, or even seeing the ancient tiki mask.

"We tried to get you to listen, Finley, so stop crying," she said, crouching down and grabbing Finley by the chin. "You've practically brought this upon yourself. The school is trying to use you, and they're all lying to your face. We've done so much to try and get you out of there."

"L-Like paying off Dean Longenecker and Wally, t-the school driver?" Finley stuttered, slowly realizing they were in fact the last piece in all this. "They told y-you when I was recruited. They helped you s-sneak in and Borrow my conscious. They h-helped you release the electric ghost!"

She threw Finley's head down and strode to the nearest window, clasping her hands behind her back.

That's why Dean Longenecker kept my ability a secret...she wanted me to feel desperate and give up! It was just another way they were going to try and flush me out of Brighton.

"Here's your first real life lesson, Finley," his attacker said. "Anyone can be bought at the right price. Your dean made contact with us the day you arrived on campus, as per our contract. She doesn't care about you, or her students, but rather the size of her pocketbook."

"It was Borrowing," Finley said, trying to sit up, but stopping when the pain was too much. "That's how Wally was c-communicating with you that d-day, behind the statue. You were probably miles away, hiding in some hole!"

His attacker chuckled, shaking her cloaked head.

"You're so observant," she said politely. "You're going to make a great asset to Olyphant's campaign."

"I'm not going anywhere," Finley said, wincing when a sharp bolt zapped his side. He needed to get out of there. He needed medical attention.

"Has this whole situation taught you nothing?" she demanded, turning from the window. "Your school doesn't care about you, Finley. They're all liars. Greedy, selfish liars. Even that Diffenbaugh isn't what he seems.

Have you used the key yet? Have you been back to his quarters? He's up to someth—"

"Y-You guys must really be desperate for help if you're going to all this trouble to recruit a thirteen-year-old," Finley said, forcing a smile. His attacker stiffened. "You're wrong about Professor Diffenbaugh, and you're wrong about Brighton Prep. There are good people there, people who care about me."

"HA!" she shrilled, whipping her cloak back and tightening her glove. "You're not that naive, are you? James is the one fighting for your loyalty, while your school is eagerly cashing his checks and selling you out. You're alone without us, and it should *terrify* you."

"I'm not t-terrified," Finley stated, his jaw set. "But you should be."

His attacker tilted her head. "Oh? And why's that?"

"If you and Olyphant don't let me do my job, bad things will happen."

" 'Your job?' "

"The Great Man$\underline{o}$ is coming," said Finley, the desire to pass out creeping upon him. "If he has his way, you'll have bigger things to worry about than government restrictions on Understanding."

There were stars dancing around his vision. He was about to faint, he could feel it. He could also taste thick, bitter bile.

Stay awake...you can get out of this...A'alona said something about "Bursting," and maybe it can help...

"You confused, foolish boy," said Finley's attacker, shaking her head. Finley did note, however, the hint of insecurity in her tone.

She left the window and drew her fist upward, channeling Understanding and raising Finley from the ground. Flashes of neon yellow sparked around her glove.

I can do this...I can use the lost phase of surging, whatever it is...

...so let go already, and Burst!

Finley had no idea what to expect, or if it would even aid him in his predicament.

"If you won't help us, you'll just get in the way," she said, winding her fist back and getting ready to throw Finley out the window and into the black ocean. "You had your chance."

Now...let go, and Burst...please...

He was starting to choke. He couldn't tell if it was saliva, blood, or his attacker's doing, but either way, despair was starting to set in.

And then, finally, his hand got extremely hot, and a blast of white neon light shot forth from his palm, like a sunray, and it smacked into his attacker's chest—sending her crashing through the ship's wall violently and hurtling toward the Pacific Ocean, where she would eventually smack onto the water's surface and undoubtedly break a limb or two.

Finley collapsed onto the deck, and then his vision was gone and there was nothing but his eyelids, and then, even those had been replaced with absolute darkness.

{book iii}

TWO DAYS LATER

Chapter 23 | Trials Around The Bend

"There he is," a friendly voice said.

Finley blinked open his eyes. His sight was a tad hazy, but eventually things sharpened and focused for him. He was lying in a strange, sparsely decorated bedroom surrounded by Ambrose, Miguel, Bridget, and Helena—who was holding his hand tightly.

"I told you he'd wake up if she squeezed hard enough," Miguel joked, leaning on his Lofstrand crutches.

"Guys?" Finley's voice sounded peculiar to his ears, and his throat was very soar. He needed a glass of water. Perhaps two. "Where are we?"

"My quarters, I'm afraid," said the professor, standing up from the bedside armchair he was sitting in. "You've been in and out of sleep for over forty-eight hours. The school nurse has been kind enough to Mend you from here."

"Because Brighton is still closed?"

"Yeah, but it reopens tomorrow!" Bridget exclaimed.

"And no one's happier than you," Helena said dryly, setting Finley's hand down and passing him a drink. He took it, thanked her, and sipped it.

"So, you guys aren't in juvie," said Finley, handing the water back to Helena. "What exactly happened?"

"After the Enhancer Force took Miguel into custody," said Ambrose, folding his arms. "They followed you onto the black ship. The Enhancer's found you passed out with three broken bones. Guess that fall did quite the number on you, huh?"

Finley's mouth dropped. When Olyphant's attacker confronted him on the lower deck, she must have stepped inside of the Great A'alona's protective time seal. Finley wondered how in the world Understanding could be used to do that, but then, it was some spiritual deity performing the surge.

I've bought us some time, the Great A'alona had said, and how he'd managed to do that was unknown.

"Dean Longenecker came clean the next day," said Bridget, sounding disgusted. "Apparently she and Wally, the driver, were in cahoots with Olyphant the whole time. That *witch*. That heartless witch."

"I called her the other itch," said Miguel, smiling. "You

know, the one that starts with a *b*—!"

"Okay, thank you, Mr. Arroyo," said the professor, cutting off Miguel.

"Explains why the dean was always trying to talk so hip and cool," said Helena, tucking her choppy yellow hair behind her ears. "It's like she was overcompensating for her sins, you know? Like it was her way of coping with her demons."

Miguel snorted. "Since when did you become Brighton's resident psychiatrist?"

Helena flashed him a scowl over her shoulder.

"I'm really sorry I didn't see this coming," Bridget told Finley, despairingly. "I'm usually so thorough with my faculty background checks"—Ambrose did a double take after that last part—"I never even found anything on Wally! He was squeaky clean! Anyway, apparently the dean felt guilty about you getting hurt, and she said everything had finally gone too far, so she exposed Olyphant's return. She even said he was probably responsible for the black ship showing up—like he was taunting the government with an omen or something. The media's going *nuts*."

Wow, Finley thought. *But now that Olyphant's a household name and he doesn't have to hide, what's his next move going to be? His accomplice has probably already filled him in about my ability, so who knows what he and his radicals are planning.*

"Professor Diffenbaugh has been promoted to interim

dean!" Bridget added. "He said not a single one of us are in trouble, can you believe that? He even said he would've snuck into the school, too, had he been our age. Oh! And you don't have to make up your final exams!"

Finley's heart soared. "That's the best news I've gotten in *months*."

Everyone laughed, including Ambrose.

"Diffenbaugh was responsible for Wally's arrest right before Christmas," the professor said. "The school board praised his action, and the vote to promote him was unanimous. The first thing he did was fire our old recruiter. Apparently Dean Longenecker paid Mr. Repairman under the table to 'persuade' your parents. She wanted to make absolutely certain they allowed you to enroll here."

Finley exchanged a look with Miguel, Bridget, and Helena. "No kidding…"

He felt massive joy for Diffenbaugh, and he appreciated that the professor was cleaning house, but then his masked attacker's words entered his mind and reinvigorated the clouds of doubt. Even that Diffenbaugh isn't what he seems, she'd said, suggesting who knew what.

Finley shook his head. *I'll go to Diffenbaugh's place when he's away—if only to cement my trust in him.*

"What is it, Fin?" Helena asked, noticing his far-off look.

"Nothing," Finley lied. "So what ended up happening

to the black ship?"

"It sunk," said the professor, stuffing his hands into his jacket pocket. "Once the Enhancers brought you back to safety on the shore, it just...fell apart and descended into the ocean."

"Have they found anything on board?" Finley asked, thinking of the Great A'alona's tiki mask.

"No," replied Ambrose, raising his eyebrows with curiosity. "Why?"

Finley said nothing.

Later in the morning, when Finley's friends left, he told Professor Ambrose everything that had happened on the black ship.

"That's...I don't believe it...," said the professor, when Finley had finished. "The Great A'alona...Delaware's going to have a heart attack."

"So you've heard of him?"

"Never," said the professor, crossing his legs after he sat back down. Finley rose up in the bed. He hadn't left Ambrose's guest bedroom yet—not even to use the restroom. "But everyone believes there's a father or mother of surging out there in the universe, even the cynics. Wait—you *actually* used a sixth phase of surging?"

Finley nodded. "Not well, though. It's called Bursting."

The professor chuckled. "Wow, this is...*wow*. Remi, my sister, specializes in surger fighting techniques. Once you're better I'm going to arrange for her to meet with you in secret every month. Your *real* training is about to begin."

Even though that prospect was exhilarating, as well as discovering the true nature of his abilities and the sixth phase of surging alongside Ambrose and the outliers, there was still Thunderlight's counsel to consider.

"What should we do about A'alona's warning?" Finley asked, rubbing his wrists under the covers. "I mean, if there's another kekoa out there, and he's dangerous enough that A'alona went to the trouble of calling me with the black ship, shouldn't we try tracking him down, like, immediately?"

The professor loosened his tie. "You said he called him the Great Man_o_?"

"Yeah. Why?"

Ambrose sighed. "That's Hawaiian for 'shark.'"

Finley felt a chill work up his back and wrap around his neck. "We have to stop him. A'alona said he's trying to find a third way to surge."

"It would appear as if the outliers have some work ahead of us," the professor said, stroking his chin with his thumb and forefinger. "I never thought I'd say this, but James Olyphant and his radicals are the least of our concerns now. I'll have Victor run Damien d'Halcourt's name through our database, and we'll start our manhunt immediately."

The professor rose. Then, after a long beat of silence, he said, "I guess the Great A'alona knew what he was doing when he foretold about his arrival in that prophecy. He knew all those years ago that eventually one of his kekoas would find the darkness, as he put it, and he'd need to choose someone to right the wrong."

Finley leaned his head back on his pillow.

"Delaware may never know how important a Gatherer's role really is."

"Oh, I think he knows," Finley said, smiling. "What's still crazy to me professor, is that of all the people the Great A'alona could've chosen to call as a kekoa, he chose me. Why?"

Ambrose's eyes twinkled. "Why *not*?"

Finley remained silent.

"I'm proud of you," the professor said, walking out the door, but then stopping and leaning on the frame with his back to Finley. "Not only have you proven to be patient, but now you have shown me that you're brave, too."

Finley cleared his throat. "I had help. I had my best friends. I had you."

Professor Ambrose left the guest bedroom. Finley let his eyes fall shut. Patient? Brave? Those words seemed at odds with each other. If Finley were patient, he wouldn't necessarily take risks, and if he were brave, he would have stared uncertainty in the face and welcomed the risks. Finley felt he had done neither.

I've just let myself get dragged through all this, he realized. *What have I really done other than accept everything with mild questioning?*

Under the covers, Finley's hands formed fists. With his eyes still closed, the room quiet, and his mind momentarily cleared, he spoke a silent promise in his head.

I'm done getting pulled along for the ride. If Professor Ambrose thinks I'm patient, then I'll be patient when I have to. If he says I'm brave, then I promise to actually be brave...

Starting now.

That afternoon, when Finley was supposed to be resting, he slipped on some clothes, called out to Professor Ambrose, and when no answer came, he grabbed the small key from his backpack, put on the surger's glove Diffenbaugh had made him, and then headed outside. His Rad Tide skateboard was leaning against the wall, and Finley snagged it in stride.

The February air hurt with coldness, like it was all a part of some punishment nature was divvying out. Finley headed down the exterior hall that split up the faculty housing building, and he was surprised to find that nearly all his wounds had healed. He must have been Mended just in time, because where there should have been soreness there was only minimal bruising.

Finley reached Professor Diffenbaugh's apartment and knocked.

Nothing.

He knocked again.

Nothing.

Finley pulled the key out and put it into the hole, praying that it wouldn't work. Then he would be forced to throw the key away and forget his attacker's wild, stupid claims about Diffenbaugh being "up to something."

Finley turned the key. It clicked. He sighed, and pushed open the door. "Professor? You here?" he said, walking down the hall. "It's Finley, sir."

Already feeling guilty for having come this far, Finley committed to his mission and began exploring the rest of the apartment. Just like the living room and kitchen, the bedrooms and bathrooms were clean and had simple, matching furniture. Everything was pale and gray and pristine. Finley even opened the closets and checked under the bed, like he was searching for monsters, and he felt extraordinarily silly.

What are you doing here? Finley said inwardly, gripping the key in his hand and heading back outside. After he locked the door, he turned just as the professor was rounding the corner.

"Finley?" he said, a large smile appearing. "You're walking, that's great! How do you feel?"

"Good, feeling good," said Finley, the key in his pocket suddenly feeling heavier than a large stone. He dropped his skateboard and rested his right foot on the tail. "I just came by to thank you for lifting my suspension."

"It was the least I could do," the professor said, squeezing Finley's shoulder gently. "You are, after all, something of a hero now."

"I am?"

"Sure! You tipped us off about Wally Grondahl," Diffenbaugh explained. "And if you hadn't have sneaked onto the ship and, well, gotten hurt, the dean would still be operating from her throne of lies."

"Your metaphors are getting better," Finley noted.

"That was actually an idiom," the professor said, winking. He then undid his bowtie. "Now, as acting dean until Brighton can find a more suitable, qualified individual, I'm being dragged to every meeting and discussion imaginable. Want to come in for a snack? I could use a break."

"Nah," said Finley, checking his wristwatch. "I promised Miguel, Bridget, and Helena I'd meet them before lunch. Rain check?"

"You got it." The professor lightly clapped Finley's arm before brushing past him, and then he suddenly stopped with his hand hovering over the door handle. "Finley?"

"Er, yes?" Finley said, staring at the professor with

dread.

"I just wanted to say I think you make a fine surger." He nodded to the glove on Finley's hand.

"Oh?" said Finley, trying to make his sigh of relief soundless.

"And you did a great job your first semester," Professor Diffenbaugh continued. "Trying to learn how to recharge when no one else knows how makes for quite the interesting schooling experience. Or so I would imagine."

Finley forced a chuckled. "Yeah, well…"

"Stay the course. There's more to your ability than meets the eye."

"I…what do you mean?" Finley turned his head at a slant.

"Oh! Sorry, gotta get inside," he said urgently. The faint beeping of an alarm was ringing from inside. He grabbed his carabineer, fished for the right key, and opened his door. "It's Tesla's feeding time. Iguanas *hate* to eat off schedule. See you soon, Finley."

Finley didn't move as the door closed. He'd just been to every room in Diffenbaugh's quarters, and there hadn't been any sign of a pet reptile within the professor's walls.

What a strange thing to lie about…

Right when Finley McComb had thought everything had been sorted out, and that now he could look ahead to the much larger tasks and responsibilities he'd taken on, he had to go and catch Diffenbaugh in a tiny lie.

What's it matter though? Finley thought, tightening his glove and skating out into the sunlight. (He would have to keep his glove on anytime he planned on surging now so as to keep up appearances.) *I just essentially* broke *into his apartment and went snooping around. Not exactly the most honest thing.*

Finley pulled the key out once more, held it between his fingers, allowed the warmth of the sunlight to flow in and around him, and then he pictured himself crushing the key with Enhanced strength. Next, Finley surged using the sunlight, tapping into the source of the Root as it shone down over the greenway, and he bent the key into a ball and tossed it over his shoulder.

It clinked pitifully when it landed on the sidewalk.

Finley pushed off the ground, skating faster and faster toward the mess hall. It felt good to be on his board. There was a time, not too long ago, when skating was about the only thing he could do with confidence.

Not anymore.

You see, he arrived at Brighton Preparatory School for Surgers with little confidence, and then, for a short time, that confidence was built up, only to be stripped away when he was suspended and he thought he'd lost his ability. But now, that seed of confidence was growing again, and he knew why…

Whatever happened next, whatever trials waited around the bend, Finley wasn't alone. No, he had his friends, he had professors at Brighton who really cherished him, and that made him confident. Sure, being a kekoa with the knowledge of some lost phase of surging helped, but something *else* made him feel practically invincible.

Friendship.

Finley clutched his gloved hand at his side, pretended to surge using the dead batteries in his glove, and mouthed: *Let. Go.* He Fueled forward, zooming across the sidewalk and around his dodging peers—off to meet Miguel, Bridget, and Helena, who were probably waiting for him in the food cart lines.

"Ready for another semester?" Miguel asked, stealing one of Finley's tacos.

He and Miguel waited at their table while Bridget and Helena stood in the drink line. The mess hall was packed, and every single Brighton student whispered and gossiped around them about Dean Longenecker's arrest, the recent light shed on what the press was calling the "James Olyphant cover-up," and how his radicals had resurfaced and were wanted persons. From what Finley gathered, the Bolt Sovereign was under vicious scrutiny for lying about the cause of his arrest in the 80s.

Political cover-ups. Surger radicals. A corrupt dean. None of it really matters, Finley thought, staring out at his peers. *No one even realizes what the biggest threat is…the rise of an evil* *kekoa...the Great Man*o*...*

"Finley?"

Finley flinched. "Sorry, um, what'd you ask?"

Miguel chuckled. "I said, can I have this taco? You were getting ready to say yes, why yes you may."

Finley smirked. "I'm not *that* out of it."

"No? Prove it."

"Okay, well, how about this: I remember that you started to tell me why you pull appliances and electronics apart, but you never finished."

Miguel took a bite out of his lunch, chewing quickly. Then, "Thought you might have forgotten about that talk."

Finley shook his head.

"Well, when the Brighton reps left my house after my calling," Miguel said, his mouth partially full, "I started looking into every piece of info I could get my hands on regarding surging. I found this one interesting article about a man who'd gone missing."

Miguel swallowed his food, then continued: "Apparently he was pulling all kinds of things apart, looking for the Root. Looking for a way to help his wife get better. She was sick, worse than me."

"What happened?"

"According to what I read, he found a 'unique' way to tap into the Root," Miguel said. Behind him, Finley saw Bridget and Helena approaching with four drinks between them. "But...he went unexpectedly missing, and hasn't been seen since…"

A unique way to tap into the Root? Finley closed his eyes, thinking deeply. *What does that even mean? Is that…is that what the Great A'alona was referring to? A* third *way to surge?*

"Miguel's finally managed to bore someone to sleep," Helena said, plopping down on the seat beside Finley, who opened his eyes.

"Helena got funnier over Christmas break," Miguel deadpanned, opening his Coke. "You guys notice?"

Finley and Bridget laughed, and Helena scowled at them for responding to Miguel's jab with amusement. When Finley stopped laughing he sighed internally, and then turned to his lunch.

"I'm still hung up on something," Bridget said all of the sudden, mixing her rice and refried beans into one steamy mound on her plate. "How were you able to make fire appear? With Mr. Repairman's test?"

"I…" Finley held one of his tacos, but froze mid bite. "Good question."

Being a kekoa meant being able to tap into the same surging phases that his friends could, except Finley utilized a different source of the Root. That didn't take away from the fact that the lighter had been empty. In other words, if his friends couldn't summon fire from nothing, how could he?

Bursting? Is that what I had done, all those months ago? Is that how I ignited the flame?

But, if that had been the case, that would mean Mr. Repairman knew Finley was a kekoa all along. It was the only explanation, right? How else would he have known that Finley could make fire appear out of thin air?

"I've noticed," Miguel said between chews, "with growing concern, that you space out a lot."

Finley forced a chuckle out of himself and then took a sizable bite out of his taco. "I'll work on that," he eventually said. "Speaking of Mr. Repairman though, did you guys hear how he reacted to getting fired?"

All three of them shook their heads.

"Why?" asked Helena, her eyebrows scrunched together. "Did he flip out or something?"

"No idea...," Finley said, his mind dashing off with wild thoughts and theories. "That's why I asked."

If Mr. Repairman really knew Finley's capabilities from the get-go, then who else did? Someone, it seemed, was pretending to believe in the lie about recharging.

"Hey, isn't that your guys' dorm mate, Quinn?"

Finley and Miguel followed the direction of Bridget's eye line. A ninth grader with a striped tank top and a buzzed haircut was standing in one of the food cart lines, talking and laughing with the Caverly twins.

Finley recognized him immediately. He was one of Dillon Trask's friends from Huntington Beach. He was one of the kids who had been with Dillon that day when they were trying to force that sixth grader into grabbing the electric fence.

He met Finley's gaze and flicked his head in a quick nod.

You were the one who surged that day, Finley realized, feebly nodding back. *You were the one who created the diversion with the fence!*

Quinn went back to his conversation with Michael and Sarah, and the line moved forward.

"Why'd he get suspended last semester?" Finley asked his table.

" 'Cause he's a jerk-face," Miguel replied, idly popping out the indentions in his Coke can.

"Miguel hasn't told you?" Helena said, a wide smile appearing. "You're gonna love this! It involves Miguel's boxers, a skunk, and a *ton* of maple syrup."

That's all it took for Finely to burst into laughter, and he almost sprayed his friends with pico de gallo in the process.

Am I ready for another semester? he thought to himself, repeating Miguel's question. *As long as I have these three at my side, you bet!*

EPILOGUE

Even footfalls echoed in the old man's chamber, and it caused him to stir from his sleep- and food-deprived daze. It was the first time since he'd been kidnapped that he had had a visitor—while he'd been awake, anyway.

The old man said after he pushed off the stiff mattress and sat up: "W-Why are you keeping me here?"

The person, whoever it was, remained in the shadows of the cement chamber so that only their dress pants and shoes were visible. They remained quiet. How had they managed to get in? As far as the old man could tell, there were no doors—not even a window slit. At least prison cells had those.

So, was this person really here, or was the old man seeing things? Given how weak and tired he was, it was quite possible his eyes—which had never been that reliable, truth be told—were playing tricks on him.

"H-Hello?" the old man tried again, gripping the single sheet on his bed. The lone, exposed fluorescent bulb above his head wavered and buzzed, like it was running on fumes.

Finally, an amused, male voice spoke into the coldness. "Your name is Neil Hatmaker."

The old man let go of the sheets. He was hard-pressed to find his voice again: "Yes. Why have you brought me here?"

"I looked everywhere for you. Had to travel through time to get you, and now you're here."

Somehow Neil managed to stand, though his knees shook with the fatigue of both old age and poor health. "What the devil are you talking about?"

The man stepped out from the darkness and into the diffused light. He was young. He had striking features and tidy hair, and he wore a polka-dotted bowtie with his clean shirt.

"The devil." He snorted, taking the newspaper he carried under his arm and dropping it onto the floor. It landed directly between the two men. "I've been called that before. Pretty unoriginal slur though, wouldn't you say?"

"You better tell me what's going on, or—"

"Sure. It's precisely what I mean to do today."

Neil was taken aback. He hadn't expected cooperation from his captor.

"I thought it first necessary to bring you more, er, *refuse deposit sheets*." He then nodded to one of the corners of the chamber, where the stink of urine and days-old feces lay in the air. Every time Neil had woken from a trance since his imprisonment, he'd found a newspaper sitting on the ground by his bed. He had been forced to use this as a means to cover his excrements.

"You can be free of all this," the young man said, spreading out his arms. "Once you tell me how you did it."

"D-Did what?"

"Found a way to surge using the most powerful, hidden wellspring of the Root."

Neil Hatmaker paused, then said, "I've no idea what you're referring to."

"Come now, don't be coy." The young man stepped forward, and the minimal lighting in the chamber casted deep shadows over his eyes and across his cheekbones. "How did you do it?"

"DO WHAT!" Neil screamed, with what little strength he had left. He panted, his eyes darting back and forth between the young man's.

"Harvested the Root from your wife's body," the young man answered darkly. "She was in the room beneath your study that night, sleeping soundly. You found a way to surge using the energy that the human body produces, and you did it while your subject was in a completely different room."

"I...what...?" Neil remembered the candle, the sway of the light, and the moving shadows. He'd been searching for the Root, yes, but the Root was found in electricity—*not* inside a human!

...Right?

"No, no, that's impossible."

"You did it, Neil Hatmaker." The young man chuckled. "Why else do you think the first responders found your wife's body in a shriveled, skeletal state the next morning? You...*drained* her. Like a surger willing power from electricity. See, the human body manufactures about the same amount of energy as a hundred watt light bulb, and you were able to tap into that."

It was quiet after he said this, and Neil eventually collapsed to his knees in tears. "No...no...no...!" he sobbed. "WHO ARE YOU!"

"I go by Brandon Diffenbaugh now," he replied. "But that's my adopted name. I prefer my real name, so you can call me Damien. Damien d'Halcourt. Now that we're on a first name basis, do be sure to respect that by being honest with me. Okay?"

"You're a monster!"

Though only the walls would hear Neil's insult, because the young man with two names had pointed at the hanging light bulb and then vanished into a strand of colorful, neon dust particles.

Damien meant to return later, and when he did, the torturing would begin. The only chance Neil had was to explain how he'd managed to draw from the energy in his wife's body. That, of course, would not happen, as Neil Hatmaker would not even know where to start...

Dark, dreadful days were on the horizon, and those days belonged to the Great Man<u>o</u>.

Finley McComb's story will continue in…
THE KINGS OF THE NIGHT!

acknowledgements

Thank you, Heavenly Father, for never ceasing to amaze me, and for allowing me to pursue my dreams. Your blessings are unending.

Thank you to my beautiful wife, who constantly gives support, creative feedback, and encouragement. You spoil me.

To my mother, father, and sisters—thank you for challenging me and always pushing me. Oh, and welcome to the family, Michael! No turning back now...

To my amazing "team" of readers. Rebecca, for catching all the food-related errors. Burn, thanks for your suggestions about A'alona and Mr. Repairman. Wesley, for calling out my telling-instead-of-showing tendencies. Thanks to Mary Beth for catching the medical related missteps, and helping me realize who Finley is. Thank you to James and Justin for accepting ARCs—you guys are my fastest readers.

Special thanks to my overworked editor, Pam. Why do you keep accepting manuscripts from me? Seriously, though, she's so good at what she does she could be a professor at Brighton Prep. (I hear they're looking for a dean.)

Two huge thank yous to Allen and James, the talented duo who made the book trailer. If you haven't seen it yet, I strongly encourage you to head over to my site. The animation and score is killer.

Lastly, I want to thank the middle school boys over at TVC Youth. You guys are such a blessing, and I look forward to hanging with you every Sunday. "SNOW, UNITED! WE LOVE YOU, WE LOVE YOU!"

soundtrack

Shout out to these bands, who provided an awesome atmosphere during my writing sessions: Blink 182, New Found Glory, Quietdrive, Angels & Airwaves, The Honeybells, Valencia, We The Kings, and The Starting Line.

about the author

Julian R. Vaca has been writing since he first learned how. He is a Long Beach, California native, and has lived in Nashville since the early 2000s. He graduated from Watkins College of Art, Design & Film in 2011, and in 2013 his second novel, *Running From Lions*, won the Novel Rocket Award in the Young Adult category.

Julian lives with his wife in Nashville, where he is hard at work on his next book.

Visit him online at www.JulianRVaca.com.

CPSIA information can be obtained at www.ICGtesting.com
Printed in the USA
LVOW10s1425260314
379043LV00010B/253/P